GLORY OF ROME

Also by Douglas Jackson

CALIGULA
CLAUDIUS
HERO OF ROME
DEFENDER OF ROME
AVENGER OF ROME
SWORD OF ROME
ENEMY OF ROME
SCOURGE OF ROME
SAVIOUR OF ROME

For more information on Douglas Jackson and his books,
see his website at www.douglas-jackson.net

GLORY OF ROME

Douglas Jackson

BANTAM PRESS

LONDON • TORONTO • SYDNEY • AUCKLAND • JOHANNESBURG

TRANSWORLD PUBLISHERS
61–63 Uxbridge Road, London W5 5SA
www.penguin.co.uk

Transworld is part of the Penguin Random House group of companies
whose addresses can be found at global.penguinrandomhouse.com

Penguin
Random House
UK

First published in Great Britain in 2017 by Bantam Press
an imprint of Transworld Publishers

A CIP catalogue record for this book
is available from the British Library.

ISBNs 9780593076156 (cased)
9780593076163 (tpb)

Typeset in 11.5/15.25pt Electra by Falcon Oast Graphic Art Ltd.
Printed and bound by Clays Ltd, Bungay, Suffolk.

Penguin Random House is committed to a sustainable
future for our business, our readers and our planet. This book
is made from Forest Stewardship Council® certified paper.

MIX
Paper from
responsible sources
FSC® C018179

1 3 5 7 9 10 8 6 4 2

For my granddaughter Lily,
who has brought a new kind of joy into our lives

BRITAIN, AD 78

North Sea

CARVETII

Irish Sea

BRIGANTES

PARISI

Mona
(Anglesey)

DECEANGLI

Canovium •

The battle against
King Owain

• Deva
II LEGION
ADIUTRIX

Lindum
IX LEGION

Venta
Icenorum •

ORDOVICES

Viroconium
XX
LEGION

CORNOVII

CORIELTAUVI

Site of Boudicca's
last battle

ICENI

DEMETAE

SILURES

DOBUNNI

CATUVELLAUNI

TRINOVANTES

Colonia •

Isca Silurum
II LEGION
AUGUSTA

Verulamium •

Londinium

DUMNONII

DUROTRIGES

BELGAE

ATREBATES

REGNI

CANTIACI

English Channel

0   MILES   100

N

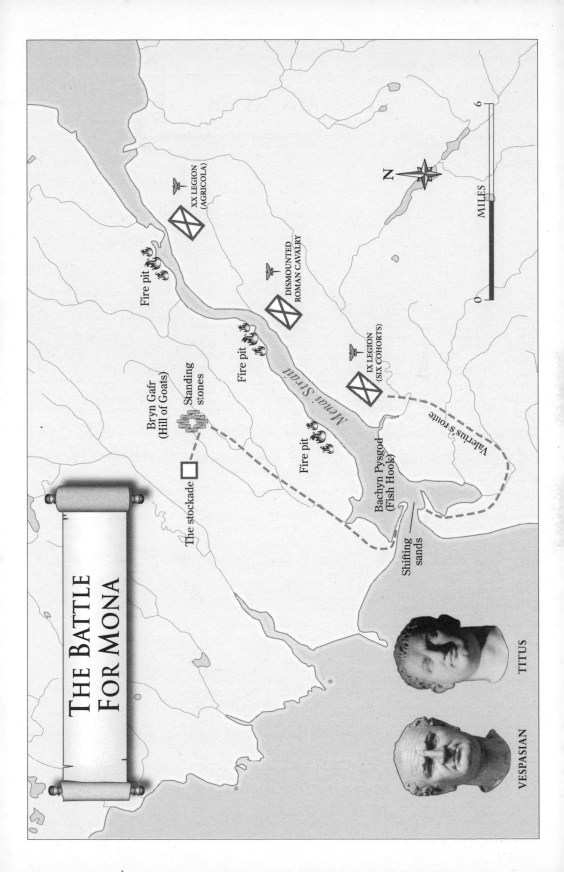

THE BATTLE FOR MONA

Bryn Gafr
(Hill of Goats)

Standing
stones

The stockade

Fire pit

Fire pit

Fire pit

Fire pit

Fire pit

Menai Strait

Bachyn Pysgod
(Fish Hook)

Shifting
sands

Valerius's route

XX LEGION
(AGRICOLA)

DISMOUNTED
ROMAN CAVALRY

IX LEGION
(SIX COHORTS)

N

MILES

0   6

VESPASIAN

TITUS

He launched them upon the enemy so suddenly that the astonished islanders, who looked for fleets of ships at sea, came to the conclusion that, to such men, nothing was too difficult or invincible.

Publius Cornelius Tacitus, *Agricola*

Prologue

Mona, AD 78

Owain Lawhir, High King of the Ordovices, suppressed a shudder as he watched the scene unfold. A warrior chief in all his splendour, standing a head taller than most men, with a heavy gold torc at his neck and an iron sword in its gilded scabbard at his waist, even he never felt at ease in this place. The great stones of the circle stood out like rotting teeth against the dying roseate light of the early summer sun. At the precise centre a similar stone, a sword-length deep and four long, lay horizontal, its upper face worn to a uniform surface by countless struggling bodies. Specks of light glittered where tiny chips of a different rock caught the last of the sunlight, but mostly the stone – the altar – was matt black where the blood of the two bulls slaughtered at Beltane had congealed to a stinking, hardened crust. In ages past some long-dead craftsman had embedded a pair of iron rings at each end.

Five druids in white robes stood facing the twin pillars of the circle's entrance. Three were men in their prime, tall and forbidding, expressions impassive and emotionless, their stillness a hint of the iron discipline that ruled them. Another was a mere youth, and despite his attempts to emulate his elders he emanated an air of agitation that told

1

the king the part he was to play in this ceremony. These four flanked the fifth priest, a shrunken, stunted figure by comparison. For the moment he kept his face hidden, but a shock of snow-white hair framed the back of his skull like a sunburst and he stood with his back hunched as if a great burden weighed down on his narrow shoulders.

A hundred other men waited impatiently outside the stone circle, forbidden to enter on pain of death. Their fine cloaks, iron swords and golden neck rings proclaimed them for what they were, an elite, the lesser kings of the Ordovices and the chiefs of their tribes and sub-tribes. On another day any one of them would have shed blood to stand in Owain's place. But not this day.

A blackbird's shrill evening song broke the silence, only to turn into the distinctive chirr, chirr, chirr of an alarm call as a murmur ran through the chiefs at the faint sound of clinking metal. The crowd parted to reveal five naked prisoners, four men and a young woman, each fettered hand and foot and held upright by two guards. The prisoners' mouths had been crudely gagged with leather thongs, but their bulging eyes spoke eloquently of their terror. The white-haired priest raised a hand and the little column stumbled to a halt. He inclined his head towards the tall druid on his left. After a whispered conversation the tall man called out, 'She is not required. Bring the others forward.'

The woman's eyes rolled up in her head and she would have fallen but for the grip of her guards as they dragged her away. Her fellow prisoners struggled vainly against their bonds as they were hustled towards the altar. One of them soiled himself at the horror of what was to come with a great spluttering fart, and his captors cursed him as their legs were spattered with ordure.

Owain's gut tightened like a coiled snake. He felt no sympathy for the doomed men. They were Roman-lovers, traitors to their people, and deserved to die. His concern was for the undoubted outcome of this ceremony and the consequences for himself and his tribe.

One of the druids must have given a hidden signal, because the guards were dragging the first prisoner to the altar, a short, fat man with matted hair and blood trickling down his cheek from a scalp wound.

Fear had shrivelled his lower parts and withdrawn them into the folds of his stomach.

The five druids broke into a low-pitched droning chant that seemed to resonate in the very air around them. As the guards approached the stone the volume grew and the prisoner's struggles intensified. Arms and legs flailed in their fetters so wildly Owain wondered they didn't snap, but the two guards held their captive with practised ease. The larger of the two stunned him with a short-arm punch to the head and he ceased struggling long enough to allow them to link his chains to the iron rings.

Oddly, the fat man's struggles ceased the moment his back touched the altar. Perhaps his horror-addled brain understood he was already dead, or fear had drained the strength from him. The chanting faded and the five druids turned to their victim. For the first time Owain looked into the face of the frail figure in the centre. The sight sent a shiver through him even though he'd prepared himself for it. At first it was as if Gwlym, arch-druid of Elfydd, stared into his soul. Only gradually did the mind register that the gleaming eyes were, in reality, two pus-filled red pits. Worse, if a man knew and believed the story behind Gwlym's mutilation: that he had plucked out his own eyes lest he be distracted by earthly sights and pleasures. The arch-druid believed his blindness brought him closer to the gods and freed his mind to divine their intentions. He lifted his hand to touch the youngest priest on the shoulder.

'Begin, Bedwr.'

Bedwr took a deep breath before stepping forward to stand over the sacrifice. The chained man had his eyes closed tight and his fists clenched so his nails must have been digging deep into his flesh. Every muscle tensed for what was to come. From the sleeve of his robe Bedwr drew a short, sickle-shaped knife and waited with the glittering blade poised above the shivering folds of flesh beneath the fat man's breastbone.

Gwlym and his acolytes resumed their rhythmic chant, pledging the soul of their victim to Taranis. Tension filled the air like a living thing and Owain found he was holding his breath. Without warning the chant ended. The knife blade swooped in a single sweeping cut that opened the fat man from breastbone to groin. A stifled cry of agony escaped the gag and the torn body shuddered and bucked against his chains.

'Aymer.'

Bedwr stepped away to be replaced by a second druid, who pulled back the torn flaps of flesh to expose the glistening coils within. A third plunged his hand into the dying victim's entrails, causing a fresh convulsion of shuddering, his fingers expertly seeking out the prize he sought. Within moments he raised a dark, gleaming mass that Owain guessed must be the dying man's liver. Gwlym accepted the dripping lump of offal and the final druid stepped forward to bring an identical sickle blade across the throat of the sacrifice. A spurt of dark blood sprayed the air and with a final heave the body went still.

They were already bringing the second sacrifice forward as the guards removed the fat man's ruined corpse.

The sky darkened with each soul's passing and the air hung heavy with the stench of blood and excrement. Gwlym and his druids studied their gory harvest beneath the light of a dozen flickering torches. Eventually they straightened.

'The gods have spoken.' Gwlym's harsh voice cut the night like a rusty saw ripping through a knotted oak. 'It is their will that the invaders be driven from this land of Elfydd.'

The druid spoke loudly enough for the men waiting in the darkness outside the stones to hear, but Owain knew the words were directed at him. He also knew that whatever the desire of the gods and the messages passed by the sacrifices it was also the will of the arch-druid that the invaders be driven from the island. No man hated the Romans more than Gwlym. It was Gwlym who had carried assurances of the gods' support across the country and urged the warriors of the Dobunni, the Cornovii and the Corieltauvi to follow Boudicca, queen of the Iceni, when she rose against the despised invaders. Gwlym who stood at the queen's side as the hated Temple of Claudius burned. Gwlym who exulted at the slaughter of the citizens of Londinium and watched their blood stain the mighty Tamesa. And Gwlym who had seen the souls of Boudicca's champions harvested by Roman swords like ripe corn in her last battle and himself taken the stomach wound that had turned him into an old man overnight.

'If it is the gods' will,' Owain said carefully, 'then so it will be.'

'The omens are good,' Gwlym continued as if Owain hadn't spoken. 'But the gods require further sacrifice. Our people's freedom will come at a blood price.' His words provoked a murmur of unease among the watching aristocrats. 'Do you deny the gods?'

'We do not deny the gods,' Owain replied. 'But we are old enough to remember the blood sacrifices of the past. My father listened to the honeyed words of Caratacus, who claimed the Silurian kingship, begged us for aid and promised to rid the island of the Romans. His reward was to have his head placed on a stake at Viroconium. Boudicca had the support of Andraste' – the king winced as Gwlym's head snapped up and he was looking directly into the weeping pits of the druid's eye sockets – 'and her warriors were as numerous as grains of sand on a beach, yet they died in their thousands, and the queen with them. Suetonius Paulinus turned the lands of the Iceni, the Dobunni, the Corieltauvi and the Cornovii into a wasteland.'

'Boudicca was betrayed!' Gwlym hissed. 'How else would Paulinus have known precisely where her army would march and arrayed his forces in the only formation capable of defeating her?'

'The gods—'

'She believed the gods wanted her to attack, but her final decision was swayed by the only one she failed to appease. A goddess more powerful even than their Jupiter or Mars. The Mother Goddess. We will not make the same mistake.' Gwlym's voice took on a new intensity and Owain felt as if someone had run a spear point down his spine. 'The message the gods send is that all it takes is a single spark to light a fire that may be fanned into an inferno. The peoples of Elfydd understand that the Romans will never stop coming. Every man among you knows he can be dispossessed as easily as Boudicca, or the Trinovantes whose land is now farmed by Roman settlers. All our people need is a sign that the gods are with them and they will join together and drown the Romans in their own blood. You, Owain Lawhir, have been chosen by the gods to provide that sign.'

'My people . . .' The words seemed to freeze in Owain's mouth. Something was happening in his head. He could hear a voice, but it was his own voice. *Owain Lawhir, they call you. Owain Longhand, whose reach and power inspire fear and respect. But lately men have taken to calling you another name, though you choose not to hear it. Owain Cadomedd, Owain who avoids battle.* It was true. He had heard the whispers. He had ordered his warriors not to attack the Roman cavalry patrols that made regular forays into the Ordovice lands. They might win a small victory, take a few heads, but he would lose men, and, worse, provoke a reaction that would cost him more. But young men's fingers itch for the sword hilt and he knew he could not control them for much longer. They would not challenge him. Not yet. But there were murmurings, and plenty of people willing to fan the flames of dissent.

'You will take your warriors and destroy the fort at Tal-y-Cafn.' Owain blinked as he realized Gwlym had resumed speaking. 'The place the Romans call Canovium. Kill every man, woman and child and wipe all trace of it from the face of the land.'

'They will retaliate. The new governor—'

'You are not listening to me, king,' the druid snapped. 'The gods have spoken. If we do not destroy the Romans, they will destroy us. When they came twenty years ago, Suetonius Paulinus was interrupted in his work by Boudicca. Our survival justifies her sacrifice, but they will return. The gods have provided us with an opportunity. You will be their instrument. The slaughter of their comrades will draw the legions into our valleys and there will they find their graves. They will be the lamb to our wolf when we fall on them from the heights.'

Owain wondered if the druid's hatred had driven him mad. The simple truth was that Paulinus had simply brushed the Ordovices aside to reach Mona, ignoring their attacks as if they were nettle stings. What had changed? Yet he also read the unspoken threat in the words. King or not, if he refused to do Gwlym's bidding there would be another sacrifice, or more likely the sting of a knife edge across his throat while he slept.

'When do the gods wish me to attack?' He struggled to keep the bitterness from his voice.

'At the dark of the moon.' Gwlym's voice held a tone of dismissal. 'You have three weeks.'

Owain Lawhir, High King of the Ordovices, stooped to pick up the iron helmet at his feet and marched from the circle past the mutilated bodies of the sacrifices. The gods had spoken. At the dark of the moon he would bring blood and fire and death to the Romans at Canovium.

I

Fidenae, near Rome

Three small boys crouched by the river, brows furrowed in concentration as they stared intently into the clear water. They wore only brief loincloths and their bronze flesh glowed with health as a result of long hours spent in the open air under the summer sun. Each held a sharpened length of stick the length of a cavalry *spatha*.

Gaius Valerius Verrens watched from a hillock overlooking the pool. He knew diminutive, wily trout lurked in the shadows of the bank, but also from experience how difficult they were to catch. It took a long time to learn that, by some strange natural phenomenon that only his friend Pliny might understand, the actual fish were inches ahead of where they looked to be. The stream was deep at this spot, a remote part of Valerius's estate at Fidenae, a few miles north of Rome, and the boys had been specifically ordered to stay away from it. But the fact that he would undoubtedly have to take the sticks to their backs in the near future did not stop him from smiling at the tranquil scene.

A shrill squeak from the smallest of the three, a tousle-haired youngster of about four, as skinny and agile as a sighthound. They'd seen something of greater interest, perhaps a rare specimen of the larger trout that haunted the deepest hollows, visible only as a dark silhouette in the depths. To a small boy such a fish would appear the size of the crocodile Emperor Nero had kept in his zoo. Catching it might save them a beating if they presented it to the villa's cook.

They jostled for position, but some hidden measure of authority gave the small boy priority. Valerius held his breath as the stick was drawn back, clutched like a warrior's spear in the lad's fist, the white of the whittled point gleaming in the sunlight. The boy waited, with a hunter's instinctive stillness, his eyes never leaving his prey. And struck.

Perhaps the fish was deeper than he'd calculated, or in his excitement he put too much power into the thrust. The result was a loss of balance that left him teetering over the river. His companions reached out desperately to arrest his fall, but they were too late. With a sharp cry the boy plunged into the pool with an almighty splash.

Valerius was already sprinting down the hill to where the two older boys stood paralysed. He pushed them aside and searched the depths until he saw a string of bubbles and a pair of startled eyes staring up at him from a face twisted into a mask of consternation. Taking a deep breath, he leapt into the pool. The chilled waters made him gasp, but they only reached his shoulders. He ducked his head beneath the surface and reached down to grasp the drowning child with his left hand. The boy struggled in his grip, choking and spluttering, until Valerius threw his catch on the riverbank like a sack of grain, where he lay with his eyes closed and his bony chest heaving.

Valerius pulled himself out of the water under the appalled gaze of the others. 'Claudius. Milo. Go back to the house. You know what to tell your fathers when they return from the fields?'

'Yes, lord,' the pair said miserably, turning away to walk downstream, glancing back occasionally to glare at the party responsible for their coming troubles.

Valerius stood over the boy as he lay on his back with his eyes still shut. 'You know what this means, Lucius?' he asked sternly.

'Yes, Father. Five strokes of the cane.'

'Was it worth it?'

One eye blinked open and the brown face slipped into a grin. 'It would have been if I'd aimed properly.'

Valerius pulled his son to his feet and cuffed him gently. 'How big was it?'

Lucius threw his arms as wide as they would go.

'Then we'll come back later with hook and feathers and see if we can get him, but first . . .'

'Yes, Father?'

'As we're both already wet,' he grabbed Lucius by the waist and lifted him up, 'we'll start teaching you to swim.' With a shout of laughter, he tossed the shrieking boy into the centre of the pool and dived in after him.

Valerius studied his wife Tabitha as she spun yarn with a hand spindle in her seat by the window overlooking the gardens. Slim, and with an exotic, eastern beauty that still took his breath away, she moved with unconscious grace as the spindle twirled to the twitch of her fingers. She sensed his gaze and looked up with a smile.

'Shouldn't you be working on the accounts, husband?'

'They can wait,' he said, continuing to oil the mechanism of the hidden knife in the wooden fist that took the place of his right hand. He'd lost the original during the rebellion that ravaged Britannia during Nero's reign, but the replacement had become so much part of him over the years he barely felt the difference. She knew that poring over the accounts was the part of an estate owner's life he least enjoyed. He could have employed someone to do them, but his father always said a man who didn't look after his own accounts was a man asking to be relieved of his estate. 'I was just thinking I have never been so happy.'

'Then I am pleased,' she said, her words confirmed by the light flush of her cheeks. 'Though I fear Lucius is less so.'

'You warned him against going near the Rock Pool,' Valerius pointed out. 'He understood the consequences.'

'Yes.' She nodded. 'But he has a way of persuading the other boys to follow him into trouble. He takes after his father, I think.' Her lips twitched mischievously.

'His father wouldn't have got caught,' Valerius said in mock dismissal. Yet her words contained a grain of truth. Even at four, Lucius was an adventurous child, always searching out some new place or testing some fascinating, and often potentially dangerous, new experience. Valerius had seen enough adventure to satisfy two lifetimes. He'd soldiered in the mountains of Britannia and on the plains of Armenia, played the spy for emperors and princes, and faced death more times than he cared to remember. But no more.

In the last four years the fates had been kind. He'd been allowed to enjoy a settled life with his family. The accession of Vespasian to the purple united Rome and brought prosperity to those he valued, of whom Valerius was fortunate to count himself one. This villa and the sprawling estate, with its olive groves, well-irrigated fields and slopes filled with vines, were the gift of the Emperor. To the south lay a second family estate, occupied by his sister Olivia and her husband, and to the north the vast palace that once belonged to the philosopher Seneca, a former owner of these lands. After Seneca's enforced suicide, Nero granted the estate to his secretary and spymaster Tigellinus. Years later, Tigellinus suffered a similar fate at the orders of Marcus Salvius Otho during the disastrous civil war known as the Year of the Four Emperors. The war that brought Vespasian to power. Valerius's friend and protector, the Emperor's eldest son Titus, commander of the elite Praetorian Guard, was currently serving his sixth consulship and had developed a deserved reputation for honesty and competence that boded well for the future of the Empire.

Valerius spent his time running the estate, attending the Senate, where he seldom spoke and then only in support of the Emperor or Titus, and took the occasional high-profile case at the law courts when it suited him.

'Have you decided whether to defend Tulius?' Tabitha's words were a gentle reminder that one of his clients had asked him for help in a case. Normally, Valerius wouldn't have hesitated. A man had a responsibility to support his followers. But . . .

'I can't.' She wouldn't judge him, but she was fond of Tulius and his young wife and he could feel her disappointment. 'His accuser Rusticus is close to Domitian. Titus has asked me not to do anything that might antagonize his brother further.'

And there lay the only shadow over their placid, rustic existence.

Titus Flavius Domitianus, Vespasian's younger son, had been Valerius's sworn enemy since Domitian attempted to steal the one-handed Roman's then lover, Domitia Longina Corbulo. The fact that Domitia was now Domitian's wife changed nothing. Domitian had accused Valerius of treason and forced him into exile. Since then Valerius had survived several attempts to kill him, all, he was certain, emanating from the same source. He'd thought Titus's favour and Vespasian's admiration, won during the siege of Jerusalem, might have brought an end to the threat, but the potential menace of Domitian hung over the villa like the cloud of smoke over a volcano. Valerius had reason to believe his household contained more than one of Domitian's spies. He and Tabitha both had experience of the clandestine world and Tabitha had ordered the sale of a slave she'd suspected, but Valerius knew that agents were easily replaced.

'He cannot touch you without harming himself, at least as long as Titus and Vespasian live.'

Tabitha's honeyed voice contained a rare suggestion of contempt. In her eyes Domitian was a coward who paid other men to do his bidding. She viewed any threat to Valerius as a threat to them all and a core of iron ran through that willowy frame. Tabitha had been a princess of Emesa, an eastern state riven by political and religious division and threatened by its neighbours. Under normal circumstances her uncle, the king, would have used her marriage to form a dynastic alliance or cement an existing one. Instead, her close bond and friendship with Titus's lover, Queen Berenice of Cilicia, had allowed her to marry for love. She had left friends and family to follow Valerius to an alien land, but he had never heard her complain. Her beauty hid the fact that she was accomplished in the darker arts of conspiracy and intrigue. Valerius knew that, given her way, she would have her own methods of dealing with Domitian. But he was the Emperor's son and Valerius had pledged his loyalty to Vespasian.

'That may be true,' he conceded, 'but he's still a very dangerous man. Another reason Lucius shouldn't go wandering off with his friends.'

She nodded. 'I will confine him to his room for the rest of the day. An extra punishment for frightening his poor mother.'

Valerius laughed. They'd fought spears and knives, faced drowning together and almost burned to death, but he'd never seen her frightened. 'Maybe it's time we employed a tutor for him?' he suggested.

The delicate chin came up and a certain light in her eyes told him he had a fight on his hands. 'But Valerius, he's so young. It would be like caging a fox cub.'

'He'd have less time to get into trouble,' Valerius grumbled. 'Two or three hours a day resolving Zeno's paradoxes would clip our little hawk's wings. And Olivia has a tutor for her boys. I'll think about it. In the meantime, he should mend his ways.'

'I will make sure he understands that,' she said meekly. Too meekly.

Being reminded of Domitian had changed his mood. Another reason for hating the scheming little bastard. In his fortieth year and with the scars and grey hairs to prove it, Valerius had better things to do with his time. He rose to his feet.

'I'll take a turn round the groves on the south slope and check how they're getting on with the drainage channels. If I find Atticus sleeping under the olive nets again, I'll sell him to Verecundus the shit collector.'

'And quite right too,' agreed Tabitha, who knew Valerius would never break up a family and that Atticus was the father of her devoted maid Helena's daughter.

Valerius's spirits rose with every stride he took up the broken path that wound between the olive trees and the vines. Halfway to the top he looked down at the sprawling villa complex. It was at least twice the size of the one he'd grown up in a few miles to the south, and lay in a great loop of the Tiber river. Fields of ripening crops carpeted the valley floor before they gave way to grapes and olive groves on the slopes. He remembered visiting groves just like this as a boy with his father and discussing the trees and their potential. Was it better to plant twenty-five to the *iugerum* or was the soil rich enough for fifty? Did this tree or that need pruning? Could a tree ever be too old? Was it worth planting vines directly beneath the canopy where the sun was unlikely to penetrate? That and the perennial problems that faced every estate owner. Low yields and dwindling profits. Why every pest under the sun liked grapes. And why did weeds grow twice as fast as any plant that could earn a man a living?

He smiled at the memory and continued climbing. His son was named for his father: Lucius Valerius Verrens. Some day all this would be his and he would have to be taught how to care for it. That had been the old man's byword, through good times and bad: *Remember this, Valerius: we may profit from the earth but we are only caretakers of the land.*

Atticus and his workers were hard at it with spades and mattocks when he reached the area where he'd decided ditches would improve the drainage. The trees and vines needed all the moisture they could get, but sometimes a thunderstorm would cause a flash flood. Better that the water was channelled to drain away to the lower slopes than that it wash away the thin red soil. He had a feeling they hadn't been working for long, but it didn't matter. Just being here made him feel better. He talked to them all, as he had the men of his many commands. How were their families? The food? Did they have any complaints?

Of course, there was always one. Didius, a slow-witted young labourer with shoulders like a bull, worried that an overseer was trying to take advantage of his mother. Valerius assured him he would deal with it and Didius thanked him with grave solemnity. When he left he heard the mattocks strike with renewed vigour. A slave always worked better when someone took an interest in who, rather than what, he was. He was their lord and master, with the power of life and death over them. They rightly feared incurring his wrath, but they also respected him, which was not always the case. Each man received a new tunic every year, and a cloak and a pair of wooden clogs every second year. They worked long hours, but they were well fed and they celebrated the same holidays as the family. Cato the Elder had advised that farmers sell 'useless things, such as worn-out cattle, diseased sheep and aged and feeble slaves'. Valerius's workers knew that when they were too old and unfit for heavy work they would still have a roof over their heads and a garden plot, and Tabitha would find them light duties around the house or the farm. Serpentius would have laughed and called him soft. Valerius felt the faint melancholy that always struck him when he thought of his old friend, the former gladiator. But he consoled himself that Serpentius would have gone mad with boredom here. Given the choice he'd have thanked his gods that he'd died with a sword in his hand and not a dribbling ancient lying in his own piss among damp blankets.

Was that the fate that awaited Valerius? He knew he shouldn't feel regret, because it meant many more nights with Tabitha, more time to watch his son grow, and, if the gods willed it, more children.

But not if Domitian had his way.

He heard the commotion as he approached the villa. Sharp cries and a child's shrieks of something between excitement and fear. The sounds came from the family quarters and he dashed through the corridors until he found a gaggle of slaves and servants gathered outside Lucius's bedroom.

'Make way,' he shouted. They parted like an enemy flank before a Boar's Snout wedge and he pushed his way to the door. Lucius was on his bed jumping with excitement as Tabitha stood by it with a hobnailed sandal in her hand and a murderous look on her face. It took a moment before he saw the reason for her fury.

Forty or fifty scorpions scuttled about the floor with their curved stings raised and ready to strike. He winced as Tabitha brought the sandal down with a sharp crack on one that came too close, leaving a mess of broken carapace on the tiled floor. She moved to strike another and Valerius saw with a thrill of alarm that her feet were bare.

'Tabitha, wait.'

The order evoked a rebellious glare, but she obeyed. She shouldn't be in any real danger. The scorpions of the hills around Fidenae were small and black and capable of a sting that would cause a few days' pain and a localized swelling. But Valerius noticed something different about some of these.

He made his way through the waving armoured claws and into position behind one of the larger specimens. The scorpion was perhaps the length of his middle finger, and the pale yellow colour of ripening barley. He stooped and gently picked it up just beneath the sting, so it hung wriggling from his fingers. A gasp went up from the watching slaves.

He showed it to Tabitha. 'Do you recognize it?'

The blood drained from her face. 'The Deathbringer. How?'

Valerius had experience of the species in Syria and Judaea, and Tabitha had grown up with a healthy respect for them. One of the few breeds of scorpion whose sting could be fatal. If one hid in your boot or your blanket, you could take a week to die in terrible agony. This changed everything. His first thought had been the revenge of a disgruntled slave. Even a child's prank by one of Lucius's companions. This was different. Whoever had released these scorpions into Lucius's bedroom had murder in mind. They had tried to kill his child.

'Marcus.' His voice sounded like a sword scraping on the lid of a tomb and even Tabitha drew breath at the savagery of his tone. 'Bring me my whip. The big one, not the toy I normally use. And have the household servants gather in the barn. Every last one, the aged, the sick, the kitchen boys and the lady's maids. All of them.'

II

Thirty slaves, servants and their overseers gathered in a frightened huddle in the barn under the terrible gaze of Gaius Valerius Verrens, flanked by two trusted ex-legionaries he retained as bodyguards. Behind Valerius, Tabitha watched impassively, with Lucius clutched to her side, her eyes unblinking as a hawk on the brink of a stoop.

'Helena?' Tabitha's maid stepped forward, her hands clutched together to stop them shaking. 'Where were you between the seventh and eighth hours?'

Valerius already knew the answer, but he and Tabitha agreed Helena must be questioned with the rest, and it gave him his starting point.

'I was with the mistress, lord, as I'm sure she will confirm.'

Valerius glanced at Tabitha and she nodded. 'You may return to the house. Julia . . .' The villa's cook stepped from the huddle, her wizened, beetroot features daring him to question her loyalty.

He began with those whose positions made them easy to track and one by one they confirmed their innocence, or had it confirmed by one of their workmates. Surprisingly quickly the group was whittled down to eight or nine. It took a while to establish who was where and when, but gradually they worked it out. And were left with two. Cassius, the estate manager, who said he was in the *tablinum* preparing the accounts for Valerius to check, but had no one to substantiate his claim, and was close enough to Lucius's bedroom to deliver the scorpions. And Rautio, the overseer, who, if his claim he was counting *amphorae* in the wine store was true, had been too far away to do so.

Valerius stared at them and Tabitha emitted a hiss of disgust. One glared back in defiance, the other stood a little aside, his face muscles twitching with either outraged innocence or fear. Valerius flicked out the whip so its length lay on the dirt floor between them. The leather tapered over ten sinuous feet to a slim tip split into three with knots that had shards of metal twisted in their loops. In his father's day he'd seen a man stripped to the backbone in a dozen lashes.

'Cassius. Did you try to kill my son with those obscenities?'

The estate manager didn't flinch. 'I would never harm Lucius, lord. If you believe I would, lay aside your whip and give me your dagger. I'll gladly cut my wrists now.'

Valerius nodded. 'That's what I thought. You may go.'

Cassius sidled past Valerius with a glance of hatred at the other man. Tabitha followed him from the barn with Lucius in tow, only to be replaced by Julia, the cook, dragging one of the kitchen boys by the arm.

'You should hear what he says, lord,' she said.

'No, lord.' Rautio's voice crackled with desperation. 'You must believe me. I couldn't have had anything to do with it. I was in the wine store. The boy will confirm it.'

'That's what he told me to say.' The kitchen boy's shrill words ended with a squeak as the cook encouraged him with a sharp twist of the arm. 'I met him between the dining room and the family quarters. He said he'd get into trouble if anyone knew, so I was to say I'd seen him in the wine store. He gave me a silver *denarius*.'

'Please, lord . . .'

Valerius remembered that Rautio was the overseer accused of taking advantage of the widow. She happened to have responsibility for cleaning the family area, including Lucius's bedroom. He would have known the boy's every movement. 'So, Rautio, give me a reason why I shouldn't flog you to death.'

'I don't—'

Valerius flicked the whip so the knotted thongs cracked within inches of Rautio's ear. The overseer collapsed to his knees, whimpering. 'Let's begin with the identity of the person who ordered this.'

'A man,' Rautio whispered. 'He said he would have me flayed alive if I didn't do what he told me.'

'Vitalis.' Valerius called one of the guards. 'Search his quarters – thoroughly, mind – and bring me anything that doesn't belong there.' He turned his attention back to the overseer. 'How long have you been working for him?'

By the time Vitalis returned, Rautio had given up all he knew and was grovelling on the floor, sobbing. His description of his contact might have fitted a hundred others. Naturally he didn't know the man's name, but Valerius had no doubts as to the source of his troubles. He dropped the whip, glad he hadn't been required to use it, but any sympathy he might have had for the overseer vanished when Vitalis placed a leather pouch in his hand. 'He'd hidden it beneath a loose tile.'

Valerius weighed the pouch in his hand, making an estimate of its value before opening the leather thongs with his teeth and pouring the contents on the floor.

'Fifty gold *aurei*.' Valerius nudged the coins with his foot. Five thousand *sestertii*. Half a year's pay for a legionary. Fresh minted, too, with a decent likeness of Vespasian's wrinkled, hook-nosed features showing sharp and clear. Further proof his suspicions were correct. 'Enough for a prudent man to start a new life. But for that I would need to be dead. How much more were you to receive when you'd killed me? I'm genuinely interested in how much my head is worth.'

But Rautio knew anything he said would only condemn him further and was prudent enough to keep his mouth shut.

'Lock him in the wine store, so he may ponder his fate through the night. Make sure no harm comes to him, but I want him ready at the second hour, roped to the saddle of my best horse. He won't be needing his sandals.'

'The gold, lord?'

Valerius picked up a coin from the dust and flicked it to Vitalis. The guard caught it with a grin. 'One for each of you. Take the rest of it to Cassius. Ten *aurei* for his manumission fund, and what's left split between the slaves. They might as well profit from their troubles. Oh, and tell him to be generous to Julia. She might have a face that would sour milk, but she's a better interrogator than I am.'

III

'Is this wise, Valerius?' Tabitha asked as he prepared to set out the next morning. It was a reprise of a discussion that had gone on long into the night. They stood in the *atrium*, Tabitha wrapped in a shawl against the morning chill. Valerius held her to him, her head resting on his shoulder.

'I can't allow him to think I will let him threaten my family and do nothing.'

'Still, the Emperor's reaction . . .'

'Is unpredictable,' Valerius accepted, 'but he is a fair man, and a man with few illusions.'

'Then be careful, my husband.' She lifted her head to kiss him on the lips, and whispered, 'I will prepare for your return with extra care.'

Valerius felt a liquid glow run through him. The words were a kind of code and contained a certain promise. 'Then I will definitely return at speed. In the meantime, make sure Lucius doesn't stray.'

'He has learned his lesson,' she said. 'I believe it was instructive to see his father in all his terrible glory. Master of life and death.'

'And his mother.' Valerius smiled. 'You frightened me as much as those scorpions. But if you hadn't been there . . .'

'It will not happen again?'

'You have my promise. I will send such a message today that the gods will hear it.'

She released him and he strode out to the courtyard where his horse waited. Vitalis held the reins at its head. Rautio stood clear of its tail, his wrists bound by a length of rope attached to the saddle. His narrow, unshaven features wore an expression of dread and his eyes darted between the twitching beast's dangerous hooves and the vengeful crowd of slaves who had gathered to see them off, hissing insults and curses.

Valerius wore his finest toga, a voluminous affair not ideal for horse-back travel, but he pulled himself up and settled awkwardly into the saddle. He reached back to test the rope, almost pulling his captive off his feet. 'Come, Rautio,' he said, loudly enough for the watching slaves to hear. 'We have a long journey ahead of us and we can't afford to dally. The exercise will do you good. You've been putting on weight lately.'

He flicked the reins and they set off up the cobbled track, the slaves jeering and Rautio half running to keep pace. It was close to eight miles from the villa to the centre of Rome, and by the time they were half-way Valerius could hear the wet slaps as Rautio's bloodied feet hit the roadway. The former overseer had pleaded for water, to stop for a rest, but Valerius kept the mare to a steady walk that suited her. He didn't consider himself a cruel man. Rautio's ordeal was nothing to the fate he deserved. The wrath of his fellow slaves would have been the least of it. He had a feeling Tabitha would have been happy to spend an instructive hour with the man who had tried to murder her child. Valerius, on the other hand, had a more fitting punishment in mind.

He closed his ears to the whines and complaints and concentrated on the path ahead. The Via Salaria was the ancient road used by the Sabines when they harvested salt from the marshes at the mouth of the Tiber. Nowadays it linked Rome with the towns of the Apennine Hills and the trading centres of Amiternum and Ausculum on the Adriatic side. At this time of the day it thronged with the last of the farmers hurrying their cattle and pigs to the markets at the Forum Boarium and the Forum Suarium, and the produce of their fields to the Forum Holitorium on the Campus Martius. Valerius pushed his way through the heavily laden donkeys and past little families herding a single cow or a pair of squealing sows. The more curious among them noticed the exhausted, half-naked prisoner with the bloody feet struggling to stay upright at the end of his tether, but his plight evoked little reaction. Nobody much cared about a slave in trouble, not even another slave.

Soon they reached the straggle of houses, factories and warehouses that had grown up outside the city walls, and the crumbling tombs that lined the road. The guards at the Porta Collina were familiar with Valerius and waved him past without scrutinizing the Imperial warrant allowing him access to the Palatine night and day. They barely glanced at his prisoner.

Down the familiar cobbles of the Alta Selita and the left fork that would take him through the Subura. As he forced his way through the crowded, narrow street in the shadow of the towering *insula* apartment blocks he wondered again at the irony that such a festering pit of humanity could survive the Great Fire of Nero's reign when so much of value had been entirely consumed. There was a sharp cry behind him as Rautio slipped on something unsavoury and fell amongst the filth and the rushing feet. Valerius reined in for a moment to allow him to struggle to his feet. He had a moment of regret that he hadn't cut the assassin's throat and had done with it, but he quickly thrust it aside. Rautio was only a minor player in this drama; a bystander to be struck down in the final act. This was not about him. It was about ensuring the safety of Valerius and his family. To disguise his feelings he gave the rope a tug to jog Rautio into movement.

In the narrow gaps between the buildings he could see the familiar outline of the Temple of Jupiter Capitolinus, completely restored after its destruction eight years earlier in the civil war. Vespasian had vowed it would be even more magnificent than before, in memory of his brother Sabinus, captured there by the Vitellians and later murdered on the

Gemonian Stairs. A great golden chariot now adorned the summit, with a likeness of Sabinus at the reins, and eagles and horses lined the roof. Valerius thought it gaudy, but he understood that an emperor's ambitions must be seen to outdo those of ordinary men.

The road widened as they reached the street known as Argiletum. Rather than his usual route by the Victory Road across the northern face of the hill, he took the Clivus Palatinus to the main entrance to the palace complex. He dismounted when he reached the gate and unhooked the rope attaching Rautio to the saddle. The former overseer slumped to his knees, mumbling to himself. Valerius handed the reins of his mount to the black-clad gate guard and asked him to call a groom to take the beast to the nearby Imperial stables. He hauled Rautio to his feet and allowed him to drink from the stone trough beside the gateway.

'Are you expected, lord?' The guard commander checked his list with one eye on the swaying, unkempt Rautio.

'The Emperor sent a courier demanding my presence,' Valerius told him. It had happened several times in the past. 'He will want to hear what this man has to say.'

The guard commander hesitated only for a moment, such was Valerius's reputation not just as adviser to the Emperor and friend of Titus, but as holder of the Corona Aurea, a Hero of Rome. There were also certain whispered tales of service to successive emperors that were no business of any soldier who wished his career to prosper in the Imperial service. Gaius Valerius Verrens was a man to reckon with, and not one to delay.

'Very well, sir. Shall I send someone along with you to keep this brute in line?'

'That won't be necessary.' Valerius pointed to the man's feet, strips of torn flesh straggling at the centre of a pool of pink water. 'As you can see, he's in no condition to trouble anyone.' He hauled at the rope and led Rautio stumbling through the gates and up the slope. A hundred years ago the Palatine had been home to anyone rich enough to buy a house on the summit. That had changed since the time of

Augustus, who had taken over the entire hill. A succession of emperors had left their mark since, building palaces that their successors had felt the need to improve and enlarge. Now it was a warren of luxurious complexes surrounded by manicured gardens. It housed not only the Emperor, his retinue and their favourites, but also the Palatium, the offices of state that took up most of his waking hours, without which the Empire would crumble and fall.

Valerius gave the guard time to watch him march Rautio towards Vespasian's palace before changing course. The Domus Transitoria, where Titus had set up home, lay to his right, but he continued straight ahead through the gardens. His destination lay in the centre of the Palatine, close to the Temple of Apollo where he'd witnessed the augury on the fateful day the Praetorians butchered Servius Sulpicius Galba and ignited the civil war that brought Vespasian the throne.

He approached a wide two-storey building with white columns, walls of pale gold and a red-tiled roof. A line of soldiers emerged from a hut near the palace entrance. Naturally, there would be a permanent guard, even here in the centre of the Palatine. It was a measure of the insecurity of the man he was about to confront.

'Gaius Valerius Verrens, Hero of Rome, seeks an interview with Caesar Domitianus, suffect consul,' he announced to the officer in command of the guard.

The centurion was young for his rank, probably not long in the Imperial service, with piercing blue eyes and a long nose. He would have been personally appointed by the Emperor and his expression said he was impressed by neither the senator's stripe on Valerius's toga nor his outdated military honours. He waved two of the guards to cover Rautio with their swords. 'What is the subject of this *interview*?'

Valerius ignored the sneer. 'I seek the consul's advice on a private matter. Please pass my request to him.'

The centurion didn't like it, but he sensed Valerius would provide no more information. He was an admirer of Domitian, a forward-looking patrician of his own age. Caesar Domitianus would know how to deal with this upstart with his airs and graces. With an irritated shake of the head he marched up the palace steps and disappeared inside. A short time later he reappeared and motioned Valerius forward into the cobbled courtyard. 'You may approach . . . that is far enough!' he snapped.

Halfway to the steps, Valerius obeyed the order without protest. Naturally Domitian would want to inspect him before he came within range of sword swing. As he waited a figure appeared on the balcony overlooking the courtyard and stood, unnaturally still, staring at the tableau below. Valerius could almost feel the throb of hatred in his enemy's temples. If the eyes had been spears, he'd already be dead. Domitian had never hidden his homicidal loathing for Valerius, especially since the day the one-handed Roman dangled him from a similar balcony on the Esquiline Hill.

'Have you searched him?' The high-pitched voice was the same, but Domitian had filled out in the shoulders and chest since their last encounter. Vespasian's youngest son was no longer the arrogant boy Valerius had scorned and dismissed. The centurion cursed beneath his breath and marched forward to run his hands over Valerius's toga. 'If he finds so much as a fruit knife,' the young consul continued, 'I would have every right to have you executed.'

'No weapons,' Valerius assured him. The guard commander nodded his confirmation. 'I'm here to talk and bring you a gift.' He pulled Rautio forward. 'On your knees, slave.'

'Centurion Polio hinted that you needed some advice. Is this some kind of Saturnalia jest, or has country life driven you mad? I seem to remember madness runs in your family.'

Valerius allowed his eyes to drift to the left. The shadowy figure standing by the curtain of a window stepped back beyond his scrutiny. 'This slave failed in his duty to not one master,' he said, 'but two. I wondered how you would deal with him.'

Domitian sniffed, but didn't hide his interest. 'Then I would beat him twice to remind him of his duties. How did he fail them?'

Valerius fixed his eyes on the younger man's. 'He owed his loyalty to the one, and the other, who had bought it, gave him a small task he

27

was too clumsy to complete.' Valerius sensed Domitian go still. Now the young patrician understood. 'When discovered he told everything, thus betraying his real master as well as his rightful one.'

Domitian was puzzled now. Whatever the slave had revealed was unlikely to threaten him, but he couldn't understand how Valerius might profit from bringing him here. It didn't occur to him that Valerius's very presence with Rautio was all his enemy sought, and, for the moment, all he needed.

'Then you should cut his throat now.' Domitian laughed. 'Or perhaps Polio should do it. You never did have the stomach.'

Valerius smiled up at him. 'No.' He dropped the rope and nudged Rautio in the back so he sprawled on the cobbles. 'I only wanted to bring him back where he belongs. I'll let you decide what to do with him.'

'Please, lord, no. Not that,' Rautio croaked.

Valerius ignored him. 'As you say, I've always been a little squeamish. Thank you for your advice, consul. ' He turned and walked away.

'Wait. I haven't given you leave to go,' Domitian cried. 'I am not finished with you. Stop him!'

But Valerius was already beyond the line of guards. This was an argument they wanted no part of.

IV

His route took him through a park where clumps of tall cypress trees masked the surrounding buildings, so he might have been in the country rather than at the centre of the world's greatest city. As he followed the path, Valerius considered what he'd just done. Domitian would always be a threat. Logically, the only course of action was to reduce that threat to its lowest possible level. He had left his enemy confused and, hopefully, off balance; perhaps even a little frightened. He'd made it clear any future attack would have its repercussions. In a few hours everyone on the Palatine would know what had happened between them, certainly everyone who mattered. Letters would be dictated. A message would be sent. Vespasian and Titus had placed Valerius under their protection. Even the Emperor's son was not immune from his wrath. At worst, he had bought his family a breathing space.

There would be a price to pay, naturally. A man did not kick over a hornet's nest on the Palatine without consequences. For all their friendship, he doubted Titus would appreciate his actions. It might even harm their relationship. But he couldn't allow Domitian to believe he could act with impunity. His honour and his duty to his family demanded he do everything possible to protect them.

'Valerius?'

His head whipped round at a familiar voice that aroused memories and ignited a whirl of conflicting emotions. She stood in the shadow beneath one of the cypress clusters, a diminutive figure in a dress of lilac silk belted at the waist with a gold chain. A cream shawl of the same material covered her shoulders. More full-bodied than he remembered, but otherwise untouched by the passing years. The same lustrous walnut tresses, artfully styled to frame the perfect oval of her features, appraising dark eyes with hidden depths of passion, and a skin so pale it was almost luminous. Domitia Longina Corbulo. Still with that cool, almost detached air. Such a contrast to his Tabitha; the difference between ice and fire. She was the daughter of General Gnaeus Domitius Corbulo, commander of Rome's eastern armies until Nero ordered him to commit suicide. Valerius had escorted Domitia to join her father in Antioch a decade or so earlier. Shipwreck and disaster threw them together and falling in love seemed natural. Unknown to Domitia, Nero had ordered Valerius to spy on the general, with a suggestion that he should kill him if the opportunity arose. Instead, Valerius saved Corbulo from assassination. Circumstances had torn them apart, only for fate to rekindle their love in the bloody chaos of the Year of the Four Emperors.

He stepped towards her, glancing over his shoulder to ensure he wasn't being followed. Hers had been the presence at the window, but how had she got here? Of course, the hill was riddled with *cryptoporticus*, the underground passages that allowed emperors, princes and their acolytes to move freely between the palace complexes without being observed. After eight years on the Palatine, Domitia would be familiar with many of them.

'My lady.' Valerius bowed. 'This is a surprise.'

'A surprise, Valerius, but not a pleasure?'

It seemed she hadn't lost the ability to disconcert him with a few well-chosen words. The last time they'd been alone together the smoke from the burning Temple of Jupiter still hung over the city and Valerius had been a penniless outcast. Domitia had bought his life by promising herself to Titus Flavius Domitianus. At the time he had felt slighted and diminished, not knowing whether to love or hate her. Now he understood that his reaction had been selfish and inconsiderate. She had saved him without thought for herself and had lived with the consequences.

She saw something of it in his face. 'What's done is done, Valerius. We cannot take back the years.'

'I thought my pleasure would have been obvious.' He allowed himself a smile. They stood less than a pace apart and the breeze brought him the lilac of the perfumed oils she wore. She studied him for a moment and he noticed her eyes drifting to his neck. She was wondering whether he still wore the little golden star of Fortuna she had given him at their parting. He hoped she wouldn't ask about it; he didn't like to lie. She was a woman and despite the years that had passed he doubted she'd appreciate knowing he'd presented the charm to a soft-handed slave girl in the baths at Apamea.

A door banged somewhere and Valerius again checked the way he'd come. 'Won't Dom— he miss you?'

'He is not interested in me.' A disdainful toss of the head accompanied her answer. 'Only the ideal of me. First, he will apply himself to discovering just how much the slave told you, and how much harm it has the potential to do him. It will take time and involve shears and glowing iron. I doubt the slave will survive.' She looked up into his face. 'Does he deserve such a fate, Valerius?'

Valerius told her about the scorpions and she grimaced. 'Ugh. I remember the filthy creatures from my father's palace at Antioch. He is truly evil.' She could have been referring to Rautio, but Valerius chose to believe otherwise.

'Yes,' he agreed.

'When he has taken his pleasure from that creature's pain he will retire to the library with a flask of wine and rail about his hatred for you, and how your every breath demeans and belittles him. He hates you and fears you, Valerius, and he believes that if he does not kill you, you will kill him.'

'Perhaps I should.'

'You are many things, Gaius Valerius Verrens, but you are not a murderer.' She shot him a look of irritation. A harder Domitia, this, than he remembered, more cynical, but how could she not be, living with a man like Domitian? 'We are safe enough for now. When the wine takes its effect he will spend another hour rambling about his favourite subject: himself. It is unfair his father heaps honours on Titus, while he must be content with a mere temporary consulship. It is unfair he must live in a twenty-room hovel while Vespasian and Titus occupy whole palaces. If his father did not want the Golden House, Domitian should have been given it. Instead he must watch it demolished. He says he will build the greatest palace Rome has ever seen, greater even than the Domus Aurea. It will cover the Palatine, absorbing everything that went before, and will have libraries and baths, and gardens, audience rooms, great halls so high clouds will form beneath their ceilings. The plans consume him.'

Valerius remembered a visit to Nero, not so far from here. A hand sweeping across a model to clear whole districts from the centre of Rome. Another man consumed with the need to be remembered in stone. A thought occurred to him. 'To carry out such a plan he would require not only wealth, but power.'

Her eyes held his. 'Of course.' A heartbeat's hesitation. 'Are you happy, Valerius?'

'Yes,' he said, surprised by the conversation's abrupt change of direction. 'I would never have believed I could be this happy.'

For a moment he saw what might be pain in the dark eyes, then it vanished.

'And they truly meant to kill your son?'

'Truly.'

'He will never stop until he sees you dead.' Valerius nodded, uncertain where this was going. 'So we must provide you with a means to make him stop.'

'We?'

'Despite what happened between us I would never see you hurt . . . or your family.'

'Thank you.' He resisted the temptation to reach out to her, but he had a question. 'What I don't understand is how.'

32

'Domitian is a plotter.'

Valerius froze. The information didn't surprise him, but the fact that she was prepared to share it meant she knew more. 'Who does he plot against?' Even as he asked the question the faces were already clear in his mind.

'Anyone in a position to oppose his ambitions.' So, there it was, unsaid, but unmistakable. Only two men held positions lofty enough to thwart Domitian. 'I cannot promise anything, Valerius,' she continued. 'At the moment all is suspicion and conjecture, but if there is a way of discovering more I will find out. If I succeed, I rely on you to deal with it sensitively.'

Do not get me killed, was what she meant. He felt a sudden surge of his old affection for her. 'You have my word. But please, Domitia, don't put yourself in any danger.'

'Do you remember the cypher we were to use to write to each other when I was staying with my uncle at Dertona?'

'Yes, I think so.' A simple substitution code – numbers for letters of the alphabet – with a symbol to indicate which letter was the number 1, and the added refinement that the first two sentences of the message were nonsense, designed to frustrate any potential code-breaker.

'If I discover anything of value, I will contact you. The messenger will carry a token.' She removed a gold ring with an enormous green stone set in a coiled snake. 'Will you remember this?'

He laughed. 'It would be hard to forget. But will you be able to trust your courier?'

She nodded. 'With my life. He served with my father in Armenia and he's entirely devoted to me.'

'What if I want to contact you?'

Perhaps the words contained an implicit message he hadn't intended, because she shook her head and her smile was tinged with sadness. 'Oh, Valerius, so scarred and experienced, but so unworldly. That is not how it works. This is the Palatine. You may count on my support, but after we part today I doubt we will ever see each other again.'

She lifted her head to kiss him on the cheek. When she disappeared into the trees, the sense of loss surprised him.

V

Valerius had just reached the gate when he heard footsteps at his back and a gruff voice announced: 'Guards. Do not let this man leave the palace.'

'I surrender.' Valerius turned with a weary sigh.

'I believe the expression is "caught in the act",' said Titus Flavius Vespasian, heir to the Empire. 'You certainly haven't lost your flair for diplomacy, Valerius. I know my advice is sometimes flawed, but . . .'

'I'm sorry, Titus, but there were pressing reasons . . .'

'There are always pressing reasons.' Titus ushered him away from the gate in the direction of the Domus Transitoria. As they walked, Valerius considered his friend of almost a dozen years. They were of a similar age and height, but different in build, Valerius lean and well muscled from his hour of exercise with the *gladius* every morning, Titus sleeker, with just a hint of bulge around the middle. Yet there could be no doubt the years had been much kinder to Titus. The close-cropped hair remained a lustrous crow black with none of the grey flecks Valerius saw when he looked in a mirror. Health and good living shone from the fine aristocratic features, the full lips had a sardonic twist which hinted that whatever happened the world would always amuse him, and a glint in his eyes confirmed it. Valerius, on the other hand, looked more like his old friend Serpentius every day. The dark eyes increasingly hawk-ish, the cheeks a little more sunken, a thin-lipped mouth that might have been drawn with a knife blade. Hard features that didn't need too much encouragement to become savage. Titus smiled, aware of his friend's appraisal. 'Your reasons will wait until we're in the shade with a cup of wine. I could have sent a servant, but I don't get out often enough these days and I thought I'd surprise you.'

'If surprise means almost giving me a seizure you succeeded. How did you know I was here?'

'The gate commander sent a guard to announce your arrival, but by then I'd already had news of what was happening at Domitian's resi-dence.' He saw Valerius's look. 'Yes, he's my brother, but I know what's happening in his household almost before he does.'

Did that mean Titus's sources kept him informed of Domitian's intrigues? Valerius thought about what Domitia had said. If Domitian's wife didn't know the details, then few others did; could Domitia her-self be one of Titus's informants? He dismissed the thought even as it formed. Duty and honour were the principles by which Domitia Longina had lived her life. She might take a risk to aid Valerius and his family, but she wouldn't play the spy for mere politics.

They followed a marble portico to one of the palace's secluded gardens, where a table and benches waited beneath the broad canopy of a stone pine. Titus invited Valerius to sit. A servant poured wine from a jug into silver cups. The consul leaned back against the bole of the tree, looking relaxed and at ease as he studied Valerius. Eventually he nodded, as if the interval had confirmed his decision.

'In a way it's fortuitous you came here today, despite your little scene with Domitian. Why did you come? I know you said you had good reason, but I'll need the details to enable me to deflect any possible repercussions. My brother is not the type to take a slight lightly. Tell me what brought you here.'

Valerius repeated the story he'd told Domitia and Titus listened in grim silence. When Valerius mentioned the species of scorpion the young consul shook his head in disgust. 'You are certain this is

35

Domitian's doing? It is difficult to believe even my brother would stoop to such a filthy trick.'

'I can't think of anyone else who hates me that much. He didn't react like an innocent man.'

'That proves nothing.'

'No, but what happens to the slave will be interesting. If Domitian is innocent he'll send him back and tell me to deal with him myself.'

'But that won't happen.'

'No, I don't believe it will.'

'Very well.' Titus nodded to himself. 'We can consider the present matter closed. As to the future . . .' He hesitated for a moment, choosing his words carefully. 'Perhaps I have a solution to your problem. A radical one, but one that will afford your family a measure of protection it does not currently possess.'

'I'm not sure I like the word radical.' Valerius eyed him warily. Was Titus making him an offer or about to give him a direct order?

Titus smiled. 'Perhaps I used it unwisely. It is a matter of distance.' He waited for the obvious question, but Valerius held his gaze. 'If you hadn't come here today, my father was about to summon you. You're acquainted with Julius Agricola?'

Valerius blinked at the name. A face tried to force its way into his head, but it was like looking through a veil and the features remained blurred and indistinct. 'Acquainted, yes, but I haven't met him for almost twenty years. We served together for a few months on Paulinus's staff in Britannia before the general brought Boudicca's rebels to battle.' Not battle, but a slaughter; a mass bloodletting that cost Valerius his first real love. 'We were never close, but I remember him as a competent, steady officer.'

'Yes, that would describe him,' Titus agreed. 'My father values him, though I find him too aloof for my liking. A little too sure of himself, and I suspect he looks down on tax farmers and mule sellers.' Valerius met his friend's eye and smiled. Vespasian's family had been tax gatherers before they rose to senatorial rank, and the Emperor himself had been forced to trade mules in the past to stay solvent. 'But that is to digress,'

36

Titus continued. 'Apart from a few questions about his time in Asia as *quaestor* to the rapacious Titianus, his record is spotless. He did well in Hispania as Galba's *praetor* and stayed out of trouble during the late war until Otho's pirates burned the family estate in Liguria and murdered his mother. Vespasian gave him command of the Twentieth where he did well enough to merit a suffect consulship . . .'

'So he's a patrician now.' Valerius smiled.

'You didn't know?'

'I've spent the last few years running the estate and fighting the occasional case in the *basilica*.' Valerius had been destined for a career in the law until events conspired to make him a soldier. He'd completed his studies on his return to Rome and an inquisitive mind and a talent for oratory ensured his success as a litigator. There'd been talk of a pact to share high-profile cases with his friend Gaius Plinius Secundus, but Pliny's political fortunes had soared with the return of Vespasian and it had come to nothing. 'I've never been one for court gossip.'

'So you're also unaware, my friend, that Julius Agricola now has a new province?'

Something in his tone told Valerius the information was significant. 'New province?'

'Britannia.'

Britannia. Rome's most northerly province, and some would say its most troublesome. A land of gloomy mist-clad mountains where the winds howled like the cries of lost souls, bottomless mires could swallow a man and his horse in moments, and near impenetrable forests saw the native priests carry out their disgusting rituals, even the trees seeming to whisper 'enemy'. A rich land, not just in gold, which was what had drawn Emperor Claudius there almost four decades earlier, but in the fertile black soil and the lush meadows, the broad rivers teeming with fish and the woods that swarmed with game. The great tribal federations of Britannia claimed that land – the Catuvellauni, the Dobunni, the Durotriges, with their tribes and their sub-tribes. In battle their champions fought naked and bore the record of their deeds tattooed on their skin; huge men, who felt no pain and feared nothing but failure.

The memory sent a shudder of dread through Valerius. He had left his right hand in Britannia, along with his youth.

'What has this to do with me?'

'My father received an initial report from Agricola a week ago – he has been in Britannia less than three months – and the governor believes the only way to guarantee the security of the province is to bring the entire island under our control.'

'No easy task,' Valerius ventured. 'I never travelled further north than Lindum, but I was in Siluria and merchants I spoke to later said the mountains of the north dwarf those of the west, and the terrain is far more difficult. Ambush territory. If Agricola isn't careful he'll end up a second Varus.'

'Precisely what he said.' Titus paused for a moment to reflect on the fate of Publius Quinctilius Varus and the legions he had led to ambush and annihilation in the forests of Germania sixty years earlier. It had taken Rome decades to recover from the ignominy of the defeat and the loss of three eagles. 'That is why it will be a long, meticulously planned campaign, lasting several seasons. And why he needs help.'

Valerius shook his head. 'My fighting days are done. After Asturica Augusta I promised Tabitha I would never risk my neck again. I'd dedicate myself to the estate and my family. I owe it to my wife and Lucius to keep that promise.'

'Oh, you won't be fighting, my friend, and I would not separate you from your family.'

'Then what?'

'I'll let my father explain.'

'Who do you favour today, Titus?'

Valerius expected to meet Vespasian in the large receiving room at his palace, or in his private quarters. Instead, Titus had escorted him to the southern side of the Palatine where a reviewing stand overlooked the seething crowds who'd flocked to the Circus Maximus to watch the Vinalia chariot meeting. Their elevated position gave them a panoramic view of the packed stands and the track. The staggered starting gates were below on the right and Valerius could see the hand-lers already pushing their teams into position while officials cleared the wreckage of a damaged chariot from the far end of the *spina*, the central barrier that divided the track. The stands were a sea of red, white and blue, signifying three of the teams the spectators supported, but the predominant colour was green.

'I have a small wager on the Whites, Father.' Titus's face glowed with anticipation and he gave Valerius a wry look that told him the bet was anything but small.

'Not the Greens? Scorpus seems unbeatable these days. It makes things quite dull.' Vespasian would be close to seventy, and he looked it. Eyes once bright with restless energy now appeared washed out, pale orbs sunk deep in a face whose every wrinkle marked a crisis or a tragedy during the seven exhausting years he had worn the purple. He'd survived one conspiracy after another seemingly unmoved, but the death of Antonia Caenis, the freedwoman who was the love of his life, had aged him overnight. The full lips were permanently down-turned, giving the impression of a constant frown, and his voice was a scratchy parody of that which once barked orders to his army commanders. Ruling the Empire would have taxed a man twenty years younger, which was why he delegated much of the responsibility to Titus, who reigned as co-Emperor in all but name.

'I watched the bay team in practice last week. Atticus tells me his lead horse Perseus was born to win and his driver is fearless.' Titus took a seat behind his father and beckoned Valerius to join him. He leaned forward and spoke quietly in Vespasian's ear. 'Valerius Verrens on the Agricola matter.'

'Ah, Verrens.' The Emperor looked over his shoulder and his lips twitched in what might have been an attempt at a smile. 'Your presence is always welcome. I could have left this to my son, but he believed there might be a certain reluctance on your part to accept the offer. After your good work in Hispania I felt it only right that I should personally convince you of the importance I attach to this mission.'

'I am always ready to serve, Caesar,' Valerius assured him.

A genuine smile and the pale eyes twinkled. 'But are you willing? That is the question. What has Titus told you?'

'Only that Governor Agricola plans a series of campaigns to pacify the north of Britannia and bring it under Roman control.'

'Precisely, and that is why . . .'

'Caesar?' An aide approached holding what looked like a napkin.

'I am afraid we must postpone our talk until the race ends,' Vespasian apologized. He accepted the napkin and Titus helped his father to his feet, accompanied by a great roar from the crowds below. Valerius searched the ranks of patricians in the reviewing stand for Domitian and his wife, but could see neither.

Vespasian held out his right hand with his arm extended and a hush fell over the multitude in the great stadium below. A hundred thousand held a single breath . . .

The napkin fluttered from the Emperor's hand and a tumult erupted that made the earlier noise seem like a whisper. Simultaneously, the starting gates sprang open and eight chariots hurtled out on to the track, instantly manoeuvring for the most favourable position closest to the *spina* wall. Valerius knew the start was one of the most dangerous parts of the race, when eight or twelve four-horse teams fought for the best line at the first corner. A collective gasp went up as two of the fragile wood and leather cars clashed wheel to wheel. Another heartbeat and one or other would have capsized. But these drivers were veterans and with a twitch of the reins they allowed the chariots to drift apart without losing advantage. A pair of carts emerged ahead of the free-for-all, the leader with a driver sporting a green tunic and a team of bays taking a wider line half a head behind. Vespasian turned to his son.

'What did I tell you?' he shouted, his voice brittle with excitement. 'Scorpus is already ahead.'

'But that's Atticus's bays and Perseus on his shoulder.' Titus's passion matched his father's. 'Ten *aurei* says he takes him by the fourth turn.'

Vespasian spat on his palm and held it out, accepting the bet. Titus grinned and slapped his father's hand.

By now the leading chariot was approaching the first fiendishly tight turn at astonishing speed. The drivers rode with the reins wrapped around their middle, leaving their hands free to wield the whip and for the more delicate manoeuvres. Valerius imagined the moment Scorpus leaned out to ease his lead runner into the turn. From above it appeared the team moved as a single unit flowing effortlessly through the corner, but he knew it took hundreds of hours of practice to achieve that effect. Each horse in the team would have an entirely different stride pattern. If one were half a stride out the chariot and team would be a heap of wreckage in a moment. The driver of the bays had to take a wider circuit and lost ground. Behind them four teams thundered for the same patch of sand and somehow came through unscathed. Green and White were neck and neck through the second turn, but Scorpus made a fractional error at the third. Vespasian groaned as the bays edged into the lead.

'Yes!' The clamour of cheers and roars all but drowned Titus's shout and the wall of noise from the stands below took on a new volume.

Now the chasing pack hit the far turn for the second time. White had the advantage, skimming the *spina* wall by a hand's breadth, with Blue and Red outside him. Scorpus's fellow Green took the wider line and Valerius watched with his heart thundering as the Red chariot eased him ever closer to the stand wall. Green must give way or . . .

One moment the chariot was a single object, the next a cartwheeling cluster of spinning wheels and splintered wood. A tumbling body flew into the air, the driver still attached to his team by the reins at his waist. Every charioteer wore a padded tunic to protect him against a crash and carried a curved knife ready to hand to cut the reins. Green must have managed it because he parted company with his galloping horses after a few moments. Yet his senses were stunned by the battering and he stood, swaying on his feet, until the horses of the second Blue chariot rode over him as if he didn't exist. Valerius saw the chariot jump as its right wheel hit an obstacle, but the driver somehow regained control, leaving a crumpled green heap lying in the dust behind him.

Seven circuits of the oval track. One by one the gilded dolphins of the lap counter dropped. Five chariots left, but Titus and his father

41

only had eyes for White and Green, who had exchanged the lead three times now. White had the advantage by half a head as they entered the final lap. The Emperor and his son looked on, puzzled, as the Green chariot dropped back so it was running directly behind the leader.

'Scorpus has no chance of winning now,' Titus said.

'Perhaps,' his father conceded. 'But there is many a slip between the cup and the lip.'

The Green team was so close their noses were actually over the back of the lead car and the White driver must have felt their breath. Scorpus had barely used his whip, but now he cracked it directly above his horses' heads, inches from the White charioteer's back. Once, twice, thrice. Valerius saw the man glance over his shoulder. Scorpus was in danger of killing them both. White's whip flicked out to urge the bays to greater speed, but Scorpus matched him. A dozen strides and they would be at the corner. The White driver knew he was going too fast, but if he slowed the Green horses would be aboard, all flashing hooves and snapping teeth.

The roar rose in a deafening crescendo as the leader entered the turn. Valerius watched the chariot drift outwards, could almost sense the moment the team felt the change. Would the lead horse change stride to compensate? Yes, but the second was less experienced. It panicked, touched shoulders with the next in line and the entire team was down in a tangle of heads and legs as the chariot overturned, throwing the helpless driver on his head. An enormous collective gasp. Scorpus and his Green team had nowhere to go; they must smash into the wreckage. But the twenty-five-year-old veteran of a thousand races had foreseen what would happen. The drift had taken the White team a chariot-width out of the racing line, leaving the narrowest of gaps. A twitch of the reins and Green was through.

Vespasian emitted a cackle of pure pleasure and Titus muttered a muffled curse as he reached for his purse. The noise level dropped as the circus officials prepared for the final race of the day. Vespasian called Valerius forward to a seat on his left. 'Come, sit by me. Governor Agricola . . . yes, Agricola.' A short pause to gather his thoughts. 'He knows that if he is to subdue the northern tribes he must exert total strategic and tactical control over his legions. You have heard of the Brigantes?'

'Yes, Caesar. The largest tribal federation in Britannia. Suetonius Paulinus persuaded them to act as a barrier against incursion from the north while he dealt with Boudicca's rebels.'

'Of course, you were in Britannia with Paulinus.' Vespasian nodded. 'After the overthrow of their queen they became an infernal nuisance. Cerialis, who was governor, decided he must deal with them once and for all. The man he chose was Julius Agricola, commander of the Twentieth. Despite the size of the territory Agricola took only a single season to subdue them. He understands the scale of the task he faces better than any other man in Britannia. I have told him he has my full support.'

'And he has asked for our help.' Titus's voice came from behind Valerius.

'He cannot simultaneously command an army in the remote north and rule the province of Britannia,' Vespasian continued. 'His procurator is a sound man who can take care of the financial details, but Agricola is most concerned about the legal aspects. As you know, the governor is called upon to give judgement in countless legal disputes as well as criminal cases. The . . . shall we call it Romanization of the province only adds to the complications. Agricola has identified five former tribal capitals as locations for self-governing *civitates*. That means choosing suitable candidates for the *ordo* and instructing individuals in their specific civic duties. There will undoubtedly be disputes over the acquisition of land for public buildings and the details of a legally binding charter for each town.'

Below, the next chariot teams were being coaxed into the starting gates and Valerius could see the aide hovering with a new napkin.

'In short,' Titus took over from his father, 'Agricola suggests sending a suitably qualified officer with the rank of legate and the office of *legatus iuridicus*. The Emperor has chosen you.'

VI

'We don't underestimate the burden we impose upon you,' Titus assured Valerius as they accompanied Vespasian back through the gardens to his palace. 'But you're one of the few men with the experience, the qualifications and qualities needed to fill this position. You will be second in rank only to the governor, and when he's on campaign you'll essentially be the civil governor of Britannia.'

'I'm flattered.'

'Don't be. This is a difficult and arduous task that will take you the length and breadth of the province. But it will have its compensations. When it's over, you can depend on a province of your own. Who knows,' the Emperor's son grinned, 'in a few years we may be consuls together.'

'I've no ambition to be a consul.'

'It is not a question of ambition, young man,' the Emperor snapped. 'It is a question of serving Rome.'

Valerius felt the blood rush to his face at the unexpected rebuke. 'Of course, Caesar.'

The Emperor's voice softened. 'Naturally you will wish to be accompanied by your family. Suitable accommodation will be provided in Londinium.'

'Not Colonia Claudia?'

Titus shook his head. 'After the rebellion, Trebellius Maximus decided Londinium had the advantages best suited to a provincial capital, though Colonia Claudia was re-established and the Temple of Claudius rebuilt. I suspect you would find it something of a rural backwater now.'

'It will certainly have changed since my time there with the Second,' Vespasian recalled. 'Londinium was a few huts overlooking the Tamesa and my Batavian auxiliaries swam across towing their armour on rafts. Claudius created his *colonia* close to where he took the surrender of the tribes of southern Britannia. They called it Camulodunum. A few farmsteads tucked in behind turf banks a five-year-old could climb. What did you think of the place? Britannia, I mean.'

'I liked it.' Valerius smiled. 'Even with the damp and the cold. Fine farmland and good grazing. I liked the people, too, at least the ones who weren't trying to kill me.' He saw Titus glance at his wooden fist. 'I can't regret my time there. Without the rebellion I would have returned to Rome and a career in the law, tucked away in sleepy Fidenae with my dusty law books, worrying about the olive harvest.' He laughed. 'No one would have offered me a consulship then.'

They'd reached Vespasian's palace. 'So you accept?'

Valerius knew he could never deny his emperor. By giving him this position Vespasian was awarding him patrician status. The Verrens family had always been equestrians and his father was the first to enter the Senate. He would never have dreamed a Verrens might become a patrician. 'Yes, Caesar.'

'Then Titus will brief you on the situation in Britannia.'

Vespasian turned and walked slowly away, followed at a discreet distance by two of his palace guard. Titus watched him go with an expression of real affection, but when he turned to Valerius the warm look had faded, to be replaced by something more sombre.

'He seems well,' Valerius said.

'Well enough. But he tires easily. I tried to persuade him to allow me to preside over the chariot racing, but he refused. His people must see their emperor, he said.'

'A question of serving Rome,' Valerius said with a wry smile.

Titus laughed. 'Yes, he can still bite. So, Britannia? How do you feel about going back?'

Valerius considered for a moment before he replied. 'Excited. Wary. Something else that I can't define. Am I up to the task.'

'No regrets, then?'

'I'm more worried about how Tabitha will react.'

Titus slapped him on the shoulder and they took their place beneath the tree where they'd sat earlier. A clerk arrived and placed a set of leather scroll cases on a campaign table set up in the shade. Titus reached for the first and retrieved the contents.

'Agricola has four legions in Britannia, the Twentieth, the Ninth, the Second Adiutrix and the Second Augusta. He intends to use three for his campaign, with Augusta dispersing to provide security across the south.' He read Valerius's look. 'The current situation differs from Boudicca's day. The south is genuinely pacified. They remember what Paulinus did after the rebellion and there'll be no repeat. Agricola will have free rein to deal with the northern savages at his leisure.'

Valerius had a momentary vision of smoke from burning villages that hung from one end of the horizon to the other, slaughtered children, and trees heavy with dangling bodies. Suetonius Paulinus was a hard, unyielding man who had put down the rebellion with pitiless brutality. 'The Reckoning', he had called it. He would have salted the fields if Nero hadn't reminded him the only point of a province was the profit that could be squeezed from it. The dead don't pay taxes.

Titus smoothed a sheet of parchment on the table. 'Gaius Valerius Verrens will be a long way from the excitement. There are already *civitates* in the south-west, at Isca and Durnovaria.' Both men had served in Britannia so the general locations Titus described were familiar enough. 'Agricola has plans for others at Corinium, in the lands of the Dobunni, and the Atrebates capital of Calleva. However, your immediate priority should be the Corieltauvi federation, who control a vast sweep of flatlands from the centre of the province to the east coast. We've decided to set up a *civitas* at Ratae, in the centre of the country, and Agricola wishes to create a *colonia* at Lindum.' He met Valerius's gaze. 'You know what that means. Trying to find land to provide decent farms for three thousand legionary veterans. We can't just commandeer it, as Claudius did at Camulodunum. He was a conqueror and the former owners were either dead or enslaved. The Corieltauvi are clients and we're on good terms with King Volisios. There's an Imperial estate to the south of the city which will give you a start, but for the rest it'll be weeks of interminable negotiations, surveys and endless fights over water and grazing rights. All that and you'll probably arrive to a roomful of unresolved case documents as high as your neck.' He grinned. 'Having a change of mind?'

'If I'd known what I was walking into I'd have left your brother alone and stayed on the estate.'

'And that is the other reason Father chose you for this position. It puts you, Tabitha and Lucius beyond Domitian's reach.'

'If someone got close enough to strangle me in Hispania, why not Britannia?'

'Because I will have my brother watched more closely than ever. And the office of *legatus iuridicus* entitles you to a substantial personal body-guard. Thirty picked men supplied by the governor.' Titus shrugged. They both knew at least one guard would be a spy tasked with report-ing Valerius's movements, but there was no helping that. 'They will be here within the week. I'll send them out to Fidenae when they arrive.'

VII

Canovium Auxiliary Fort, Conwy Valley

Twenty-five summers had passed since the conquerors laid the initial layer of turf for the walls and put mattock to soil to dig the first ditch. Not Romans, it turned out, but Tungri, hard-eyed, heavily bearded German auxiliary cavalrymen, quick with sword and spear, who spoke a different language among themselves from that used by their officers. Their horses were twice the stature of the small native breeds and the riders liked to tie the severed heads of their victims to their saddle pommels by the hair. Canovium squatted on a low rise overlooking the river. A rough square surrounded by a pair of ditches and a stout timber wall half as tall again as the height of Owain's champion Cadwal. It guarded what had always been an important trade route, for the river was fordable here, but high tide allowed Roman ships to ply their way to Canovium with essential supplies for the garrison. The silver in the soldiers' pouches attracted craftsmen to supply them with the luxuries Rome would not provide and a settlement quickly grew up outside the walls.

Owain Lawhir had used the weeks since the gory ceremony on Mona to gather spearmen from every corner of his realm at his capital,

Dinas Affaraon. Each warrior carried enough dried fish and rough barley cakes to last ten days. He'd reckoned on two thousand, but the fear inspired by Gwlym ensured his force was closer to three. No tribal leader would risk the wrath of the arch-druid by failing to give his support. It had taken them three days to reach the secluded valley a few miles south of Canovium where Owain left them while he made his final plan of attack. Three times already he'd crept up to the little settlement outside the walls and waited in the darkness listening to the Tungrian sentries making their rounds. Tomorrow six of his best men would visit the tavern which served the soldiers of Canovium thick, dark local beer and provided the use of a back room when they wanted their women. The Ordovices would pose as traders waiting to make the crossing with packhorses loaded with sacks of wool and beaver and otter pelts.

The guards were the key. These Tungrians were well versed in the art of defence and snug behind their wooden palisades. They'd raised the ground level inside the walls to create a walkway and fighting platform. If the defenders reached that platform in numbers any attack would cost Owain more casualties than he could afford. Even Gwlym recognized a night attack was the only way. Yet, veterans though they were, the defenders had one great weakness: they had been here too long. The Tungrians who frequented the settlement and the sentries he'd listened to at night had the relaxed air of men comfortable in their surroundings. They were surrounded by their enemy, unloved and resented, but Owain's unpopular policy of live and let live had worked in his favour. Night after night the guards patrolled these walls and in five years they had never faced a threat. The only things that disturbed their sleepy, mind-numbing vigil were the occasional barking of rival foxes or the howl of a lone wolf in the far mountains.

Owain slipped away before dawn and arrived on the ridge above the Ordovice camp as the sun rose. Below him, the rough meadow on either side of the stream was a mass of movement as men woke shivering to brush off the morning dew. No fires, because a single wisp of smoke would attract a Tungrian patrol like horseflies to fresh dung. They would force down the barley cakes with a scoop of water from the river, praying someone wasn't pissing in it upstream. Ten or more distinct bands, some of whom would have been tearing out each other's throats if he hadn't ordered their leaders to make camp at opposite ends of the valley. He saw faces look up at his little group descending the winding track and a soft murmur rippled through the mass of men as they recognized the High King. Already the thud of axes was audible from the tree-lined slopes as the men tasked with providing timber got to work.

Owain was tired and hungry, but he called his war chiefs together in a rough shelter beneath the trees. They sat in a circle as a serving boy handed round a leather bucket filled with thin beer. Owain waited till each man had drunk his fill before he began.

'Madog?' A short, savage-looking man in a leather jerkin and plaid trews looked up. He held a broad-bladed axe across his knees and his pale, narrow eyes glared at Owain from beneath a shock of dark curls. 'You will take the east wall.'

Madog's craggy features creased into a grin. Owain had honoured him. Assaulting the wall facing the river was the most hazardous assignment of the night. His warriors would be hemmed into a narrow strip of marshland and forced to lie motionless in the muddy pools until the attack began. Owain didn't need to stress the necessity for absolute silence. He could depend on Madog because he had a reputation for cruelty and his men feared him as no other.

'A token of my esteem.' He handed over a neck ring of pale yellow gold and Madog's thick lips parted in a smile that revealed a single blackened tooth.

Owain turned next to a tall young warrior with dark hair falling to his shoulders who sat to Madog's left. 'Tudfic. Yours is the south wall.' The slightest nod of acknowledgement. Tudfic was here in his injured father's stead. An Ordovice princeling of the most southern tribe, Tudfic had been one of the fiercest opponents of Owain's policy of non-aggression. 'Remember. A few men to pave the way, the others well back, but within rushing distance. Not a movement before you hear the signal.' Tudfic shrugged at advice he clearly deemed unnecessary. Owain experienced a pang of concern. Should he send Cadwal to ensure his instructions were followed? No. Tudfic would regard it as an insult and might withdraw his men altogether. In any case, he had another job for his champion. He handed over another neck ring and Tudfic accepted it as his right.

'Dafyd? The west.' Another grin of consent. Dafyd, balding, with a grey moustache that fell below the level of his chins, was Owain's closest ally in this company. They'd already discussed the attack and it needed no further debate.

At a given signal each man would lead five hundred warriors to assault the walls. A thousand more would join Owain in an attack on the main gate and the settlement. 'We will leave at noon.' A risk, but one that had to be taken if they were to be in position at full dark. They would each travel by a different route, along ancient hill paths where the Tungrian patrols seldom ventured. 'Tell your men to get what rest—'

He saw Madog's face freeze and felt a presence behind him.

'You have done well, Owain Lawhir.' Gwlym's harsh growl was little more than a whisper, but its effect was as chilling as the first winter frost. 'Soon men will call you Owain y Cedyrn, Owain the Mighty. With a host so vast Canovium will be nothing but a beech nut to your grindstone.'

'You are accompanying the attack? I thought—'

'You were solicitous for my health?' The words had a mocking quality. 'But the gods have provided me with the strength to join your warriors. When you have achieved your victory certain specific require-ments must be met.' Owain felt a moment of dread exacerbated by the druid's next words. 'I have further instructions for you, Owain Lawhir, but they will wait. First I will lead our brave spearmen in the Victory Song of Beli Mawr.'

Dusk was falling as Owain and his war band reached the old hill fort at Pen-y-gaer to the west of Canovium. Roman engineers had once built a signal station within the collapsed turf walls, but it was long gone, the timbers overgrown and rotting beneath their covering of moss. The river twisted across the plain below like a discarded silver belt and he could just make out the fort and the settlement beneath a haze of smoke in the distance. Cadwal and his men would have been there for the last hour, mingling with the customers in the tavern. For the thousandth time he reassured himself he could trust Cadwal to succeed. The champion had the look and manner of a jovial bear, but he was the deadliest fighter Owain had ever seen, lightning quick with spear and knife. The men he led were similarly adept.

It wasn't fear that gnawed his guts, but the waiting. The waiting and the responsibility of leading such a vast host; the greatest gathering of Ordovice warriors since his father had joined Caratacus. As he waited for darkness and prayed that the other war bands remained undiscovered, he reflected on the puzzling instructions issued by Gwlym. Individual auxiliaries taken alive and kept for a special purpose. Certain civilian captives set aside for later use.

Less than two Roman miles away, Cadwal unwrapped the pretty whore from where she'd attached herself to his waist. She was a big lass and on another night her attractions would have been a temptation, but not tonight. Four bearded Tungrians with swords on their hips sat in a corner drinking with a morose intensity, but they were accustomed to the changing faces of traders and paid Cadwal no heed. The owner was cleaning up and as he approached Cadwal tossed a silver coin on the table. 'Is there anywhere we can sleep, friend?'

'There's a barn out the back and a couple of straw mattresses.' The man smiled and swept up the coin, and nodded at the girl. 'I'll throw in a little entertainment for another. A night with Brana will set you up for tomorrow.'

Cadwal grinned. 'Nothing I'd like better, but this is my woman's brother, Geraint. He has a big mouth and if she catches me straying again she's like to take a shearing knife to my essentials.'

As he led his packhorse into the barn Cadwal caught the eyes of the four traders already lying in the flickering shadows thrown by a single oil lamp. Two of them were slim, dark-haired young men who could have been brothers to Geraint, and were in fact twins, Idwal and Eurig. The two others were short and solidly built, one with a shock of red hair. Apart from their physique, what united them was their eyes, which reminded Cadwal of a hawk he'd once caught and tried to train to hunt. They held a piercing intense ferocity that made him wonder the Tungrians hadn't slit their throats just in case. But without Bryn and Bran the attack wouldn't go ahead.

He went to the door and studied the fading light. The flame of the oil lamp fluttered in a draught. It was a ceramic type in the shape of a human foot, a style popular with the Romans. His eyes hardened as he reached up and snuffed out the flame.

VIII

Owain's scouts led his warriors down the mountain in a compact column. He had always planned to make the final approach in darkness. His pathfinders had spent the last three weeks repeating the journey in daylight and dark till they'd fixed every stone and potential hazard in their minds. Sticks painted with limewash marked the most treacherous stages of the route and the scouts roamed the column whispering instructions.

Not that he believed any of his warriors would stumble or fall aside. Apart from a few unblooded youngsters every man was a veteran of the night raid to steal cattle or sheep from his neighbours. Such raids were a rite of passage, almost a way of life among the Ordovice people. In times of drought or famine, rival tribes and clans would combine to carry out raids on a larger scale against Silurian border villages, taking slaves and supplies and slaughtering any who resisted.

Owain marched at their front with the men who would make the actual attack. A hundred to take and hold the gate, ten times that number to follow up the assault and subdue the defenders, who would by then – if everything went to plan – be under attack from all sides. Groups of warriors carried the trunks of carefully selected birch trees left with the stumps of their branches to act as makeshift ladders. Others hefted wood and wattle panels for crossing the ditches. Owain knew the defenders would have sown them with sharpened sticks angled to impale any man unfortunate enough to fall on them and thorn bushes positioned to slow the attackers' progress while they were slaughtered. But that slaughter would only occur if he gave the Tungrians time to man the walls. Owain didn't intend to let that happen.

Which was why he had sent Cadwal in first.

Cadwal didn't have to give any order. The six men rose together and crept to where their packs lay beside the resting horses. Sure fingers unfastened the leather straps and searched the contents by touch until they found the weapons hidden among the wool and the furs. Cadwal and the dark-haired twins pulled out long knives similar to the short swords Roman legionaries carried. Cadwal would have preferred a spear, but he reckoned he'd find one quickly enough if things went to Owain's plan. Geraint retrieved a short, odd-shaped object in a leather sack. Bryn and Bran emerged with the slings that had made them famous in song and story for their deadly accuracy. Each slinger also carried a pouch filled with lovingly polished lead spheres the diameter of the top joint of a man's thumb. Idwal and Eurig picked up the straw mattresses they'd been lying on and Cadwal led them silently from the barn.

He'd taken the noisy departure of the Tungrians from the tavern as his signal, waited for the count of a hundred and then the same again. It was early in the sentries' stint and their minds would still be partly within the barrack room. The six Ordovice warriors wore dark clothing and slipped unseen from one shadow to the next as they approached the fortress gate. Owain had wanted to send more men, but Cadwal had insisted they would only attract attention. If it couldn't be done with six another four or five would make no difference. He paused. Somewhere out there in the night thousands of men should be on the move, but all he could hear were the usual nocturnal sounds of owls and nightjars. Still, no point in worrying. He had his own job to do.

A pair of torches illuminated the gates, closed nightly at dusk. Owain had chosen the main gate because the settlement, what the Romans called the *vicus*, had encroached close to the entrance. The first house on the east side, where a cobbler did business on the ground floor, lay just outside the circle of light cast by the torches. It had been built on Roman lines, with shuttered windows on both floors, but roofed with thatch instead of tile. The men crouched in the shadow of the building. Cadwal nodded to Geraint and he moved forward with the twins. There'd been a dog which would have complicated things, but it now lay in a ditch with its throat cut. A pity, Cadwal thought; he liked dogs. Soft rustling and the snap of wood. A choked-off cry from inside the house.

Cadwal slipped towards the door. It opened a moment later and Geraint beckoned the three men forward. Cadwal stepped inside with Bryn and Bran at his back. The sharp metallic scent of new-shed blood made his nostrils twitch. An infant's cradle lay on its side just visible in the gloom, the motionless contents spilled on the earth floor. The mother and father side by side, their pale faces like twin moons at the centre of a pool of spreading darkness.

'Upstairs,' he told the two slingers.

The upper storey of the house was at the same level as the palisade above the gate. Cadwal carefully eased the window shutters open. It seemed a long way to the walls. He studied his two companions. He'd seen Bran put a lead slingshot between a man's eyes at forty paces, but could they do this? It was on the tip of his tongue to ask, but they pushed past him to stare at the gateway through the open window. The two guards talked quietly together in the open tower above the gate, their faces visible as pale circles in the light of the torches below. Bryn and Bran exchanged a glance and carefully unwound their oiled leather slings. Cadwal would have stayed to watch them, but he had work elsewhere. He ran downstairs and slipped out into the street.

Geraint and the twins were crouching in the shadows outside the torchlight when he joined them. And waited. He muttered a soft curse as the two guards drifted apart. Behind him he thought he could hear the whisper of dozens of running feet in the distance, but the sound faded long before the men at the gate became aware of it. Cadwal closed his eyes and thanked Taranis. They weren't alone. He saw the glint of a helmet as the second guard moved back into view. Cadwal sensed he was laughing.

The two impacts were so close they sounded like one. A distinct snap like two stones clicking together. The heads disappeared. Cadwal winced at the clatter of a helmet on the wood floor of the tower. But he was already on the causeway leading to the gate, veering at the last moment to approach the section of wall to the left. He put his back against the rough wood and clasped his hands in a cradle. Idwal had been following close behind. Now he ran forward with a straw mattress in his hands and placed his bare foot in the cradle of Cadwal's fingers. One quick heave and Cadwal's enormous strength boosted him upwards so the Ordovice could throw the mattress across the sharpened ends of the wooden timbers and clamber over. Cadwal cursed at the clatter of feet on the walkway behind the palisade. Above him Idwal cried out, anticipating a blow, but another slingshot found its target and Cadwal heard the sound of a falling body. Idwal disappeared from view. Cadwal looked to his right to see Eurig slipping over the rampart, similarly boosted by Geraint.

He stood by the gate, breathing hard, his heart thundering. Logic told him the noise must have reached the other guards, but there seemed to be no immediate reaction. Quickly now. Every second counted.

At last he heard the muted rumble of a wooden bar being withdrawn. The gate shifted a fraction and Cadwal put his shoulder to the seasoned oak to help it along. Behind him the sound of more movement. A mass of men carrying spears and painted shields raced across the causeway with no attempt at stealth. The gate opened to reveal the broad sweep of the cavalry parade ground and Cadwal stepped back to allow the first attackers to pour through the entrance. In the same instant Geraint slipped a short trumpet from its leather sack, put it to his lips and blew a long, blaring challenge.

In the darkness outside the fort walls the very earth seemed to rise up as Madog, Dafyd and Tudfic urged their warriors forward. Owain's men surged through the settlement in the wake of the vanguard, while others battered in the doors of the houses and shops and rounded up the inhabitants.

Inside the fort the guards at last raised the alarm. The distinctive bray of a Roman cavalry trumpet echoed Geraint's blast. Roused from their beds, auxiliaries dressed only in tunics and armed with swords burst from the neatly spaced barrack blocks and sprinted for their assigned defensive positions on the walls. Too late. The Ordovice warriors had already swarmed across the ditches on their makeshift wattle bridges and over the undefended parapets.

Eurig threw Cadwal a spear dropped by one of the dead guards and Owain's champion stepped into the line hastily formed by the first men through the gate. He took his place behind two overlapping shields and waited for the first rush of defenders. They came in a makeshift, staggered line that broke against the Ordovice shields. The heavy cavalry *spathae* they carried were brutal weapons when wielded from horseback. Long, edged bludgeons that could crack a man's skull like an egg or cleave neck and shoulder. On the ground only an exceptionally strong man could wield them with any skill. The auxiliaries hammered desperately at the enemy shields, but they carried none of their own to fight behind.

Wielding his spear two-handed, Cadwal darted the iron point at an exposed throat. A bearded auxiliary went down in a spray of blood. Another took his place, stabbing the point of his *spatha* at Cadwal's eyes. Owain's champion swayed back and the man with the shield on his left shifted it slightly and stabbed through the gap with a curved knife, ripping upwards and twisting the blade so the Tungrian's entrails were torn from his stomach. The blood drained from the man's face in a heartbeat. He dropped his sword and turned away, trying vainly to cram his vitals back into his torn body. More and more Ordovice warriors poured through the gate, joining the line and forcing the auxiliaries back over their dead and dying comrades. The defenders were equally hard pressed from the north and west flanks, only holding their own among the barrack blocks on the eastern side where Madog battled to break down their resistance.

The Tungrian commander, a prince of the tribe brought up and trained in arms by Rome, struggled into his helmet and armour, trying to make sense of the chaos. Timber buildings to the west of the *principia* blazed in a single enormous beacon. In the diabolical shadows cast by the flames he was able to make out overwhelming enemy numbers that might have struck fear into a lesser man. His first instinct was to fight his way out, but the Celts beset his command on every side leaving no obvious line of retreat. *Testudo*? If even a quarter of the men had shields he would have ordered them to form the armoured carapace that was the Roman army's defence of last resort, but barely one in ten had snatched up a *scutum* as they ran from their barracks. He called his second in command across.

'We must buy time, Priscinus. We're losing too many men. The patrol beyond the river must be able to see that.' He pointed his sword to the glow above them. 'They'll send to Deva for reinforcements. Have the signaller sound form square.' He saw the look of dismay the *decurio* shot him. 'Just do it,' he hissed. 'It's our only chance.'

Priscinus shouted the order and a new blast of the cavalry horn rang out above the clamour of sword on shield, screams of mortal agony and barbarian roars of triumph. The Tungrians disengaged as best they could and trotted back to the centre of the parade ground to form a ragged square in three ranks, a prickling hedgehog of swords and spears. Priscinus and his commander stood at the centre in the midst of a carpet of wounded men who groaned with pain and cried out for water. The *decurio* cursed the day he'd been sent to this place. Another month and they were due to hand over to an infantry cohort. Another year and he'd have retired with a pension and enough put away to buy the farm he'd always coveted. They both knew it would take reinforcements from Deva at least two days to reach them. Priscinus reckoned they might last two hours if Fortuna favoured them.

As the men in the square shuffled closer for protection, the battle seemed to pause for breath. Then Owain opened his mouth to call for an all-out attack, but Cadwal, his face turned into a nightmarish mask

59

by the streaked blood of the men he'd killed, advised: 'Why risk more casualties, lord? They're not going anywhere.'

Owain saw the sense in his champion's words. They would sing about this victory for a dozen lifetimes and sing all the louder the fewer men he lost. 'Bran?' he called. The little slinger appeared at his side. 'Get as many of your folk together as you can and make them suffer.' Bran grinned and ran off, shouting for slingers.

'Why don't they attack?' the Tungrian prince whispered.

'Why would they need to?'

It was like tormenting a felled aurochs, the great bull they hunted in the remote river valleys. In the light of the burning buildings Bran and his men flayed the Tungrian formation from all sides. Men flopped out of position, their brains leaking from circular holes in their skulls. The Ordovice warriors added to the bloodletting by occasionally darting forward and hurling a spear to take an auxiliary in the chest or the belly.

'Why won't you fight, you cowardly bastards?' a man in the front rank roared in frustration. A slingshot rattled off his helmet and he rose with a scream to charge at Owain, identified as a leader by the great gold torc at his neck. When he was within three paces Cadwal stepped forward, knocked the sword from his hand and spun him to cut his throat, all in a single fluid movement.

'Attack or surrender,' Priscinus muttered to his commander through clenched teeth. 'They're slaughtering us like sheep.'

'We're finished either way,' the prince raged. 'At best we'd be slaves.'

'Better a slave than dead,' his second in command insisted. 'They'll keep you as a hostage and the legate will eventually strike a bargain to free the rest of us. He doesn't like to leave a man behind. It's our only chance.'

The prince had his doubts about that, but he knew Priscinus was right, even if his outraged sense of honour quailed from the decision. The choice was between certain death and slavery. At least a slave had a chance. He stifled a groan of anguish and pushed past Priscinus to lead the way through to the front rank closest to where Owain stood.

The prince knelt and laid his sword on the bloodied earth of the parade ground and Priscinus followed suit. Owain motioned for his slingers to stay their weapons and a hush fell over the burning fort.

'I ask for mercy for my men,' the Tungrian commander called. 'Keep me as a hostage and allow them to return to Deva.'

'And who are you?' Owain's Latin was so poor it took a moment for the prince to answer.

'Claudius Vindex, prefect commanding First Ala Tungriana.'

'Have your men lay down their arms,' Owain said evenly, 'and you will be my guest while we negotiate terms.' He turned to his body-guard. 'Bring food and drink.'

He led the way to one of the surviving barrack blocks. The ease with which the Ordovice king acquiesced to his terms of surrender surprised Vindex.

It was only when Gwlym walked into the room that he realized the truth.

Five hours later, in the first light of dawn, Claudius Vindex, prince of the Tungri, prefect commanding First Ala Tungriana, pleaded for his own death as they impaled his naked body on a four-foot spike set in the gateway of the fort he had commanded.

He was the last of his men to die. Gwlym's executioners had dis-embowelled Priscinus and his fellow officers and strangled them with their own entrails. Their bodies now hung like obscene trophies from the palisade on either side of the gate. Cadwal had often heard it threatened, but he'd never believed it possible. The expertise of the druids impressed him, but their endeavours left the whole fort smelling of shit.

Gore spattered his leather jerkin to the shoulders and he looked a fear-some sight as he set off along the causeway away from the horror. In the settlement, dozens of Ordovice warriors herded Canovium's civilians into three of the largest houses. Brana, the pretty whore, looked at him, her terrified, imploring eyes pleading with him to save her, but Cadwal kept walking. By the time he reached the outskirts he could smell the fresh smoke and hear the screaming.

It took two days for the patrol Claudius Vindex had depended on to return. They never did see the glow in the sky or send to Deva for help. Their commander's hands shook uncontrollably as he sat his horse in front of the shrivelled blackened things decorating the fort's gateway. In three houses flanking the roadway the domes of dozens of charred skulls poked through the blackened ruins. After two days of summer heat the stench of death was so thick it stuck in the throat. He called to one of his senior troopers.

'Take two men and ride with all speed to Deva. The legate must see this with his own eyes. No matter what he is doing you must make him come. I will touch nothing until you return.'

He forced himself to walk his horse past Claudius Vindex and into the fort. It was only then he saw the pyramid of a hundred heads stacked in the centre of the parade ground.

They never found the others.

IX

'*This* is my personal bodyguard?'

'Yes, lord.' The young decurion sat straight in the saddle, but he spoke with weary resignation and Valerius guessed he'd already had this conversation with Titus. Behind him thirty-two mounted troopers stood in two untidy lines across the courtyard of Valerius's villa. They wore cavalry uniforms: chain link armour, iron helmets with cheek-pieces and narrow neck guards. The familiar *spatha* swords, longer and heavier than the infantry version, hung at their waists. But something wasn't right.

'They informed me crack legionary cavalry would escort my family to Britannia, but that's not what I see, is it?'

'No, lord.'

'What *do* I see?'

'Governor Agricola ordered his legates to provide eight cavalrymen from each legion's mounted contingent for your permanent escort.'

'But . . .'

'But no legate would willingly give up his best soldiers to . . .'

'Act as nursemaids to a jumped-up lawyer with a fancy title?'

'No, lord. Well, yes . . . so he chooses men he can spare.'

Valerius closed his eyes. He knew exactly what that meant. The dregs.

Misfits, troublemakers, criminals and cowards, men who wouldn't take orders, or who could barely hold a weapon.

'You.' He marched up to a trooper in the centre of the first line, one of two with bandaged heads. 'Name, rank and unit.'

The man's chin snapped up. 'Rufius Florus, trooper, third squadron, legionary cavalry Ninth Hispana, sir.'

'Length of service?'

Florus gave him a puzzled look. 'In the cavalry, sir?'

'That's right, trooper.'

'One month and two weeks, sir.'

One and a half months. The time it had taken these men to get to Rome from Britannia.

'And before that?'

'Legionary, second rank, third century of the Third cohort.'

'Reason for transfer?'

Florus hesitated, but decided it wasn't worth lying. 'My centurion said I stole a *pugio*, sir.'

'And did you?'

'No, sir.' The cavalryman's lips twitched. 'I stole it back.'

Valerius walked along the line. The cavalrymen stared straight ahead, but he knew they were studying him as he was them. He doubted the senator's toga with the purple stripe he'd worn for the occasion would impress them. Nor the grey hairs or the scars. He kept the wooden fist hidden in the folds of the toga. Let that wait. What did *he* see? Weariness. Resentment. Resignation. A big man who sat in the saddle like a sack of grain, all jutting, unshaven chin and burning eyes. A hater, this one. One face that stirred something in him. Had they met? It seemed unlikely. Someone in the rear row hawked and spat. He ignored it, but made a mental note of the likely culprit.

'You.' He chose the unlikeliest cavalryman in the front rank, a flabby, hulking giant who barely fit in the saddle.

'G-g-gellius P-p-pudens, trooper, second squadron legionary cavalry Second Adiutrix, sir.'

'Length of service?' Valerius sighed.

'One month and two weeks, sir.'

'And what did you do in your legion?'

'I was a cook, sir.' Pudens straightened as much as he was able. 'I cooked for the legate.'

'So you were either selling the rations or you tried to poison him?'

Pudens's various chins quivered with indignation. 'I didn't try to poison him, sir.'

Valerius turned and walked back to the escort commander. 'And you, decurion?'

'Cornelius Felix, first squadron, Twentieth Valeria Victrix, lord.'

'And what crime brings you here?'

'I was accused of fornication, lord.'

Valerius laughed. 'Fornication doesn't seem a sufficiently serious offence to sentence you to command this shambles.'

Felix failed to suppress a smile. 'It is if it was with the legate's daughter, lord.'

Valerius shook his head. 'Have your men dismount and water their horses in the stream. I'll have food and drink sent out to them. In the meantime, I'm sure you'd welcome a cup of wine.'

'I'd appreciate it, sir.' The decurion slid from the saddle. He passed on the order to a trooper who'd been hovering close by and handed over his mount's reins. Valerius patted the horse's neck.

'Your horses seem worn out?'

'I thought it best not to change them at the way stations,' Felix admitted. 'Some of these men could barely ride. Better to keep a horse they know and that knows them.'

'How many of them are true cavalry?'

'About half, and they're good. But they're all men their commanders didn't want for one reason or another.' The decurion raised a cultured eyebrow. 'One of them is probably a murderer. You've seen the five men in the second rank who look like brothers?' Valerius nodded. A row of remote, emotionless faces that might have been carved from granite. He doubted the plaited sidelocks hanging below their cheekpieces fitted part of any legion's dress regulations. 'I think they're auxiliaries from a Pannonian unit, but they don't give much away so I can't be certain. They were among the quota from Second Augusta.'

'You said some of them couldn't ride. But they can now?'

'Oh, yes. They've had six weeks in the saddle and I had the dullards riding with our best horsemen. Pudens still struggles to keep his seat at anything faster than a trot, but they'll do.'

'So they can ride.' Valerius handed Felix a cup of wine. 'But can they fight?'

'They can certainly fight each other,' Felix said. 'They've been at each other's throats since we left Londinium.' Valerius laughed, but Felix shook his head. 'I think the governor calculated that providing an escort from all four legions would mean there'd always be at least one man familiar with the country. He didn't take into account the rivalry between the units. The two Second legions are always trying to prove they're superior to each other, but pick on one and you pick on all sixteen of them. Our contingent from the Ninth don't like it when someone mentions their reputation for bad luck and will generally fight anyone, but they hate the Twentieth's guts because of some horror that happened when they took different sides in the civil war. The Twentieth has never forgiven the Second Augusta for refusing to leave camp when Boudicca was on the rampage.' He hesitated. 'You would have every right to send us away.'

Valerius smiled. 'No,' he said. 'A soldier must always make do with what he is given. It will take me two weeks to wind up my affairs here. In the meantime, you can use the meadow by the river to set up camp. Give men and horses a day to rest then continue their training. I want them able to manoeuvre as a unit. And fight.'

Felix downed his wine, snapped an arm across his chest in salute and turned to join his men.

'And Felix?'

'Yes, lord?'

'Keep them out of trouble.'

*

Tabitha was waiting for him in the shade of the portico. 'What do you think?' she asked.

'I've never seen an uglier or less soldierly company of men in my life.'

'Oh, I don't know. The young decurion is very handsome.'

'Is he?'

'Oh, yes.' She smiled at his confusion. 'Those deep blue eyes and a certain air of innocence some women would find a challenge. Tall too, and athletic.'

'I hadn't noticed.' Valerius bit his lip to stop himself laughing.

'You must invite him to dinner.'

'A challenge, eh?'

Her lips twitched into a smile and she kissed him on the cheek. 'Invite him to dinner.'

X

Tabitha accepted the change in their circumstances with her usual equanimity. 'At least this time I can come with you,' was all she'd said. Now her mind focused on the more practical issues. 'Would it be possible to find someone recently returned from Britannia, and preferably Londinium? Someone who has run a household there.'

'A woman?'

'Yes, Valerius, a woman. You tell me I am to be the wife of the second most important official in the province. That means entertaining and being entertained. What dresses should I take? A hostess cannot be too drab, but neither can she consciously outshine the wives of her husband's guests. I need to be aware of the kind of society we will mix with.'

The Palatium tracked down a *quaestor* and his wife who'd returned to Rome from Britannia three months earlier. Tabitha invited them to dinner at the house Valerius owned in the city and the two women spent the evening talking fashion, food and the names of people who might be helpful. Valerius remembered Londinium as a sea of blackened timber and grey ash, with the charred bones of its inhabitants still lying where they'd been butchered by Boudicca's horde. Their guests assured Tabitha it was now a cosmopolitan city, provincial, but perfectly civilized. The *quaestor*'s wife, an older woman, had one important piece of advice. 'It will still be summer when you arrive, but do not let that deceive you. You will require at least four sets of woollen underwear to survive your first winter in Britannia.'

Valerius's preparations kept him away from the estate and it was a week before he inspected Felix and his troopers again. He noted that, whatever the limitations of his motley unit, the decurion knew his business. His men had erected their tents close to the river, but on high ground clear of the marshy banks. The latrine pit was the recommended distance away and the horse lines were downstream where they wouldn't foul the drinking water. Common sense, and second nature to any veteran, but Valerius had come across plenty of aristocratic junior officers who refused to listen to advice.

They'd set up a pair of wooden posts in the centre of the meadow. When Valerius arrived Felix had just divided his cavalrymen into two squads and placed them in single line formation opposite each post. They wore their chain armour and iron helmets and each man carried a flat oval shield on his left forearm.

'Legate.' The young man welcomed him with a smart salute and Valerius smiled at the first use of his new rank. 'You've arrived just in time for sword exercise. Marius?' he called to the *duplicarius* checking the lines.

Marius raised a hand. 'Ready, decurion.'

Valerius noticed that the man at the front of each line had the look of a veteran, relaxed in the saddle and sword held upright at the ready. Their narrowed eyes never left Marius.

'We've made it a competition today,' Felix murmured. 'But if you were a gambling man, I'd advise you to put your money on the far team.'

Valerius studied the closer line of horsemen and smiled. 'I see why. Carry on.'

Marius's hand dropped and the two horsemen dug their heels in, urging their mounts to a fast trot. 'We're practising the backhand cut,' Felix said.

'That should separate the old soldiers from the recruits.' Valerius had enough cavalry experience to know that a backhand cut from horseback required a particular technique that ensured you didn't tangle with your shield or chop off your horse's ears.

The two troopers reached the posts in the same stride, simultaneously chopping downwards with a diagonal cut from above the left shoulder and drawing the edge across the front of the post as they rode past. Once clear they spun their horses and galloped to where the next man in line waited. Only when each mount's nose passed an invisible line did Marius release the second rider. The first five pairs included the Pannonians, who impressed Valerius with their horsemanship and weapons skill, and the exercise went smoothly.

The far team were slightly ahead. Florus was the next man. His awkward strike left his sword embedded deep in the wood and his momentum almost plucked him from the saddle before he released his grip. The delay while he recovered the sword allowed the hooting nearside team to make up ground and overtake him. Three more pairs, the tentative approach and awkward swordplay marking them as novices, apart from one.

'Who's the trooper on the black gelding?'

'His name is Julius Crescens.' Felix's lips twitched with distaste. 'Another from the Ninth. Knows his job, but you get one in every unit. A troublemaker. If he's not causing it, he's encouraging someone else to do it. Clever, too. Always has an answer or an excuse, or someone else to blame.'

Valerius nodded.

By now they were down to the last few pairs. Felix sighed as the penultimate rider in the near team came forward. They had a lead of almost half the length of the field that increased with every stride of the mount approaching the finish. 'Go,' Marius shouted.

The look on Gellius Pudens's plump features matched any man in the unit's for determination, but neither his temperament nor his physique fitted him for the saddle. He nudged his mount into a walk that gradually increased to something approaching a trot. Where others rode in a direct line, Gellius's course wavered as his mare responded to the shaking of his well-padded knees. He held his sword as if he intended to use it to stir soup, and when he struck at the post the edge of his blade chipped a splinter from his shield. As he tried to adjust, he lost his balance and rolled from his saddle to an ironic cheer from the opposing team and groans from his own.

The final two competitors were veterans, but the near team's rider had to watch in disgust as his opponent swept from one end of the course to the other, made his cut and returned while Gellius was still struggling to get back in the saddle. Eventually, the fat man gave up and led his horse back to the start line. Valerius heard the muttered curses as he approached his comrades. 'Our friend won't be popular tonight.'

Felix smiled. 'It's just as well he's a good cook.'

'Why not rest the horses for an hour and let him feed the men? I'd like to join them, if I may?'

'It would be our pleasure, legate.'

'And I have a request. If nothing else it'll give them a bit of entertainment.'

The first thing Valerius noticed was that the men ate in distinct groups, with little or no conversation between them. In any legionary unit it was usual for tentmates from the same *contubernium* to mess together, but most would indulge in banter and insult.

'Is it always like this?' he asked Felix.

'Yes, they stick to their units. I've tried to encourage them to mix, but all they do is fight.'

They approached the group that included the five Pannonians. The men started to get to their feet, but Valerius motioned them to stay where they were. He sat beside a tall, slim cavalryman with close-cropped sandy hair and the distinctive sidelock hanging by his right ear. The trooper had serious grey eyes and handsome, regular features, marred only by the white pucker of an old scar on his right cheek.

'You rode well today, trooper, but I'm willing to bet this is the first time you've visited Italia.'

'Then you would lose your money, lord.' The cavalryman's Latin had a distinct accent, but he spoke it well, with a solemn gravity. 'I came here eight years ago with the First Pannonian Horse as part of the vexillation Legate Rusticus sent to support Emperor Vitellius against the renegade Otho. When Titus Flavius Vespasianus declared for the purple he believed our loyalty suspect and posted us to the Rhenus frontier for a year before we returned to Britannia.'

'I'm interested in how you and your comrades came to be part of my bodyguard.'

'We are volunteers, lord,' the trooper said with a hint of a smile. 'When our legate granted us Roman citizenship, he honoured us with a place in the legion's regular cavalry. Sadly, his cavalry commander felt differently and considered us uncouth barbarians. Given the choice of volunteering or becoming stable hands, we chose the former.'

Valerius returned the smile. 'I'm glad you did. But I'm surprised they encouraged you to leave. You must have carried out a feat of great valour for your commander to grant immediate citizenship.'

A shadow fell over the Pannonian's eyes. 'You are familiar with what happened on the Rhenus during the late war, lord?'

'The Batavian revolt?' Batavian auxiliaries under the command of their tribal leader had risen against Vitellius, but the rebellion had swollen into a full-scale war for overlordship of the Batavian lands west of the Rhenus. Vespasian's forces eventually defeated the rebels, but not before they'd proved Rome's legions weren't invincible.

'Yes, lord. Enemies and betrayal on every side. Whole legions mutinying or fleeing without orders. The Batavians surrounded our camp, with more arriving every day. The commander ordered my squadron to lead the breakout. We five are all who survived.'

Valerius nodded his understanding. He'd been in enough last stands to know the combination of Fortuna's favour and fighting skill it must have taken for these men to get out alive. 'What is your name, trooper?'

'They call me Shabolz.'

'I will remember you, Shabolz.' Here at least was one man on whom he could depend.

He continued his inspection of the camp. Sullen silence and eyes that avoided contact. Not everyone was as pleased with their posting as the Pannonians. At least two expressions of bovine stupidity. One man studied him as if he expected to be noticed. That face again. Where had he seen it before?

Valerius approached the little circle of men from the Ninth. Florus the thief made to stand up, but Julius Crescens put a hand on his arm and he remained seated with the rest. Gellius Pudens knelt by a pot simmering on the central fire and a mouthwatering scent hung over the camp. He filled a plate and rose to join the group from the Second Adiutrix. As he walked past, Crescens stretched out a foot to trip him and he stumbled, spilling his food.

'Do you no harm to miss a meal, fat boy,' his tormentor sneered. 'Especially this pigswill.'

Felix would have reacted, but Valerius shook his head and addressed Crescens himself. 'You don't like the rations, trooper?'

'He's trying to poison us with his weeds.' Crescens looked to his comrades for support, but they were all concentrating on their plates.

Valerius went to the pot. It contained a simple meat stew of good fatty pork, but Pudens had added herbs he must have collected from the fields. Felix handed him a spoon and he tasted the stew, which was a step above the standard legionary rations he'd eaten.

'Seems fair enough. Crescens, isn't it?' The man studied him with wary eyes. 'You impressed me at the sword exercise, Crescens. A proper cavalryman. How much service do you have?'

Crescens pushed himself to his feet. 'Five years.' He didn't hide the bitterness in his voice. 'Trooper, third squadron, Ninth legionary cavalry, based at Lindum, which is where I'd like to be now.'

Valerius ignored the muttered complaint and raised his voice so he was addressing all the men. 'You did well today, but I don't expect to be ambushed by many wooden posts when we get to Britannia.' Smiles, and a few of them laughed. 'Your decurion assures me you know how to manoeuvre, to charge, wheel and countercharge, but what will happen when you face a man sword against sword in the saddle? That is the test of the true cavalryman.' He nodded to Marius. 'Break out a pair of practice swords.'

Marius marched off to a tent and returned with two identical wooden swords. Replica cavalry *spathae* in every way, but cut from planks of oak.

Valerius accepted one and hefted it in his left hand. Shabolz rose from his position with a wry smile, but Valerius tossed the sword to Julius Crescens, who caught it with a puzzled frown.

'Let's see just how good you really are, trooper.'

Now the frown turned to incredulity. 'You?'

'That's right, Crescens. You have no objection to fighting a superior officer, I'm sure.' Valerius shrugged off his toga and stepped out of its folds in his short tunic. He heard the collective intake of breath as the watching men noticed the wooden fist that replaced his right hand. 'When we're out there it's just man against man.'

'Man against half a man.' Crescens grinned at his companions.

Valerius took the second sword and called for his mount. When Felix led the horse to Valerius he carried a mail shirt across his arm. 'You'll need armour, legate?'

Valerius considered for a moment before shaking his head. 'I haven't worn mail for years. Better to have more freedom of movement, I think. And no shield for obvious reasons, but I'll take a helm.'

'Are you sure this is sensible, lord?' Felix's voice dropped to a whisper as he helped Valerius into the saddle. 'Crescens may be a troublemaker, but he's a fine horseman and dangerous with a sword.'

'That's something we'll find out, decurion.' Valerius looked around at the ring of faces, eyes bright with anticipation. Crescens might not be popular, but he doubted any of them would be averse to seeing a patrician dumped on his backside with blood dripping from a nasty scalp wound. It hadn't only been years since he'd worn chain armour, but since he'd fought on horseback. He still practised for an hour with a sword every morning and all his horses were cavalry trained to react to touches of knee or thigh, but he was no longer the veteran cavalryman of Corbulo's Armenian campaign. What he did know was that if these men were to protect his family for what might be three or four years he needed their loyalty, and if you wanted to gain a man's loyalty, first you must win his respect. The one thing in his favour was that when he'd fought the Parthians he'd been in a true battle, fighting for his life. In the five years Crescens had been a cavalryman the Ninth Hispana had been on garrison duty at Lindum. That meant patrols and the occasional punishment raid, but the only men he'd have fought on horseback would be those of his own unit. He'd never faced a killer. Valerius remembered the advice of Marcus, the *lanista*, on the day he'd first met the gladiator Serpentius. *Don't fight like a one-handed man, or a two-handed man. Fight like a killer.*

Fight like a killer.

He felt the heat rising inside him at the prospect, but attempted to still it. The most dangerous men on the battlefield weren't the berserkers who charged you with blood in their eye, they were controlled, calculating and cold-blooded. The thought made him smile, a savage rictus that would have surprised him if he'd seen it. It had been five years since he'd experienced this sense of anticipation. Was it wrong to feel such joy at the prospect of violence?

He looked to where Florus was helping Crescens on to his horse. The cavalryman wore full armour and carried a shield in his left hand. He was grinning and boasting to his friends, but when their eyes met Valerius saw something that cheered him further. Doubt.

Until the prefect commanding Ninth Hispana's cavalry volunteered him for the *legatus iuridicus*'s escort things had come easily to Julius Crescens. His father had been a legionary in the Ninth and it seemed only natural that his son should follow him. But young Julius had an affinity with horses and a gift for riding and he didn't plan on marching the length and breadth of Britannia. Instead, he applied to join the hundred and twenty strong cavalry unit that provided the legate's couriers and carried out scouting and patrol duties. A man could lose himself polishing brass or oiling leather; it helped pass the time. Other people could be persuaded to muck out the stables in return for a favour or the promise of one (seldom fulfilled). He had a way of impressing his officers without doing anything to justify it, and he cultivated friendships with comrades who mattered and ignored those who didn't. Women liked him until they realized he was as free with their possessions as with their persons. Lindum wasn't too bad, once you got used to the damp, and the service was far from onerous. Then he'd made the mistake. He'd underestimated the influence of a man he'd tried to blackmail and the trooper had gone to his decurion. An investigation led to further probing that uncovered his other activities: the gambling ring he encouraged and the oddly weighted dice; the women smuggled into the stables and rented out to whoever could pay. The not so subtle hint that he might want to volunteer with Florus and the rest instead of marching behind an eagle with the loss of two years' seniority was impossible to ignore.

There hadn't really been any choice.

Now he was here on this patch of dusty ground about to face a crippled old lawyer who seemed to think he was some kind of warrior. Well, he was about to find out differently. Crescens couldn't afford to hurt him too much, but a few strikes here and there would put him in his place.

And yet a few things about this situation made him uneasy. Fighting without armour and a shield spoke of either confidence or stupidity, and the old man didn't look stupid. Then there was the wooden hand. For the first time it dawned on Julius Crescens that he faced a left-handed swordsman and his mind struggled with the complications generated by that imponderable. It opened the right side to the lightning attack Crescens had trained for these five years past, but where would the defensive stroke come from? But Crescens carried a stout wooden shield and wore chain armour. What did he have to fear? The old man couldn't hurt him. Make it quick, then. Best to keep complications to a minimum.

Valerius trotted to the far side of the field, choosing to make his opponent fight with the sun on his face. A small advantage, but sometimes small advantages could be the difference between winning and losing. He might have ordered Crescens to fight without his shield, but that would have been a sign of weakness, just as the watching men would think the lack of a right hand a weakness. He would prove them wrong.

His purpose was not to hurt his opponent, but to make a point. They looked upon him as a toothless old bureaucrat. But he was Gaius Valerius Verrens, Hero of Rome and holder of the Corona Aurea. Julius Crescens was about to discover that.

Marius marched to the centre of the field, and in an echo of Vespasian at the chariot race held out his hand with a piece of cloth between his fingers. Beyond him, the men of the escort watched eagerly. Valerius urged his horse into motion as the cloth fluttered to the ground.

A hundred paces away Julius Crescens glared from beneath the rim of his polished iron helmet. He held his shield in his left hand and the heavy wooden *spatha* in his right. The most direct point of attack for a left-handed swordsman was from Crescens's left side. Valerius took precisely that line, automatically calculating his opponent's possible countermoves as he rode. Crescens would be confident in his ability to fend off a blow with his shield while simultaneously wielding the back cut he'd shown so effectively earlier. Valerius must beat the shield and somehow find a telling strike on armour or helmet.

Fifty paces. Valerius held his line.

Twenty-five.

Crescens raised his sword for the backhand cut.

Valerius nudged his mount in the left flank and before Crescens could react the left-handed swordsman was approaching the black gelding's right shoulder. Too late to swing the shield across. Instead, Crescens brought his *spatha* round to strike Valerius's unprotected chest. Wooden sword or not, a direct thrust to his chest combined with the closing speed of the horses could be fatal. Crescens expected Valerius to swerve away. Instead, Valerius used the edge of his sword to flick the point aside and lashed out with the wooden fist.

77

If he'd struck Crescens in the face, the oak fist would have broken his jaw or pulverized his nose and smashed the bone into his brain. But the fist took the cavalryman just above the helmet rim, so the iron dome rang like a bell and the impact knocked the wits from him. Valerius half turned into Crescens's intended blow so the other man's sword arm brushed his shoulder instead of knocking him from the saddle.

Fight like a killer.

He heard an ironic cheer, but he was already spinning the horse in a tight wheel that brought him behind his stunned enemy. The wooden sword clattered into the back of Crescens's helm, knocking him forward in the saddle. The cavalryman tried to protect his back with the shield, but all it did was expose his shield arm to Valerius's relentless attack. A well-aimed cut above the elbow and the shield fell from paralysed fingers. Crescens flailed with his own sword and tried to turn into Valerius, but the older man forced his mount close so Crescens had no room for manoeuvre.

By now the battle joy filled Valerius's head and the wooden sword hammered against Crescens's helmet like a bludgeon. The stricken cavalryman's world whirled and he lost the capacity to think or defend himself. With a despairing cry he toppled from the saddle out of range of his tormentor, to slam into the hard earth with a force that knocked the breath from his body.

Valerius slid from his mount and stood over his fallen opponent. Crescens's chest rose and fell beneath his mail in frantic, spasmodic movements. Valerius used the tip of his sword to push the fallen trooper's helmet from his head. Crescens's eyes were closed and blood ran from his ears and nose. Men ran towards them and Valerius waited till they were within hearing distance.

'Some of you, perhaps most of you,' his raised voice held a savage, post-combat harshness, 'do not want to be here. I can understand why. You left behind sweethearts, friends and good lives at Lindum, Isca and Deva. Believe me, given the choice I'd send you back.' He swivelled to meet the eyes of those standing in a half-circle behind him. 'But know this. Until we reach Britannia, you are mine. You are soldiers and your

78

orders are to protect your legate and his family. You may think it is a soft job. An easy task. But every soldier knows that if you allow your guard to drop you invite trouble. So you will act like professionals. No soft living in *mansiones*. We will make camp every night as if we were marching through enemy territory. We will sleep in tents.' He saw their looks of disbelief and allowed himself a grin. 'Yes, even me. Some of you are good. Some are barely able to stay in the saddle. That's why your decurion and I will mix up tentmates. So the very good can help the very bad.' The first soft murmur of dissent. A growl from the big man with the permanent scowl that could mean anything. He stared them down. 'There will be no fighting and no trouble. Because the first man who steps out of line will find himself lying there like Trooper Crescens. Marius? Help him back to his tent. The rest of you ready your mounts. And remember. Never let your enemy get behind you. You won't find him as merciful as I was.'

He picked up the reins of his horse and Felix fell into step beside him as they walked back to the camp.

'You certainly know how to make an impression, lord,' the decurion murmured.

Valerius smiled. 'I needed the exercise.'

Julius Crescens opened his eyes and winced at his aching head. As he watched the two men go he made an inner vow. When they reached Britannia, Gaius Valerius Verrens would never take up his post. He was a dead man.

XI

'You said we'd be living in tents.' Tabitha counted the line of wagons and confirmed she'd been right the first time. Twenty, including the luxurious sprung carriage that came with the title of *legatus iuridicus*. Wagons packed not only with the necessities she'd identified for the journey, but also a full-sized dining table and couches, enough food and wine to get them to Londinium and back three times, a cook from the Emperor's own kitchens, and . . .

'Titus insisted we have his pavilion.' Valerius smiled. 'I know it takes up two of the wagons on its own, but it has four or five individual rooms. We'll be sleeping in our own bed. You're the wife of a legate now.' His voice took on a note of self-mockery. 'A patrician. And that demands a certain style.'

'And all that food?'

'My orders are to act as Vespasian's envoy to Germania. That's why we're travelling down the Rhenus.' Normally Roman officials would sail to Narbo in southern Gaul and cross overland to Burdigala to take ship direct to Londinium, but Vespasian was still not completely certain of the morale and loyalty of the frontier garrisons. 'We'll be entertaining men of consular rank and the governors of the German provinces.'

Servants scurried back and forth between the villa and the wagons carrying the contents of Tabitha's dressing room. They heard a high-pitched cry of delight and turned to see Lucius leading the new pony – a little white mare – Valerius had bought for him as a surprise. The boy approached with a broad smile, but as he reached his parents he forced his pink features into what he believed to be a mask of solemnity.

'Mother, Father.' Lucius bowed from the waist and Valerius suppressed a smile. 'I thank you for my gift. I promise to look after her and I will ride her every day.'

'You certainly will, boy.' Valerius struggled to keep his voice stern. 'You'll oil and polish her harness and, when she's in stables, you'll muck them out every day.'

'A horse needs a name,' Tabitha suggested. 'What will you call her?'

Lucius looked up into the mare's face. Clearly he hadn't considered naming her. She was a pretty animal, with a bright eye and a steady temperament. Valerius had chosen her for her quickness of foot and her stamina. 'May I make a suggestion?' he said.

Lucius nodded.

'I once had a horse like her. Loyal and fast and she never let me down. I called her Khamsin after the swift winds that scour the Syrian desert. It would honour me if you would do the same.'

'Thank you, sir.' Lucius's voice quivered with emotion.

'Now saddle her up. We leave within the hour.'

'Khamsin?' Tabitha smiled. 'I didn't know you were such a romantic, Valerius.'

'It was when I was with Corbulo in Antioch. She was a fine horse. A gift.' He felt a twinge of guilt. The reply was disingenuous at best. Not a gift from the general, but from his daughter, Domitia Longina Corbulo.

'Will he be safe, do you think? You know how impetuous he can be.'

'He's well taught and she is well schooled,' Valerius assured her. 'By the time we reach Britannia he'll be as at home in the saddle as you or I.'

'Even so . . .'

A hint of humour softened her words, but Valerius knew this was an argument she wouldn't give up. 'I'll have Felix put a good man in charge of him and they'll never be out of our sight.'

He found Felix making a last-minute check of his men's equipment. For the cavalry troopers, tied to the pace of the slowest bullock cart, the first two weeks of the journey threatened to be interminably dull. To combat the boredom Valerius and Felix had worked out a series of exercises they could carry out on the march without tiring the horses overmuch. They would travel across the spine of Italia and north over the River Padus and the gods-cursed plain of Placentia. The journey through the Alps in the summer would be safe enough on a well-found road all the way to Augusta Raurica.

'Who is your steadiest trooper, Felix?' he asked. 'I need your best man to look after my son.'

'The Pannonians are the best horsemen, but they're a rough-and-ready crowd.' Felix ran a hand through his dark hair and frowned. 'Didius Gallus, who came with me from the Twentieth. A genuine volunteer. Though the gods only know why because he was due a promotion if he'd stayed. He has manners. Knows his trade. And he's a reader. Yes, lord, you could do a lot worse than young Didius.'

'Which one is he?'

'The tall sandy-haired trooper checking the girth on the bay.'

Valerius followed his gaze. It was the cavalryman who looked so familiar. Felix called him over. 'Your officer speaks well of you,' Valerius told him.

The shy grey eyes blinked at the unexpected praise. 'Then I thank him for it, sir.'

'I have a request for you. I cannot make it an order because it's a personal matter.'

The young man straightened. 'Anything, sir.'

Valerius grinned. 'Don't be too eager until you've heard what it is. I know from experience it may be no easy task. You see the boy with the white mare?'

'Your son, sir?'

'Yes. He'll travel in the coach for some of the journey, but when the going is easier I want him to spend time in the saddle. He's a good boy, but he can be apt to stray. I need someone reliable to watch over him, teach him some proper horsemanship and what it means to be a cavalryman.'

'I'd be pleased to, sir.'

Valerius studied him. An honest open face, but no fool. He knew his tentmates would make fun of him for babysitting the legate's son, but he was prepared to do it anyway. 'Tell me, Didius, have we ever served together?'

'No, sir.' Didius grinned. 'But you served with my grandfather.'

Valerius gave a snort of disbelief. 'I'm not that old, boy.'

'He was in the Colonia militia, sir. I'm named for him.'

It felt as if someone had dipped him in ice water. All that remained of the Colonia militia was a mound outside the city where the bleached bones of their anonymous owners lay buried in a mass grave. Seventeen years since Boudicca's horde swept the retired veterans of the Twentieth legion aside in a haze of blood. Valerius had commanded the militia for a few short hours. Now their blurred faces ran through his head and he tried to put names to them. Falco, senior centurion. Corvinus, the armourer, who'd sacrificed his honour to save his wife and child. Octavian, with the flashing dark eyes and bushy beard. Then it came to him. 'Didius, the moneylender?'

'Yes, sir.'

'I remember him.' An image formed of the grizzled centurion taking an Iceni spear point in the throat. 'A good soldier and a good man. He annulled all of his comrades' debts the night before he died.'

'He did, sir,' Didius said wryly. 'The family didn't much appreciate that.'

'You must have been what? Four or five years old? I'm surprised . . .'

'That I'm here, sir?' The cavalryman laughed. 'My father used to tell the story every year on the anniversary of my grandfather's death. How you ordered the civilians to be evacuated the previous night. Because

83

he had a young family, my father received dispensation to escort them to safety.'

Valerius remembered the evacuation well enough, but he was even more surprised the boy and his family had survived. 'I was told they'd been wiped out.'

'The Celts ambushed us on the Londinium road.' Didius's face turned sombre. 'Many died, but the auxiliary cavalry escort kept the rebels back long enough for my father to lead a party into the woods. He always said we owed our lives to your foresight.'

Valerius would argue differently. He'd made one mistake after the other, driven by foolish pride and a false sense of duty. A more sensible man would have ignored his orders and got them all out alive long before Boudicca arrived. He managed a smile. 'Well, I'm glad of it. And I can see my son will be in good hands.'

'Thank you, sir.'

'Come, I'll introduce him to his new bodyguard . . . and Didius?'

'Sir?'

'When you get round to telling him about the cavalry leave out the bit about troopers sometimes having to eat their horses. He can find that out for himself.'

They'd been on the road for three days before Valerius realized they were being followed. He spent his mornings in the sprung carriage with Tabitha, reading through the documents Titus had provided detailing the legal history of Roman rule in Britannia. In the afternoons he'd take to the saddle in mail and helmet, indistinguishable from his escort. Normally, he rode with Felix in the vanguard, but often he'd take the chance to drop back and talk to individual troopers. As long as they were in Italia he saw no need for scouts or outriders, but Felix felt it prudent to post a rearguard. Valerius was with them the second day when he noticed a single horseman keeping pace with the convoy. He'd thought little of it, expecting the rider to overtake them when they camped for the evening, but here he was again. Just an occasional glimpse from a height, or on a long, straight stretch of road, and always at the same distance. Valerius called Felix down from the front of the column.

'What do you make of that?'

Felix stared back down the road at the black dot in the far distance. 'Just another traveller?' he suggested. A forced carelessness to his voice made Valerius persist.

'You think so? He was in exactly the same place yesterday.'

The decurion shifted in the saddle. 'I wasn't certain how to tell you.'

Valerius shook his head. 'Why don't we wait for him among those trees?'

At the next bend, the two men and two of the rearguard slipped away into a nearby olive grove. One was Shabolz, the Pannonian, and the other the man with the permanent scowl, known to his comrades as Hilario. Valerius noticed Shabolz reach back to the pouch attached to his saddle to retrieve a fletched and weighted dart about a foot long.

Valerius turned to Felix. 'We don't want him dead, do we?'

'Mars save us, no.'

'I can part his hair at thirty paces,' Shabolz assured them. 'If he makes a run for it I'll lame the horse.'

'That won't be necessary, trooper,' Felix growled.

'You seem to know a lot about our stalker?' Valerius's suggestion drew an angry grunt from Hilario.

'You'll see.' Felix didn't hide his misery.

'He's taking his time,' Valerius mused. 'That horse is barely moving. He's probably asleep in the saddle.'

A few minutes later they heard the slow clop of the animal's hooves. Soon the horse was visible through a gap in the trees, its rider cloaked and hooded despite the summer heat. Valerius waited until it was just past their position.

'Now,' he hissed.

They urged their mounts into the road and surrounded the rider. Valerius expected an instant surrender to superior force, but the horseman's hand whipped to his belt. Before he could reach the weapon,

Valerius reached across with his left hand and hauled the man from the saddle, puzzled by a lack of weight and bulk. The figure in the cloak was so light he could hold him in the air between the horses, legs kicking. A wriggling lurch and the hood fell back to reveal a boy, a remarkably beautiful boy with high cheekbones and long lashes, his thick dark hair cropped tight. Did one of his escort have pederasty to add to their many vices?

'Leave me alone.' With the shrill cry the boy fell clear of the cloak to land sprawling on the packed dirt of the road. He bounded up and would have fled, but Valerius dropped from the saddle and wrapped an arm around him. Iron-shod sandals kicked against Valerius's legs, but the legate ignored the pain. He had made a surprising discovery. The boy was not a boy at all, but a rather well-endowed girl.

'I told you we should have cut her throat,' Hilario growled.

'I should have mentioned it earlier, lord.'

'She's yours?' Valerius asked. Hilario and Shabolz flanked the girl, her hands tied to her saddle till Valerius decided what to do with her.

'Oh no, lord. If she belongs to anyone, she belongs to Florus. She's from some wild tribe that lives in the marshes east of Lindum. Around sixteen, as far as we can gather, with a name no one can pronounce, but she shortens to Ceris. She followed him on foot all the way to Londinium, then stowed away on the ship to Gesoriacum. One of the crew discovered her and the captain would have thrown her overboard had Florus not pleaded for her life. He relented, but I insisted she leave us when we reached shore.'

'Yet here she is riding one of your remounts, decurion.'

'Yes, lord.' Felix hung his head. 'Florus claimed she had great powers in the healing arts. One reason the captain spared her was because she mixed up a poultice that reduced a great swelling on his jaw.' He glanced at Valerius. 'She also mixed a potion that cured my ship sickness.'

'So you kept her.'

'It's good for morale for a squadron to have a *medicus*.' Valerius hid a smile as Felix's voice took on a veteran's tone. 'The men know they can rely on being dosed if they get the shits or camp fever and that someone will stitch them up if they're wounded. She sewed up Florus's arm after an unfortunate knife fight, and you can barely see the scar.'

'I'm willing to bet she caused it.'

'True, lord, but that was more than a month ago. The lads are used to her now. They're not all bad. She helps Pudens with the rations. In a few days you'll barely notice she's around.'

'You think I'll keep her?'

Felix kept his eyes on the road and his face straight, but Valerius could hear the smile in his voice. 'You've commanded soldiers, lord. I don't believe you'd ever rob them of their talisman and that's what she's become. You can send her home when we get back to Britannia and you break up the unit.'

'Why would I break up the escort?'

'We haven't exactly covered ourselves in glory, lord.'

'No, you haven't,' Valerius agreed. 'But who knows when you might get the chance.'

XII

Augusta Raurica sat on a plateau just south of the Rhenus, bounded by the valleys of two lesser streams which formed a triangle whose tip closed at the great river. The city's origins lay in the fort on the bank of the Rhenus, but unlike many such communities Augusta Raurica hadn't developed in haphazard fashion around the military centre. Its founders had planned it on firm architectural lines, with wide intersecting streets and the Temple of Jupiter dominating from the highest point. A thriving city, situated at the crossroads of two important trade routes. Stout defensive walls at the top of steep slopes protected the riches of those who occupied it.

Valerius had intended to stay only a single night before sailing for Moguntiacum, but he discovered his hopes were in vain. In all honour he couldn't refuse an invitation to dine with the leading members of the *ordo*, the council of a hundred leading citizens. In any case, no ships of the Rhenus fleet were in dock, so they'd have to wait for the next convoy of merchant vessels.

During the banquet, the city's *duoviri* took their opportunity to lobby a man with direct access to the Emperor. It was all very well defeating the Batavians, but they would never feel safe until Vespasian dealt with the tribes east of the Rhenus. Valerius promised to pass on their concerns before making his excuses at the earliest opportunity to leave with Tabitha. They walked back to the camp by the light of two flickering torches, escorted by six of Felix's troopers. 'So the price of your legate's sash is to be trapped between two of the biggest bores in Germania Superior.' Tabitha laughed. 'I hope it was worth it.'

'Oh, it wasn't too bad.' Valerius took his wife's hand. 'They agreed to give us the use of three merchant ships that will arrive tomorrow. What they told me may come in useful when we visit Moguntiacum and Colonia. I suspect they have a point about the eastern tribes, but the real reason they want the Eleventh moved here from Vindonissa is the amount of profit they can squeeze from five thousand soldiers instead of five hundred.'

She laid her head on his shoulder, unconscious of the men surrounding them, and Valerius thanked the gods this was his woman. He loved her in so many complicated ways and she made his heart thunder the moment she stepped into a room. For all their new riches he knew it didn't matter to Tabitha whether they lived in a villa or a one-room apartment high in a Suburan *insula*. All that mattered was that they were together.

'And how did you fare with the ladies of Augusta Raurica?'

Tabitha laughed. 'Naturally they had their instructions to impress upon the legate's lady the virtues of their husbands, but it was simple enough to turn them away from politics. They plagued me about the latest fashions in Rome, their troubles with their servants, and their babies.'

'Babies.' Valerius smiled. 'I wouldn't have thought old Justus and Tiberius had it in them.'

'I doubt they do.'

The way she said it, softly, but with a certain unmistakable conviction, made the hair on the back of his neck stand on end. He stopped dead in the street. 'You're . . .'

'The girl Ceris noticed a week ago, but I wanted to be certain before I told you.'

'But this means . . .' He struggled for breath. 'You can't continue. All this travelling can't be good for the baby.'

'You would abandon me here?' She pulled him by the arm towards the city gates, laughing at his fears.

'Then you should go back to Fidenae. Olivia will look after you.'

She turned to face him, a hawkish glint in her eye. 'If you think either I or your child will let you travel to Britannia without us, Gaius Valerius Verrens, you may think again. It will be another six months at least and Ceris can look after me on the journey.'

Valerius sensed the men around them trying to keep their faces straight. What more could he say that wouldn't be wasted breath? She had the coach. The pavilion was as comfortable as any *mansio*. And she was right: Ceris had proved as skilled and useful as Felix suggested. She would be as safe among her friends and servants as at Fidenae, perhaps more so.

Tabitha took his hand and squeezed it, and they continued along a street lined with crowded bars. Valerius had agreed with Felix that some of the men could taste the dubious delights of Augusta Raurica while they waited for the ships. He'd kept them on a tight leash during the journey north, with constant exercises that he'd hoped would bring the men of the different units together. An overloud, slurred voice told him it was a forlorn hope.

'You bastards from the Twentieth have always thought you're better than the rest of us.' The familiar carping tones of Julius Crescens echoed in the street. 'You, Marius, you're worse than the rest, with your tongue up the decurion's arse and yes, sir, no sir. You're happy playing nursemaid to a has-been cripple. Well fuck you. As soon as we get back to Londinium, I'm gone.'

Valerius motioned Tabitha into the shadows and ordered the escort to douse their torches.

'And we'll be well rid of you and your constant whining.' A shadow appeared in the doorway of the bar and a push propelled Crescens bodily into the street, muttering threats and curses. He stood for a moment trying to get his bearings before disappearing into an alley. The familiar sound of rushing liquid followed.

'I could cut his throat and no one would be any the wiser, lord,' Trooper Shabolz suggested quietly.

'I'm grateful for the offer, but I don't think so, Shabolz.' Valerius held Tabitha close. 'Let's not taint an auspicious day with the blood of a fool.'

'Thank you,' Tabitha whispered.

Valerius bent to kiss her head. He had a feeling it might be a decision he'd live to regret.

It took two full days of back-breaking work to load the bulk of the horses and wagons on to the three available merchant galleys. Felix sold the bullocks to a local trader – they could hire or buy more when they were needed – and the other carts and most of the servants would follow when suitable transport arrived. Valerius selected a section of eight men to protect the supplies he was forced to leave behind.

Still, the ships were cramped as a result of the cargo and passengers they carried. Accommodation was of the most basic kind, with a cloth tent for Tabitha and her servants, and everyone else sleeping on deck. The captains were happy to accept Valerius's suggestion that they anchor early each day to allow the cavalrymen to exercise their mounts before making camp.

They set sail on the third morning and the strong current carried them swiftly downstream. Felix and seven of his men accompanied Valerius, Tabitha and Lucius in the leading galley. Each ship was equipped with a single central mast, a bank of seven oars to each side and a larger steering oar at the stern. Thick woodland carpeted the countryside they travelled through, with small farmsteads providing occasional signs of life among the trees. Where the woods thinned the broad, fertile flatlands flanking the river were given perspective by low hills just visible in the hazy far distance. Brigo, the captain, a taciturn, bearded Ligurian, told Valerius he was keeping to the centre of the river because of reports of suspicious activity on the east bank further downstream.

'It'll get worse after Argentoratum. Any ship that strays within bow range is like as not to get a shower of arrows for a welcome, so we'll hug the west bank. If the current forced us east and we ended up stranded on a sandbank a cut throat would be the best of it.'

Valerius used the six days it took to reach Moguntiacum, two hundred Roman miles downstream, to get to know Felix and his escort. The decurion had chosen his steadiest men to travel with the legate and his wife. Didius Gallus was one, virtually inseparable from Lucius these days, Shabolz and Licco, one of his Pannonian comrades, two men who had followed Felix from the Twentieth, Florus, who it seemed couldn't be separated from Ceris, and, most surprisingly, the threatening Hilario.

'He's angry at life,' Felix explained. 'He lost his woman and newborn son just before we left Britannia. I think the reason the legate sent him was that he was frightened of him, and what he was capable of.'

'Then why is he with us?' Valerius glanced towards the brooding presence in the bows, where Hilario stared menacingly across the dark waters to the east.

'Because when it comes to a fight Hilario is a force of nature,' Felix said cheerfully. 'A combination of whirlwind and battering ram. He rode at Governor Agricola's side in the northern campaign to tame the Brigantes six years ago. The men of the legion still talk of the day his patrol was ambushed and he singlehandedly cleared a way for the survivors to make their retreat. He was covered in so much Brigante blood they called him the Butcher.' Hilario turned as if he could sense them talking about him. He fixed Valerius with a narrow-eyed glare. 'Besides, I think he likes you.'

They harboured for three nights below the bridge at Moguntiacum, provincial capital of Germania Superior and the base for two legions. Valerius and Tabitha dined with the governor, Lucius Acilius Strabo, at his palace, along with the legates of the First Adiutrix and the Fourteenth Gemina. All three men assured him Vespasian had nothing to fear about the morale or loyalty of the legions or their auxiliaries, but Strabo echoed the suggestion of Augusta Raurica's *duoviri* that the time was ripe to force the Germanic tribes away from the Rhenus.

He pointed to the window. 'That river mouth you can see from the balcony leads like a spear into the heart of the Chatti. If the Emperor would agree to a combined operation with the legions of Upper

Germania, I could transport fifteen thousand soldiers thirty miles into their territory before they could react. Between us we would crush the Chatti and the Tencteri like grapes in an olive press, then combine to destroy the Cherusci.'

Valerius thanked them for their hospitality and returned with Tabitha to the house where Strabo had insisted they stay. While Tabitha slept, he worked on his report to the Emperor and reflected on the individual characters of the men of his escort. While they'd improved as soldiers – even Gellius Pudens could stay in the saddle – the divisions between them had deepened rather than healed as he'd hoped. Not all, it was true. He could depend on perhaps fifteen or twenty out of the thirty-two, but the others, encouraged by Crescens, wanted nothing to do with their new master.

At dawn the next day they continued their journey north towards Colonia Agrippinensis.

XIII

Two hours after they left Moguntiacum the great river entered a deep gorge and the tree-lined slopes soared above them to east and west. A soft, all-enveloping drizzle began to fall that even a lanolin-treated cloak struggled to keep at bay, and wisps of mist or cloud caught in the tree-tops like pieces of wind-blown spider's web. Driven by the current, they sailed in perpetual silence through a landscape of rugged, fractured beauty, yet their eyes seldom left those dark, preternatural forests with their hint of constant threat. Valerius was reminded that it was in these very same forests that Publius Quinctilius Varus had lost three legions and their eagles. One thing was certain: nobody would ever again underestimate the fighting qualities of the Germanic tribes.

Felix saw it first. A slim, multi-oared galley moored in the centre of the current. A man stood in the bows waving a flag while another motioned that the ships should veer towards the left bank. As the ship slowed the galley reinforced the signal with a piercing trumpet call.

'What's this?' Valerius demanded.

'River patrol of the Rhenus fleet,' the captain explained. 'They want us to moor in the inlet where they've set up a tent, see?'

'Does it happen often?'

'Not often, but I've seen it before. During the revolt they suspended all merchant traffic on the river for a month.'

'Can you ignore them?'

Brigo gave him a sour look. 'Not without losing my reputation and my livelihood.'

'Very well.'

'Back oars and steer for the bank!' The ship slowed dramatically and veered to the left, with their consorts following suit.

They anchored as close to the tent as they could without grounding and a young officer appeared. 'You can't continue past Baudobriga until we've cleared the way,' the man told the captain. 'The Chats have a pair of captured *ballistae* and are up to their usual mischief. They're covering the narrows and have sunk one cargo ship already. Moor outside the fort and wait for instructions.' His tone changed as he noticed Valerius in his distinctive legate's sash. 'My apologies for delaying you, sir, but I have my orders.'

'How long will it take?' Valerius asked.

'We can't tell, I'm afraid.' He pushed a flick of damp hair from his brow. 'It could be a few days or a week. They've done this before. When we attack them from the river they just shift the catapults somewhere else. We may have to wait for a century to come up from Confluentes, but they won't be in any hurry to be ferried across in case it's a trap.'

'I can't afford to wait on the ship for a week.'

The young officer was more used to dealing with the merchant ship captains whose livelihood he controlled than with patricians who could break him on a whim. A horse whinnied in the depths of the hold and he brightened. 'If I can make a suggestion, sir, you could disembark at Baudobriga. They still have a usable dock from when they rebuilt the place. From there you could ride to Confluentes below the obstruction. It may be that you could charter more ships' – his voice faltered as he saw Brigo's jaw come up and the dangerous glint in his eye – 'or stay in comfort until we've dealt with the situation.'

'How far from Baudobriga to Confluentes?' Valerius asked the captain.

'About three hours' ride, lord,' Brigo estimated. 'He's probably right. We couldn't accommodate you in any comfort on board and Baudobriga's hardly a fort at all. A few auxiliaries behind a wooden wall protecting the trading settlement. But they tell me there's a decent road these days. You can't miss Confluentes. Just cut the arc of the river bend until you reach the Mosela, then follow it downstream. The place has a decent *mansio* and baths. If you wait there I'll pick you up as soon as I can.' He shot the officer a look designed to shrivel his essentials. 'I doubt you'll find three ships with the cargo space to carry you in any case.'

Valerius studied the mist-shrouded heights around him as they proceeded cautiously downriver. Though the delay irritated him it was fortunate they'd been forewarned. A well-aimed *ballista* from among those trees could fire directly down into the ship and put a missile straight through her bottom. While the crew struggled to keep the ship afloat the enemy would swarm over the sides from small craft, cut their throats and tow the cargo ashore.

Baudobriga was as the shipmaster described it, a small civilian settle-ment protected by a wooden palisade. Judging by the charred remains of buildings lining the river it had been a much more substantial place before the Batavians destroyed it and slaughtered the occupants. They tied up at a rickety wooden pier below the town and the crew and the auxiliaries began unloading the cargo.

'The horses will be easy enough,' Brigo growled. 'But the carriage and your supply wagons will be a bastard without winches or a crane.'

'Leave the carts where they are then,' Valerius ordered. 'We should reach Confluentes before dark and it's pointless to land them for such a short time.'

They managed to heave Tabitha's carriage ashore, using every man they had and with the aid of a ramp. Didius and Hilario helped the driver hitch the team to the carriage under the watchful eyes of the auxiliaries manning the town walls. Valerius saw his wife and son aboard while the others helped the remainder of the escort to disembark their horses from the second and third ships. Tabitha would have one serving girl;

the rest would stay on board until the way was clear to Confluentes.

'But Father,' Lucius cried. 'Can't I ride Khamsin?'

'Not today, Lucius.' Valerius rumpled the boy's damp curls. He knew his son lived for his time in the saddle with Didius at his side, but with the light beginning to fade they'd have to move fast to reach Confluentes before full dark. 'We're likely to be in camp for two or three days and Didius will take you out as often as you like.'

Valerius went to say his farewells to Brigo.

'I was talking to one of the sentries.' The captain jerked a thumb towards the fort. 'He reckons you have two choices. You can take the old road that flanks the river, but it's more or less a farm track and there are some swampy patches that will give you trouble in this weather. Or you can ride half a mile west and pick up the Via Mosela, which is a better road, though with some tricky stretches. He recommends the second.'

An hour later Valerius was cursing the guard's helpful advice. If the river road was a farm track the path they followed through the hills to the Via Mosela had been little better. The 'tricky stretches' turned out to be sections so steep that Felix and his men were forced to dismount and use their shoulders to help push the carriage over the next summit. The Via Mosela was nothing like the great roads that traversed Italia and Gaul, or even the comparatively rough tracks of Hispania. The track was so narrow and hemmed in by forest Valerius couldn't post a flank guard. Instead, the escort split to ride sixteen in the van ahead of the coach, with a section of eight men bringing up the rear. Worse, the close-ranked trees and overlapping canopy made it seem like night although they still had at least an hour till darkness. Didius rode at Valerius's side, alert as an Iceni hunting dog, and Felix nervously fingered his sword. Behind them, men cursed as they attempted in vain to pierce the gloom, and whispered of forest beasts. Felix hissed at them to stay quiet. If nothing else, Valerius reflected, his escort was receiving a lesson in its true role.

Eventually Felix lost patience and ordered Shabolz to scout ahead. 'Maybe we should stop if we reach a clearing, lord, and camp for the night,' the decurion suggested.

Valerius shook his head. 'No. It can't be as bad as this for the entire route. Once we're out of the hills we'll be able to move faster. It's still possible we can reach Confluentes before dark.'

They travelled another mile before Shabolz reappeared, leading his horse from the gloom like a wraith. He raised a hand to signal the column to halt and Valerius slipped from his horse and handed the reins to Didius. 'Stay with the carriage,' he whispered.

When he reached the Pannonian, Shabolz stepped in close and spoke quietly into his ear. 'The road is blocked by a fallen tree a hundred paces ahead. It could have been natural, but I thought it worth checking. They're in the woods to the east of the track.'

'How many?'

'It's difficult to tell because the forest is so thick, but fewer than twenty, I'd reckon. I doubt they were expecting a column in this strength. By the tattoos I would say they're Chatti, a raiding party to pick off a wagon or two and cut a few throats.'

Valerius considered the position. Clearly the *ballistae* threat had been a diversion to draw the navy away from the point where the ambushers crossed the Rhenus. Now they were his problem. The question was how to deal with them. The convoy was strung out on the narrow road and he doubted they could turn the carriage without alerting the Chatti. Much depended on the mood of the enemy. He could take a chance and push through to remove the road block, gambling the ambushers wouldn't attack a force which outnumbered them, but there was no telling how they'd react. Twenty warriors screaming from the trees could still do plenty of damage even to a column that had been alerted in advance. 'You did well not to show them we were here,' Valerius said to the quiet Pannonian, and signalled Felix forward so he could explain the position.

'We'll leave the horses here and move into the woods to take them in the flank,' he told the decurion. 'Shabolz says they're about thirty paces back and fifty paces ahead. We'll have to move quietly. Leave Pudens and one other man a little way up the road to guard our rear.'

While Felix organized his men, Valerius led his horse to the coach

98

where Tabitha was watching from the curtained doorway. 'There may be trouble,' he warned her. 'Didius and Florus will stay with you while we investigate.'

Typically, she neither protested nor complained. Instead, she rummaged in a bag at her feet and came out first with a cloak which she wrapped around Lucius, and then a belt with a sheathed dagger attached which she buckled around her waist.

'I hope it won't come to that,' he said.

'Better to be prepared.' Tabitha leaned forward and her lips brushed his cheek. 'I won't let them harm Lucius.'

They locked eyes and Valerius felt a moment of regret at leaving her, but if he was going to act it had to be quickly.

'Didius?' he called softly.

'Yes, lord?'

'You and Florus will stay with the lady and Lucius. If anything happens when we're gone take them into the forest and find somewhere to hide. If I don't return you know what to do?'

'Yes, lord. I get them to Confluentes, whatever happens.'

'Good lad.'

The remaining cavalrymen tied their horses to the nearest branch and formed up in a rough skirmish line with Shabolz in the centre and a few steps ahead. Valerius stood where they could see him. 'We outnumber them and we're better than them,' he called softly. 'When it comes to it, make it quick and make it certain. Shabolz will lead; keep your eyes on him. We need absolute silence so check your equipment now. If anything rattles leave it behind. Tread carefully – a single snapping twig will kill you. For Rome.'

'For Rome!' The response was necessarily restrained, but no matter how often he heard it the words sent a thrill of anticipation through him. But he had much more at stake than ever before. 'For you,' he whispered.

As they set off into the forest he had to fend off the doubts that always plagued a commander before any battle. The rain had increased and great drops fell from the canopy on to the crouching men. The close-ranked trees and perpetual gloom reduced visibility to a few feet. What if Shabolz had miscalculated? These woods could hide an army. Perhaps he should have retreated back up the road and sent a messenger to Baudobriga or Confluentes for reinforcements. There was something else, too, a certain reluctance he'd never experienced before. He didn't have to be here with a sword in his hand. Felix was perfectly capable of leading these men. Valerius could have stayed at the wagon with Tabitha and Lucius and no one would have thought any the less of him. Perhaps fatherhood and the years of peaceful existence at Fidenae had changed him? He shook the thought from his head and concentrated on placing his feet. Very little undergrowth here, thank the gods, just fallen leaves and fungi to soften the tread. The sound of the rain on the leaves above would drown out everything except a snapping branch. This was better. Forget about the might have beens; all that mattered was what was to come and how you adapted to the challenges. He looked along the line of men. They seemed steady enough, but he knew they too would be feeling a mix of emotions, especially those who'd never been in a proper fight. The Pannonians he could depend on. Shabolz stalked through the forest like a ghost, balanced on his feet in a slight crouch so he could dance one way or the other at the first sign of a threat. But for the sword held ready in his right hand, Hilario might have been on a country stroll and Valerius was astonished to see what passed for a smile on his forbidding features. There were others who looked equally confident, but that confidence could vanish in a dozen heartbeats. A man never knew how brave he was until his courage was truly tested in the balefire of battle.

Shabolz signalled a diagonal to the left and the line halted. Valerius watched with a critical eye as they shuffled into position before setting off once more. Impossible to keep station among the trees, of course, and they looked like what they were. A set of cavalrymen missing their horses.

Slowly, now. Very slowly.

He looked towards Shabolz: they must be close. Of its own volition Valerius's left hand tightened its grip on the sword, and he experienced the odd sensation of the missing right echoing the movement. He glanced at the man next to him, a trooper called Paulus, but he was staring ahead with bulging eyes and Valerius could see his throat working.

He counted the paces. Ten. Twenty. Thirty. Shabolz raised his hand to signal and motioned to the men behind to drop to a low crouch. When the order had been followed he scurried across to where Valerius waited and put his mouth to the legate's ear.

'They are less than twenty paces ahead, waiting among the trees,' he whispered. 'I think they're restless, because they're making as much noise as a pack of boar. Let me take my Pannonian brothers to attack from the far side. Give me to the count of one hundred.' Valerius was going to protest that it would over-complicate the assault, but Shabolz continued relentlessly. 'We will take them between the hammer and the anvil. More certain. Fewer casualties. No survivors. Yes?' He held Valerius's gaze. The Roman hesitated only a moment. There were men you just had to trust.

'Yes.'

Shabolz's face split into a grin. He motioned to the other Pannonians and they stepped out of line and followed him to disappear away to Valerius's right. Valerius saw some of the other men staring at him in consternation. He slipped across to take Shabolz's place. And waited.

Tabitha and her serving girl were attempting to teach Lucius the rudiments of the board game Caesar when she heard the sound of approaching hooves. Ignoring the rain, she slipped through the curtained doorway as Gellius Pudens and a trooper she recognized as Julius Crescens rode up from the direction of Baudobriga.

Pudens dismounted clumsily from his horse. 'They're here,' he hissed, wide eyes betraying his alarm. 'Dozens of them. Coming up behind us.'

Tabitha felt a thrill of panic for her son. She opened her mouth to question the plump cook, but Didius preempted her. 'Gellius, warn the legate,' he snapped. 'Our boys are in the woods to the right of the road. Follow them, but do it quietly. Understand?'

'Yes, Didius.' The big man slipped clumsily from the saddle, and lumbered into the trees.

'Julius, help the lady get anything she needs from the coach, and follow me. Leave the horses.'

'Who are you to give me orders?' Crescens demanded, but he was already dismounting.

'Lady, you must do exactly what I say.'

Tabitha took a deep breath, but she nodded.

Didius reached into the coach and took Lucius in his arms. 'Come, Lucius,' he said, smiling. 'We're going to play a game of hide and seek.'

Florus stood at the rear of the carriage with his sword drawn watching the road, with Ceris at his side. Tabitha and Crescens helped the bewildered serving girl from the coach, and they followed Didius into the trees on the opposite side of the road.

'What about Khamsin?' Lucius pointed to the white pony tethered to the rear of the coach.

'She'll still be here when we get back. Rufius,' Didius called softly. Florus turned to stare at him. 'Cover our rear.' Florus nodded and began to back towards them. He hissed an order at Ceris and she ran to help Tabitha.

'Where are we going, Didius?' Tabitha asked.

'I scouted the woods earlier and I found somewhere you can hide until it's safe.'

'I can hide?'

'You and your maid and Lucius. The rest of us will spread out and protect you.'

'What about Ceris?'

Didius was about to say that Ceris was perfectly capable of looking after herself, but he had a feeling that would only encourage the legate's wife to put herself in harm's way. 'There's room for Ceris,' he said. 'But we must hurry.'

After a hundred paces or so they reached a steep slope where the roots of a fallen oak tree had torn out a hollow in the hillside. It was only a shallow depression in the dirt, but partly concealed by the toppled trunk. 'This is where you will hide, Lucius.' Didius bundled the boy up the six or so feet to the dirt hole. 'But you must not make a sound.'

Tabitha scrambled up beside her son and pulled her maid into the sanctuary as Crescens pushed from below.

Florus appeared through the trees and ran to Didius. 'They're looting the carriage, but it won't keep them busy for long. There must be upwards of thirty of them.'

'Maybe they'll just steal the horses?' Crescens suggested.

Florus shook his head. 'They just released them and drove them back up the road. What do we do?'

'We'll make a line about forty paces east. They may only send two or three to investigate this side of the road. If they do we'll take them out.'

'And if not?'

Didius studied his surroundings for a moment. 'We'll retreat back here and try to keep them at bay until the legate sends help.'

'We should all have gone with Pudens,' Crescens said resentfully.

'I had my orders,' Didius said. 'Ceris? I need you to stay with the lady.'

Ceris looked to Florus. 'I'll be safe enough,' he said. She nodded and went to take refuge with Tabitha. When she climbed into the crowded earth shelter she pulled a short dagger from her sleeve. She noticed Tabitha already had her blade drawn.

XIV

'Now!'

Valerius and his men trotted silently through the wood. Twenty paces, Shabolz had said, but it seemed much further.

Between two trees he caught a glimpse of a group of warriors crouched low and staring intensely in the direction of the road. Naked from the waist up, their well-muscled bodies were covered in tattoos and they carried spears or long, heavy swords similar to the Roman pattern. They were young, but every man wore a full beard and long hair fashioned in a curious topknot.

A piercing scream from the far distance drew the attention of the crouching Germans and they turned in confusion towards the sound.

Valerius ran slightly ahead of his men. So close now he could see the crude eagle tattoo on the closest German's back and count the knots on his spine. At last, the warrior registered the sound of running footsteps. He rose and half turned, shouting a warning that turned into a shriek of mortal agony as Valerius ran his *spatha* into the exposed flesh above the hip. Without breaking stride the legate ripped the long blade clear so blood sprayed bright and guts spilled in a slippery pink-blue coil to the forest floor.

In the same instant the men of Valerius's escort fell on the dying warrior's companions. Caught entirely by surprise, the enemy barely had time to raise their swords before the disciplined cavalry troopers chopped them down. Valerius saw Hilario smash his heavy blade on an unprotected head in a blow so powerful it almost sliced his victim's skull in two. Another German howled as two Romans hacked at his body until his chest was a bloody mess of splintered ribs and exposed viscera. 'On,' Valerius roared. Somewhere up ahead Shabolz and his companions would be fighting for their lives. They had accounted for just five of the twenty enemy the Pannonian estimated were in the forest. From nowhere a German appeared at full tilt, swinging a massive axe at Valerius's head. Valerius brought his sword up to parry and the shock of the blow sent a dart of agony down his arm and into his heart. No time or space to bring the point round. Instead, he rammed the German warrior chest to chest, the weight of his mail hammering his enemy backwards. They smashed to the ground together, pummelling each other as they tumbled down the steep slope of an unseen gully. Valerius's helmet went flying and his sword followed it. A thumping impact as they hit a tree knocked all the breath from him. In the same instant his vision was filled with a mass of dark hair and eyes burning with hate, a spittle-flecked mouth so close Valerius could smell the sewer stink of his enemy's breath. He rammed his head into the twisted features and blood spurted from the ruined nose into Valerius's eyes. Yet the blow seemed only to galvanize the German. A pair of incredibly strong hands closed on Valerius's throat. Someone was growling like a dog, but he couldn't be sure who. With his left hand he felt for the familiar protrusion on his right wrist where the cowhide stock met the oak. A sharp snick went unnoticed by his strangler. Valerius ignored the choking fingers to smash his head into the German's face a second time, creating enough leeway to bring the wooden fist round into his enemy's neck. At first the blow induced no reaction and he struggled against the German's iron grip, his vision beginning to go. Mars' sacred arse, had he left it too late? Very gradually the fingers relaxed and the fire in the murderous eyes faded. After a few moments

105

Valerius was able to roll clear and lay gasping beside his enemy. Blood soaked the dark beard and the chest below, pulsing in fading spurts from a small wound below his right ear. Valerius studied the little knife blade projecting from the middle knuckle of the wooden fist and, not for the first time, gave thanks to Dimitrios, the Emesan armourer who had created it for him. He fumbled around in the leaves at the sound of crashing feet on the slope, but when he looked up it was Hilario standing over him.

'Are you hurt, lord?'

Valerius realized his chain armour was slick with his enemy's blood. 'No. It's his. Why are you here and not killing Germans?'

Hilario helped Valerius to his feet. 'Because there are no more left to kill.'

They scrambled up the slope and Hilario recounted how the cavalrymen had hunted the panicked German warriors through the woods like chickens. A few of the more agile escaped towards the river, but any brave enough to stand and fight were slaughtered. Valerius's men had accounted for ten and Shabolz and his Pannonians six. The troopers knelt by the scattered bodies stripping the fallen warriors of any valuables. Shabolz handed Valerius a fine gold neck ring. 'It must have come from their leader.'

Valerius handed back the gold ornament. 'Keep it. You deserve it. Any casualties on our side?'

'A few cuts,' Shabolz said. 'But nothing that will trouble the witch.'

'The witch?'

'Ceris. Crescens says she's some kind of priestess.'

'She's certainly cast a spell on our young friend Florus, but I'd have thought you'd know better than to listen to Crescens.'

Shabolz shrugged. 'He—'

'Lord, you should see this!'

The shout came from Nilus, the group's signaller, his brass trumpet never far from his right hand.

'I thought I sent you back to tell the carriage everything was all right,' Valerius said.

For the first time Valerius noticed his face was as white as parchment.

'What is it?'

'It's Gellius, sir . . .'

Valerius felt his heart stutter as he recognized the crumpled body in cavalry armour lying among the leaves. Nilus heaved the massive corpse on to its back. He paused for a moment, knelt and very gently brushed a leaf from Pudens's plump features. A ragged, pink-lipped gash ran beneath the cook's chin from one ear to the other.

'Minitra save us,' Shabolz whispered. He turned to Valerius. 'He was with the rearguard. What was he doing here?'

But Valerius was already running back towards the road. When he reached the carriage the horses were missing and the contents strewn across the road. He fought a wave of panic as he pulled back the curtain. The coach was empty.

Tabitha held her son close and stared through the tree roots at the ranks of oaks separating them from the road. She would have felt more useful with Didius and the others. She had killed before and she had no doubt she could take at least one of the German tribesmen with her. But more important to be here to give Lucius what comfort she could. She could feel the boy's beating heart as she held him close, her throat as dry as a desert salt flat. If it came to it would she be able to do it? She knew just where to place the point. He would feel nothing but a tiny sting. But the thought sent a shudder through her.

'I'm bored with this game,' Lucius whispered.

'Just a little longer, Lucius,' she assured him.

'What games do you like?' Tabitha blinked. Ceris hadn't said a word since entering their den and snuggling down between Lucius and Vacia the maid.

'I want to ride Khamsin.'

'You can do that later.' Ceris smiled. 'Do you like magic?'

Four-year-old eyes narrowed in suspicion. 'Can you do magic?'

'We'll just have to see. Do you have a coin?' This to Tabitha.

She reached beneath her dress for a purse and pulled out a gold *aureus*.

Ceris laughed as she rubbed the buttery yellow coin between her fingers. 'A little on the large side. I could have bought a small farm with this back in Lindum.'

'What is it like there?' Tabitha asked.

'Flat and wet.' Ceris held up the big coin so Lucius could see it and began to twirl it between her fingers, increasing the speed so it appeared to have a life of its own and changing from one hand to another with bewildering dexterity. Suddenly her fingers were empty.

'Where has it gone?' Lucius demanded. 'You're hiding it.'

Ceris opened first one hand, then the other, but there was no sign of the coin. Tabitha watched just as closely, for she had no idea where the *aureus* had gone.

'I think you must have stolen it,' Ceris said with narrowed eyes. 'I think you magicked it into your head.'

'No,' the boy gasped.

'Yes,' Ceris said. She reached across with her right hand and rummaged in Lucius's dark hair beside his right ear. 'Look, here it is.' She seemed to pluck something from his head and when he looked he saw the gleaming coin in her hand. His finger shot to his ear and a look of pure astonishment flashed across his face.

Tabitha laughed and Ceris tossed the coin in the air so it tumbled four or five times. 'Would you like to see more magic.'

'Please.'

But not for long. Within minutes Lucius had fallen asleep in his mother's arms. 'Thank you for keeping him amused, Ceris,' Tabitha whispered. 'Some day you must show me how you did it.'

Ceris shrugged, all the lightness of her performance replaced by her normal sullen demeanour. 'It was nothing.'

Tabitha stared at the trees. 'Perhaps they won't come.'

The sound of the rain on the leaves above masked any noise, but there was no disguising the stealthy movement amongst the trees to their front. 'They're coming,' Didius whispered. 'We should go back to the women.'

'Fuck that,' Crescens said decisively. 'They can look after themselves.' He was already running towards the left past a startled Rufius Florus.

Didius watched him go, uncertain what to do. 'Rufius,' he called urgently, 'for all the gods' sake persuade him to come back and help. Join me at the fallen tree.'

Rufius nodded and ran after the fleeing Crescens.

Didius found the slope and followed it south until he reached the fallen tree. The women were nowhere in sight. He had a moment of terrible irrational fear that they'd been taken until he clambered up to the hollowed-out chamber and saw the determined faces of Tabitha and Ceris and felt the prick of a knife point beneath his chin. He gulped. 'The others will be with us soon.' The words were said with more hope than conviction. Rufius would certainly return. He'd never leave Ceris, but something told him that that coward Crescens was gone for good. A pity, because they had a perfectly good defensive position that Didius reckoned could have been held by three men until Valerius returned. Their refuge was high enough to be reached only with difficulty, and the tangled network of tree roots would protect them from all but a very fortunate spear.

All they could do was wait and hope.

Not five minutes later the rain slackened and in the eerie silence that followed they could hear the sound of men moving stealthily through the forest towards them. Didius tightened his grip on his sword.

Julius Crescens hesitated, uncertain of his direction, and Rufius finally caught up with him.

'Which way is the road?'

'Don't be a fool, Julius,' Rufius hissed. 'Even if you did manage to join the squadron what do you think will happen when the legate finds out you abandoned his wife and son? Like as not he'll tie you between four horses and take the whip to them himself.'

'It's our word against that fool Gallus. As long as you back me no one will touch us.' He set off in what he thought was the right direction, but Rufius didn't move.

'I'm going back,' he called softly. 'I won't leave Ceris.'

'Suit yourself, but remember, I got lost in the woods.'

Rufius muttered a curse and was about to turn away when a shadow appeared from the scrub behind Crescens. As if in a dream he watched hands rise and fall before the Roman cavalryman collapsed among the tree litter. Before he could decide whether to help his comrade or run back to support Didius Gallus and Ceris something seemed to fall on him and his own world turned black.

XV

Shabolz knelt by the patch of disturbed ground and ran his hand over the leaves. 'Two men in *caligae* stood here, lord.' He rose to his feet and walked twenty paces. 'One moved this way, but something happened when he reached this point. The other didn't move from here on his feet. See the signs of something being dragged? That's all I can be sure of. For the rest there is evidence of many men in the felt-soled boots the German tribes wear.'

'So they've been taken?'

Without a word Ceris, who had been standing with Tabitha and Lucius, set off in the direction of the road. Valerius grabbed her arm as she marched past and she turned on him with a look of fury, hissing like a trapped wildcat.

'There's nothing you can do on your own,' Valerius snarled. 'You'll get yourself killed and that won't help Rufius. Stay where you are and let me think.'

Ceris dragged her arm free, but she went back to Tabitha.

'You will find them, Valerius?' his wife said.

'I need to know a lot more than I do now before I decide anything. Shabolz?' The Pannonian nodded. 'Take ten men and follow the tracks as far as you're able. Don't risk a confrontation, but I need to know

111

if they're on this side of the river and still alive.' Their eyes met and Valerius knew the Pannonian's thoughts mirrored his own. The most convenient outcome would be if the patrol came back with two corpses. 'Send a messenger when you get to the river, and if they haven't crossed we'll join you when we've rounded up the rest of the horses.'

'And if they have?'

'Then we'll meet at Confluentes.'

Shabolz ran off shouting the names of the men he wanted for the patrol. Valerius nodded to Felix and they walked a little way aside. 'What do you think?' he asked.

'You're planning to go after them?' The decurion sounded incredulous.

'I've never left a man behind if there was a way to avoid it.'

Felix considered for a moment. 'Not even his own tentmates would be too concerned to see Crescens's head on a spike, but they like Rufius despite his light-fingered habits. They wouldn't be happy to abandon him.'

'That's what I thought.' Valerius stroked the scar on his cheek. 'But it will depend on what we hear at Confluentes.'

'All I'm asking is an assessment of the situation on the far side of the river and likely places the missing men of my escort may have been taken.'

The commander of the fort at Confluentes stared out across the dark waters of the Rhenus at the thickly wooded slopes on the far bank. Sextus Regulus was an overworked and surprisingly elderly senior military tribune from the Twenty-first Rapax stationed at Bonna. His garrison consisted of a detachment from the legion and a cohort of Rhaetian auxiliaries. He had barely seven hundred men to secure almost forty miles of the west bank, and the constant strain showed in the lines on his weathered face. The raid in which Crescens and Florus had been abducted reflected badly on his leadership and he knew it. He'd allowed the *ballistae* below Baudobriga to distract him and left it to the navy to deal with. This visiting legate with his warrant

112

from the Emperor could make trouble for him if he didn't cooperate. On the other hand, losing two insignificant legionary cavalrymen was one thing, losing the Emperor's personal envoy quite another.

'I repeat, my advice to you is to forget them.'

Valerius knew it was good advice. Any prudent commander would make an offering to Jupiter in their memory and continue his journey. But Crescens and Florus were *his* men and for all their faults part of the unit. Leaving them to their fate would send a message to their comrades that would never be forgotten. He was depending on these men to be prepared to sacrifice themselves to save his wife and child. Continuing without even attempting to save two of them would prove there was a point beyond which Valerius wouldn't go to protect his troopers. Oh, he could argue, as one of his former commanders had predicted, that there came a time when a soldier's life was only a coin that must be spent, but that wasn't the point. Every moment he'd spent with Felix and his escort he'd been trying to create a special bond between them. A face swam into his head: smouldering dark eyes, a gleaming head as smooth and black as a river boulder, full lips and a blunt nose like a ship's ram. Juva and the crew of the *Waverider* had volunteered to be part of a naval legion formed by Nero and they had scorned massacre and ignominy to make it a reality. What grew between them was more than a bond. It was a brotherhood. Valerius had seen them swept away at Bedriacum by the swords of the very legion Regulus served. The troopers of the escort would never become a brotherhood if he were to order them to abandon two of their comrades. And he had another, much more personal reason to risk all. He was Gaius Valerius Verrens, Hero of Rome. With that accolade came a responsibility that had guided his course from the moment Nero had placed the Corona Aurea upon his brow. It had been no idle boast when he told Felix he had never left a man behind. His old friend Serpentius would have told him he was a sentimental fool, but he would have been first in the boat at Valerius's side.

'Let's assume that I don't intend to take it.'

'I cannot authorize you to cross the river.'

'I don't require your authorization, tribune,' Valerius pointed out. 'If I choose to do so you can't stop me. I happen to outrank you, and that scroll you're holding orders you to give me every assistance to carry out my mission for the Emperor. If I choose to believe that mission is best served by a visit to your neighbours that's entirely my responsibility.'

Regulus stared at the document and the Imperial eagle on the seal. 'Will you sign a letter accepting full responsibility for the consequences?'

'If that will ensure your cooperation, I'll be happy to do so.'

The tribune sighed and went to a cabinet where a series of yellowing and torn pieces of parchment hung from wooden dowels. 'These were begun in Varus's time,' he said, finding the one he wanted. 'Subsequent commanders have added to them over the years, so what you have is a reasonable approximation of the terrain and geography on the east bank and up to twenty miles inland. We're fortunate that the then commander buried them in a sealed container before Civilis and his rebels chopped his head off and burned the place down.' He laid the parchment on the table and used four metal discs, obviously manufactured for the purpose, to weigh down the corners. 'The faded red dots are settlements, although some of them may no longer be there. The Germans have a habit of moving on once they've fouled the nest to an extent that nauseates even them. There are no roads as such, but the main trails between the villages are marked. The rest is mainly impenetrable forest.'

Valerius's heart sank when he saw the extent of the territory he would have to search if he were to find Crescens and Florus. It would take weeks, even months, and he didn't have weeks.

'One of my men identified the warriors as members of a tribe called the Chatti. Does that help?'

'If he's right, it would, but the gods only know how he'd do it. They all look the same to me with their filthy beards and barbaric tattoos.' He ran a finger across the map to indicate a general area. 'This is Chatti territory, but I'm afraid there's no doubt where they've taken your soldiers.'

'How can you know?'

114

'Because it's not the first time it's happened. They discovered an appetite for abduction after the civil war, when Civilis sent her prisoners as tribute.'

'Her?'

'Their witch.'

Valerius felt as if someone had run a sword point up his spine. The second time in two days he'd heard that word. Was it an omen? He bent low over the map. 'And where does this witch live?'

Regulus bent beside him and pointed to a pink dot far inland. 'Her temple complex is here in a settlement they call Guda.' He looked up and their eyes met. 'But from what we hear she's well guarded, legate, and surrounded by several hundred loyal followers.'

Valerius studied the map. No way of riding that far into enemy territory undetected, even if they could ever find the place. It would be suicide even to attempt it. He was just about to admit defeat when he noticed something. 'And this is?' He pointed to a dark line that curved into Chatti country like a fish hook and passed within what appeared to be a short distance of Guda.

'The River Logana.'

'How far upstream is it possible to travel by boat?'

'I will only take volunteers.' Valerius allowed his gaze to roam across the men in the barrack room, meeting each eye to eye. 'It will be dangerous and the chances of success are low. Anyone who wants out should leave now.'

'You make it sound like a visit to the brothel at the Grapes in Isca,' Marius grinned. 'But we've already decided. If you're going we're all going.' His words brought a growl of assent. 'Besides, we need to pay those bastards back for Gellius. He may have been a sack of lard, but he was a good cook and he was one of us.'

Valerius saw Didius Gallus looking at the floor and knew the young soldier was thinking he'd be left behind to guard Lucius and Tabitha. 'Didius? You're with us?'

The dark head snapped up. 'Of course, sir.'

'Good. I'll need an aide to pass on messages, so you stick close to me. Felix? Someone has to stay behind and meet Brigo and his ships.'

Felix nodded glumly. They'd had their argument earlier.

'The good news is that Tribune Regulus has agreed to provide us with a galley, so we'll be travelling in style.' He returned the smiles. 'The bad,' he stepped forward and uncovered the ancient map Regulus had loaned him, 'is that we'll be travelling twenty miles into territory crawling with Chatti warriors. We'll leave tonight and only travel by dark. I'm assured our sailor knows the river and we'll be able to hide up by day. According to this, it's about three miles from the river to Guda.'

'What can we expect when we get there?' Nilus, the signaller who'd found Pudens's body.

'We have a guide who knows the area,' Valerius assured him, leaving out the fact that the man had never been inside the witch's settlement. 'The temple is at the heart of the village and the people think of her as a prophetess and a god. We can't fight our way in, because they'll out-number us by at least ten to one. If we're to save Rufius and Crescens we need to do it by stealth.'

That sobered the mood. In the silence that followed he waited for the inevitable question. Hilario didn't disappoint him. The big man rose and approached the table where Valerius had spread the map. Studying it intently, he ran a finger thoughtfully down the curve of the river from the settlement back to the Rhenus just above Confluentes. 'Would I be correct in saying, lord, that getting there is the easy part?'

Valerius nodded slowly. 'I'm glad you mentioned that, Hilario. Once we've walked into Guda, freed the prisoners and strolled back to the boats through hundreds of, hopefully, sleeping Germans, we have the small problem of retreating twenty miles down the river. Only this time every warrior on the Rhenus frontier will be after us.'

'And how do we do that, lord?'

'I have no idea.' Ceris had been standing by the door unnoticed. Now Valerius watched as she slipped away, unseen by the others. 'In the meantime I suggest you make ready. Pick up rations for five days from the quartermaster. Don't worry about going hungry, because if we're not back by then you'll be dead, or wishing you were. And soot.'

Their faces turned to him in consternation.

'Soot, lord?'

'Yes, find some soot.'

Tabitha had insisted Ceris be assigned a room in the guest accommodation they shared. Valerius entered without knocking and found the Corieltauvi girl dressed in German *bracae* and a plaid tunic. He recognized the clothing from one of the raiders they'd killed the day before, but it had been altered to fit Ceris's slim frame. Tabitha was helping her strap an iron sword to her waist.

'You knew about this?'

'Of course,' Tabitha said.

'And you approved?'

'You would have expected me to do likewise if it was you they'd taken over the river.'

Valerius sighed. He could have depended on it. Sometimes he wondered who was in charge of this band of misfits. Without another word he went to the open hearth in the centre of the room and bent to rub his hand over the blackened bricks. He returned to Ceris and put his hand to her face. She flinched away with a grunt of disgust, but Valerius persisted, smearing the black soot until it covered both cheeks and her forehead.

'That's a start,' he said to Tabitha. 'But she'll need more to cover her clothes.'

Tabitha gave him a look of puzzlement, but then understanding dawned. 'Yes.'

There were many things Valerius should have been doing in the last few hours before night fell, but one outweighed all the others. He sought out Didius and told him to take Lucius riding on Khamsin, with strict instructions not to return before dusk.

When he returned to his quarters, Tabitha was waiting. She saw the look on his face and without a word walked into their small bedroom and unclipped two brooches and allowed her dress to fall to the floor.

An hour later they lay tangled amid the sheets, their sweat-sheened limbs haphazardly splayed across each other. Valerius ran his fingers over her right breast, intrigued by the small but noticeable changes that confirmed her condition. Tabitha lay back with her eyes closed, a look of contentment on her face and a pleasing flush to her cheeks. 'If you keep doing that you may have to postpone your madness for another day,' she said drowsily.

'If I don't—'

Her fingers went to his lips to silence him.

'You will come back, Gaius Valerius Verrens. This Chatti sorceress is not the only woman on the Rhenus with the sight.'

'Go to Titus. He will keep you safe and make sure the right things are done for Lucius and our daughter.'

'Daughter?'

'Your beauty is eternal, Tabitha of Emesa. She will be the gods' guarantee of it.'

She took his left hand in hers and laid it flat on her stomach. 'You will return,' she repeated. 'Ceris has foretold it.'

'Ceris?'

'That's why I helped her. It will take a witch to find a witch.'

XVI

'I don't know if your night stalkers will scare the enemy, but they certainly put the fear of death in me, sir.'

Valerius stood on the quayside with Antonius, the young officer of the Rhenus fleet who'd stopped the convoy above Baudobriga. In the light of a dozen flickering torches he could see the slim and, to Valerius, worryingly fragile oak frame of the galley bobbing gently in the shelter of the quay wall, held steady by the oarsmen who sat seven to each side on their benches.

Behind the two officers the men of the escort waited to board by the narrow gangway connecting the quay to the ship. They were indeed a sight to strike terror into any who crossed their path, but, more important, able to operate more or less unseen in the dark. Each trooper had covered himself in soot – flesh, clothes, chain armour, and weapons – so that in the darkness he was an indistinct shadow only identifiable by a pair of white staring eyes. No helmet, to reduce the weight the oarsmen would have to propel, and no shields, because they'd only be a liability in the thick woods they expected to encounter. Valerius was as black as any of his men, with the soot stink thick in his nostrils.

He had to keep reminding himself these were cavalrymen, more at home on horseback than on their own feet. Yet a number of them had been legionaries less than two months ago; truculent, barely govern-able legionaries in some cases, but legionaries still. Was he expecting too much of them? Regulus clearly believed Valerius was leading his soldiers to certain death, and the cheerful young galley captain treated him as if he were an aged, but respected, relative who wasn't quite right in the head.

Yet Valerius thought he now had the measure of the men he led. Every member of the escort was committed to the rescue of their two comrades, whatever the cost. Rivalry between the various factions still divided them more than he cared for, but it was competitive rather than murderous. They'd fought well in the woods, not a man taking a step back, and Valerius knew it had nothing to do with his leadership. He'd pointed them at the enemy and they'd done what was needed.

'Tell the men to get ready,' Valerius ordered Didius, almost unidentifiable at his side. 'But I'll talk to them first.'

Valerius looked up towards the looming shadow of the fort. They had said their farewells while he was donning his armour, but he sensed Tabitha was up there watching.

He approached the line of blackened figures. Only two were identifi-able. Hilario's enormous frame would have stood out in any company, and Ceris seemed a childlike figure tagged on to the end of the front rank.

'You will board by twos.' The occasion seemed to call for a discreet whisper, but the enemy was far away and there was no likelihood of hearing anything less than a normal speaking voice above the rush of the great river. 'You know your positions, so take them quickly. Get into the centre of the ship and stay there. If you need to piss do it now; there won't be any chance once we cast off.' Two or three of the anonymous figures slunk guiltily into the outer darkness. 'If anything happens, do not panic. You can trust our water rat friends to get us out of trouble. If they can't there's no point in worrying either' – he slapped his chain armour – 'because we're all eel bait in any case. But that won't happen. Antonius and his men will get us across and with Fortuna's favour will carry us up the Logana to the witch's lair.' He sensed a shiver of unease run through the men at the mention of their quarry. 'Just remember that once we're across, every man, woman and child is your enemy. Discovery means death. Do not hesitate. Kill first and kill quickly. Now get on board.'

They shuffled down the wooden planking led by Marius and Hilario, nervousness making their steps tentative and almost childlike. Two sailors waited at the bottom to help them into the boat and they clambered over the benches to their assigned positions.

'Regulus tells me you have the most experience of the eastern shore of any sailor in the Rhenus fleet,' Valerius said to Antonius.

'That's true enough, I suppose,' the other man agreed. 'We've run up the Logana in *Rapid Racer* on no less than three occasions. Delivering the likes of your spy there.' He motioned to the guide Regulus had provided, an insignificant, hairy creature dressed in soiled brown sackcloth. 'But we have never been more than six miles upstream, whereas today you expect me to row you as far as twenty.'

'Can you do it?'

'That is for the gods to decide,' Antonius said with grave formality. 'A river is a creature of ever-changing geography. What is a navigable pool today could be a gravel bank after the next flood. It depends on the shoals and the shallows and whether your men are prepared to carry her over them. Whether the Chatti have suddenly been motivated to do what they should have done a decade ago and put a barrier across the river. Even a bastard fish trap in the wrong place could hole her. But time will tell, legate.' He met Valerius's gaze. 'What is certain is that I will get you across the river and into the mouth of the Logana. After that it is up to Fortuna and the sorceress.'

Valerius waited till Ceris skipped lightly down the gangway and hurdled the ship's side before following at a pace commensurate with his age and dignity.

He took his place at the back of the boat, close to Antonius, mildly concerned to find himself ankle deep in water. *Rapid Racer* had a sharp bow, a broad stern with a pair of short steering oars attached one to each side, and a central mast.

As they cast off Valerius murmured encouragement to his men and tried to stifle his own nerves. They sat, rigid as statues, as Antonius quietly issued orders in a calm voice and his sailors manoeuvred the galley slowly out into the stream. The total darkness – the night sky entirely devoid of stars – and the constant drag and whisper of the river was unnerving at first, as if they were no longer in the hands of human-kind, but of the gods. He tried to make himself comfortable on the hard bench, but he froze as the men propelled the little craft first eastwards, then downriver.

'I thought the mouth of the Logana was upstream of Confluentes,' he whispered to Antonius.

'Only a fool would tell the enemy precisely where he intended to go.' He heard the smile in the other man's voice. 'I have a feeling you never charged straight into the maw of the lion, legate.'

Valerius felt the spray from the oars on his face. 'Only when I needed to, captain.' He laughed. 'But you have my apologies. We are in your hands.'

A few minutes later, Antonius whispered a new order. The galley spun within its own length and headed back upstream, hugging the east bank, the force of the current immediately apparent. Soon they passed Confluentes on the right, pinpointed by the soft glow of a hundred oil lamps. Valerius had a momentary pang for Tabitha before the darkness closed in again. He marvelled at Antonius's ability to read the river when it was impossible to see a dozen paces ahead.

A soft whisper in the night and he realized the galley master was speaking to him. 'It is all about the current,' he heard the other man say. 'Swift as a galloping horse and soft as a woman's touch. Sometimes a little to the east and sometimes to the west and then that jerk, as the Logana pushes you west as if you've been hit by a bullock cart. Wait, wait. Hard left.' The men at the oars responded instantly to Antonius's low shout. Within moments they were aware of a darker darkness and the oarsmen slackened their speed. 'Easy, easy,' the steady voice cautioned. 'Wait for the sandbar.' A momentary check and a flurry of oars and Valerius sensed Antonius's relief. 'That's the easy part. The worst is yet to come. Straight ahead. But slowly. Kronos? Put out the pole.'

'The pole?' Valerius hissed.

'Sometimes they string ropes across the river,' Antonius replied from the darkness. 'Better to know it's there before it rips your head off.'

No ropes, just the constant swish of the oars and the rush of the stream. As far as Valerius could tell the river was around three boat-lengths wide, but beneath the cloak of the all-enveloping night that was all he knew. He marvelled at the stamina of the oarsmen as they pulled hour after hour against the current. Their only respite came when Antonius sensed a backwater to the left and they rested for what felt like all too short a time.

'Can we help?' he asked the young sailor.

Antonius laughed. 'Not unless you can change the direction of the current. A stream joins the river three miles ahead. We anchored there last time. There wasn't a sign of life within a day's march, but you never know with the Germans. They move at a whim, or when the stink gets too much for them. We have to get there well before daylight and hide the boat.'

Again, Antonius sensed their destination by the change in the current. By the time they reached the inlet the rowers were slumped over their oars with exhaustion and Hilario jumped into the shallows and dragged the galley in to the river edge. The cavalrymen scrambled ashore to set up a perimeter on the bank of the tributary stream and Shabolz and five others went deep into the woods to chop branches and used them to camouflage the ship. When the work was done Marius set guards and the others, soldiers and sailors alike, lay on the hard ground beneath the trees and got what rest they could. Dawn revealed a narrow platform of flat land at the bottom of a steep tree-lined slope and Antonius swam the river to be certain his craft was completely hidden from the other side. When he returned he collapsed without a word into the sleep of the dead. Valerius found a cloak to cover him.

'My captain has been awake for the last thirty-six hours,' one of the oarsmen said, dragging a bundle of ferns across himself. 'He's spent half the night on the oars himself.'

'Who's on guard?' Valerius asked Marius.

'Hilario, Nilus and two from the Ninth.'

'Wake me in an hour and I'll take the second watch.'

'Lord . . .'

'Wake me in an hour.'

It must have been the seventh hour, with a weak sun slanting through the trees, when they heard voices. Valerius came instantly awake. Marius was already hustling the men further back into the forest. 'Send Shabolz and three of his Pannonians to me.' Valerius squirmed through the knee high grass to where Antonius watched over his ship like a mother hen.

'What is it?' Valerius whispered.

Antonius gently parted the grass in front of them to give Valerius a view across the Logana. In the shallows on the near side, so close that Valerius almost jerked his head back, two ragged children worked over what looked like a wicker eel trap. Beside them, moored to a nearby rock, was a small round boat. As they checked the trap they argued in loud, shrill, but none the less good-humoured voices. Valerius saw that one was a scrawny waif of a girl of about eight, and the other a dark-haired boy about a year younger.

'Maybe they'll go away,' he whispered.

Antonius shrugged, but his eyes went to the galley. Close up their camouflage was a wispy confection of leaves and branches that did little to conceal the lines of the ship. All it would take was one look in the wrong direction and the entire mission would be compromised.

Valerius felt a stealthy presence move up beside him. Shabolz and the men he'd asked for. He raised two fingers on his left hand and motioned with his right that two should go upstream of the children and two downstream. Shabolz nodded, but he hesitated for a moment. He drew a hand across his throat in an unmistakable gesture. Valerius could feel Antonius's eyes on him and he knew the rest of the men would be watching.

He shook his head. Not yet. It might not be necessary, and if it was, that decision could wait.

When he looked again the boy was pointing directly at the inlet. The girl shook her head. The boy picked up a lithe wriggling eel from the boat and made as if to eat it. The girl hesitated, her thin features suddenly uncertain. Valerius remembered a little patch of scorched grass he'd seen earlier. It hadn't struck him as a threat.

He breathed a sigh of relief as they slipped with surprising dexterity over the side of their clumsy-looking craft and set off downstream using a pair of short oars . . . only to turn immediately into the inlet.

Antonius sucked in a breath. Valerius heard a little squeal of surprise. A pair of sudden splashes and a scream of fright. He got to his feet as Shabolz and one of his men dragged the squirming children up the bank and threw them at his feet.

Valerius closed his eyes. 'What in the name of all the gods are we going to do with them?'

'I'm glad that's not my problem, legate,' Antonius said with some feeling.

Cavalrymen and sailors emerged from the wood and gathered in a half-circle around Valerius and the terrified prisoners. The two children looked in horror at captors who appeared to have just emerged from some Stygian wormhole.

'Tie them up,' Valerius said. 'And feed them. I'll decide what to do with them later.'

'What's to decide?' A harsh voice from the back of the crowd of cavalrymen. Serenus, one of Crescens's and Florus's tentmates from the Ninth legion. 'Discovery is death, you said. Every man, woman and child is our enemy. I say kill them.'

Valerius looked round the half-circle of men. Serenus had a few allies, but not many. Some couldn't care one way or the other. One or two wouldn't meet his eyes and he knew the foolish words he'd used to put fire in their bellies had cost him their respect. Hilario's angry features had taken on a thoughtful cast that Valerius found difficult to read. He turned and went to the two huddled figures sitting on the grass.

They had their heads bowed, but he crouched beside them and lifted their chins one at a time so he could look into their faces. The boy was still terrified and wouldn't meet his gaze, but the girl's eyes glittered defiance and her lip curled. He wouldn't have been surprised if she'd spat in his face.

'I think—'

'This is not a matter for discussion.' Valerius cut Antonius off. 'It will be my decision.' He turned back to the waiting men. 'We will take them with us.'

'No.' Serenus shook his head. 'We have Gellius to avenge.'

'They're just children,' Valerius snarled. 'Gellius is the last person who'd want them to die.'

'They're the enemy. One way or the other, when they don't return their people will come looking for them. Probably before dark.'

'Children on a river? They won't look here. They'll believe they drowned.'

'Discovery is death, you said.' Serenus threw Valerius's words back at him.

Valerius stared at him until the other man couldn't meet his eyes. Eventually, he shrugged and plucked the dagger from his belt. He flicked it so it buried itself point up between Serenus's feet.

'If you're so keen to cut their throats,' he said, 'why don't you do it? I won't stop you.'

The defiance in Serenus's eyes turned into a mixture of confusion and suspicion. He looked to left and right to see how much support he had. Valerius saw him square his shoulders.

Before Serenus could move Hilario stepped forward. Not a man breathed as the big cavalryman marched up to Valerius. The one-handed Roman felt a moment of confusion. Had he miscalculated? What would he do if Hilario stepped past him towards the children? But when the trooper reached him he spun to stand by Valerius's side.

'If you won't stop him, I will.' The harsh grating voice was filled with something like contempt.

'And I.' Softer this time, but the words carried just as much force.

Ceris stood by Valerius's left hand with her fingers on the hilt of her sword and her eyes daring Serenus to move.

'We're taking them with us,' Valerius snapped. 'Now get what rest you can. We leave an hour after dusk.'

But they were already dispersing. Only Hilario didn't move.

'You should have killed him,' the trooper growled. 'Instead you humiliated him. He won't forgive that.'

Valerius picked up his knife. 'Then you'll just have to watch my back.'

'Ha!' Hilario's bark of laughter echoed through the trees.

XVII

A night so dark it could have been the inside of a grave, yet the air had a soporific quality, a gentle warmth that kissed the skin. Combined with the unceasing cadence of the oars and the whisper of the river beneath the keel, the atmosphere made it difficult to keep your eyes open. Again and again Valerius had to shake himself awake when he found his chin resting on his chest and his eyelids closing, his mind far away in Confluentes and his fingers stroking the soft contours of Tabitha's hip.

He suspected many of his men were already asleep, but he decided there was no harm in it. They'd wake quickly enough if anything happened. They knew their lives depended on it. Each stroke of the oars was accompanied by a low grunt, the only sound inside the galley apart from the soft murmur of the guide as he questioned the two young prisoners.

Valerius had ordered him to seek out any information he could glean on the sorceress. The further inland they travelled the more the lack of specific intelligence about their target concerned the one-handed Roman. He felt like a blind man groping his way towards the edge of a cliff. All they knew for certain was that the witch's settlement lay an unspecified number of miles north of the river. According to the guide a distinctive cliff of red sandstone on the south bank would give him his mark. It meant they'd have to make the final short leg of the river journey in daylight, but Valerius could see no other choice. The river gorge deepened the farther east they sailed and the chances of being seen were low. Once on land they'd make their way close to the settlement by night and find somewhere to lie up the following day. What happened next depended on what they found when they got there. Antonius would conceal the ship in some inlet and return to the red cliff at dawn the next two mornings. If they didn't reappear by the height of the sun on the second day he had orders to return to Confluentes without them.

A rustle and muttered complaints from the direction of the bow and the guide appeared on the bench in front of him. A native of the Tencteri tribe with a heavy brow and a nose like a well-used hatchet, the man had been vouched for by Regulus, but he had an evasive quality that made the Roman wonder whether he was quite as familiar with the area as he claimed.

'They are of the Chatti, lord, as you suspected,' the man whispered. 'From a village an hour or so upriver by their reckoning. Their father is dead and their mother's new bedmate takes no notice of them, so they will not be missed overnight.'

'What of the sorceress?'

'They know of her, lord.' Valerius sensed a note of uncertainty in the guide's voice. 'She is called Aurinia.'

'And?'

'They say she does not live on earth, but has a house in the sky.'

'Just a story.' Valerius laughed, but he made the sign against evil with the fingers of his left hand.

'The girl said it is where Aurinia devours her victims.'

'I asked for information, not fairy tales. Is that all? Nothing about the settlement?'

'No, lord.'

'You will say nothing of this to the men.'

Valerius could tell by the stars that the river twisted and turned through the mountains like a giant serpent. Once more he marvelled at Antonius's ability to feel the subtle changes in the current that allowed them to make good progress through the night. Only once did his instinct desert him. The galley lurched as it struck bottom and Valerius was all but thrown from his seat.

'Every man not at an oar must get out to lighten the ship,' Antonius hissed. A flurry of splashes and Valerius was up to his waist in the freezing water with the rest, heaving at any projection they could find to haul *Rapid Racer* over the hidden obstacle. When they were clear Antonius threw out the anchor and the cavalrymen clambered aboard with the aid of ropes lowered by the oarsmen.

While they were still shivering, a great glow in the night sky forced them to back oars and hold position in the centre of the river.

'What is it?' Valerius whispered.

'Some kind of fire,' Antonius said. 'But the gods only know what at this time of night. Should I anchor until it dies down?'

'We don't have time. Move ahead slowly and as close to the left bank as you dare.'

The light grew brighter as they rounded the next bend. On a low mound above the river three great pyres threw towers of flame and sparks into the sky. As they came closer they could see that three houses were on fire. A large crowd of people had gathered to watch, but not a man made a move to extinguish the flames. It all took place in an eerie silence and the light cast by the blaze seemed to reach out across the surface of the river to the galley. Valerius heard muttered prayers and more than one man fumbled for the talisman or charm at his throat. It seemed they must be discovered, but very gradually the galley slipped upstream through the shadows beneath the far bank and the welcoming darkness closed about them.

It was only when they were past that Valerius realized he'd been clutching the bench so hard with his left hand he could barely unclench his fist.

Antonius, unfamiliar with this stretch of river, found it more difficult to find a sheltered position to lie up for the day, and it was only in the first light of dawn he saw what he was looking for. The action of the river had cut away the earth bank almost back to the roots of a large clump of trees whose branches hung close to the surface of the water. By deft manoeuvring he was able to guide the galley between the branches and the river edge and tie up against an exposed root. The only disadvantage was that the bank here was so steep it was impossible for anyone to go ashore. Valerius and his men wriggled into the least intolerable position and attempted to get what rest they could. Eventually the one-handed Roman gave up even trying to sleep and joined Antonius where he sat, red-eyed, in the bow, staring upstream through the lattice of branches. In the next few hours they saw three or four native river craft, tree trunk canoes heaped with merchandise in two cases, and a pair of the odd leather and willow craft the two children had been sailing. These were crewed by two men who drifted on the current a short spear-cast apart with a net between their boats. Antonius's right hand slipped towards his sword hilt at the sight of them, but all kept to midstream and none of the crews even looked in the direction of the trees.

'Let's hope they're home in their beds by the time we have to move,' Antonius said. 'I don't like the idea of moving about in daylight up here, but there's no help for it. We won't find the red cliff in the dark.'

'You seemed confident enough when we talked earlier.'

The sailor looked over his shoulder to where his oarsmen slept at their benches. 'That was for the benefit of the crew. You don't get the best out of them by telling them they're all going to die.'

'You really think that?'

'I think you're going to get us all killed, legate. Even if you do rescue your men we'll never get back to the Rhenus alive. Every tribesman in Germania will be after your head.'

'And yours.' Valerius smiled.

'And mine. We have a stack of *pila* in the bilges. They're for the marines who usually sail with us, but I plan to issue them to your men tonight. I take it they know how to use them?'

'Of course.'

'So if we do happen to meet any peaceful traders or fishermen when we're looking for the red cliffs I want your assurance there won't be any more misplaced mercy.'

The words were so innocuous that it took time for Valerius to understand their true meaning. 'You think I was wrong to let the children live?'

'I think they complicate things. If you don't mind my saying so, you are an odd character, legate.'

'And if I did mind?'

'I'm only a humble river rat and you could squash me without a thought, but even so I don't think you're the vindictive type. On the one hand you're prepared to risk your own rather valuable life and those of thirty odd other men to try to retrieve two dispensable cavalry troopers who are probably already dead. On the other you appear too squeamish to cut the throats of two members of a tribe our venerable empire regards as rather less than vermin.' He nodded at Valerius's wooden hand. 'If my guess is right, you've spilled blood before. It would have been much simpler to kill them. You could have drowned them and tossed the bodies back into the river and no one would have been any the wiser, but of course you know that.'

Valerius trailed his single hand in the water, enjoying the sensation of being caressed by nature. Was it his vanity that had brought them here, rather than a desire to save Crescens who – if he was being entirely honest – wasn't worth saving, and Florus, who was little better? He looked up and met Antonius's steady gaze. 'I've killed enough people to believe that you don't draw a sword unless it's truly necessary. Don't misunderstand me, I'll kill if I have to, but this would have been murder. I am many things, Antonius, but I have never been a murderer.'

'They tell me some people get a taste for it.'

'That's true.' He'd known men who revelled in butchery from dawn to dusk and woke up the next morning still with an appetite for death. 'But it gets to them in the end. How did it affect you?'

Antonius laughed. 'I've never killed anyone. The Germani don't come near naval craft. All I do is transport killers like you where they want to go. Are you superstitious, legate?'

'Why do you ask?'

'Because,' said Antonius, 'the only thing that's got us this far has been Fortuna's favour. Pure luck. Every man on this ship wears a charm around his neck.' He reached up and pulled out a tiny winged phallus on a leather thong. 'Every man except you.'

Valerius laughed. 'I think a man makes his own luck. Besides,' he held up the wooden fist, 'this is my lucky charm.' He reached across and pressed the little metal protrusion on the wrist. With a sharp snick the four-inch knife blade appeared, the point glittering needle sharp.

Antonius blinked, but a broad grin spread across his face. 'I too think a man needs to make his own luck,' he said. 'Do you trust your guide?'

'Regulus said we could rely on him. Do you think he's mistaken?'

'I think our friend spends too much time looking around him with a look of frank bewilderment. The look of a man who has no idea where he is. He may have been east once, but he is no guide. Someone has told him about the red cliffs and the valley that leads to this village. I think the lure of the tribune's silver was too much for him. It is my belief he will not be able to guide you to the settlement in the dark.'

Valerius nodded thoughtfully. Antonius had voiced his own unspoken doubts. 'What do you suggest?'

'I think there would be no greater risk setting off now than in three or four hours. If we can find the red cliffs quickly, we'll land you with a few hours of daylight to spare. Enough perhaps to let you get close to the witch's settlement before dark.'

'We have no idea whether the valley is inhabited,' Valerius pointed out. 'Whether there is a road, or a track, or how well used it is.'

'All the more reason to pass through it in daylight. From what I've seen you have men who are well capable of finding a way undiscovered.'

Valerius thought of Shabolz and his comrades and the way they'd slipped so effortlessly through the woods to thwart the Chatti ambush. He made his decision. 'Very well. We'll leave as soon as you can make the ship ready.'

Antonius started issuing orders, and his men went into the well-practised routine of preparing to cast off. Two sailors disappeared into the bowels of the little ship and reappeared with armfuls of *pila*. Valerius watched as they distributed them among the mystified cavalrymen. 'If we meet a Chatti river craft,' he told them, 'no one must be left alive. Cast straight and do not fall overboard because we won't be coming back for you.' They laughed, all except Serenus, who spat over the side.

Antonius kept well into the left bank and they rowed upstream in a tense silence, eyeing the wooded hills that loomed over the river. Valerius had never felt so exposed as they pushed against the current in the afternoon sunlight, the river glittering like molten silver ahead. All it would take was one enemy to see them and the whole country would be alerted. At any moment he expected a boat to appear round the next bend, or the one after.

'Not far now,' the guide announced for the third or fourth time. Someone in the bows produced a scornful laugh, but when they turned the next loop in the river Antonius pointed ahead to where a sheer pink slope was visible among the trees on the southern bank.

'The red cliffs.'

XVIII

Antonius barked an order and the galley swept left to land them dryfoot on a gravel beach on the north bank. Valerius stepped ashore four hundred paces downstream from the cleft in the wooded hills the guide claimed would carry them towards the settlement.

'Are you certain you want to continue, lord?' the young sailor asked quietly. 'Like as not they're already dead.'

The same thought had crossed Valerius's mind. But . . . 'It's only four days since the Chatti took them. Thanks to you and your crew we've made good speed upriver. In country like this it would take a man on foot at least three days to get here from the Rhenus, perhaps more. My instinct tells me they're still alive.'

'Then I'll bid you farewell,' Antonius said. 'The less we're on the river in daylight the better. I'll be here at dawn tomorrow. Then dawn the day after. We'll beach her here, camouflage her and remain until noon.'

Valerius offered his wooden fist. 'You have your orders. If we're not back by then we're not coming back. Release the children as close to where we found them as you can.'

'You'll be back.' Antonius clasped the artificial hand. 'Your kind always gets back. And when you do you'll really see how quickly *Rapid*

Racer can fly.' He boarded the ship and ran to the steering platform. 'If you're in real trouble and need to get out quickly,' he called, 'we'll be anchored behind the trees where we stopped today.'

Hilario and four or five others helped push the ship off the gravel and the oars flashed. Within a dozen strokes *Rapid Racer* was out of sight and they were alone.

Valerius turned and found every man staring at him. 'Don't just stand there,' he rasped. 'Get everything back into the trees. We'll eat now and fill our water skins, but be ready to move within the hour. Shabolz?'

'Lord?'

'Take the guide and check out the valley. If there's a road, is it a busy one? If the answer's yes, can we find an alternative route through the forest?'

Shabolz called softly to the guide and they set off upstream. The Pannonian returned before Valerius had eaten his rough porridge, with the guide trotting behind gasping for breath. 'There's a road, lord,' Shabolz confirmed. 'More of a dirt track, four hundred paces east. It's well worn and leads to a wooden jetty upstream, but there are no fresh tracks. I scouted north for almost a mile without seeing any sign of life, but the valley narrows and the scrub is thick. If we're going anywhere in a hurry we need to use the road.'

'All right.' Valerius waved him to a grassy mound. 'Sit down. Didius, get him something to eat.' The guide hovered close, but Valerius waved him away. 'What did you think of our friend?'

Shabolz accepted a bowl from Didius and muttered his thanks. 'He knows as much about this place as I do, lord.' He took a spoonful of porridge and gulped it down. 'Moves with all the stealth of a buffalo and he would have marched out into the road without checking. He may be a good spy, but he's no guide.'

So Antonius's instincts had been correct. 'Then you'll have to be our guide,' Valerius said. Shabolz nodded without interrupting his intake of porridge. 'Wash off the soot and take your pick of the clothes we took from the Germani we killed. You and two others. Two of you will scout four hundred paces or so ahead of the column, with one

136

man two hundred paces behind you. At the first sign of anyone on the track signal back and have the rear man report to me. Unless they're on horses that should give us time to disappear into the woods.'

'No horse tracks that I could make out, lord.'

'Good. I hesitate to ask, given your opinion of him, but should you take the guide with you? At need he could talk you out of trouble.' Shabolz dropped his head and concentrated on finishing his food. 'Say your piece, trooper. You don't need to be shy with me.'

'I'd rather he stayed.' The Pannonian's chin came up. 'A man like that. Who would know what he was saying? I know the Germani from the rebellion, lord. They're a surly people. A snarl and a spit and give way to none. No need for conversation.'

They marched in a compact column of twos, with Valerius in the lead. He concentrated on what lay ahead, on the strengths and weaknesses of his little command, and the perils they would undoubtedly face. Stealth would be the key. No charging into a settlement of five or six hundred Chatti and hoping to get out alive. This would be like Jerusalem, where he'd twice slipped unnoticed inside the city walls, but there would be no convenient Conduit of Hezekiah to smooth his passage. *She has a house in the sky where she devours her victims*, the girl had said. But what did it mean? Regulus had suggested the Chatti and their allies considered Aurinia a goddess. Perhaps her temple was a house on stilts, of the type he'd seen in the Batavian lands. It would make things complicated, but not impossible.

His mind went back to what Antonius had said as they parted. *Your kind always gets back*. Another riddle. *Your kind?* A leader. A veteran. A proper soldier. Whatever the sailor meant, he was right. Valerius had lost his hand to an Iceni blade in the maelstrom of Boudicca's rebellion and suffered a dozen honourable wounds since. He should have died more times than he could count, but he had always survived. Yet he wasn't so vain as to believe Antonius had been flattering him. What he'd meant was a man ruthless enough to do what was needed. A man prepared to keep going when every other man had given up. A man who could look death in the face and be uncowed. And he was right. Valerius had inherited all these traits from his old friend Serpentius, the former gladiator. Yet there had come a day when Serpentius lay lifeless in the dust after sacrificing himself for Valerius and a Rome the one-handed legate was uncertain even existed.

Gradually, he settled into the familiar rhythm of the march, a world of tramping feet, clinking chain and buzzing insects, sweat running into your eyes, the straps of your water skin and your pack cutting into your shoulders, and your aching legs reminding you of every change in incline and that you were no longer twenty years old.

Twice in the next hour Shabolz sent back word that they should take to the trees, provoking a hurried but disciplined rush up the flanking slopes. Valerius delayed long enough to ensure nothing had been left to mark their position before joining the cavalrymen in the forest.

After about an hour Shabolz himself appeared, and Valerius ordered the men into the trees while he spoke to the Pannonian.

'The situation is this, lord.' Shabolz used the point of his dagger to draw the shape of a T in the dust. 'A few hundred paces ahead this track meets a much wider road used by carts and horse traffic. I sent Licco to climb the hill next to the road and he reports that there is smoke from the fires of a settlement to the east.'

'Did he manage to get any impression of the size?'

'No, lord, but there is a second hill much closer to the settlement. Licco believes he can take us there before dark, but we must move without delay.' He pointed to the trees where the men were concealed. 'If we push upwards across the line of the slope we will meet the others. Licco will lead from there.'

The going was much harder in the trees, with their route dictated by outcrops and rock falls and the steepness of the slope. They found Licco and the other man waiting on a knoll, grinning at the sight of their red-faced, gasping comrades. Licco led them across the shoulder of the hill, and Valerius saw the smear of smoke in the blue sky that he prayed marked Aurinia's settlement.

A steep gully blocked their way and they paused while Licco searched for a way down. While they waited, Hilario approached Valerius with a look of concern on his face.

'The guide is gone,' he said quietly.

'Gone?'

'He said he needed to piss and would catch us up, but he never reappeared. I went back to search, but there's no sign of him.'

Valerius called Shabolz over and explained the situation. The Pannonian grimaced. 'He will sell us to the Chatti,' he said. 'I think he always intended to.'

Valerius cursed silently. 'This is my fault. I should have set someone to watch him,' he said. 'He will try to reach the road. Can you get to him first?'

Shabolz shrugged. 'If I can't we're all dead.'

'I'll come with you.' Hilario unslung his packs and pulled his chain armour over his head.

Shabolz looked at Valerius, who nodded his assent.

'You'd better be quick and quiet, my Roman friend,' Shabolz sneered. 'I won't be waiting around for you.'

'You won't have to slow down for me, you Pannonian mountain monkey. I'm only coming along in case the weasel decides to take your head to the witch as a gift.'

They continued to bicker as they set off up the hill. Valerius shook his head and went back to the lip of the gorge where Licco had just reappeared. 'There's a deer track that's just about passable, lord, and a fallen tree that we can use to cross the river.' He looked around the waiting men. 'Shabolz?'

'Shabolz is busy. He'll meet us on the next hill.'

It took another hour before they emerged from the trees just below the rocky summit. The cavalrymen slumped on the ground and Licco led Valerius through the boulders to a point where the landscape was laid out before him like a mosaic.

He was astonished to discover that Guda, probably four miles from the position Antonius had landed them, was built on one of the few pieces of flat ground adjacent to the bank of the Logana. A huge loop of the river curved through the thickly wooded hills and their four-mile trek had crossed the base of it. The Chatti settlement was surrounded by a flimsy palisade and bisected by a small stream. Perhaps two hundred turf-walled longhouses were scattered haphazardly across an area the size of two legionary encampments, and smoke from cooking fires seeped through their thatched roofs. A double gate in the western wall mirrored a second on the river side. Valerius could see people moving about between the buildings and the animal pens.

Only one thing set Guda apart from any other Germanic settlement.

An area in the centre of the town had been left clear so that the curious structure which occupied it was visible from every angle. It resembled a Roman signal tower, but was at least twice – possibly even three times – the height. A skeletal timber structure rose to a first platform perhaps fifty feet up, and a second a further twenty-five. Valerius's initial reaction was that it must be some kind of lookout position, but then he noticed the lower platform was occupied by a roofed building.

A house in the sky.

He was still considering the implications of his discovery when a commotion broke out among the cavalrymen below. His first thought was that it was yet another argument between the men of the Ninth and the Twentieth, but he saw Shabolz at the centre of the group. He slithered down through the rocks to join them.

'You were right, lord.' The Pannonian grinned. 'He was heading for the road, presumably hoping to add to this.' He threw Valerius a leather purse that landed heavily in his left hand. 'The commander of the fort at Confluentes obviously valued his services highly.'

Valerius weighed the purse in his palm. 'You're right.' He tossed the silver back to Shabolz. 'You can put it to good use when we get back to Confluentes by buying your comrades the best wine the place has to offer.'

A murmur of appreciation from the watching troopers. Even Serenus joined in the laughter. Valerius noticed Hilario hadn't reappeared.

'I hope he didn't slow you down too much?'

'Oh no, lord,' the Pannonian said with genuine respect. 'For a big man he can move fast. It was Hilario who stopped the guide from reaching the road. When the German tried to flee he ran into my sword. Hilario volunteered to take him further into the woods and bury him while I returned with the welcome news.'

'And I have more welcome news.' Valerius led him to the top of the hill and the Pannonian scout whistled softly as he saw the scale of the settlement.

'So this is the witch's lair? The building on that curious platform must be where she performs her ceremonies. I see no other structure that looks like a temple.'

'You have the best eyes in the unit,' Valerius said. 'Do you see any building that's guarded as if it might be being used to hold prisoners?'

Shabolz's grey eyes narrowed in concentration. He shook his head. 'It's impossible to tell for certain. Any guards might be hidden by the houses.'

'Then I think we have to assume Crescens and Florus are being held in the temple.'

'Lord?' Shabolz looked unconvinced.

'There's no way we can check every building. Do you have any better ideas?'

'No, lord.'

'Then concentrate on finding a way to get us inside.'

'Tonight?'

'If it can be done.'

Shabolz returned to his study of the settlement below. 'We could probably get over the palisade almost anywhere. There's no walkway and it's not really built for defence.'

'But there will be some kind of watch. And even if we manage to get in undetected we still have to reach the tower.'

'And there'll be dogs,' Shabolz muttered. 'The Germans always have dogs.'

'I'm thinking three groups. One to cover our escape route outside the wall. A second to guard it inside the wall. The third, you and Licco, myself, Hilario, Didius and Serenus . . .'

'You're taking Serenus?'

'I want somebody from the Ninth involved in rescuing their comrades.'

Shabolz nodded. 'And Ceris.'

'Ceris?'

'If you don't take her she'll follow anyway.'

'I keep forgetting she's with us,' Valerius said wryly.

'Because that's the way she wants it,' Shabolz grinned. 'She stays out of the way, quiet as a mouse, because she fears you'll send her back. But I've watched her. She moves like a shadow and she's fearless. She won't let us down.'

'Ceris then. I just pray that what we find is what she hopes.'

'If it's not,' Shabolz's voice turned sombre, 'then I wouldn't like to be the witch.'

'But first we have to get inside.'

XIX

Shabolz led them down the hill just before dusk, so full darkness brought them to the edge of the forest perhaps two hundred paces from the settlement wall, just across the stream from the west gate. The Pannonian had spent the remainder of the afternoon scouting the position and plotting the safest way to approach Guda in the night. A pair of torches marked the location of the gateway, but Valerius ignored the flickering circles of light.

When Shabolz had proposed the idea it seemed so obvious Valerius wondered that he hadn't thought of it himself. Perhaps weariness was the answer. Apart from Marius and Hilario he was almost twice the age of the men he led. If you can't go over a wall, and you can't go through it, what was left but to go under it? They would use the stream.

'There will be some kind of barrier,' Shabolz admitted. 'But I'll wager that purse of silver we can get through it. The stream is barely knee deep and the bed will help provide cover until we reach the centre of the village.'

They sat in the three groups Valerius had chosen. Valerius had mixed the men from different legions and impressed on them the need to work together.

'When you're in a fight you won't worry whether the man next to you is from the Ninth or the Second,' he whispered. 'All you'll want to know is that you can trust him to keep his shield high and his sword arm swinging. Before we go into battle we say "For Rome", but we don't really fight for Rome, or even the Emperor. We fight for each other, because when some hairy-arsed barbarian has his spear point at your throat it won't be Rome or the Emperor that saves you, it will be some weary, bleeding bastard like Nilus here, whose stinking feet you curse every night and whose farts keep you awake.' He could see the white glow of their teeth as they grinned in the darkness. 'Marius, you'll cover our escape route from the outside. Split your men on either side of the stream. Nilus? Your group will be on the inside. We don't know what we'll find there, so you'll have to work out a way to make yourself invisible. If everything goes well, we'll be in and out before they know we're there.'

'And if it doesn't?'

'If we're discovered make your way back to the river and find Antonius.'

They waited another hour. Somewhere in the hills behind them a wolf howled. Men hissed and reached for their charms, but Valerius declared it was a sign that the gods were with them.

Shabolz led the way across an open field of recently planted crops. The smell of the human and animal manure used to enrich the black earth filled Valerius's nostrils as he squirmed across the damp ground. A little way to their left he could hear the sound of water trickling over the stones. Before he knew it the settlement wall loomed above them. Shabolz slipped into the stream and Valerius followed, the cold water barely up to his calves. They crawled to the point where the stream ran below the palisade. There would be a barrier to prevent men like them from entering, they were all agreed on that. Everything depended on just how secure that barrier was and how long it took them to remove the obstacle. Valerius probed with his left hand and he sensed Shabolz doing the same to his right. Nothing.

He fumbled among the stones of the river bed, wary of the wooden spikes he would have expected, but all he found was a row of stumps. Puzzled, he reached up to the base of the palisade and felt along the

144

underside. The fittings for some kind of gate or fence existed, but of the thing itself nothing remained.

A trap? A door left open to lure them inside to slaughter? No, the slimy wood he could feel had been worn smooth by the action of the stream. It had been like this for years, probably tens of years, through flood and drought.

Flood. Valerius felt a surge of elation. Winter spates would bring down leaves and branches and constantly block the barrier. Unless it was cleared quickly the stream would overflow and deluge the entire area. At some point in the past whoever was responsible had decided that maintaining the barrier was more trouble than it was worth. He tapped Shabolz on the shoulder and the Pannonian slipped under the palisade. The others were waiting a few paces behind and Valerius crawled back to them. He felt Hilario's bulk and pushed him towards the culvert, hissing: 'Stay low.' Licco next, wiry and alert and needing no urging. Didius, wound tight as a bow string. Serenus, more willing than Valerius had expected, and finally the slight figure of Ceris.

Valerius followed, bent double in a low crouch and concealed from the surrounding houses by the banks of the stream. Around them, Guda slept on unaware its defences had been breached. From some-where nearby a woman cried out in ecstasy and a dog yipped twice in answer. Valerius had half expected the stream to be little more than an open sewer filled with the detritus of years. To his surprise the water smelled clean and the river bed beneath his feet was free of any obs-tacles, and they were able to make good progress towards the centre of the settlement. No flickering torches or rasped commands of a watch being changed.

From ahead came the sound of scuffling feet as Shabolz left the sanctuary of the river bed and scrambled up the bank. The Pannonian waited at the top while the others followed and Valerius crept to his side. By now their eyes had become well accustomed to the darkness, and Shabolz could make out enough light and shade to give him his directions. Valerius guessed that three or four longhouses lay between them and the open square, and the Pannonian led them between two of the buildings. They passed through a garden. From their right came the unmistakable stink of a pigsty, and the grunting snuffle of its sleeping occupants. Another dog either sensed or scented the intruders and barked a warning. Valerius froze at the sound, anticipating inevitable discovery and the bloody horror that would follow, but the only reaction was the smack of something striking the beast and a whine of resentment that it had only been doing its job.

Shabolz stopped in the shadow of the next house and whispered an order for the others to remain where they were. A soft glow silhouetted the corner of the building and the Pannonian dropped to his stomach and crept warily forward until he had a view of what lay beyond. Valerius heard a soft intake of breath before Shabolz wriggled backwards and stood up.

'Two guards,' he whispered. 'One each side of the stairs and facing this way. There's not a scrap of cover for thirty paces in every direction.'

Valerius nodded. He'd known there was a possibility the temple would be guarded, but he'd hoped otherwise. 'Could we rush them?' he asked.

'We could.' Shabolz's tone said the opposite. 'But they'd have plenty of time to give the alarm before we overpowered them.'

There had to be a way. Valerius wriggled his way to the corner and looked for himself. Big men, dressed in leather tunics and plaid *bracae*, armed with seven-foot spears. The pair stood a few paces apart at the centre of a circle illuminated by a pair of torches that also lit the narrow stairway that zigzagged its way into the darkness. If he squinted he thought he could just see the boards that made up the temple platform. Shabolz was right. No chance of reaching the guards before they raised the alarm. Yet they were looking from light into the shadows. If Valerius and his men could get a little closer without being seen . . .

He retreated back to the others.

'Could you and Licco get behind them?' he asked Shabolz.

Shabolz worked it through in his head before replying. 'We could, but they're alert enough. You've seen how they scan the whole area every few moments. We'd have the same problem.'

'What if we could attract their attention?'

'Wouldn't they just raise the alarm?'

'Not if the distraction was obviously innocent and harmless.'

The Pannonian nodded slowly. 'All we'd need is a few seconds.'

'Go then,' Valerius ordered, and Shabolz and his fellow countryman disappeared into the night like shadows.

'I will provide the distraction,' Hilario offered. 'I'll pretend I'm drunk.'

'You're the opposite of innocent and harmless,' Valerius said. 'Send me Ceris.'

Valerius waited until he was certain Shabolz and Licco would be in position before he sent her out.

At first the Chatti guards didn't see her, then they noticed the pale, wraithlike figure emerging from the darkness, the flicker of the torches giving her flesh the hue of a midsummer moon.

'What will you do to get Florus back alive?' he'd asked her.

'Anything,' she'd said.

A childlike figure until you noticed the curve of her breasts and the dark tuft at the base of her stomach, she seemed to be part of the very air, her feet barely disturbing the surface of the square and her arms held wide. At first the men were struck dumb by the sight, but then came the inevitable challenge, unintelligible, but the meaning clear enough.

Ceris ignored the order and kept coming. The two men looked at each other, each expecting the other to make a decision.

Too late. Their attention was entirely focused on Ceris when Shabolz and Licco attacked. They struck from behind, crossing from darkness into light in a silent rush. In a heartbeat practised hands stifled any opportunity to cry out even as blades as sharp as any razor simultaneously sliced through windpipes. In their eagerness the Pannonians came close to decapitating their victims and two great fountains of blood spurted into the lamplight. The guards were dead before their blood-soaked killers lowered them to the ground.

Valerius was already running towards them, followed by Hilario, Serenus and Didius, who handed Ceris her clothes.

'Hide the bodies and take their places,' Valerius ordered as he passed. 'I'll leave Serenus on the stairs to cover you.'

He'd removed his sandals so that he climbed the narrow stair sword in hand with only the faint slap of bare feet to announce his coming. Four flights alternating back and forth across the face of the tower, until he reached the lower platform. The temple, if that's what it was, was constructed of wood, apart from the thatched roof. Valerius ran to the far end where a curtained doorway provided the only entrance, with a human skull nailed above the lintel.

He pulled back the curtain, but the interior was in total darkness. An odd musty scent tickled his nostrils.

'Crescens? Florus?' he called quietly.

He blinked as light flooded the chamber from a torch Didius had snatched somewhere on the way. And froze.

Whatever he'd been expecting it wasn't this. Of Crescens and Florus there was no sign. Most of the interior was taken up by an ancient, four-wheeled chariot. Sheets of bronze covered the body and it must once have been an astonishing sight: a polished, glittering symbol of wealth and power to these primitive people. Now the metal fittings had turned green with age and the leather harness had disintegrated. A front wheel lay at an angle, so the whole thing tilted to one side. It was oddly chilling, an object that had once been revered but whose time had passed, which now lay all but forgotten. Chilling, but not so much as the stone altar at the far end of the room and the gilded tray in its centre which held two wicked-looking curved knives, sharpened so often the blades were almost translucent. Beyond the altar two more curtained doorways could conceal opportunity or threat.

'Search the place,' he ordered.

They took a room each, but were back within seconds shaking their heads. Valerius had a moment of confusion before his eyes drifted upwards. If not here, perhaps . . .

He was out of the door before the thought fully formed, dashing up the rickety stairway to the high platform and trying not to think about how far down it would be if he put a foot out of place. The sound of footsteps to his rear told him Didius and Hilario weren't far behind. His heart stuttered as he reached the top. Two pale bodies lay spreadeagled in the gloom. Had it all been for nothing?

'Water, for pity's sake,' a voice croaked in Latin.

Crescens. Valerius was at his side in a heartbeat, unstopping his water skin and putting it to the bound man's lips. Hilario worked at the rope that pinioned his wrists and ankles to the platform. The freed man groaned as Valerius helped him to sit up.

'Thank the . . .'

'Quiet.' Valerius clamped a hand over Crescens's mouth. 'You'll bring the whole village down on us.'

Didius and Serenus untied Florus and helped him to his feet. Both men were naked, and by the stink of excrement they'd been left to lie in their own filth.

'Can you walk?'

'I'll crawl on my hands and knees if I have to,' Florus rasped. 'But first give me a sword. They won't take me alive again, that's certain. Not after what they did today.'

Valerius helped Crescens to the stairs. 'What happened?'

'When they took us they gagged us and bound our wrists,' the cavalry-man said in a croaked whisper. 'We were dragged through the brush and thrown into boats. Thank Fortuna they removed the gags when we crossed the river for it meant we could drink from any stream we passed, even if it cost us a beating. Otherwise they gave us no food or water for four days. When we reached this place they stripped us naked and encouraged people to abuse us before they brought us up here.' The words caught in his throat and he coughed. 'We knew that . . . We prepared ourselves for death, urging each other to be brave Roman soldiers, but . . . Oh—' He vomited over the edge of the rail. 'They taunted us and said they would show us how we were to die. A man was brought, another prisoner, and their sorceress appeared. She cut him open and put her hands into him. All the time the crowd below watched in silence. She showed them something from inside him and pointed to us and they bayed for our blood. She hacked . . . hacked off his manhood and threw it to them and they laughed.'

'Mars save us,' Valerius whispered.

149

'But that wasn't the worst of it.' Crescens looked directly into Valerius's eyes and the Roman flinched at the horror he saw there. 'While he still lived they pulled out a coil of his guts, tied it to a hook and threw him off the platform and ripped the rest out of him. His screams will live with me to the end of my days.'

Valerius felt the bile rising in his throat. 'You're safe now, trooper,' he said with more confidence than he felt. 'We'll get you out of here.'

'I hope so.' Crescens stared at him. 'But if not . . . Your dagger, lord?'

Valerius nodded and handed him the knife. As they reached the door of the temple the curtain parted. Valerius raised his sword, but it was only Ceris, now fully dressed in her Germanic clothes once more. In front of her she pushed a tiny, wizened old woman dressed in a filthy smock and crowned by a verminous mop of grey hair.

'That's the bitch.' Crescens lunged at the prisoner with the dagger, clearly intent on slicing her from breastbone to crotch. Ceris knocked the knife contemptuously aside with the point of her sword.

'Don't be a fool.'

Valerius's mind raced. The last thing they needed was a prisoner to slow them down. If anyone deserved killing, as Crescens's story confirmed, it was the Chatti witch, but Valerius hesitated. The implications of cutting Aurinia's throat had the potential to be devastating for the whole Rhenus frontier. Stones in pools. You never knew what effect the ripples would have. Sulpicius Galba had signed his death warrant when he'd dismissed Otho's claim to be his heir with a sneer. Would Vitellius ever have picked up Divine Caesar's sword if he'd known it would lead to the Gemonian Steps? 'Tie her up and leave her,' Valerius ordered.

Ceris glared at him. 'It seems he is not the only fool.'

Hilario raised a hand to her, but Didius and Serenus appeared with Florus and Ceris rushed to take her lover in her arms. They stood gazing into each other's eyes for a moment before Hilario parted them. 'We don't have time for this,' the big man urged.

'Why am I a fool?' Valerius demanded of the British girl.

Ceris turned to fix him with her luminous eyes. 'Because without Aurinia we will never return to Confluentes.'

XX

Crescens and Florus had to make do with the blood-soaked and soiled clothing of the dead guards, but anything was better than nakedness and the terrors of their captivity. Valerius emerged from the tower into the square. Shabolz confirmed the area was clear and cast aside the guard's spear to take the lead once more. He set off into the darkness at a trot and let the others follow as they could. Didius and Serenus supported Crescens, whose legs were virtually useless, while Licco and Valerius did the same for Florus. Hilario picked up the witch Aurinia, by now gagged as well as bound, and carried her as if she weighed nothing, while Ceris brought up the rear.

They were halfway back to the stream when the dog barked again, close and startlingly loud. Shabolz dropped to the ground and the others did likewise. This time the warning was followed by the sound of a woman's voice from within a neighbouring house. Ceris lay by the corner of the building, tense and waiting. Without warning a shadow loomed over her, immediately engulfed from behind by an even greater shadow. A moment of muffled complaint before she rose up to force the point of her sword into the struggling body. She felt the momentary obstruction as the flesh closed round the blade and tried vainly to withdraw the sword for a second strike.

'Finish him,' a voice hissed.

The body bucked against her and she used both hands and all her strength to ram the point home until the man went rigid and she felt the warmth of his lifeblood flood over her hands.

'Hurry.' Hilario dropped the body and ran to where he'd left the witch, whispering to Valerius that they were discovered. Ceris made an ineffectual pull at the sword hilt, but it was stuck fast and she abandoned the blade before bounding after the others.

The urgency of their situation had communicated itself to Shabolz and he abandoned the shelter of the stream for the quicker going along the top of the bank. They dashed heedless through gardens and across soil pits, stumbling over low fences. Crescens and Florus had recovered sufficiently to manage a stumbling run. More dogs took up the call, but there was still no general outcry. Valerius knew it couldn't last.

As they approached the wall Nilus rose out of the shadows with Bato, another of the Pannonians. 'This way,' he called softly. Shabolz swerved to his left and dropped into the stream with a splash.

'What . . . ?' Nilus, who'd spent what felt like an eternity maintaining complete silence, opened his mouth to protest, but Valerius pushed him towards the opening.

'Gather up your men and save your breath for running.'

He waited in the stream and counted them through, Hilario with his tiny burden, and Ceris last of all, before he ducked under the palisade. Marius had sent his men ahead while he waited for Valerius. As they ran for the trees the one-handed Roman breathlessly explained the position.

'So they'll be on our tail?'

'It will take them time to work out exactly what's happened, but when they do every able-bodied man in the settlement will be looking for us. We have to put as much distance as possible between ourselves and Guda before then.'

Shabolz had halted the others beneath the trees and Valerius and Marius joined them. Crescens and Florus were breathing hard and

Valerius decided he had no option but to allow them a few moments to recover.

Shabolz approached him. 'What now, lord?'

'The galley as fast as we can. If we reach the river early we'll turn west to where they've anchored for the night.'

'What if they overtake us?'

'They won't overtake us. When the men hear what the witch had planned for Crescens and Florus they'll run through Hades to avoid the same fate.'

The Pannonian's eyes strayed to where Hilario had laid Aurinia. 'We would move faster without her.'

'That's true,' Valerius agreed. 'But we need her, more so now than before. Even if we reach the galley we still have to get back to the Rhenus. When they realize she's gone they'll send their fastest horses and their swiftest craft to spread word of her abduction. Every settlement on the river will be looking out for us. If we take her, we have a chance. Cut her throat and we have next to none.'

He went to where Hilario sat beneath a tree. 'If you're tiring let me know, and I'll have someone else carry her for a while.'

'She's but a feather to me,' the big man grunted. 'Have someone carry my packs and I'll get her to the river.'

'Should we remove the gag?' Valerius bent over the tethered bundle, only to flinch back as he became the focus of a pair of malevolent eyes glaring at him with visceral hatred from their nests of wrinkled skin.

'I took it out to give her some water and had a piece removed from my hand for my pains. The witch still has her fangs.'

Valerius helped him to his feet. 'You are a credit to your legion, soldier.' Hilario's gap-toothed grin shone in the dark. 'Get the men ready.'

Shabolz set a fast pace, but not a man faltered, nor Ceris who matched Florus stride for stride. Hilario rumbled on with a dogged, high-kneed gait and Aurinia bundled in his arms. As they advanced the Pannonian dropped back beside Valerius. 'We could take to the woods. Stay out of sight and work our way west until we reach the Rhenus,' he suggested.

Valerius considered the possibility before rejecting it. 'They know these mountains better than we do, and the chances of getting lost or being discovered are too great. If we stick to the path we can be back at the river well before daylight. Antonius and *Rapid Racer* give us our best chance.'

They reached the path more quickly than Valerius had anticipated and turned off the road towards the river. Shabolz and Licco dropped back to brush away any tracks they'd left.

A soft mist formed, turning the black night a silvery grey and coating clothing and equipment with tiny droplets of water. The treacherous, undulating dirt track through the forest was less inviting than the road, but Valerius had the topography in his head and he refused to slacken speed. A fully laden legionary could march twenty miles in a day and build a defended camp at the end of it. Even in the dark, he reckoned the four miles shouldn't take much more than an hour. He cast hopeful glances at the sky, looking for the hint of gold that would herald the first sign of sunrise, but he looked in vain.

Lungs bursting, they marched onwards with the mist thickening to an impenetrable fog. Valerius stalked the little column like a centurion, snarling encouragement and threats until at last Shabolz called to them to halt and they collapsed, gasping for breath. Somewhere ahead, Valerius could hear the familiar rush of the river in the fog-dulled silence.

Valerius sent Shabolz to find a route to where they'd landed. As they waited, he sat with the others, reassuring them all was well and it was only a matter of time before Antonius arrived to pick them up.

But when Shabolz reported back there was a note of consternation in his voice. 'I can't be sure, lord. In this fog one piece of bank looks just like another. Better to lie up and form a perimeter here, and I'll check again as soon as it gets light.'

Valerius hid his disappointment. 'Find me a place we can defend, at need, with our backs to the river.'

Shabolz returned a few minutes later and led Valerius to the site he'd chosen. Valerius had been expecting a height or at the very least the mouth of a gully where he could set up a defensive wall. 'This is it?' the Roman whispered as they inspected the position, a low hill that, if it hadn't been for the fog, would have overlooked the rough jetty the natives had built on the bank of the Logana.

'It's the best I could find, lord.'

The hill was perhaps twenty paces by ten and barely a dozen feet high. Steep-sided and covered in trees, it reminded Valerius of the grave mounds where the barbarians had interred their dead in ancient times. Now that Crescens and Florus were back with them his little force counted twenty-five, including himself and Ceris. He put them to work collecting a barrier of thorn bushes which grew in abundance in the forest and cutting pointed stakes to place among the heavy scrub on the land side of the hill. Dawn – and rescue – couldn't be far away, but the danger grew with every passing moment and he would not make it easy for his enemies. He bitterly regretted leaving the galley's *pila* with Antonius. The heavy spears would have slowed them on the march, but he'd have been confident of holding the hill against any number of barbarians.

When he was satisfied with the preparations he scrambled down to the river and stared out into the fog with the soft burble of the water filling his ears. For the first time it struck him that unless the weather cleared it would be almost impossible for Antonius to find the rendezvous.

By now the Chatti would have discovered that Aurinia's kidnappers hadn't escaped by river at Guda. They would know east wasn't an option because it would take the Romans further into danger. That left the hills to the north and the western road, and eventually the western road would lead them here. Was there anything else he could have done? If Antonius was coming he should have left his hiding place by now. Perhaps they should have been cutting wood for rafts, but that would leave them at the mercy of the natives and the river, and in any case they only had a few feet of rope. No, he'd done what he could. Despite the threat of imminent danger it was oddly peaceful standing in the darkness with the sound of the river lulling his senses. His thoughts turned to Tabitha and the unborn child growing inside her, enduring another night without him in Confluentes. They would be asleep now, or perhaps Tabitha was staring out over the river wondering whether he was alive or dead. For a moment it seemed all he had to do to reach her was to cast off his chain armour, walk into the river and let it carry him away. The fog seemed a lighter grey now, and he guessed dawn was close. He bent and picked up a pebble from amongst the gravel on the river bed. Considering it for a moment, he threw it out into the stream, then walked after it; six or seven strides until the chill water reached his thighs and the current threatened to pull his feet from under him.

'Movement in the woods, lord.'

Valerius splashed his way back to the bank and picked his way up the slope behind Shabolz. The Pannonian had already alerted the others and they stood behind a wall of thorns four feet high and just as thick, swords at the ready. Licco ran in from his position beside the road.

'They're coming.'

'How many?'

'I saw twenty or thirty in the fog, but I could hear more in the woods on both sides of the road. More than enough.'

'Then we'll make them pay for every inch of this hill until Antonius reaches us,' Valerius said loudly enough for all to hear. 'They'll come all the faster when they hear the sound of battle. These bastards are doing us a favour.'

He doubted he'd convinced anyone, but it was an officer's duty to keep up the spirits of his men even if he knew they were all likely to be dead within the hour. It must be almost light now, because he could make out Hilario standing close by holding Aurinia by the arm.

'I need you in the line,' he said. 'Give the witch to Ceris.'

'I can fight,' the Corieltauvi girl protested from her position beside Florus.

'I know you can fight,' Valerius said patiently. 'But can you follow orders?' Ceris rose and took Hilario's place. 'If they break through you know what to do?'

She drew her dagger and placed the point against Aurinia's neck. The sorceress flinched, but her expression didn't change.

'If they attack at once,' Shabolz whispered, 'they could overrun us in a moment.'

'They won't do that,' Valerius assured him. 'They don't know how many we are, or how strong this position is. Their leader could lose a lot of men and it might be for nothing. They may probe us, but there's an easier way.'

The Chatti warriors made little attempt to conceal their approach and the crack of twigs and rustle of leaves from the fog was almost constant. Valerius could feel the tension rising. 'Steady,' he whispered to the defenders. 'They can't reach us until they've climbed the hill. Kill them while they're fighting their way through the thorn bushes.'

'I wish to talk.' The disembodied voice from the fog spoke a guttural but intelligible Latin.

Valerius motioned to the defenders to crouch down behind the barriers where they couldn't be seen. 'I'm listening,' he replied.

'May I approach?'

'Only if you're certain I won't put a spear through you.'

'Surely you are anxious to see the face of the man who could save your life.' A shadowy figure appeared through the fog and walked into the dip between the hill and the trees.

'That's far enough.' Valerius studied his enemy, a tall bare-chested Chatti warrior with long dark moustaches and a topknot. Torcs of gold decorated his arms and declared his high rank. His eyes glittered like shards of obsidian. A twist of his lip suggested he found the whole situation amusing, but Valerius knew the smile was an illusion.

'You took a woman from our village.'

'We took your witch.' Valerius allowed a confident sneer to tint his voice. 'I'm going to give her as a present to the Emperor. Either that or slit her throat the moment your first warrior steps on this hill.'

'Send her to me and I will spare your lives.'

Valerius laughed. 'If I send her to you I'll have nothing to bargain with. There'll be nothing to stop you attacking and, to be honest, I'm not sure I believe you'll spare my life if you succeed.'

'That may be, Roman.' The Celt stared up at him. 'But you have my word that your end will be quick. You will have heard from the cowards you rescued of the fate we intended for them?'

'Your word is worth as much as the turd that comes out of my arse in the morning.'

The Chatti leader ignored the insult. 'I have five hundred men, all warriors and all pledged to the service of the sorceress. If you make me send them for her I promise I will make you eat your turds before we cast you from the sky platform. Think on that, Roman. Think on what it feels like to have your guts stripped from you as you fall to your death.'

'We have talked enough,' Valerius said. 'My spearmen's hands are itching and I cannot guarantee your safety any longer.'

The warrior stood for just long enough to prove the threat didn't frighten him before he stepped back into the fog.

'Five hundred warriors?' someone whispered. 'We're dead.'

'Give them the witch. What difference does it make?'

'The difference between living and dying,' Ceris hissed.

'We should get out while we can,' Crescens's distinctive voice. 'Take our chances on the river.'

'Quiet,' Valerius snarled. 'We are Roman soldiers. If we fight together we stay alive together. They couldn't gather five hundred warriors in four or five hours. I doubt Guda held sixty. The rest will be farmers and potters and tanners. Fodder for your swords.'

'You don't know that,' Shabolz whispered so only Valerius could hear. It was the first hint of dissent from the Pannonian and a sign of how desperate he believed their situation to be.

'No,' Valerius admitted. 'But I know they don't have five hundred warriors. If we can survive for another hour we can get out of here.'

'How?' the Pannonian demanded. 'The galley will never find us in this.'

The blast of a trumpet sent a bolt of lightning down Valerius's spine.

At first he thought it was the signal for the Chatti attack, but it came from downriver and the familiar tone suggested the instrument was a Roman one. Antonius!

'Nilus?' he cried. 'Answer it and keep repeating the call every ten seconds.' He rushed to the front of the hill. Visibility had increased to the extent that he could see individual trees, with vague shapes moving between them. The sound of the horn would have confused the Chatti chieftain as much as it had Valerius, and Nilus's frantic blasts were no doubt compounding it. Did they herald the arrival of twenty Roman galleys carrying two hundred legionaries, or was it some trick to draw him into an ambush? The question was what he would do about it.

Another blast from the river, much closer now.

Valerius made his decision. 'Florus, help Ceris get the witch down to the river. I need to know the moment the galley appears. The rest of you hold your positions and I want to hear you cheering.'

He could see their faces now and every man stared at him. 'Cheer, you bastards,' he snarled. At last they obeyed. A faltering cry at first, but one which grew into a great triumphant roar that poured scorn on their enemy.

And the Chatti attacked, rising from the forest in one great wave.

Which was precisely what Valerius wanted them to do.

XXI

The chieftain with the gold torcs had faced a dilemma. His first priority was to recover the sorceress Aurinia, the source of his tribe's prestige and prosperity, their guiding hand for four generations. He'd hoped to do so by negotiation or intimidation. When they failed, his only options were to attack and take the hill, or besiege it and starve the enemy out. Yet either risked the Roman commander's fulfilling his promise and killing Aurinia. Then the horns blared out and he knew he had to make a decision. The horns meant potential rescue and the loss of the prize. If he'd been given a moment to consider he might have remembered that this was one of the few places the river shelved gently from the shallows to the centre, and that by outflanking the position on either side he could cut off the Romans' escape. But the taunting cheers from the little redoubt robbed him of that moment. His proud warriors responded by rising from their concealment without his command to meet the challenge.

Valerius's estimate of the force facing him had been surprisingly accurate. Of the hundred and twenty or so men who accompanied the chief barely half were seasoned fighters, with the rest made up of artisans or farmers. It was the warriors, bare-chested and tattooed, who charged screaming from the trees and hit the slope at the run, clawing

160

their way through the scrub. The chief ran in their midst, Aurinia's fate all but forgotten, his whole being bent on slaughtering the arrogant Roman who had insulted him.

Valerius watched them come, sword in his left hand, positioned to the right of the defences where he could see the entire line. Hilario stood closest to him, with three men from the Ninth and one from the Second Adiutrix. Shabolz and his Pannonians were in the centre, alongside Crescens, while Serenus and the rest made up the left flank. His heart raced, but his mind was entirely calm, senses attempting to assess everything around him. He became aware that the timbre of some of the Chatti screams had changed. A warrior reared up as one of the concealed stakes ripped into his groin. Another fell back with blood pulsing from the gaping hole in his throat. The charge slowed, the men suddenly aware of the hidden danger. He heard a sharp snap that reminded him of the strike of a sling pellet and one of the leading attackers dropped like a stone with a Pannonian throwing a dart in his brain. Yet the rest came on, more eager than ever, determined to avenge their comrades. The first of them reached the top of the slope and began hauling at the thorn wall, oblivious of the inch-long hooked claws that tore into his flesh. Shabolz almost casually reached across and stabbed the point of his sword into the exposed neck and the warrior disappeared in a haze of scarlet. A concerted attack might have overrun the meagre defences in those first moments, but the Chatti advanced piecemeal, some braver than others. The time spent hauling at the barrier left them momentarily defenceless and easy practice for the Roman swords. Hilario reached out and pulled a screaming warrior on top of the thorns before sawing his sword across the Chatti champion's throat. In the centre Valerius was conscious of Crescens hacking the head from a man who came too close. It was going well, but he knew it couldn't last. A burst of frantic shouted orders and now the warriors were attacking in pairs and fours. Spearmen protected the warrior who tore at the barrier allowing him time to make a difference. Valerius saw the Chatti chieftain halfway up the slope urging his men on.

161

'Shabolz, I want that bastard dead.' The Pannonian's arm came up, but before he could throw a warrior lunged at him with his sword and when the chance came again the chieftain had disappeared.

Valerius concentrated all his senses on gauging the ebb and flow of the fighting. Warriors swarmed the slope, and now the more timid, the farmers and the millers and the carpenters, scented an opportunity to share in the slaughter. Outnumbered four or five to one the defenders were only being kept alive by the strength of the position and the barrier of thorns. Timing. It was all about the timing.

He turned to look at the river. Florus and Ceris were pushing the sorceress into the shallows, about to be swallowed by the bank of fog. Where was Antonius? It had to be soon, before the enemy breached the barrier. A scream and Serenus reeled back with blood spurting from his forearm. One of the big Chatti warriors threw himself across the thorns to make a bridge and another leapt on his back and into the perimeter. The warrior's sword came up and Serenus raised his uninjured hand in a despairing attempt to protect himself. Before Valerius could react the closest Pannonian turned and whipped one of his weighted darts through the air and into the swordsman's back. The man dropped his blade and clawed vainly at the missile before collapsing and trying to crawl away. Nilus stepped forward and finished him with a cut to the base of the skull.

'Who gave you permission to stop signalling, trooper?' Valerius demanded.

'There's no need, sir. Look.'

Valerius turned in time to see *Rapid Racer* emerging from the fog bank. Antonius came in as close as he dared and dropped anchor. Florus threw Aurinia bodily into the ship and helped Ceris after her. He hesitated, and the Corieltauvi girl called out to him, but he was already on his way back to the hill.

'Get Serenus to the galley,' Valerius ordered Nilus. The young signaller helped his wounded comrade to his feet and they staggered towards the river.

'Lord?'

'You should have stayed with the galley, Florus.'

'Yes, lord, but the captain thought you might find these useful.'

Valerius turned. Florus was standing with his arms filled with *pila*. Valerius felt a surge of elation. 'The captain was correct.' He sheathed his sword and picked up one of the weighted javelins. Four foot of ash, topped with two and a half of iron that ended in a pyramid-shaped point, it was designed to pierce the outer layers of a shield and then stay there. Valerius had seen a *pilum* go through human flesh as if it didn't exist. He planted the point of the javelin in the hard-packed earth and picked up a second. 'Shabolz, Crescens and Licco, to me,' he roared above the din of the battle.

The cavalrymen were struggling to keep enemy opponents from crossing the thorns, but they responded immediately, sprinting to where Valerius stood. All three were breathing hard and Licco had a cut across his cheek that turned his mail scarlet. Valerius nodded to the *pila*. 'Two casts and then we go. But wait for my order. Form line.'

They made a rough line on Florus two or three feet apart and waited, while their comrades fought for their lives not twenty feet away. Valerius stepped to one side.

'Prepare to disengage.' His cry echoed across the hill. A moment's pause for a final assessment. 'Disengage! Back to the galley.'

Most of them had no idea of the galley's arrival. They'd expected to die on the hill and they needed no second urging. Backing out of range, the defenders raced across the hilltop and down the steep slope to the river. The enemy howled with new enthusiasm as they saw the Romans turn and run and clawed all the harder to pull the thorns aside.

'Ready,' Valerius ordered as soon as the men were clear. Five arms came up and back, the *pila* clutched in their fists. 'Throw.'

The javelins whistled through the air and each struck its chosen target. Warriors along the line saw their comrades pinned by the heavy spears and hesitated.

'Throw.' The second cast met with equal success, but Valerius had no time to witness the result. The moment the spear left his hand he turned and sprinted for the river. Antonius and his oarsmen were hauling cavalrymen aboard as fast as they were able. Most managed to discard their chain armour as they ran to make it easier to board the ship. The men with Valerius did likewise, but for their commander, with his single hand, it was impossible. They were together as they hit the water, but within a few steps he'd fallen behind.

The galley lay less than twenty paces from the shore and those already aboard shouted encouragement to the rearguard. Valerius saw Hilario standing by the bow roaring and Antonius shouting orders to his crew. Suddenly the cries became shriller and he could hear splashing at his back. A line of men rose up on the ship and a flight of javelins whipped just above his head. Someone screamed a few feet behind him and he surged on, floundering the last few paces. He was almost at the galley when he slipped and plunged face first into the water. With the heavy chain mail on his back he felt as if he was pinned to the river bottom. Water filled his mouth and nose, but almost immediately something large splashed into the water beside him and he was hauled bodily to the surface. He blinked as Hilario's glaring features came into focus.

'This is no time to go for a swim, lord.' The big man lifted him up so eager hands could drag him aboard the galley. They were already under way as Hilario heaved himself over the side and Valerius had the chance to look back at the shore for the first time. Dozens of screaming Chatti warriors stood in the shallows howling their frustration, while four or five of their comrades floated face up in the river, the heavy javelins that transfixed them swaying like masts in an ocean swell.

They were safe. For now.

Antonius set a fast rhythm to take *Rapid Racer* and her passengers out of danger. With the aid of the current the little craft fairly flew across the surface, powered by her fourteen oars. When he was happy with her course he left the steersman and clambered over the seating benches to join Valerius, who'd stripped off his armour and tunic and sat shivering along with his men, naked but for a loincloth.

Ceris moved among them treating their wounds, but, by some

164

miracle, the only serious injury was to Serenus, who had a deep slash on his forearm.

'We were lucky,' Valerius said to the sailor. 'If you hadn't arrived when you did we'd all be dead.'

'I almost didn't,' Antonius admitted with a wry smile. 'We were groping our way up the river like a blind beggar and I had no idea where we were. I was on the point of giving up and coming back tomorrow when I remembered what you said about making your own luck and ordered our signaller to sound the call.'

'Fortunately for us,' Valerius said. 'You have my thanks.'

'Who is the woman?' Antonius nodded to the bow where the two children stared in patent terror at Aurinia. Her gag had been removed and she sat in silence, staring ahead as if she was unaware of her surroundings. As they watched her head slowly turned and her eyes fixed on Valerius.

'I will never be the plaything of your emperor, Roman who is only part man.' Her voice was high and shrill and contained a loathing that sent a shiver through every man on the boat. More surprisingly, the words were in a Latin that could be understood by all. 'Return me to my people,' she continued, 'and I will see to it you return safely to yours.' From the corner of his eye Valerius saw Ceris shake her head. 'Do not and I will lay such a curse on you as will destroy you and every-one you love.'

Antonius's hand shot to the charm at his neck and she smiled contemptuously as if the Roman gods were of no consequence to her, and turned away. 'That,' Valerius said, 'is their witch. Florus and Crescens wanted to cut her throat, but Ceris convinced me she might come in useful. How long before we reach the Rhenus?'

'That depends,' Antonius said, his face suddenly grave.

'Yes?'

'On them.' He pointed to the mouth of a tributary stream, where a pair of long slim shapes emerged. Canoes, each carrying five tribes-men, and paddling swiftly to intersect *Rapid Racer*'s course.

'Can we outpace them?'

Antonius shook his head. 'We need to avoid those rapids because of our draught. They'll paddle straight through them.'

'What, then?'

The young sailor looked thoughtful. '*Rapid Racer* isn't built for ramming. All we can do is make them keep their distance.'

Valerius shrugged on his tunic and replaced his chain armour. 'Shabolz. Hilario. Into the bows with a pair of *pila* each, but don't throw unless they try to board. Didius, tie the witch to the mast where they can see her.'

The canoes came within spear-throw, but kept their distance when they saw the two men in the bows. Only when Aurinia began a high-pitched keening did they make any kind of threatening move.

'Lord?' Didius prompted.

Valerius nodded and the screeching stopped abruptly as the young soldier reapplied her gag. The two canoes veered away.

Two miles further downstream they passed another inlet, this time on the south side of the river. Three craft waited in the mouth. One was much larger than the others, some kind of trading vessel, twenty paces in length, and carrying about thirty men armed with everything from spears to axes and hay scythes.

Valerius and Antonius exchanged a glance. Without waiting for the order Marius began handing out the remaining *pila* to the men of Valerius's escort.

'How did they know?' Antonius whispered.

'Some kind of signalling system,' Valerius guessed. 'Or maybe a relay of fast couriers.'

The biggest craft came directly towards them. 'Marius?' Valerius called. 'Choose ten men in the centre of the boat. On my order they will stand and make ready to throw.'

Marius called out the names and Valerius waited, hoping the Germans would veer away when they recognized Aurinia, but they kept coming.

'They plan to ram us.' Antonius slipped from the bench and returned to the steering oar.

'Stand.'

The ten men rose and drew back their throwing arms.

'Save your spears. Tell them to get down.' Valerius thought he was hearing things, but Antonius repeated the order, watching the cargo boat intently as it closed with every stroke. So close now that Valerius could see the glaring eyes of the man in the bow and the gleam of the blade he carried.

'Wait. Wait. Slow your stroke,' Antonius ordered, making subtle adjustments to the galley's course and speed. Less than a boat's-length now. 'Brace yourselves,' the sailor called. 'Back oars!' The oarsmen changed instantly from the forward stroke to the reverse and men were thrown from their seats as the galley stopped dead in the water. The cargo boat shaved the bow and Antonius waited until it had almost passed. 'Now, row for your lives.'

The oars bit and the galley accelerated with the current, its speed taking it up and over the stern of the cargo boat. The impact threw the men seated there into the river and the other occupants began to bail frantically with anything they could find as the boat filled with water. A great cheer went up from the galley. Within a few strokes they were past and Valerius looked back to see the other craft going to the larger boat's aid.

'It appears the witch isn't as precious to them as you thought,' Antonius called.

'You may be right,' Valerius smiled. 'Do you want to throw her overboard?'

They looked to where Aurinia sat and she must have sensed their gaze, because she turned and stared at them with such loathsome malevolence they had to turn away.

'No.' Antonius's voice held a nervous edge. 'But we're close to where we picked up the children. If you want to land them now is a good time, while we don't have any company.'

Valerius agreed and they anchored off a gravel beach that backed on to an area of relatively flat ground. They landed the children and Valerius left them some food, a silver *denarius* each to make up for the loss of their boat, and a knife, which the girl snatched before her brother could get it.

When they rounded the next bend the two small figures still stood watching them out of sight.

'Do you think they'll survive, Antonius?' Valerius asked.

The naval officer shrugged. 'They're half wild and they know the river. One thing's certain: they're safer on their own than they are with us.'

The truth of his words was borne in upon Valerius an hour later as dusk was falling.

'Back oars,' Antonius said quietly.

Valerius looked ahead. About two hundred paces downstream the river writhed and seethed in an unnatural fashion right across its width, and he saw that someone had created a crude barrier of tree trunks linked together in some way. On a bluff to their left ten or so warriors watched the galley's progress and Valerius thought he caught a glint of gold in one man's hair. Along the shoreline some twenty small craft waited, each one filled with armed men.

'We're dead,' someone said quietly. Valerius was surprised to find the voice belonged to Hilario.

Antonius looked to the right bank, hoping to discover somewhere he could land the galley and give them a chance to escape, but the woods were filled with watchers. One glance told him that if he tried to run the barrier he'd tear the bottom out of the galley. 'What do you want to do, legate?'

Valerius felt a moment of panic. If Antonius, in his natural element, couldn't get them out of this, what chance did they have? Every eye in the galley was on him, but two with an intensity that drew him to them. Ceris.

Valerius rose to his feet and went to stand beside the mast where Aurinia was tied. He bent to remove the gag from her mouth. She worked her jaw for a moment before hawking and spitting in his face, a smile of triumph wreathing her wizened features. Valerius turned to Antonius. 'Approach the barrier as slowly as you're able,' he ordered.

The only sound was the rush of the river and the surge as the current forced itself beneath *Rapid Racer*'s stern. Aurinia's harsh voice broke the silence, apparently giving instructions to the men on the shore. Her words stirred a ripple of movement through the moored boats. The occupants looked to their leader on the bluff, anticipating his signal.

'For Mars' sake, shut her up,' Florus pleaded. Didius rose to replace the gag, but Valerius waved him away and drew his long sword. They were level with the height now, close enough to make out the chieftain's splendidly coloured cloak and the gold circlet in his dark hair. Valerius looked up, and thought he could almost feel the heat of the man's hatred. A hundred paces to the foam-flecked line of the barrier. 'Stop her,' he whispered to Antonius.

Only the galley's oarsmen breathed, fear and tension etched on their faces as they strained at the oars. Valerius stepped in front of the mast and turned, bringing the point of his sword level with Aurinia's throat. Still she harangued the men on the shore. When he placed the point against her flesh she dropped her gaze from the height, her tiny dark eyes pinpoints of malice that never left his face. 'This is your last chance, Roman,' she spat. 'Heed my warning or your gods will forsake you for all eternity. I will plant a plague of . . .' Her words sent a shiver through Valerius and he pushed a little harder until the screeching ended with a sharp choke.

He turned his attention back to the group on the headland. 'If a single boat so much as stirs the only thing you will recover of your sorceress will be her head.' The shouted threat echoed in the silence. Aurinia squirmed under the sword point and her mouth opened and closed, but no words emerged. 'Continue, Antonius, but slowly.'

They inched towards the barrier. Valerius's eyes never left the man on the height. Had he even understood the words? Valerius suspected he had, but if not their import was clear enough. Fifty paces. Twenty. A shout from the bluff froze the blood of everyone in the galley.

Valerius risked a glance towards the shore, but there was no sign of an impending attack. Instead, a single man ran towards the place where the barrier was anchored. So close that Valerius could make out every knot and splintered branch of the line of great logs, which he could now see were linked by inches-thick leather ropes. At the periphery of his vision the glint of an axe flashed in the dying sunlight. He heard the thud of the blade striking the rope. Once. Twice. Thrice. Slowly at first, but with ever-increasing speed, the barrier fell away like a door opening.

'You may continue, Antonius.' Valerius pulled his sword away from Aurinia's throat as the galley surged ahead. Before her head dropped forward he could see where the blood had pooled in the hollow below her throat. Behind him he heard the sound of someone vomiting over the side.

They pulled into the dock at Confluentes just before dawn and for a long time they sat slumped in their positions, too exhausted to move.

Torches flared on the bank and Valerius heard an urgent voice call, 'Quick. Fetch the commander.' He forced himself to his feet as one of the crew leapt ashore and dragged a wooden gangway to link the galley to the landing.

Julius Crescens caught up with him as he was halfway to the city gate. 'I haven't had the opportunity to thank you for coming for us, sir,' he said.

Valerius looked for some of the old mockery or condescension, but could find none. He smiled and shook his head. 'Don't thank me, boy; thank them.' He waved his wooden fist to the straggling line of weary, blackened, red-eyed cavalrymen.

Before he reached the gate Regulus burst through with two aides. 'I thought you'd be dead by now.'

'Not yet.'

The tribune counted the men behind them. 'You got them out?' He noticed the tiny figure being handed over to his guards by Hilario. 'Who is this?'

'The Chatti witch.' Valerius's attention was caught by Tabitha as she appeared in the gateway. He began to walk towards her.

'What am I supposed to do with her?' Regulus demanded.

Valerius stopped for a moment, remembering his words to the Chatti warrior chieftain. 'Send her to the Emperor with my compliments. He'll find a use for her.'

Two slave boys were filling lamps outside the gate when one of them dropped the *amphora* they were using. An overseer snarled a rebuke for the carelessness that had left them standing in the midst of a spreading pool of oil. The guard leading Aurinia was ten feet short of the gate when chaos erupted. Without warning he reeled back, screaming and clutching his side. Aurinia's bonds fell away beneath the knife she had somehow concealed and she ran towards the slave boys, snatching a flaming brand from its holder as she went. Before anyone could react she was standing in the middle of the viscous pool of oil with the torch held ready to drop.

'It's only olive oil. It will barely scorch her skirt,' someone laughed as a group of guards ran towards her.

'No,' Regulus's powerful voice halted the men in their tracks. 'We get the oil for our lamps from the shale pits to the south.'

'What does that mean?' Valerius demanded.

'You'll find out soon enough if she lowers that torch another inch.'

'Gaius Valerius Verrens.' Aurinia's shriek and the shock of hearing his name from her lips froze Valerius in place. How could she know? 'I warned you to turn back. I will not be put on display in Rome as some trophy of war. This curse I place upon you. An old enemy and an old friend will take from you that which you love most. A servant of the old gods will haunt your waking hours and occupy your nightmares.' The torch flashed out to point directly towards him and the air above the oil seemed to shimmer in its light. 'I have seen it. An eagle flies over you. The hand which has laid down the sword will raise it once more. You will fight your battle and taste your victory, but it will turn to ashes in your mouth. You will have your legion. But it will be the legion of the damned. All that awaits you in the end, Gaius Valerius Verrens, is darkness and death.'

'Wait.' Valerius raised his hands to show he was unarmed. He began walking slowly towards the sorceress. 'There is no need for this. I spoke

171

in haste when I talked of sending you to Rome. It was a mistake. You have served your purpose. Your people will ransom you and we will return you unharmed.'

He stopped ten paces away, just outside the shallow circle of oil. The torch spluttered in the soft breeze and the flames were reflected on the surface of the pool.

'Why should I trust a Roman?' Aurinia's voice dripped contempt.

'If you know so much about me, you know I am a man of my word.'

He saw the hesitation in Aurinia's eyes and prepared to take the few steps that would allow him to remove the torch from her hand. His ears barely registered the movement of air as something passed a few inches from his head. The sorceress cried out as a stone struck her on the shoulder. It wasn't a large stone, but the impact was enough to make her drop the torch. Valerius watched it fall.

Flames reached up almost caressingly from the pool to meet the torch. In the same instant the oil exploded with a roar matched only by the power of Aurinia's accompanying screams. For one heartbeat she was recognizable as a living, breathing entity in the centre of the inferno. The next transformed her into a writhing, twisting column of fire. Her filthy hair turned into a halo of orange and gold. Her plaid smock burned with a fierce intensity till it disintegrated and fell away from her thin form. Valerius stepped back from the wall of heat that scorched his face and singed his hair and eyebrows. He watched horrified as the skin melted from her body and her very flesh seemed to feed the flames. Her mouth hung open in a single endless shriek. And all the time her eyes never left his.

Unseen hands dragged him away from the inferno as the pillar of flame that had been Aurinia finally collapsed, to be consumed in the conflagration. 'Who was responsible?' He turned on his men. 'Who threw the stone?' But all that confronted him was a wall of blank faces.

He shook his head and walked to where Tabitha stood, her face pale and grim. 'Did you see what happened?'

She shook her head. 'I was too busy watching you. Poor woman.'

172

'Don't waste your sympathy on her. She was a torturer and a murderess. A witch.'

'And a prophet.' Tabitha shivered. 'All that awaits you is darkness and death.'

A burst of scornful laughter interrupted the conversation. 'You do not have to be a witch to predict darkness and death for Gaius Valerius Verrens,' Ceris said. 'In the end the only thing that awaits any of us is darkness and death.'

XXII

The brooding iron-grey clouds that hung over the port of Gesoriacum were a perfect match for Valerius's mood as they waited for the ship that would carry them to Londinium. The witch had predicted his days would be haunted by a servant of the old gods, and she was right. Yet it was no shadowy figure from the future who tormented him, but Aurinia herself. He would never forget the words of her prophecy or the fiery end she had failed to foresee. Ceris assured him the elements of the curse were mere word tricks. Of course she would want him to believe he would lose what he loved most, because that would strike fear into his heart. Darkness and death were life's only certainty. The suggestion he would command a legion? The same conversation that had provided her with his name would also have given her his rank. He shook his head. Fool, to allow the words of a barbarian crone to dismay you.

'Our ship is the *Concordia*, lord.' Didius Gallus returned from the port office. 'She's being unloaded at the end of the wharf and will be ready to sail again on the morning tide.'

'Very well, Didius. Go back to the *mansio* and inform the lady Tabitha. Tell Felix to bring the wagons down. In the meantime I'll introduce myself to the captain.'

The young cavalryman eyed the bustling quayside uncertainly. 'Is that wise, lord?'

Valerius smiled. 'I'll be safe enough. This isn't Germania.'

He was halfway to the wharf when he sensed someone taking step beside him. 'You ought to be more careful,' a hard-edged voice growled. 'A port like this is full of hungry men who'd slit your throat for the price of a loaf.'

Valerius turned to find himself the focus of a pair of deep-set blue eyes. A lived-in face, jaw like a shield boss, boxer's crooked nose and a thin-lipped mouth given a permanent sardonic twist by twin scars from cheek to chin on the left side. Cropped grey hair and a bruiser's solid body beneath the travel-stained tunic. 'I'm grateful for your advice, friend.' His eyes scanned their surroundings for possible accomplices, but everyone else seemed to be going about their business. Still, he allowed his left hand to creep towards his dagger. 'But I'm perfectly capable of looking after myself.'

'Is that a threat?' A grunt of laughter accompanied the words.

'You can take it any way you like.'

'They tell me you're interested in jewellery.'

'What?'

'I have this ring to sell.' The man opened his fist to reveal the glint of gold in his palm. Valerius instantly recognized the design and the glittering green stone.

'Yes,' he said. 'I'm definitely interested. Maybe we should find somewhere private to conduct our business?'

'I know a place.'

The darkest corner of a dockside bar whose only customers were a trio of prostitutes who left them alone when they declined the offer of a 'quickie' in the back room. The messenger pulled a scroll from the sleeve of his tunic and handed it to Valerius. 'You know what it says?' Valerius unrolled the single sheet of parchment.

'Best not.'

An unintelligible mass of numbers until you recognized the symbol that would allow you to unlock the code. A short letter, when you discarded the first two sentences.

'I must get back to my rooms to decode this.' Valerius reached for his purse.

'There's no need,' the stranger insisted. 'I serve our mutual friend and that is all the payment I need.'

'Then you have my thanks, as does . . . our friend.'

An hour later he had it. *He keeps his business close these days, but know this. I have learned that the name of Verrens was mentioned in a dispatch to an official in Britannia with the rank of legatus. Beware, Valerius. Great danger may await you.*

Another dull, grey dawn when the only thing that separated ocean from sky were the white caps that flickered across the water's surface like sea sprites riding the waves. Lucius, always curious, joined his father in the ship as a soft, misty rain combined with the salt spray to seep through the thick cloaks they wore.

'So this is Britannia, Father?' Lucius pointed to the soaring white cliffs a mile or so away off the port side.

'Yes.' Valerius smiled at his son. 'But we still have far to go. Another half a day's sailing north before we enter the river that will carry us to Londinium.'

'Is it always this wet?'

'I hope not.' Tabitha's voice came from behind them. 'Or it will be a short visit.'

She had her arms clasped around her waist against the cold and the hood of her cloak covered her hair. The unusual paleness of her features was evidence she'd been sick more than once during the crossing. Nothing to do with the sea, she insisted, but something that had to be borne along with the child she carried. The first thickening of her trim waist had become apparent in the last few days. In the night he'd placed his hand on her belly and she'd laughed. 'You'll be looking for another woman now that I'm old and fat.'

The memory made Valerius smile and he put an arm round her shoulders. 'What a bleak place,' she said.

'Oh, I remember the sun shining once or twice in the time I was here.'

'How long was that?'

'About two years.'

She nudged him in the ribs with her elbow.

Valerius could hear Felix's voice from the cargo hold where the cavalrymen had spent the night. Apart from Khamsin, they'd left the horses in Gaul, along with the Emperor's carriage and Titus's pavilion, but the young decurion was determined they should look their finest when they escorted Valerius from the ship to the governor's palace. Valerius had used his influence to ensure the mail lost fleeing the Chatti was replaced from the armoury at Colonia Agrippinensis. From the muttered curses below he gathered they were polishing the close-knit mesh of hundreds of iron rings with fine sand collected from the beach at Gesoriacum.

Around midday the waters around the ship turned from grey to a thick, murky brown. 'The Tamesa,' the *Concordia's* captain announced. 'You can smell her from a mile and more.' He ordered the steersman to change course into the face of the flood and deployed his oars as they lost the following wind. Soon land became visible on either hand. Flat, treeless and unwelcoming, a sight so oppressive Tabitha wondered aloud that Claudius hadn't turned back the moment he saw it. As they continued upstream the river narrowed and Lucius pointed excitedly to three dark mounds on one of the endless mudbanks. Soulful dark eyes turned to follow their progress and the mounds became a family of seals.

In the estuary proper they met a steady flow of merchant vessels, from large ships like the *Concordia* to smaller coastal barges and even canoes filled to overflowing with sacks and packages. The occasional skeletal frame sticking from the mud was a reminder that these waters were far from benign, and the ship twisted and turned to follow the deepest channel and avoid native fish traps.

As they wound their way inland, Valerius pointed to a haze of smoke in the distance.

'Londinium.'

Londinium. Seventeen years and more since he'd last seen the place, first as a bustling commercial and industrial township, a work in progress where every second building was roofless and surrounded by scaffolding. Later, Boudicca had turned those same buildings into blackened ruins and their inhabitants to mere piles of bones amongst the ashes. He remembered drinking wine with old Decimus Castus, commander of Londinium's fort, and his warning never to underestimate the British tribesmen. 'They can be subdued, but they can never be tamed,' Castus had said. He'd given the same advice to the governor, but Suetonius Paulinus had laughed at the old soldier. Castus had died on a rebel spear before he had the opportunity to point out Paulinus's error.

Beneath her cloak Tabitha was already dressed in the finery that would be expected of a Roman lady of her class and status. Valerius went to the sleeping cabin and emerged in a fine white toga with the senatorial stripe and the scarlet sash of the *legatus iuridicus* knotted around his waist.

The city came into view as they rounded a sharp bend in the river. Ahead of them an impressive wooden bridge stretched from one bank to the other, the massive supports creating dozens of arches. To their right, the eastern outskirts and, just short of the bridge, the city's port, where several merchant ships were already moored.

'At least it looks civilized,' Tabitha whispered as a number of large stone-built buildings came into view, towering above the sea of red-tiled roofs.

Valerius saw it at once. Nothing had changed, but everything had changed. All that Boudicca's wrath had swept away had been replaced, but on an even greater scale. He felt an upsurge of excitement in the pit of his stomach. What challenges awaited him here? And what opportunities? He realized that getting to this point had been all that had absorbed him. What happened afterwards hadn't seemed real, and therefore worth concerning himself with. Until now.

How would Julius Agricola receive him? The last time they met, the governor had been a junior officer on the staff of Suetonius Paulinus, and Valerius, barely twenty-three, a shocked and damaged survivor of

Boudicca's destruction of Colonia Claudia Victricensis. Valerius knew the years had changed him almost beyond recognition, the young man replaced by a veteran soldier who had seen the very best and the very worst of the Empire. One who could be as hard as the iron of the sword he wielded. This Valerius had been forged in the fires of war and made wary by intrigue and conspiracy. Agricola, too, would have been altered by his experiences. He had lost his mother, butchered during the civil war. Vespasian had made the family patricians and rewarded Agricola for his loyalty with the province of Gallia Aquitania and a consulship. Now he'd been given the responsibility of governing a province notoriously difficult to rule, and, just as important, impossible to wring a profit from. The strain of running Britannia had killed one governor and ruined the careers of several more. From what Titus had said Agricola hadn't asked for Valerius by name. It made the forthcoming meeting interesting.

The *Concordia* manoeuvred into the dock and two deckhands threw ropes ashore where men waited to moor the ship. Valerius scanned the quayside, but he could see no sign of the reception committee a newly appointed official of his rank might expect. A mistake, or a deliberate omission to remind him of his place? The sailors ran out a gangplank and a centurion with a gleaming *phalera* that identified him as a customs officer marched aboard demanding to see the captain's cargo manifest. A sailor took him aside and after a whispered conversation the centurion approached Valerius.

'My apologies, sir.' He saluted. 'We expected you a week ago, and had a guard of honour waiting for three full days. I'm sure Governor Agricola would have been here himself if he'd known.'

'No need for apologies, soldier,' Valerius assured him. 'Please send a messenger to let him know we have arrived. There's no need for any fuss. I have an escort of my own. All that will be required is a guide to show us the way.'

While they waited, Valerius pointed out to Lucius the bounty of the Empire that flowed through Londinium to the rest of the province. Clearly the port here had replaced Colonia as the gateway to Britannia, and by some measure. From the deck of the ship they could see *amphorae* of wine, olive oil and garum recently arrived from Italia and Hispania, stacks of gleaming red pottery from factories in Gaul, and trays of fine glassware from Asia and Syria. A line of slaves carried sacks of African grain from the hold of a ship direct to one of the great storehouses behind the dock. That grain was destined for the quartermaster stores of the island's four legions, along with the chain and plate armour, swords and spears and saddlery all stockpiled in Londinium before distribution. Bales of furs, traded from the primitive northern tribes, were being loaded into an adjacent merchant vessel. And Valerius knew that freshwater pearls and ingots of tin, silver and gold would be stored nearby ready for transport to Rome. Truly, Londinium had become one of the great crossroads of the world.

Valerius's request for a quiet reception had been made more in hope than expectation and so it proved. Before long he heard the familiar sound of marching feet and a century of legionaries appeared at the far end of the quay, followed in the distance by a carriage pulled by four white horses and surrounded by a milling crowd of servants. The legionaries came to a crashing halt fifty paces away and moved to one side to allow the carriage and a single toga-clad dignitary to approach.

'Is this the governor?' Tabitha asked.

Valerius shook his head. 'One of his aides, I should think. Agricola won't move without a cloud of officials and a full cohort.' Felix shouted an order and ten of Valerius's escort ran down the gangplank to form a guard of honour. Valerius followed, accompanied by the decurion carrying his polished helmet under his right arm. The official, a young man with a frank, open face, intelligent blue eyes and crimped dark hair, arrived at the escort just as Valerius set foot on shore. They bowed in greeting, the young man deeply, and Valerius with the slightest nod of the head that acknowledged his seniority.

'The governor sends his regrets that he could not meet you personally,' the young man said. 'But he is sure you will understand the burdens of office. Metilius Aprilis, the governor's aide, at your service, sir. I have a coach waiting and an escort from the governor's personal bodyguard to accompany you through the city to the palace.' He eyed the men at the bottom of the gangway. 'Perhaps your own escort could act as rear-guard,' he said tactfully.

'I think that would be wise.' Valerius smiled. He had felt Felix stiffen at the perceived slight. 'We don't want your lads frightening those fresh-faced legionaries from the Twentieth, do we, decurion?' Aprilis's handsome features took on a certain expression and Valerius had a feel-ing they might have met before. He turned to the young officer. 'May I ask you to inform my escort commander of their billeting arrange-ments and where we can access horses and remounts.'

'Of course, sir, and I will arrange the transfer of your baggage to the governor's palace.'

'Thank you.' Aprilis waved the carriage forward and Valerius bowed to where Tabitha waited at the top of the gangplank. 'My lady? Lucius?'

The carriage rattled over the rough cobbles of the port on to a street that hugged the river. A partially built temple complex lay to their right, and, far off, Valerius could see the roof of a massive *basilica* that vied for scale with anything he'd seen in the Empire. Somewhere in that mass of buildings was the headquarters of the *legatus iuridicus*, where he would be based, and the staff of lawyers and clerks he would command. Tabitha stared at him and he realized he'd let out an undignified snort at the thought of 'commanding' office workers. He smiled an apology. But this was what he was here for. It was time to act his age and remember the days of glory were behind him.

The governor's palace lay a short distance ahead, surrounded by gardens and perched on a series of terraces overlooking the river. Like most of the city's public buildings, it was still in the midst of con-struction, but three of the four wings had been completed and a team of builders worked steadily to complete the façade of the fourth. Armed guards stood at every corner and more formed an avenue through the gardens to the steps where a small delegation was waiting.

The carriage rolled to a halt and Valerius helped his wife and son to the ground. He took Tabitha by the hand and they walked slowly towards the palace. Valerius recognized Gnaeus Julius Agricola immediately. The slim, athletic young officer he remembered had grown stouter and his sparse hair was a steely grey, but the essence of the man remained in the shrewd appraisal and steady grey eyes that promised determination and resolve. Beside him stood a tall, slender woman of similar age who must be his wife.

'Well met, Gaius Valerius Verrens,' the governor called before Valerius could present his credentials. A smile accompanied the words, but Valerius thought it contained an element of . . . not quite suspicion, perhaps, but a certain wariness. 'No man has ever been more welcome. I congratulate you on your elevation and promise you will more than pay for it in labour.'

'And you, governor.' Valerius bowed. 'I remember our service together with nothing but pleasure.'

Agricola covered up a disbelieving laugh with a cough. 'May I present my wife Domitia?' The woman held out a slim hand that flinched only a little when her fingers touched the chill of Valerius's wooden fist. Tabitha saw her confusion and stepped forward. 'A gift.' She handed over a pouch of soft leather and the governor's wife tugged at the strings, gasping with pleasure when she saw what was inside. 'A small token of our esteem,' Tabitha continued, as Domitia withdrew a beautifully fashioned gold bracelet in the shape of a coiled snake. Domitia slipped it over her wrist and held it up to admire it.

'It's beautiful,' she said. 'And this must be Lucius.' She turned her attention to the boy hovering behind his mother's skirts. Lucius stepped out and bowed from the waist and Valerius noticed a liquid gleam in the corner of Domitia's eye as she patted his dark hair.

'Perhaps we should go inside,' Agricola said gruffly.

'Yes.' Domitia straightened with a forced smile. 'I will show Tabitha and Lucius to their rooms. I insist you stay in our guest quarters for a few days while we put the final touches to your villa. I know these men have much official nonsense to discuss. There will be time for conversation later.'

'Thank you,' Tabitha said. 'I'd also count it a favour if you would show me somewhere I can wash this horrible salt from my hair.'

'Of course.' The other woman led her past the two men. 'Fortunately the bathhouse was one of the first areas to be completed. You wouldn't believe how . . .'

Agricola ushered Valerius after them. 'Come, we have much to discuss before dinner. I've invited a few people I think it would be beneficial for you to meet.'

'I'm very grateful,' Valerius said.

The governor led the way to a room in the south wing overlooking the broad expanse of the river. A jug of wine and two silver cups had been laid on a table. Agricola filled the cups with a liquid that glowed green and gold. He handed one cup to Valerius and they stood looking at each other for a long time, the only sounds the rasp of saws and tap of hammers from the men working outside.

'"I remember our service together with nothing but pleasure"?' Agricola growled. 'I remember a man with one hand who looked as if he'd come back from the dead.'

'I seem to have learned the language of diplomacy.' Valerius took a sip of the wine, savouring the tart fruit on his tongue. It was very good, as he'd have expected.

'That's not all you've learned, from what I've heard.'

'Yes?' Valerius held his gaze. 'Does that mean you don't appreciate the Emperor's choice?'

'Let us dispense with the language of diplomacy, Valerius.' Agricola laid his cup aside and counted off the words on the fingers of his right hand. 'Assassin, spy, conspirator, exile . . .'

Valerius helped him with the word he seemed reluctant to utter. 'They called me a traitor once too.'

'One way or the other, wherever you have served, men have died. Friend or enemy, it seems it is dangerous to know you, Gaius Valerius Verrens.'

It hit Valerius with a shock that Agricola was frightened of him. 'But we are neither.' He smiled to lighten the mood. 'And perhaps it's better it stays that way.'

'Very well.' Agricola's tone didn't soften. 'Let me put it to you directly.

If Vespasian wishes to know anything about Julius Agricola and you have been tasked with discovering it, ask now and I will answer with complete candour.'

Valerius would have laughed if the governor's expression wasn't so serious. 'I am not your rival, Julius,' he assured the other man. 'It is only six months since the Emperor appointed you to this province. You have his complete confidence, and that of Titus. The reason I am here is that they believe I have the qualities you need in your legal officer. I am here to help you, not to spy on you. You have my word on it.'

Agricola picked up his cup and went to the window, staring out over the grey expanse of the Tamesa. He seemed to stay there for a long time. Valerius watched him, knowing that if he'd failed to convince the governor of his sincerity he'd be as well taking the next ship back to Rome.

'Good.' Agricola swung round. A twitch of a smile appeared fleetingly on the thin lips. 'Then let us deal first with the practicalities.' He let out a long sigh. 'I'm sorry, Valerius, but I had to know.'

The practicalities. Valerius, Tabitha and Lucius would move into a villa just outside the line of the old city walls, newly built and one of the few to have heated floors and walls. It was close to the fort, and for convenience, his escort would be billeted with the auxiliary garrison and source their mounts and remounts through the normal channels. 'They're satisfactory? The men? I know commanders can use this kind of thing as an opportunity to get rid of their problems.'

'Perfectly,' Valerius assured him. 'We had a few adventures on the way here that rubbed off any rough edges.'

'You can tell me about them later.' Valerius bowed his head in acknowledgement. 'Your headquarters is in the *basilica*. You must have seen it – the biggest building in the city by far. Petilius Cerialis began it and I think he must have taken his lessons in architecture from Nero because everything's on a grand scale. On the positive side it means there's plenty of room for the clerks and all the province's administrative documents.'

'I doubt they'd have had any trouble with the archives,' Valerius said grimly.

'You're right.' Agricola met his eye. 'Everything was turned to ash in Boudicca's balefire. There was no point in trying to replace them; just about everybody was dead. The rebels killed every Roman and loyal Briton they could lay their hands on, and, as you know, Paulinus did the same to the rebel tribes.'

'May I make an observation, governor?'

'Of course.'

'After what happened, I would have thought the first thing your predecessors would have built was a city wall.'

'And you would have been right, had there been a city. You remember that sea of ash with just the occasional oven chimney left upright? Everything – houses, people, animals and stores – burned, and then the walls and gates pulled down and thrown on top for good measure. Any former inhabitant left alive wouldn't come near the place because of its history. We still find blackened bones when we dig the foundations. When they put in the terrace here the builders unearthed an entire family not ten feet from where we sit. So, no city, no citizens, and no one could persuade replacements to come from elsewhere in the Empire after what had happened. Trebellius Maximus had the fort rebuilt to try to entice people back into its protection, but it wasn't until Petilius Cerialis arrived that they were able to start rebuilding.'

'But no wall,' Valerius persisted.

'By then Cerialis felt there was no reason for one. Paulinus had crushed the rebellion with such barbarous enthusiasm that I doubt any Briton will ever take up arms again.'

'You had to take the Twentieth against the Brigantes.'

'True, but that was more of an internal dispute. When they saw the legion marching upon them they mostly fled. No, Paulinus may have been a brute, but he did his successors an inestimable service, as you will find when you begin your tour of the country. And I intend to finish what he started.'

'Titus told me of your plan for subduing the hill tribes.'

'Yes. Claudius's last instruction to Aulus Plautius was "Conquer the rest", and here we are thirty-odd years later still talking about the threat from the north.' Agricola hesitated. 'But by necessity, and probably for the best, my original plan has changed.'

'Necessity?'

Agricola nodded. 'My spies have reported rumours that the druids are back, contaminating the tribes with their lust for blood vengeance. Fortunately, there is no reason to believe they are being listened to. But . . .'

'You've had trouble?'

'Worse than trouble. A massacre. An entire auxiliary garrison slaughtered on the edge of Ordovice country. The kind of obscenities we haven't seen perpetrated since the Iceni witch's day. Here is the report from the officer who went to investigate.'

Valerius read the scroll Agricola handed him and a shudder ran through him as he read of Claudius Vindex's fate. He'd seen a man die on the stake on the Dacian frontier and it hadn't been pleasant. He carried on until he reached the officer's conclusions.

'An attack from every side and only a handful of enemy casualties. That suggests overwhelming force. Not hundreds of men, but thousands. This wasn't just a raid.'

'No. It was a challenge. One I am minded to accept. A war cry intended to show the druids are still a force in the west. This beastliness is their mark. I originally planned for one legion to remain at Viroconium to cover the frontier, but I can't leave this unfinished business to fester behind me. It would only encourage them to try something similar further east. In two weeks I will march in overwhelming force on the Ordovices, and destroy their power once and for all. But Mona is the key. Mona is not just the druids' stronghold, it is the granary that feeds the Ordovices and their allies, and a centre of weapons manufacture. I intend to wipe this barbaric stain from the island of Britannia for ever.'

Valerius had a feeling he was listening to a speech Agricola had already made, but one thing troubled him.

'I'm sure you've considered it, governor, but isn't it a little late in the campaigning season to march against the Ordovices? Paulinus reckoned on a month to fight his way through the mountains. They would defend every hill and every river crossing. You've been there. In a month you'll have the morning frosts turning your toes blue and the north wind cutting through your cloak like a knife. Two weeks later there'll be snow on the mountains.'

'Nevertheless,' Agricola said stiffly, 'I will lead Roman soldiers west to destroy the druids.'

XXIII

An officer with the rank of legate. Was it by accident or design that Valerius now shared a room with the four men in Britannia who commanded Agricola's legions? They lounged on couches round a table the size of a small ship in a room built to scale. Nymphs, dolphins and strange sea creatures chased each other across the plastered ceiling and the deep terracotta tones and vibrant greens and blues of the wall paintings had clearly been chosen to remind Agricola of his home in Forum Julii.

The governor introduced them one by one. Tiberius Julius Ursus, *legatus augustus* of Agricola's old command, the Twentieth Valeria Victrix. A short, compact man with crow-black hair and sharp, angular features who punctuated his conversation with swift, darting hand movements. Caristanius Fronto, Ninth Hispana. Fronto's deep-set eyes stared bemusedly at the world in a manner that suggested he'd already been drinking for hours. He had a querulous voice that demanded to be heard and a face the colour of a terracotta tile and the shape of a melon. Terentius Strabo, Second Augusta, tall and thin, with a lugubrious manner but bright, intelligent eyes. And Herenius Polio of the Second Adiutrix, young for his rank, perhaps only in his mid-thirties. A mark of the Emperor's favour, or, Valerius mused, the favour of someone else in Vespasian's circle. Polio had a pampered, well-fed look that might, wrongly, be mistaken for softness, and the kind of manners that only came with generations of patrician ancestors. Fronto apart, the legionary commanders studied the newcomer with undisguised interest, but Valerius could detect no outward malice. Nevertheless, one of these men was his enemy, and, until he discovered which, they must all be treated as such.

The girlish tinkle of Tabitha's laughter reminded him that this was meant to be a celebration of his arrival in Britannia. The two wives shared a couch on one side of the table while the six men shared the other three. Fine wine flowed freely from Agricola's store, but Tabitha's cup barely touched her lips and Valerius sensed a growing understanding in the governor's wife's grave eyes.

When the last of the food had been cleared away, Domitia stood and thanked her guests for their understanding and hoped they enjoyed the rest of the evening. The lady Tabitha was tired and must rest after her long journey, and she would escort her guest to her room.

It was clearly a predetermined agreement between Agricola and his wife to allow the men to talk alone. Valerius watched Tabitha leave, as always taking pleasure in her regal bearing and, despite her best intentions, sensuous carriage. As he smiled and turned back to his neighbour he heard someone slur: 'She's a rare piece, that one. I like a bit of dark meat myself.'

It took a moment for the words to sink in, but when they did Valerius felt an upsurge of dark rage and his vision filled with red. He half rose from his seat before his neighbour, Julius Ursus, drew him back on to the couch. 'I beg you, legate. He's not worth it. A boor, a drunkard and a fool. A fine combination for the general of a legion, you might say, but not unknown. Please, join me in another cup of wine. Soon we will be talking strategy and no doubt he will fall asleep.'

Valerius accepted the cup and allowed his rage to lie dormant, but he told himself there would some day be a reckoning with Caristanius Fronto. In the meantime, the others discussed mutual acquaintances, of which it turned out they had many across the Empire. Ursus had actually served as aide to Vespasian during the early part of the Judaean revolt and this command was his reward.

'Gentlemen.' Agricola tapped his cup on the gilded table top to command their attention. 'Now that the ladies,' he gave the word special emphasis and Fronto a look that made him drop his eyes, 'have left us we come to the true purpose of this gathering. Once again I thank you for coming such long distances, from Lindum, Isca, Deva and Viroconium, but I felt we needed to be together so I can properly emphasize the prodigious effort that will be required of you and your soldiers in the coming years.'

'Does this jumped-up clerk have to be here,' Fronto said in a loud whisper. 'Won't be leading anyone. Won't be risking a spear up his arse.'

'For clarification.' Agricola didn't disguise the irritation in his voice. 'Gaius Valerius Verrens is my trusted adviser and a man with a long and distinguished military career. The Emperor has sent him to Britannia to allow me to concentrate on strategy during this vital period. In my absence he will be the acting governor of the province, and should I fall the province will be his.' In the long silence that followed Valerius felt the eyes of the other men on him and the blood rush to his face. This was a step beyond what Titus had suggested and an enormous honour. Part of him was elated, but another part wondered if Agricola was only saying it for effect. 'I expect you to give him the same loyalty and respect you do myself,' the governor continued. 'Is that understood?'

A murmur of agreement and one petulant shrug.

At one end of the room a curtain hung over a large alcove and now Agricola drew the heavy cloth back. A wooden frame had been set up with a large piece of parchment stretched across it. They saw immediately that the white surface was sparsely marked with what appeared to be the lines of rivers and mountains. The soldiers craned forward to study the markings, Valerius as eager as any of them.

'I had this drawn up by our best cartographers,' Agricola said. 'Behold Britannia as you have never seen it before. It is as accurate as we can make it based on the information gleaned from our previous campaigns, and from merchants, spies and native traders.' Britannia appeared to be made up of two triangles stacked point to point on top of each other. Most of the bottom triangle – southern Britannia – had been filled in with rivers, forests, hills and settlements. By comparison, the inverted triangle on top was almost bare, with two or three rivers and a mountainous centre. 'Of course, given our past experiences with the northern tribes some of it will be exaggeration, some lies and some nothing but fantasy, but we will only discover that when we reach it.'

Agricola allowed his legates time to digest what they were seeing before he continued.

'I expect to complete the subjugation of Britannia in four campaigning seasons. In the first, or what remains of it, we will finish the job Suetonius Paulinus began seventeen years ago. The Ordovice raid on Canovium has given us the perfect opportunity to cleanse the west of the druid poison.'

'With respect, sir,' Herenius Polio interrupted. 'As I said in my report, there is a suspicion that the attack on Canovium was calculated to inspire exactly this response. The Ordovices and whoever is directing them will hope to draw you into the mountains and . . .'

'You think I am a second Varus, Herenius?' Agricola softened his words with a smile and shook his head. 'There will be no eagles lost to the Ordovices. You are in a better position to know their loathsome ways than anyone in this room, but if what you say is true, I welcome it. Yes, they will try to draw us in, but eventually they will mass their forces against us and I will slaughter them.'

'But . . .'

'The details can wait.' Agricola dismissed his lieutenant's concerns with a wave of the hand. 'So, first the west. In the second season we will consolidate what we have in Brigante country. They are cowed, but given the opportunity they can still put a formidable force in the field and I don't want that kind of threat at my back. I have ordered my spymasters to discover and record every infringement of Roman law amongst the tribes of the Brigante federation. Every bushel of grain that's not reported, every government horse that's stolen or cow butchered, every hidden sword and chariot. We will bring the forces at our command down upon them like a sledgehammer. Raid the villages, take hostages by the hundred from their ruling classes, empty their corn stores in retaliation, and then give it back so they love us as much as they fear us.'

The legates were grinning now. This was the kind of campaigning they understood and liked. An enemy that didn't know what was coming, light casualties, and who knew what profit might be picked up along the way.

'As far as possible we will replenish our supplies from the sea, which means bases here in the west' – he pointed to the chart – 'where our *exploratores* have confirmed this estuary cuts well inland, and again in the east, where this river provides access on the same line. This will provide the platform to move north again.' He gave them a significant look. 'North into the unknown. The only information we have comes from coastal traders. Beyond this line of hills – they are too insignificant to be called mountains – lies a fertile plain. It's said the tribes who inhabit it constantly squabble and fight over land and water rights.'

'Divide and conquer.' Julius Ursus spoke for the first time.

'Precisely.' Agricola smiled. 'Why fight the enemy when you can get them to fight each other?'

'And this feature?' The legate of the Twentieth pointed to a mark two-thirds of the way up the map.

'One of the few definite things we know,' the governor answered. 'A distinctive formation of three hills visible all around, said to be sacred to the natives. I have called it Trimontium and I hope you and I will become better acquainted with it, Julius.'

'How far do we expect to advance?' Polio asked.

'As far as here, where the two rivers form what may well be the narrowest point in the northlands.'

'The narrower it is, the better to defend,' Second Augusta's legate pointed out.

Agricola shrugged. They would cross that hurdle when they came to it. 'And in the fourth season we will conquer what's left. The true primitives of the island.'

'Then they must be primitives indeed, if the filth in the south is anything to go by.' His comrades smiled dutifully at Fronto's intervention, but Agricola ignored him.

'None of this can be achieved until we secure the west. Forgive me for cutting you off earlier, Herenius, but I felt the need to expand on . . . should we call it my grand plan, before setting out my thoughts on the initial phase. The Ordovices will expect us to advance by the route taken by Paulinus. I intend to confound them by attacking from Viroconium with the Twentieth,' Julius Ursus bowed, though he knew Agricola would be sharing not only his command tent, but his command also, 'and a strong *vexillatio* of the Ninth.' A few grunts of surprise. Like its legate, Fronto's Ninth was known to be the weakest of the legions in Britannia, with a poor record and significant leadership flaws. Fronto knew this as well as anyone and the expression on his face mirrored his surprise. 'The remaining cohorts of the Ninth will move north to Eboracum and prepare winter quarters for the legion. Herenius, you and the Adiutrix will remain at Deva. I want you to bring in every ear of wheat and oats and every cow the locals can spare. Be firm. I don't want my men going hungry because we fretted over a few empty Deceangli and Cornovii bellies. A stockpile every day's march to the border of Brigantia, but hide them well. I don't want them to know we're coming. Once we've dealt with the Ordovices the Twentieth will winter at Lindum, but march north to Eboracum at the first thaw.'

He turned to Strabo. 'My apologies for neglecting you. The Second Augusta will move up from Isca to Deva in the spring and be ready to reinforce my advance or support my withdrawal at need. Now,' he looked at each man in turn, 'I'm sure you will wish to make an early start tomorrow and begin your preparations. Caristanius? See me in the morning before you leave.'

The legates got to their feet, and Valerius turned to go with the rest. 'A moment, Valerius. I have some guidance for you.'

'Governor.'

Valerius watched the other four men leave. Ursus and Strabo invited him to visit their bases as they made their farewells, Fronto only scowled, and Polio seemed lost in his own thoughts. Still no clue as to which of them was Domitian's man. Agricola waited until they were alone, toying with an ornate metal tower decorated with a short text. The tower rattled as he turned it and he noticed Valerius's interest. 'A gift from my staff after the Brigante campaign. It helps add a little spice to a game.'

Valerius studied the inscription. *Brigantes Victos Hostis Deleta Ludite Securi.* 'The Brigantes are defeated, the enemy is destroyed, play in safety,' he read aloud. The gambler placed the dice in the top so they fell through a series of steps to little doors hung with bells that would ring as they emerged. 'A fine gift,' he observed.

'A token of genuine esteem, I think.'

Valerius smiled. Did Agricola not see that it could also be a hint that his officers believed their commander was prone to cheating at games of chance? The governor took back the tower and placed it on the wooden chest it came from. 'You didn't have much to say for yourself. Your reputation is of a man who is more forthright.'

Valerius laughed. 'I wasn't aware I had a reputation, never mind that it had travelled so far.'

'But you do have an opinion?'

Valerius hesitated, uncertain what this had to do with Fronto's 'jumped-up clerk'. 'As for your overall campaign . . . Your generals seem satisfied. I am not here in a military capacity and it's not my place to question their judgement or yours.'

'But . . . ?'

'If you really want my view, I think your timetable is optimistic. You could very easily get bogged down in the west, especially in winter. I applaud your strategy in Brigante country, although I doubt our allies will. They are still our allies?'

'Nominally.'

'After that you're in the unknown. You say the place of the three hills is believed to be sacred. In my experience people fight for their sacred places and they fight to the death.' He went to the map. 'You'll be wintering among people who hate your guts and then you reach this narrow isthmus between the two rivers. But then you'll have taken all this into consideration.'

Agricola smiled. 'Of course.'

'Then I only have one question. Why the Ninth?'

'Was it so obvious?'

'To me, yes. Even Fronto couldn't believe the honour you'd done him.'

The governor nodded slowly. 'The Ninth isn't a bad legion, or certainly not as bad as their reputation would suggest. They haven't had Fortuna's favour, but of course you know that.' Valerius had a momentary flashback to the white corpses scattered like maggots along the road between Lindum and Londinium, butchered by Boudicca's allies. 'I need them if I'm to conquer the north,' Agricola continued. 'The trouble is they've been in Lindum so long they've put down roots. They think they can do things their way. That story you told at dinner, about abducting the Chatti witch – not something I would have condoned, I might add – made my point. The best way to change their attitude is to put them in harm's way and let them learn the reality.'

'I can't fault your logic,' Valerius admitted.

'Good. Now, as to the guidance I mentioned . . .'

XXIV

Valerius slipped into bed and pulled the sheet over him. He had thought Tabitha was asleep, but she took his left hand and placed it over the warm, silky flesh of her stomach. When they'd lain like that for a while she said: 'So what do we think of Governor Agricola?'

'If we were wise we would delay having a view until we knew him better.'

'He seems to value your opinion.'

'Who told you that?'

'His wife told me there was no one of rank on the island he could trust until you arrived. You don't like him?'

'It's not a question of liking. He's a competent administrator and a successful general. That hasn't always been the case in Britannia. I still don't fully understand why he feels he needs me. He has three first class generals in Ursus, Polio and Strabo. Any one of them is capable of defeating the northern tribes with three full legions.'

'It's simple,' Tabitha said drowsily. 'He wants the glory.'

Valerius laughed. 'Julius Agricola already has all the laurels any man would need.'

'No one is going to erect a statue of him in the Forum because he subdued the Brigantes. But if he sends the kings of every northern tribe he defeats to Rome in chains Vespasian will award him a triumph.'

'You seem to know a lot.'

'I told you. Domitia likes to talk. There are very few women of rank in Britannia, and none she cares to confide in.'

'Yet she took to an exotic eastern princess in a matter of hours.'

'Of course.' He heard the smile in her voice. 'I chose her gift with great care. She says Agricola has been on edge lately.'

'I'm not surprised. He thought I was sent here either to assassinate him or to spy on him.'

'See, your reputation goes before you.'

'He said that.'

'But you convinced him he could trust you?'

'He introduced me to his senior officers and briefed me on the detail of his plans. He didn't have to do that. But trust? I'm not sure he trusts anyone.'

'I think you're wrong, my Hero of Rome.'

He turned and kissed her. 'I'm not here as a soldier but as a lawyer, or as Legate Fronto put it a jumped-up clerk.'

'Domitia despises the man, and I didn't like the way he looked at me.'

Valerius thought it best not to tell her what Fronto had said about her. Tabitha's reaction to a slight could be both unpredictable and dangerous.

'So when do you start your clerking?'

He smiled and moved his hand a little lower. She stirred beneath him and wriggled her hips so his fingers were in a certain position she liked. What he felt now produced another kind of stirring.

'As soon as I check that the men of the escort are settled in tomorrow. The governor says I should take as long as I need to get to know my people.'

'Good. I'm interested in exploring Londinium. There was a little goldsmith's shop on the way here . . .'

'Then there are two or three complex cases in Colonia the local magistrate doesn't feel able to deal with.' She heard something in his voice when he said the word Colonia, but decided not to pursue it for now.

'So we're going to this Colonia?'

'We?'

'Of course. Lucius needs to be with his father. Domitia says I can use the governor's coach whenever I wish.'

Valerius could tell there was no point in arguing.

'Valerius?'

'Yes?'

'If this is the governor's palace there will be a spy listening at every door.'

'True,' he agreed.

'Well,' she raised the sheet and rolled on top of him, 'let's give them something to report.'

'So tell me about Colonia,' Tabitha suggested, as they walked in the sunshine beside the carriage. Valerius led his horse and was heartily glad of the fresh air after seven days inhaling the scent of old leather and decaying parchment in the cramped rooms of the *basilica*. Soot, too, because despite what Agricola had said some of the archives had been recovered – charred fragments in most cases – and the little information they contained informed the law as much as those which came later. Much of his time had been spent trying to understand the complex network of grants, dispensations and monopolies which dated back to just after the Claudian conquest. King Cogidubnus of the Regni, who had ruled a great swathe of land on the south coast, had been granted something close to self-rule for his support of the invasion. His successors enjoyed the same privileges, with some apparently controversial modifications imposed in Nero's time. Likewise, the citizens of Verulamium, who had been left destitute by Boudicca, had been given the right to levy taxes on goods carried up and down the road between Londinium and Lindum. On the other hand *municipia* like Verulamium had fewer rights than *coloniae*, such as their present destination, Colonia Claudia. To the uninitiated, Roman law applied equally to all the cities, but the reality was very different.

'I said tell me about Colonia.'

'I'm sorry.' He smiled. 'I was thinking. My head seems to be filled with a huge spider's web linking one piece of apparently useless information to another.'

He looked ahead to where the vanguard of his escort were walking their horses, happy to see men from the four legions talking together. At first he'd been concerned that Tabitha's carriage would slow them down, but when he'd thought about it he'd realized that a well-driven carriage on a good road could easily maintain the same pace as a cavalryman in no hurry. And Valerius was in no hurry. He was content to take his time and get a feel for the country again.

'Colonia is where they took this from me.' He raised the wooden fist. Tabitha knew he'd lost his right hand in battle, but she'd never asked for more detail. The oak replacement was part of him and that was all she cared about. 'I'd spent the winter there, but I was in Londinium preparing to return to Rome when word came of the rising. Because I knew the area, the governor appointed me to command the reinforcements for the local militia.'

'How many were you?' she asked.

'Two hundred: auxiliaries, men on leave and a few of my comrades come to say goodbye.'

'And Boudicca?'

'They say seventy thousand, but I didn't count them,' he said.

They heard a child's delighted laughter and Lucius flew past on Khamsin, closely pursued by Didius, trying desperately not to catch him. Tabitha watched them with a mother's smile, then turned to look her husband in the eye. 'Yet you survived.'

'I survived, by Fortuna's intervention.'

'Tell me.'

So he did. How the civilian inhabitants of Colonia had been herded together into a convoy destined for the supposed sanctuary of Londinium. The anguish when the bloodied remnants of the Thracian escort returned to report ambush and massacre. A long night of waiting, punctuated by what appeared to be fireflies on the opposite slope. Knowing the fireflies were actually burning villas and farms. And in the first light of dawn, accompanied by the sound of a million bees, Boudicca's horde, tribes and sub-tribes and clans, countless thousands that stretched to the horizon.

'We fought them, and we fought them again as they forced their way across a bridge of their own dead. Iceni and Catuvellauni champions naked but for sword and spear, who feared nothing but dishonour. The veterans of the Colonia militia, old men,' a bitter laugh escaped his throat as he realized it, 'not much older than I am now. Falco and his men were the true heroes of Colonia. They fought like lions until they were slain where they stood. They saved us.'

Tabitha reached out to take his hand, understanding the anguish the words were causing him and the bloody reality that lay behind them. Men like Didius's grandfather, worn down and finally overwhelmed by the merciless Iceni rebels, torn by swords or transfixed by spears. And at the centre of it all, surrounded by horror, her kind, caring husband. Now she understood the tortured cries that sometimes punctuated his sleep and the names that populated his noisy dreams. The names of long dead comrades. 'They held the Iceni until we, the supposed true soldiers, formed *testudo* and managed to reach the last refuge: the Temple of Claudius. For three days we held out in the heat and the stink, our tongues cleaved to our palates by thirst, before the door burned through and they came with fire and sword.'

'But you survived,' she repeated, but now there was awe in her voice, and the pain etched on his face made her want to weep.

'I survived,' he agreed. 'But I will speak of it no more.'

'I don't understand,' Tabitha said. 'If it causes you so much anguish, why return?'

He stared at her. 'Because unless a man can face the ghosts of his past he is not the man he hopes he is.'

They halted at a village Didius named as Durolitum where they watered the horses and the inhabitants emerged from their mud and wattle houses to gawp at the carriage. A woman approached Felix and offered bread and wine, but would take no payment for it. When he shared it with the escort later, Valerius, who had drunk the worst tavern piss known to man, thought his throat was on fire and had to drink a whole water skin before he could speak again. That night they crammed into the *mansio* outside the walls of the fort at Caesaromagus, the midway point between Colonia and Londinium.

In the room he shared with Tabitha and Lucius, Valerius struggled to find sleep, his mind spinning with memories and half-memories and images that couldn't be memories at all because he was viewing the events from inside another mind. He must have dozed off eventually because he opened his eyes to find Tabitha leaning over him in the gloom and the sound of movement outside the room.

'You had a poor night of it, my husband.' She smoothed a wisp of damp hair from his forehead.

'Just dreams. After this,' he held up the mottled purple stump of his right wrist, 'I had them every night for two years. It took a Judaean called Petrus to convince me that it wasn't self-pity that caused them but guilt at surviving when everyone else didn't. When I understood that, the dreams stopped.'

Tabitha reached over, picked up the clay bottle of oil that was never far from Valerius's bedside and poured a little on to her fingers. She took the stump in both hands and rubbed the oil gently into the puckered skin covering the bone of his wrist and then moved upwards along his arm. The sensuousness of her touch made something that might have been humiliating seem almost erotic. He smiled and she sat back and studied him without stopping the movement of her hands.

'It always surprises me that it doesn't hurt,' she said. 'You can see how the shock of the blow has travelled upwards, causing bruises on the skin, but ones which never go away.'

He handed her the oak fist on its stock of thrice-tanned leather and she slipped it over the wrist until it was firmly in place before knotting the leather thongs.

'I don't remember the pain so much as the sense of loss; the feeling of not being a whole man.' He shrugged. 'I was delirious for days after the temple fell.'

'So it didn't happen in the battle?'

Valerius shook his head. 'They said my hand was the price I must pay them for saving my life.'

'They?'

'It's a long story. For another day.'

She took him in her arms and laid her head on his shoulder.

'Can I go and see Didius?'

'We'll see to the horses first.' Valerius slipped out of bed as he answered Lucius, all but forgotten on a couch in the corner of the room. He pulled his tunic over his head as his son struggled into his clothes. 'I'll send Vacia with more water,' he told Tabitha.

When he pulled back the curtain the outer area of the *mansio* was already abuzz with activity. Some of the men had been able to cram three to each of the small rooms that opened off the main courtyard, but other members of the escort had been forced to sleep in the stables. Now they sat in their tunics in any space they could find, polishing mail and helmets and all the dozens of minor pieces of horse brass that were part of a cavalryman's equipment. Didius put down the strip of leather he'd been oiling and looked up with a smile.

'I'll take Lucius to feed the horses, lord.' He got to his feet and the boy ran to him. 'Remember, Lucius, not too much or they'll get too fat and you can't have a fat cavalry horse . . .'

'And not too little or they won't be able to carry a fat cavalryman in full armour.'

Valerius watched them go with a glow of pride. He saw Felix watching him. 'You're keeping them busy.' He gestured to the men around them as they rubbed until the iron shone, laughing as they worked and occasionally stopping for a drink of small beer from a leather mug, or to cram a bite of bread into their mouths.

'I don't need to keep them busy. All I did was remind them that Colonia is an old soldiers' town and some of the reception committee will be legionary veterans. They're determined to do themselves justice.' He grinned. 'And you, of course, legate.'

'And they don't mind that they'll have to do it all again when it gets covered in dust before we reach Colonia?'

'No, sir. They're soldiers; all they know is it beats digging ditches.'

Valerius saw Ceris sitting beside a pile of equipment polishing a bronze pendant from a piece of horse harness. 'Where's Florus, decurion?'

Felix pursed his lips and studied a point beyond Valerius's shoulder. 'Foraging, legate. He saw some apple trees by the road on the way here.'

Valerius had seen them too: the ordered rows of an orchard, the fruit just coming to ripeness. He sighed. 'He can't just help himself. Ceris?'

'Yes, lord?'

'Get Marius to give you enough money for two sacks of apples from the ration fund and find Florus before he ends up on the point of some farmer's pitchfork.'

'Yes, lord.' She dashed off to find the *duplicarius*.

'And tell him we'll be in the saddle before the hour's up!'

It was another of those soft, sunlit days that made Britannia a place worth fighting for: feathery white clouds drifting across a sky of eggshell blue, the dew clinging to spiders' webs in the hedgerows shining like minuscule gemstones, and the fields and forests a patchwork of so many greens it was difficult to tell where the one ended and the next began. Agricola had offered the use of a guide, but Valerius had travelled the road between Colonia and Londinium a dozen times, and where he threatened to go wrong Didius was always on hand to point them in the right direction. They stopped short of Colonia around midday to wash off the dust of the journey in a narrow stream. Valerius changed into his ceremonial toga in the carriage, with Tabitha fussing at him to ensure the legate's knot was perfectly tied. The escort fitted bright red horsehair plumes to their helmets and gave their equipment a last polish.

'Shabolz,' Valerius said. 'Take one man and ride to Colonia and give them warning of our coming. We'll wait here for your return.'

XXV

Colonia had learned its lesson even if Londinium had not. As he approached the city through the avenue of tombs on the western road the first thing Valerius noticed was the substantial defensive wall that surrounded the town. He'd seen higher – it was nothing to compare with Jerusalem or even Placentia – but it could only be scaled by long ladders or siege machines and no native assault would ever carry it. Lookout posts dotted the stone battlements every two hundred feet. Two more towers, circular and much more substantial, flanked the great double-arched gate at the head of the long street of suburban houses, shops and workshops which were much as Valerius remembered. The fact that the gate had survived intact astonished him: it had been as much a symbol of the old Colonia as the Temple of Claudius, and a similar focus for Boudicca's wrath. Away to his left, where the ground sloped towards the river, columns of smoke rose from blacksmiths' forges, iron furnaces and pottery kilns in a workers' settlement.

A welcoming party stood outside the gate and Valerius was thrust back in an instant to the day he'd brought his pathetic little band to reinforce Colonia's veterans. The city's leaders had been waiting for him in precisely the same position: Petronius, the long-nosed *quaestor*;

old Falco, commander of the militia; Agrippa the temple keeper; Numidius, the engineer who had built it; and Corvinus the goldsmith and militia armourer. The memory sent an involuntary shiver down his spine and he fought to control his emotions. They'd welcomed him with a fanfare of horns and drums that had died away slowly as they'd realized how few he'd brought. What could two hundred do against the tens of thousands marauding south towards them?

Slowly the small crowd became individuals and he automatically scanned their number seeking a familiar face, cursing himself for a fool as he did so because of course they were all dead. Claudius Gemellus, the official who'd been sent to escort him, whispered indistinct names in his ear as they approached so he could respond accordingly. Julius Liberalis, head of the *ordo*, someone Florentius, the *quaestor*, Terentius Cantaber, tribune commanding the Colonia militia, the High Priest, name unintelligible, but Roman of course. They would never dare give that financially onerous position to a native again. The names meant nothing and the faces blurred into each other. He had to blink before his vision returned. No native chieftains, as there once would have been; Suetonius Paulinus's great purge had seen to that. It was only now he noticed the walls were lined with people, curious families come to take the measure of the fleeting visitor who held the power of life and death over them.

An honour guard of militia had formed up on either side of the road. Much better equipped than in Falco's day, but the same grizzled, alert features and determined expressions. Their armour and weapons glittered like bullion in the sunshine and he saw that it wasn't just his escort who wanted to prove a point today. He met them eye to eye and the veterans returned his look in a certain way – something beyond respect – and he realized they *knew*. Gemellus might be unaware of his visitor's pedigree, he couldn't see beyond the legate's sash, but these men were aware of his history.

Valerius dismounted and handed his reins to Cornelius Felix. Liberalis and Florentius stepped out to meet him, with Cantaber, in militia uniform, and the High Priest a little behind. Liberalis, of medium height and running to fat, had the air of a successful merchant, but Valerius knew that, like many of these men, he would be a former legionary.

With the sparse strands of his pale gold hair flickering in the breeze, the head of the *ordo* pulled a scroll from his sleeve and began to read in a hurried, monotonous drone.

'The people of Colonia Claudia Victricensis welcome the distinguished *legatus iuridicus* Gaius Valerius Verrens, Hero of Rome and bearer of the Corona Aurea, holder of senatorial honours and direct representative of Titus Caesar Flavius Vespasianus Augustus . . .'

A long oration followed in which Liberalis imparted his detailed and firmly held views on the role of justice in a fledgling community surrounded by potential enemies, the history of Colonia's mercantile classes since what he termed 'the revival', and, with a hopeful mention of Valerius's close connection to the governor, the iniquitous benefits awarded to that nest of thieves and rogues on the Tamesa (a hint only, not a direct accusation), and the need for a fairer spread of subsidies to allow Colonia to resume its rightful position as Britannia's pre-eminent trading port, as befitted the home of the cult of Divine Claudius. Oh, and the transfer of one of the bureaucratic arms of government from Londinium would help too.

Valerius maintained a fixed smile as Liberalis murmured on. He allowed his attention to wander as the horses fidgeted and shook their manes, rattling their metal harness decorations and pawing at the ground. An unlikely pause and he realized his host had ended his peroration and was studying him with a look of hopeful enquiry.

Valerius thanked him for his kind words in equally courteous terms, and made a speech of his own as memorable for its brevity as its content. He pledged to bring the *ordo*'s concerns to the ear of those who needed to hear them – nods of approval all round – and ended by complimenting Liberalis on the improvements made to Colonia since his last visit, a sentiment met with blank looks apart from the militia officer who responded with a grave nod of the head.

Liberalis introduced him to the procurator, a man as dull and humourless as the tax returns he spent his day sorting. The High Priest was less arrogant than most of his kind and greeted Valerius civilly. Terentius Cantaber, the militia commander, didn't hide his delight at being introduced.

'I remember you well from the battle when we finished them for good and all, sir,' he said softly. 'Everyone was talking about the only man to survive the defence of Colonia. I was a centurion then and you were younger and a lot paler, if I may say so, after what you'd been through. You were on the general's staff just behind the Fourteenth and I must have walked within three feet of you bringing the reserves forward. It's good to see you again.'

'And you, tribune.' Valerius smiled. 'It seems a long time ago now and, as I remember, it wasn't quite the finish.'

'No, sir, you have the right of it. But it was the last of the proper soldiering. The rest, and let's not be coy about it, was just butchery.'

Proper soldiering? Perhaps the first quarter of that long day when they held the line, but butchery described the rest well enough. Valerius hadn't taken part in the fighting, but he'd witnessed Boudicca's last battle. Legionaries with sword arms bloody up to their armpits and so exhausted or sickened by the killing that their officers had to beat them into continuing, while their defeated victims waited like sheep for slaughter. So many that he guessed their weathered bones still lay where they died. All but one.

A face flashed into his head, startlingly clear for the first time in almost two decades. Maeve, the Trinovante girl he had loved and lost. He had wanted to show Maeve the glory of Rome, but all he'd done was drive her into the arms of Boudicca, another disaffected Briton who had lost everything. Astonishingly, he'd found her among the countless dead, her long chestnut hair fluttering like a fallen banner beneath an overturned cart. With the help of two legionaries he'd buried her beneath an oak tree.

'What?'

'I asked if you would honour us with your presence at the banquet tomorrow, legate. The court will not convene until the day after at the earliest. We hold it every year to honour the men who fell in defence of Colonia. Attendance has fallen over the last couple of years, but when they heard you would be visiting the city every man wanted to be there. We had to draw lots to decide.'

Valerius was ready to decline. The last thing he needed was to spend time with a hundred drunk, maudlin former soldiers reminiscing about the glories of the long years in uniform that had actually been purgatory at the time. But the words that emerged were: 'I'd be very pleased to, tribune.'

Why? Valerius had learned long since not to go on a mission or plan an attack without the best possible intelligence of the potential difficulties ahead. He had the bare, bureaucratic bones of the two most complex cases he would preside over in Colonia's *basilica*, but little sense of the undercurrents that had brought them about, or the personalities involved. Here was an opportunity to gently probe men at the very heart of the community and gain an insight untainted by favouritism, flattery or bias.

A moment of comedy worthy of Plautus. Tabitha's coach proved too wide to fit through the double-arched gate. Consternation on every hand until Valerius returned to help his wife from the carriage. Liberalis was full of apology; she should be carried to the east gate which was much wider. But Tabitha silenced him with a smile. 'I will happily walk, sir, the better to see the wonders of your beautiful city. They say the Temple of Claudius is the finest building in Britannia.'

Liberalis fairly glowed with pride at the compliment, but his place at Tabitha's side was instantly usurped by the High Priest who pushed through to take step beside her. 'It may also interest you, lady, to know it is the first public building constructed by Rome on this island. On the black day when the Iceni witch brought her rebels to our gates it provided a last refuge for the brave defenders of Colonia.'

'And did it prove a sanctuary for them?' Tabitha turned her head so she could see Valerius's reaction.

'Alas, no. In the end the doors gave way and the barbarians entered with fire and sword. There is a story of a single survivor, a child, but it is only that; a story. Most likely all died.'

Valerius saw his wife's look and shrugged. Those who knew the truth of it were long gone. Old soldiers, like Cantaber, who had served with Suetonius Paulinus would be aware the governor had honoured him as the last of Colonia's defenders, but not the details.

Inside the gates, a much more ordered Colonia than he remembered. The city had been the direct descendant of the original fortress built to guard the river crossing below, with barrack blocks converted into homes and shops and the *principia* and its environs acting as *basilica* and *forum*. All turned to ashes by Boudicca's horde. Now the streets formed a uniform grid pattern and the buildings that lined the *decumanus maximus* were three and four storeys high with shops on the ground floor. The fruits of every trade seemed to be represented, from simple woven cloth to the finest worked gold, and no city of this size would be complete without the pisspot stink of the tannery and the dyeworks, or the bars whose customers helped provide the liquid so central to their craft.

At the first intersection, Valerius noticed that beyond the main street weed-infested gaps remained in the neat rows of buildings. He guessed they were remnants of Boudicca's ravages. Even a generation on the ownership of townhouses and gardens would continue to be disputed amongst relatives, and if the records had burned with the rest of the town the provenance of some sites would be entirely unknown.

His step faltered as he had his first sight of a massive red-tiled roof that towered above the others to his left front. What had he expected? The temple had still stood, ravaged and fire-blackened, but as solid as ever, when he'd left Colonia for the last time, his vision blurred by Celtic potions, tears and pain. Boudicca would have ordered it torn down stone by stone, but the far greater loot of Londinium beckoned. No doubt whoever she'd left with the task had been lured by the scent of gold rather than staying and completing the thankless task of demolishing the temple. Now it appeared, a magnificent confection of shimmering white and ochre, the huge fluted columns exactly as

Valerius remembered them and the great bronze door with its image of Sol Invictus polished to a golden sheen. A life-sized bronze statue of Claudius had stood at the top of the temple steps. The one that replaced it was double the size.

Tabitha moved closer to Valerius's left side. He felt her hand touch his and realized that she'd sensed some of his apprehension. As they came closer he saw that the run-down buildings of the temple complex which had served as a bulwark against Boudicca's forces had been replaced by an elegant roofed walkway. Opposite the entrance a field that had once held vegetable gardens was now occupied by the city's *basilica* and *forum*. From between the *basilica* pillars several men dressed in togas watched the little procession approach.

How did a man's defensive instincts work? Valerius would swear his old friend Serpentius could sense the position of his enemy even if he couldn't see him. Valerius felt something similar now. The polite inspection from the temple steps wasn't the only interest. At least one pair of eyes had a much more limited focus. They were intent only on one man.

'Are you all right, Valerius?' Tabitha whispered.

He used the question to casually look around, as if he was studying the *basilica* architecture. The usual mix of lawyers between cases, moneylenders and beggars. A few men seeking work and one or two women who could have been courtesans looking for trade, but he might be doing them an injustice. No one appeared to be overtly studying him.

But whoever he was he had a feeling someone was taking an unhealthy interest in Gaius Valerius Verrens.

XXVI

After the welcoming ceremonies, Claudius Gemellus led Valerius and Tabitha to a handsome townhouse in the centre of Colonia, close to where the original *principia* of the fortress had stood. It belonged to Liberalis, the head of the *ordo*, who had moved out with his family to an estate he owned on the slope on the far side of the river. From Gemellus's description Valerius guessed the land had once been the property of Lucullus, a long dead Trinovante prince who had befriended him. Lucullus was also the father of Maeve, the Celtic girl he'd loved. Memories everywhere he turned.

'I am honoured,' he told Gemellus. 'Please pass on my thanks to the *duoviri*.' He turned to Felix, who accompanied them. 'What arrangements have been made for my escort?'

'The militia have a hall close by that they use for storing equipment and for exercises during the winter,' Gemellus said. 'Cantaber has had it cleared and procured sufficient cots. The amenities are basic, but . . .'

'We're soldiers, sir,' Felix assured him. 'Anywhere with a roof and four walls is a luxury to us.'

'While we're in Colonia we only need ten men on duty at any one time,' Valerius told the escort commander. 'With a guard of four on this house through the night and five to act as lictors on the morning of each court session.'

'Of course, sir.' The decurion saluted. 'I will arrange it.'

'And,' Valerius had a sudden thought, 'I'll need Hilario with me in court.' He saw Felix's look of surprise. The surly trooper was the last person he would have chosen as a legal aide. 'I'll explain his duties tomorrow.'

Tabitha waited till they were alone. 'Why Hilario?' she asked.

'You'll find out tomorrow, just like everyone else.' Valerius grinned.

She gave him a sideways look but didn't press further. 'What will you do now?'

'I'd like to have shown you the city, but I need to talk to the local clerks about the cases I'll be overseeing.' He shrugged off his ceremonial toga and a servant handed him a lighter version, more suitable for working in. Tabitha helped him arrange the folds and tie the legate's sash. 'Hopefully it won't take too long.'

A blur of movement erupted through the curtained doorway, skidded to a halt and bowed from the waist. Tabitha frowned. 'Lucius, what have I told you about entering a room with decorum? What if your father and I had been entertaining guests?'

'I apologize, Mother.' Lucius dropped his head for a respectful second, only to raise it again with eyes blazing with excitement. 'Didius took me to the market by the river. They had a pair of hunting dogs taller at the shoulder than Khamsin.'

'Pfft.' Tabitha blew out her cheeks. 'And now you're exaggerating.'

'No, Mother,' the boy pleaded.

'It's true,' Valerius assured her, ruffling his son's hair. 'The deer hounds of Britannia are famous for their size, strength and stamina.'

'Then you will take me to see them later.'

Valerius walked to the *basilica* surrounded by six of his escort, led by Shabolz. It was a busy hour on the *decumanus maximus* with carts unloading supplies to the shops and bars, and custom aplenty from the farmers and estate owners and their families who'd streamed into the city to see justice done at the courts. As the Emperor's direct representative

Valerius carried the authority to impose a sentence of death, and at least one of the cases he would oversee had the potential to produce an execution. Word had somehow spread that the *legatus iuridicus* was just the type of strict disciplinarian to exercise that authority. No one wanted to miss the sight of blood being spilled.

Many people turned to watch as the little procession of armoured men passed, but once more Valerius had the feeling of being the focus of a singular and very specific pair of eyes. Shabolz must have sensed it too, because at a whispered order the escort moved closer and Valerius saw knuckles whiten as fingers tightened on sword hilts. He swept the street for the cause, but only a faint shadow in the mouth of an alley caused him any kind of unease and it vanished before he could alert Shabolz.

Gemellus awaited him outside the *basilica* and led him through the columned entrance and down three steps into the great pillared hall. It was here Valerius would hear cases deemed too sensitive or important for the local magistrates.

'We will set up your chair next to the altar.' Gemellus pointed to a raised dais where a statue of Jupiter stood beside a carved stone platform. A row of desks had been arranged to one side. 'The court clerks,' Gemellus confirmed. 'With any pertinent evidence ready to hand. The complainants will be to your right front and the defendants on the left. The *ordo*, obviously, in a roped area and beyond them, behind a guard of local militia, the citizenry. Is there anything else you wish to know?'

'How many cases will I be hearing?'

'Four.' He sounded apologetic. 'There were originally only three, but a rather nasty and potentially inflammatory case came up after we petitioned the governor to convene a court here. The clerks will give you the details.'

A stairway led from an annexe to an upper floor and a well-lit office where four clerks sat at desks studying or copying documents. The men rose to their feet and bowed as Valerius entered, but he waved them back to their desks. Beside each lay a wooden chest part filled

213

with scrolls and leather scroll cases. The chief clerk, a thin, balding man with stooped shoulders and ink-stained fingers, explained that the chests contained witness statements, evidence and the detailed claims and counterclaims of each side in a case.

'But,' he held up a piece of parchment, 'we have prepared a condensed summary of each case to give you an outline of the charges and the arguments.'

'I'm grateful,' Valerius said with some feeling; it would have taken him weeks to read all the documents. 'May I see them?'

'Of course, lord.'

He went to a spare desk and sat down. The clerk brought him four sheets of parchment and placed them before him. He studied them one by one. The ruler of a sub-tribe of the Trinovante complained that a group of veterans had seized one of his estates and divided it up amongst themselves. The argument had been going on for some years and the case stood or fell on whether he could prove his claim that he'd supported Suetonius Paulinus during the Boudiccan rising. Agricola had given Valerius some of the background, along with the instruction that he wanted it decided once and for all. Next, an inheritance case that would be of little interest except that one of the parties had Imperial favour. A veteran accused of murdering his Trinovante neighbour in a dispute over water rights. This was the capital crime on the list. The late entry Gemellus had mentioned was actually a pre-trial hearing. A farmer claimed his neighbour's son had kidnapped or murdered his wife. The case was complicated by the fact that there was no body, and, on first viewing, little evidence.

'Have you decided the order of the cases?' Valerius asked.

'No, lord,' the clerk said. 'We thought you'd wish to decide yourself.'

Valerius nodded thoughtfully. 'I'll let you know tomorrow.'

He ordered two of the chests to be carried to the house and spent the next morning reading through the documents. At the sixth hour the *atriensis* announced the arrival of a young boy sent to guide Valerius to the militia meeting hall.

'Find him something to eat while I change,' he ordered.

The meeting hall was in a narrow street by the river behind the temple complex. Terentius Cantaber was waiting by the doorway, dressed in a formal toga and with a look of anticipation on his ruddy features. After the formal greetings he led Valerius inside and along a narrow corridor. A brightly coloured painting filled one wall and Valerius had a moment of recognition. He'd seen it before on a similar occasion years earlier, when he'd been introduced to Colonia's *ordo* in an annexe of the temple complex. Divine Claudius accepting the surrender of ten British kings and one queen. The artist portrayed the Emperor as a tall, imposing man, standing on a gilded dais surrounded by his generals as the British rulers knelt before him. Valerius had a feeling something was different about this mural, but he couldn't quite place what it was. He was still pondering the thought as they passed through a second door to be hit with a wall of sound. There must have been a hundred men seated at rough trestle tables, and as Valerius entered every one hammered at the boards with his pewter cup, setting up a clatter that was an assault on the ears. Cantaber paused to allow Valerius to take in the scene and the one-handed Roman found him self grinning at the red-faced mass of veterans. Here too the walls were painted, but these murals depicted a defeat, not a victory. Yet there was a glory in them that sent a shiver down Valerius's spine. In one that filled the entire far wall, three sparse lines of soldiers in legionary gear stood in a grassy meadow confronted by thousands of Celtic warriors, with more swarming across the river in front of them from a great mass on the slope beyond. The accuracy of the depiction impressed Valerius, for not a man who witnessed it had survived – bar one. A few omissions. There were none of the fearsome war dogs or the chariots he remembered roving among the great horde. No flame-haired Boudicca with her malevolent presence driving her warriors forward. And, more surprisingly, no great mounds of writhing bodies on the bridge. By the time the rebels had crossed the river in force they had had to negotiate the dead and dying of a dozen previous assaults, spitted by the weighted javelins of the militia cohorts.

'Legate?'

As the noise died away Valerius followed Cantaber to a table on a raised platform and the militia commander introduced him to his centurions before they sat down. Murmured conversation continued as the plates came and went carried by a stream of slaves. A simple *gustus* of fresh oysters accompanied by chopped lettuce, onion and beans. Roast chicken and vegetables for the main course and a *secunda* of preserved fruits. Wine, of course, in copious quantities, but Valerius sipped with abstemious restraint. As they ate Cantaber spoke of the changes he'd witnessed in Colonia since retiring ten years earlier to a farm south of the city. Fewer than half the number of ships now docked at the harbour downstream from the bridge. Bars that had depended on the sailors closed. Merchants were struggling to survive and threatening to move to Londinium.

'The roads we built as legionaries are now the ropes that strangle us.' He produced a bitter laugh. 'From the port at Londinium you can have a cart load of *amphorae* in Venonis in just over ten days. From Colonia it takes eighteen. I doubt we would be little more than a market town were it not for the temple. They still come in their hundreds to sacrifice to the god and everyone must have somewhere to sleep and something to eat. It is the one thing Londinium cannot take away from us.'

The conversations around them grew louder with each cup of wine and when the last dish was cleared the militia tribune rose to his feet and called for silence. Valerius stifled a wry smile. Plainly, this was when he paid for his victuals.

Cantaber introduced Valerius by his various titles and continued: 'We are fortunate to have a guest who knew Colonia as it once was. A man who fought shoulder to shoulder with our predecessors. What we know only as myth or legend or fireside tale, Gaius Valerius Verrens lived through. Sir, if it is not too much to ask, perhaps you might tell us of your part in the defence of Colonia?'

A great cry of 'Yes' went up from the veterans at the tables and the cups hammered on wood once more, only to fade away as Valerius rose to his feet and shook his head.

'No, Terentius,' he said, to groans of disappointment. 'I will not speak of my part in Colonia's defence. The true Heroes of Rome sit not at this table, but,' he threw out an arm in a gesture Cicero would have been proud of, 'are immortalized here on your walls. Marcus Quintus Falco led them and they died where they stood. I owe them my life.' He told them how the men of the Colonia militia lay in the darkness and watched the firefly sparks of distant fires grow ever closer. The way the dawn broke to show not an army as the Romans knew it, but an entire people on the move. 'We gave them the bridge,' he continued, and a murmur went up as they imagined the sky above the narrow crossing filled with *pila* and the butcher's block sound of the points striking home into flesh. They groaned as the Iceni champions inexorably began to swamp the defences, could almost feel the flanks of the militia lines bending back with the strain. Not a man present had not heard another soldier's death cry. Not a man who didn't know the gut-wrenching terror of the battle line.

'And when all hope was lost with barely a man unwounded,' Valerius continued, 'I ordered the retreat. Falco turned to me. He said: "I fear that is an order I must disobey, tribune. We old men have walked as far as we intend to this day. We will stay where we stand and buy you what time we can." It was the hardest decision of my life to give the order,' he had to swallow to save from choking, 'but to have done anything else would have been to squander their sacrifice. The survivors of the Londinium contingent formed *testudo* and retreated to the Temple of Claudius.'

They waited expectantly for more, but Valerius did not care to remember the events of the next three days. They had all heard the stories: how the defenders had held the complex walls until they were overwhelmed; how the last survivors had retreated into the temple building and barred themselves inside; and what their comrades in the Fourteenth had discovered when they retook the ruins of Colonia.

A long sniff from the back of the hall broke the silence and they began banging their cups in appreciation. Valerius stood for a moment and allowed his gaze to drift over the stern, approving features until eventually the banging died away and he could bow his thanks before taking his place beside Cantaber. The militia tribune nodded gravely and handed him a cup of wine.

'My thanks, legate. Most inspiring for us to hear of the sacrifices of our predecessors from one who witnessed them. I doubt we'll have many absentees from our training sessions for the next few months.'

'I'm pleased if I've done some good, Terentius,' Valerius replied quietly. 'Tell me, do you know of a veteran called Sextus Marcellus?'

Cantaber went very still. Clearly the question was unexpected. 'Yes,' he said at last. 'He is in the third century, Second cohort. Not one of our most enthusiastic militiamen. He currently has some personal problems.'

'So I understand.' Valerius held his gaze. 'Tell me what you know of him.'

When he returned to the townhouse, Valerius was surprised to find a smiling toga-clad figure waiting for him in the vestibule under the watchful eye of Marius and Didius.

'He says he wishes to talk to you on a private matter, lord,' Marius said, his grizzled features wrinkled with distaste. 'The lady agreed he could wait here until your return.'

'Larcius Dexter, lord, member of the *ordo* and friend to Roman justice, at your service.' The visitor introduced himself with an oily flattery that made Valerius immediately dislike him. The narrow pointed nose and simpering, buck-toothed smile reminded him of a self-satisfied rat.

'Take him through to the library,' he ordered. He bowed. 'I will join you in a moment, sir, but you must excuse me. I have to change my clothes.'

Valerius walked through to the *tablinum*, where Tabitha sat by a window reading a book borrowed from Liberalis's collection. She rose and kissed him on the lips with a smile, then stepped back to look into his face. 'You seem troubled, husband. Is it the man waiting outside?' She sighed. 'I would have sent him away, but he claimed it was important.'

218

'No, you did right,' Valerius assured her. 'I have a feeling I know why he's here. Best to deal with it now. Have a jug of wine sent through – we must observe the proprieties.'

By the time he'd changed and walked through to the library the wine had been placed on a table. Larcius Dexter stood nearby, studying the shelves. 'Old Liberalis does himself well,' he sniffed. 'All a bit clever for me. Personally I prefer a bit of Horace.'

Valerius poured him a cup of wine and then one for himself. 'So, Larcius Dexter, friend to Roman justice, what brings you to see Gaius Valerius Verrens, *legatus iuridicus,* on the eve of the courts?'

Dexter's smile froze at Valerius's directness and the use of the full title. Clearly he was accustomed to more in the way of preamble to his business discussions. He hesitated, considering the other man, taking in the scars of old wounds and the missing right hand.

'I wished to honour you with my own personal welcome.' He put down his cup and his hand reached into the sleeve of his toga. Valerius tensed and stepped a little closer to make any attack more awkward, but relaxed as the hand emerged holding a leather pouch. A substantial and patently weighty leather pouch. Dexter placed it on the table between them with an audible chink. 'I discussed it with a friend and we thought you might well wish to make a sacrifice at the temple. This small donation would go towards the purchase of a white lamb for the purpose.'

Valerius considered the purse for a moment before he reached down to pick it up. Weighty indeed. As Dexter watched he returned it to the table and held it down with his wooden fist while he worked at the ties with the fingers of his left hand. When he opened the leather mouth he could see the buttery glint of gold inside. Enough golden *aurei* to buy a whole flock of lambs.

'You and your *friend* are very generous.'

Dexter bowed his head in acknowledgement.

'Perhaps I should know his identity,' Valerius persisted.

The other man smiled. 'His name would mean nothing to you, but should you meet him while you are in Colonia you would know him by this ring.' He held out his hand so Valerius had a clear view of a thick gold band with a massive ruby at its centre. 'He also commends to you his cousin by marriage, Titus Flavius Clemens.'

Valerius choked on a laugh and managed to turn it into a cough. Did they really think he could be swayed by a powerful name and a few gold coins? He nodded slowly.

'I thank you for your gift and your welcome.' Valerius ushered Dexter towards the door. 'You may tell your friend that I will take this into consideration should we meet over the next few days.'

'He will be pleased to hear it.' Dexter gave him what he obviously thought was a conspiratorial smile.

When Valerius was alone, Tabitha appeared from behind the curtained doorway to the *tablinum*. 'They are not very sophisticated in Britannia.' She shook her head with a smile. 'We conducted things much more subtly in Emesa.'

'Oh, you can guarantee there'll be a trail of witnesses that will place the money here, just in case I'm thinking of changing my mind.'

'Titus Flavius Clemens?'

'Vespasian's nephew. A very powerful young man these days. He was with Sabinus when the temple burned down on the Capitoline. If I remember correctly I persuaded Vitellius not to have him executed, though it might have been his brother.'

'And what will you do about this?' She pointed to the purse.

'I have an idea.' He grinned, despite the anger that boiled inside him. 'But first have Felix buy a plump white lamb and tell him we'll be parading to the *basilica* from the temple tomorrow at the third hour.'

XXVII

Hilario led the procession carrying the *fasces*, the bundled birch rods which symbolized Valerius's right to dispense justice. A gleaming axe at their centre showed that he wielded the power of *imperium*, directly granted by the Emperor, which included the licence to sentence a man to death. His status as a legate entitled him to five lictors. The others, Shabolz and three of his Pannonians, flanked the one-handed Roman and Tabitha, her face and hair hidden by the folds of her *palla*. Behind them marched the clerks who would assist him in the court, followed by the hundred members of the *ordo* ranked in pairs.

The scent of roasting meat perfumed the morning air. Valerius's sacrifice had been pronounced a success and the day unusually auspicious. As they approached the *basilica* he had a vivid memory of looking down from the temple steps and seeing Larcius Dexter *wink* at him.

'I wish you'd tell me what you have planned,' Tabitha whispered. 'Sometimes, husband, you can be very impulsive.'

He reached down and squeezed her hand. A century of militia veterans lined the route to the courts, keeping the hundreds hoping to attend the proceedings at a safe distance. Accusers and defendants in the four cases stood in separate groups on the *basilica* steps. They broke off from eyeing each other with wary suspicion to stare at the man who would decide their fates. What they saw matched their expectations of the legal might of Rome. Stern, scarred features and close-cropped, iron-grey hair. A man who walked with the confidence of worldly experience and carried the wounds of his military years without embarrassment. A few looked upon the narrowed, pitiless eyes and felt a shiver, but one man whispered reassurance to his companions.

Inside, Valerius escorted Tabitha to her seat, set to the right hand of the dais, before taking his own. Hilario handed the *fasces* to Shabolz and extracted the long-handled axe. He looked to Valerius, who answered with a nod. Hilario stepped on to the dais to stand at the right hand of the *legatus iuridicus* with the axe held easily across his massive chest, brutish features set in a grim scowl. Valerius heard a murmur of unease as the members of the *ordo* filed into their places on four rows of benches. No man in this court would be under any illusion about who was in charge or the extent of his powers. They looked upon Hilario and saw the legate's executioner.

The clerks stood beside their desks as the defendants and accusers and their representatives took their positions at opposite sides of the hall. Their witnesses would be kept out of earshot until called to give evidence. When the participants were in place one of the clerks signalled to a militiaman guarding the door and a wave of citizens from Colonia and the surrounding farmlands surged in to jostle for the best positions behind the *ordo*. When they were more or less settled the clerk approached the dais and whispered to Valerius that they were ready.

'Have you decided the order of the cases, lord?'

Valerius nodded grimly. 'I had thought to take the Marcellus trial first, but circumstances have changed. We will decide the Prince Claudius land dispute.'

He saw the clerk's look of surprise. This was the case that had been going on for years and was undoubtedly the most complex. It could take days.

'Very well,' the clerk said after a moment. 'On the Marcellus affair

222

I must tell you that the defendant's counsel has asked to make an application.'

'Does he say what it is?'

'I believe he seeks a postponement, lord.'

Valerius nodded. It was a usual tactic in such serious cases. The client's lawyer trying to keep him at liberty until he could come before a lesser court or a local judge who might prove more sympathetic. 'Very well, have him approach.' The clerk went off and returned with a tall thin man who walked with a curious high-stepping lope that reminded Valerius of a stalking heron. He was quickly joined by the prosecutor.

'I'm told you have an application to make,' Valerius prompted.

The thin man bowed. 'I regret to inform my lord that I require more time to prepare my client. Potential new evidence. Change of circumstances of certain witnesses . . .'

The prosecutor grunted and took a deep breath, but Valerius raised a hand before he could speak. 'This – incident – occurred six months ago. According to the court papers, the *denuntiatio* was served two months ago. If you haven't been able to prepare your client by now I doubt you ever will. The application is dismissed.'

The lawyer made a choking noise, drowned out by the prosecutor's triumphant 'harrumph', and both men retreated to their places. Valerius rose to his feet and announced to the packed hall: 'We will now take the case of Prince Claudius Tasciovanus against Priscus, Severus, Victor and Silenus, and the countercharge of fraud by the aforementioned against the prince.'

A murmur ran through the crowd and the clerk called for silence. As he sat down Valerius noticed a hooded figure in ragged clothing slip in at the back of the court. The man was checked by a militia-man, who pulled back the cowl but then retreated and allowed the latecomer into the body of the court. Valerius wasn't certain why the incident registered, but he had little time to dwell on it. Four prosperous-looking men stepped forward to stand to his left and a single silver-haired elder in an ill-fitting toga approached from his right. Of those on the left, three had the weary, troubled faces of men uncertain of the outcome. The fourth wore a garish ruby ring on the middle finger of his right hand and a look of smug self-confidence. In contrast, Claudius Tasciovanus stood straight-backed, long moustaches drooping below his lips and head held high, radiating a natural, unforced dignity that stirred a distant memory in Valerius's breast.

The clerk read out the details of the case. Before the Boudiccan rebellion, Claudius Tasciovanus, a prince of the Trinovante tribe, had owned a substantial estate north of Colonia. In the chaotic aftermath of the insurrection the lands had been confiscated and parcelled out between the four defendants. Claudius claimed he had fought on the Roman side and had been assured his estate was safe, and he wanted the lands returned, with suitable compensation for seventeen years of lost revenues. The four farmers accused Tasciovanus of fabricating evidence, which, if proven, would merit a ruinous fine. Previous courts had failed to reach a conclusion and simply deferred the case time after time.

As the opposing lawyers laid out their cases Valerius studied one of the four almost identical documents lodged on the part of the Romans. In it, Priscus, Severus and Victor, former centurions of the Twentieth legion, ceded a twenty-five *iugera* portion of land, identified by its various boundary marks, to their old comrade Silenus, in perpetuity, and asked Colonia's registrar to record the transaction in the land register. It concluded: 'The public treasury in no way suffers detriment or loss. It is for the information and protection of Your Honour and of the treasury that we have directed to you this communication which, duly signed, is to be valid and binding.'

On the face of it, a perfectly proper and legal land transfer – if the signatories owned the land in the first place. It was replicated by three others in which only the beneficiaries and the land boundaries differed.

Valerius looked up and found himself the focus of Tasciovanus's emotionless grey eyes. What was the Briton thinking? This must be the fourth or fifth time he'd suffered this ordeal. A rich man, he had other estates; why not just give up a fight so obviously weighted against him?

The answer, of course, was pride. The Celts Valerius remembered had all been proud regardless of status or class. Men who reacted to a slight by drawing a sword and could hold a grudge for generations. Some ancestor had fought to win this land. His father would have held it, and his father before him. It would be a personal humiliation to lose it.

Tasciovanus's counsel came to the end of his outline. 'As my first witness I would call upon . . .'

Valerius raised a hand and the lawyer's voice drifted into silence.

'I have studied transcripts of the evidence and cross-examination from previous appearances of this case before the courts and I see no profit in going over it all again.' He saw the lawyers' look of consternation mirrored on the face of Priscus and his co-defendants. 'Certain facts are not in dispute. The land in question was once under the ownership of Prince Claudius Tasciovanus. The transfer of the lands to the defendants in the aftermath of the rebellion is recorded in proper legal fashion. As I see it the only salient point at issue here is the claim that Princc Claudius supported the Imperial forces against Boudicca and that therefore his lands should have been protected. I'm told a letter exists?' he asked Tasciovanus's counsel.

'Yes, lord.'

'Then why isn't it with the rest of the evidence?' Valerius demanded. 'Why haven't I seen it?'

'The defendants dispute the authenticity of this letter, lord,' Priscus's lawyer interrupted.

'So I understand,' Valerius said. 'Well?'

'It is my client's only proof of his service to the then governor. He has vowed never to let it out of his sight.'

Valerius turned to the Trinovante. 'May I see it, sir?'

Tasciovanus hesitated for a heartbeat before approaching the dais and pulling a leather scroll case from the sleeve of his toga.

'Open it, please.' As the prince worked at the straps Valerius continued: 'It is the defendants' contention that this letter is a fabrication,' he said. 'And should that be the case they seek to have Prince Claudius Tasciovanus prosecuted for misleading the court. Previous courts decided that the letter could not be properly verified because no one could be found who could confirm or refute the signature.' This wasn't exactly true. One man had been perfectly capable of validating the letter, but he was travelling westwards to join his generals for the assault on the Ordovices. It was now clear to Valerius that Julius Agricola had not cared to risk his career by getting involved in such a contentious case. Prince Tasciovanus had power and influence among the tribal chiefs of southern Britannia; finding against him would be seen as a slight against every Celt south of Eboracum. Priscus, on the other hand, had connections that reached to the heart of the Palatium who could cause trouble even for a man like the governor. No wonder Agricola wanted to keep his hands clean.

Finally, Tasciovanus removed the scroll from the case. His hands trembled as he set the yellowing piece of parchment in Valerius's palm. Valerius placed the scroll on his knee and held it down with his right fist so he could unroll it.

'Suetonius Paulinus,' he read in a voice loud enough to echo through the great chamber, 'governor of the Province of Britannia, thanks Prince Claudius Tasciovanus for his gallant service in support of the forces of the State against treasonous native elements bent on subverting the rule of law in the province. This letter exempts the lands, property, goods and slaves of the said Prince Claudius Tasciovanus from any general punishment imposed in the future against the native population for the treasonable actions outlined above.' He paused to allow the import of his words to register. 'It is signed Gaius Suetonius Paulinus, governor.'

'An obvious fake,' Priscus barked, ignoring his counsel's signal to be quiet.

'What makes you say that?'

'It has no seal. Any document from the governor would carry his seal.'

Valerius nodded as if he was considering the suggestion. He could feel Tabitha's eyes on him and knew she would be wondering how this was going to end. 'Any official document,' he agreed. 'But this could be construed as a personal letter.'

Priscus spluttered dangerously, and his lawyer hastily intervened. 'But it is impossible to verify the signature,' he pointed out.

'Perhaps,' Valerius agreed. 'Let us find out.' He raised his voice. 'Is anyone in this room in a position to verify or otherwise the signature of the former governor Suetonius Paulinus?' A murmur went through the crowd and a few of the *ordo* looked to each other and shook their heads. Valerius waited long enough for someone to come forward, allowing the tension to build. 'Then it is fortunate,' he continued at last, 'that I spent nine months serving as aide to the governor Gaius Suetonius Paulinus . . . and this signature,' he had recognized the almost savage sweep of the pen in an instant, 'is genuine.' A collective gasp from the audience and an outraged shout of 'No' from Priscus. 'Accordingly, by the power of *imperium* granted me by the Emperor, I hereby order that all the lands identified in the court documents should be returned immediately to Prince Claudius Tasciovanus, and recorded in the land register as his property. Any question of compensation should take into consideration improvements carried out to the land by the defendants.'

Priscus's fleshy features were crimson with fury. He looked wildly to where Dexter stood among the *ordo*, his face white as weathered bone.

'In addition,' Valerius continued relentlessly, 'I fine the defendants fifty *aurei* for the spurious accusation of fraud against the claimant.' He pulled a leather bag from the voluminous sleeve of his toga and placed it at his feet. 'Fortuitously this sum has already been lodged with the court.'

Tabitha was struggling to keep a straight face. Priscus looked as if he was ready to rush the dais, but Hilario took a threatening step forward and the farmer hesitated long enough for Shabolz and the lictors to surround the defendants and usher them away. Prince Claudius Tasciovanus's lawyer whispered that his client begged leave to approach the dais.

Valerius nodded and Tasciovanus stepped forward. 'You have my thanks, lord.'

'I only did what justice required. Once I established that the letter was genuine your case was not in doubt.'

Tasciovanus looked back to where Priscus was being pushed out of the doorway. 'Others might have been less certain,' he glanced at the leather bag, 'especially given the proper incentives. You have restored my faith, and that of my people, in Roman justice. If there is ever any service I can do yourself or the governor, please do not hesitate to ask.'

Valerius thanked him for his courtesy, but he was pleased when he saw Tasciovanus leaving the court. If the Trinovante stayed he had a feeling his faith in Roman justice might be sorely tested.

'Call the case of the State against Sextus Marcellus.'

XXVIII

A hater, Terentius Cantaber had said. One of the legion's finest soldiers. A man to have at your side in any battle line, but one to respect rather than like, Marcellus subscribed to the view, popular among certain legionary circles, that any native who raised a hand against Rome should be regarded as vermin. 'Fearless and pitiless,' Cantaber said. 'Working the land would mellow some men, but not Marcellus.'

Like most of his militia comrades, Marcellus had retired from the Twentieth legion in the aftermath of the Boudiccan rebellion. He had been rewarded with a generous stipend and twenty-five *iugera* of prime farmland to the south of Colonia. Marcellus had never married, insisting he preferred 'slaves to sons', and he ran his farm with a harsh discipline that over the years had wrung healthy profits from the land. Yet when Marcellus rose each morning to break his fast and whip his workers into a frenzy of activity, two things combined to spoil his appetite.

The first was the knowledge that his neighbour was a despised Celt, Emeran, who had survived the Boudiccan rebellion and Paulinus's 'reckoning' by providing sanctuary for a Roman family who had fled from Colonia. This act of kindness had exempted him from the wrath that had consumed the property of most of his neighbours and consigned their lands to the likes of Marcellus. Emeran had a large family who hunted the forests and farmed the land in the desultory, and to Marcellus wasteful, Celtic fashion. Worse, Emeran's lands included a small lake and a stream that ran tantalizingly close to the boundary of Marcellus's farm, while Marcellus relied on brackish, barely drinkable water from a well he'd dug to supply his wattle and daub farmhouse, and his livestock were watered at a pitifully inadequate spring that had a habit of drying up at the height of summer. When the spring ran dry it was natural that Marcellus's cows would be drawn to the stream and the Roman did nothing to stop them.

This had happened on the morning Emeran died. According to Emeran's son, he and his father had attempted to drive the animals back on to Marcellus's land, but were quickly confronted by the legionary veteran, who was alone. Marcellus insisted, as he'd done on many similar occasions, that as a former Roman soldier he had a right to water his cattle in a stream on land he'd conquered. Emeran was a native, a barbarian, who should have been slaughtered with the rest after Boudicca's last battle.

Whatever happened next, Emeran ended up face down in his stream with his skull shattered and his brains splattered over a rock the size of a man's head.

Here the accounts diverged. Marcellus claimed Emeran had attacked him and he'd been forced to defend himself, a story confirmed by the overseer and two slaves who said they were with him. Emeran's son said his father had lost patience with his neighbour's harangue and turned away, at which point Marcellus picked up the rock, battered Emeran to the ground and kept hitting him till he was certainly dead. Such a disparity in the weight of the evidence, and the fact that Emeran and his son were mere Celts, would normally be enough to assure Marcellus's acquittal. The matter was complicated by the fact that two nights before the incident, after a militia practice, three people in a bar testified they'd heard Marcellus saying he was going to kill Emeran.

Marcellus rivalled Hilario for bulk and ferocity of expression, glaring at the prosecutor across the *basilica* floor as if daring him to make a direct accusation. The prosecutor, a local magistrate, was nervous to begin with under the malevolent gaze, and became more so as he questioned the three men from the bar. For some reason they seemed less certain now about the form of words or even what had been said. The victim's son was more impressive, meeting Marcellus's gaze without flinching and recounting the events as he remembered them in simple unvarnished fashion in a melodic sing-song Latin, only faltering when he listed his father's injuries. Valerius had no doubt he was telling the truth. Not that it would make much difference.

The boy was about seventeen and slightly built, with long dark hair. 'I have a question for you,' Valerius said. 'Would you say your father was a big man?'

The witness stared at him in confusion. 'Big?'

'In stature.'

'No, lord,' the boy said. 'He was smaller than I am, though of a similar build.' Valerius nodded. 'And he had one leg shorter than the other.' A searing glare at Marcellus. 'He walked with a limp.'

Emeran's son resolutely maintained his story under cross examination from Marcellus's counsel, not even condescending to reply to the accusations of lying. Then it was Marcellus, who told his version of the story exactly as it was written in the statement he had given. 'He flew at me,' the former soldier rasped. 'His hands were at my throat, but I managed to get a hand to the rock and hit him. I didn't mean to kill him.'

'His skull was smashed into fourteen pieces,' Valerius pointed out.

Marcellus frowned. 'I must have hit him harder than I thought.'

'Did he have a weapon?'

The frown deepened. 'A weapon?'

'As I understand it you are much taller and heavier than the victim. It would take a very brave, or foolish, man to attack someone your size, a former soldier.'

'He was a Celt,' Marcellus said airily. 'And therefore a fool, but they do not lack courage. He came at me like a wildcat.'

'So no weapon?'

Marcellus looked to his counsel for support, but found no help there. Valerius could see tiny beads of sweat appearing below his hairline. His mouth opened and closed. 'Perhaps he had a knife?'

'A big knife? A small knife?'

'It must have been small,' Marcellus shrugged, 'or I would have mentioned it earlier.'

The first witness was Marcellus's overseer, a brute of a man in his master's image. Like Marcellus he repeated his statement word for word in a slow, determined monotone. Valerius asked about a weapon. 'Your master is a big man. Surely no one would be foolish enough to attack him with his bare hands?'

Again the desperate look towards Marcellus's counsel, who looked on with gritted teeth. Eventually the man shook his head. 'I didn't see a weapon.'

Such was his terror that the first of Marcellus's slaves had to be half carried into the court by Shabolz and another of the lictors, and he let out a cry when he saw Hilario's axe. His fear was perfectly justified because, under Roman law, if Valerius doubted any part of his evidence he had the power to order the slave tortured to get to the truth. In a shaking voice the man outlined a scenario that precisely mirrored the testimony of the overseer and his master. When the slave reached Emeran's frenzied attack on Marcellus, the farmer's counsel quickly interjected: 'And did you see the knife?'

The slave's features froze in the startled look of a rabbit trapped by a stoat. The lawyer repeated his question with a deliberate emphasis on the word 'knife', and comprehension dawned on the man's face. 'Yes, lord. I saw the knife.' He nodded so enthusiastically it was a wonder his head didn't fall off. 'Emeran attacked the master with a big knife.'

By the time the second slave had completed his testimony the knife had become a small sword and there were murmurs from the crowd. No one doubted that Marcellus was guilty, but he was an old soldier, their comrade who had shared the battle line with them, bled and tasted blood at their sides. They didn't want to see his head rolling in the dust in the forum.

Marcellus's florid features had paled as he watched his defence collapse. His eyes flickered to Hilario, who returned his stare with a look of savage concentration, as if he was already measuring the girth of his victim's neck.

Valerius addressed the accused and his counsel. 'Sextus Marcellus, I find you guilty of the murder of Emeran the Celt.' He allowed the words to hang in the air for a moment. 'Your crime merits a sentence of death, but in view of your record of service to the State and a certain element of provocation on the part of the victim, I commute the sentence to an order of compensation for five thousand *sestertii*. In addition, you will provide the family of Emeran the Celt with the services of two field slaves, to be chosen by the court, to aid with the running of the estate.' Marcellus hung his head, entirely defeated. Five thousand *sestertii* was half a year's wages for a legionary; finding it would come close to ruining him. Valerius saw the murdered man's son staring at him with something like hatred. Sometimes even the best justice had to be tempered with pragmatism, but it left a bitter taste in the mouth. 'I also issue an order preventing you from setting foot on the Emerans' land for two years on pain of death.'

'So my clever husband can find a way to turn the corruptors' gold against them.' Tabitha didn't hide her disapproval as Hilario and his fellow lictors escorted them back to the townhouse. 'But a murderer goes free. We would have done things differently in Emesa.'

'I'm sure you would,' Valerius replied mildly. 'And Marcellus certainly deserved to die. But Terentius Cantaber told me he was a follower of Mithras, and a high-ranking one at that. If I'd had him executed his comrades in the militia who worship the bull-slayer would have driven the boy and his family out, or more likely killed them all. Agricola sent me here to do his dirty work. If he'd been presented with the Marcellus case he would have dismissed the charges before it ever came to trial.'

'What will happen now?'

'If the boy has any sense he'll use the money to hire a couple of handy veterans to protect the family. But the best thing he could do is let Marcellus stew for a few months then offer some sort of limited access to the stream.'

'But wouldn't the killer just see that as a sign of weakness?'

'Perhaps.' Valerius allowed his gaze to drift across his surroundings. They were approaching an intersection on the narrow street, with apartment blocks towering over them to either side. 'But by then we'll be far away. I hope to finish up tomorrow and we'll leave the following morning for Lindum. I—'

Without warning a cloaked and hooded figure stumbled from an alleyway into the road, heading directly for Valerius. Shabolz effortlessly kicked the man's legs from under him and he fell face down with Hilario looming over him, axe held high ready to strike at Valerius's order. One of the Pannonians picked something up from the dust. 'He was carrying this.' He showed Valerius a small knife, insignificant in its way, but lethal enough if you knew what you were doing.

'Get him to his feet.' Only now Valerius recognized the ragged cloak as the one he'd seen in the *basilica*. 'Pull back the hood and let's see his face.'

Shabolz dragged back the all-encompassing cowl.

Even Hilario took a step back at the sight that greeted them. The face of a monster. A sword edge had taken him high on the left side of the forehead, splitting scalp and skull before it cut diagonally across his face. The force of the blow had destroyed the left eye socket and turned the eye into a festering, pus-filled sore. Relentlessly the blade had continued its course to carve through the bridge of the man's nose, shattering bone and cartilage to leave a gaping cavity through which breath and snot whistled noisily. Finally, the blow had stripped the flesh from his right upper lip and removed half his teeth before breaking his lower jaw so it hung loose, giving his face a permanently lop-sided cast. An old wound, all puckered scar tissue and weeping fissures, but the horror of it transfixed even men inured to battle. The old man's undamaged features were filthy and wrinkled and covered in thick grey stubble, and strands of greasy, matted hair drooped like rats' tails from a weathered skull. Dried mud coated the flapping rags of a cloak so verminous a man could almost see the legions of lice marching up and down the threads.

Valerius stared at the face and the single burning eye that transfixed him like a spear point.

'Cearan?'

'Valerius, do you know this man?'

Valerius's eyes never left the ruined face as he answered. 'He saved my life, Tabitha.'

'Oh, Valerius . . .'

'And he took my hand.'

XXIX

Valerius had felt the ghosts of the past stirring from the moment he landed in Britannia. Now he began to doubt his sanity. Cearan? Cearan should have been dead years ago. He should have died with Maeve and Boudicca, and a hundred thousand Britons who had followed the Iceni queen, and a hundred thousand more who had paid the price for her barbarous lust for revenge. His wound should have killed him, or disease, or starvation. Yet he'd survived, and he was here, where it had all begun. Why?

Hatred. His whirling mind found the answer in an instant. As he sought to recover his composure in the sheltered courtyard garden of the townhouse, he shuddered as he remembered the mix of loathing, disgust and downright madness in the depths of that single eye. And Cearan had reason to hate. Rome had robbed him of everything. His wife, his family, his lands, his rank and his honour.

'You should send him away, Valerius,' Tabitha insisted. 'He tried to kill you.' Shabolz and Hilario had taken an unprotesting Cearan to the bathhouse with orders to clean him up, find him fresh clothes and something to eat.

'If he'd wanted me dead he wouldn't have done it in the middle of the street with guards all around me. There was something else.' Valerius tried to visualize the moment again. The hooded figure stumbling towards him in a shambling run, arms outstretched. Almost welcoming. Or more accurately seeking welcome. 'I think he recognized me and it stirred some spark of memory in him. A memory of friendship or of better times, even if it was just for a moment. For seventeen years Cearan has lived the life of a starving beggar. An abomination to be sent away with a kick. Never experiencing a woman's touch or another man's affection. Driven mad by his loss and his suffering. And tormented beyond sanity every time he touches the ruin of his face. It is difficult to believe, but Cearan was probably the handsomest man I ever met. A woman might even have called him beautiful. I need to talk to him. Alone.'

She reached up and touched his cheek. 'You're a good man, Valerius, but one day your goodness will be the death of you. At least keep Shabolz with you.'

'Cearan won't speak if he feels threatened.'

'And what does it matter if he doesn't speak?' A hiss of exasperation escaped her lips. 'What is it you want from him?'

'I don't know,' he admitted.

'Forgiveness? Is that it? You seek his pardon for some imagined slight? Or crimes committed in your name by the soldiers of Rome? From what I understand, if he marched with Boudicca's rebels he may have crimes of his own for which to atone. Have you thought of that? Ceris told me what happened here and in Londinium. As always in your men's wars, it was the women and children who suffered most. Feed him and clothe him by all means, Valerius. Indulge your compassion. Give him a purse and a horse and the gods' blessing. But send him away. I see no good coming from any further contact with this man.'

Valerius reached out to hold her by the shoulders and kissed her on the forehead. None the less, Tabitha couldn't rid herself of a terrible foreboding when he walked from the room.

'Leave us,' Valerius ordered.

Shabolz went to the curtained doorway. Hilario hesitated, glancing at the man hunched over the kitchen table, a spoon moving between a wooden bowl and his lips with rhythmic determination. As much food – some kind of stew – sprayed from the shattered mouth as went down his gullet.

'He won't hurt me,' Valerius assured them.

Shabolz jerked his head towards the door. Hilario obeyed with a scowl and a glare at Cearan that promised terrible retribution if Valerius were wrong.

When they were gone, Valerius took his seat on the opposite side of the table, taking care to stay out of range of the spatter of meat and gravy. The other man continued eating with the singleminded application of one uncertain when he'd see another meal. As he ate, Valerius studied him. A barber had cut his hair and shaved him and they'd provided him with a new tunic. Still, it was difficult to recognize this skeletal, broken creature as the great lord he had once been; the man Valerius had called friend. The only man who could have saved Britannia from Boudicca's ravages and Paulinus's reckoning.

'Cearan?'

The spoon froze midway between mouth and bowl. In the seconds that followed the silence stretched out until it was as taut as a bowstring. When the Iceni spoke at last, the words were so garbled it took Valerius time to recognize the language as Latin.

'It is a long time since anyone called me that,' the Briton slurred. 'Scum. Filth. Monster. They are the names I answer to now. Or traitor, should I be unfortunate enough to fall in among my own people.'

As the words trailed away Cearan descended into some kind of reverie. Valerius resisted the urge to reach out and touch him. His head filled with a nightmare vision of the moment Boudicca's champions smashed their way into the Temple of Claudius. A flare of light and glittering iron coming at him from every side and then only darkness. Cearan had stood over his defenceless body, though Valerius had no memory of it, driven to mercy by the knowledge that Valerius had saved his grandson from drowning. Yet – Valerius winced at the familiar sting where his wrist had been – life came at a price. The strong right hand that wielded a sword for the hated Romans would wield one no more. A vivid image of the terrible moment the blade fell and his life changed for ever flashed through his head like a lightning bolt.

Cearan's mumble brought him back to the present. 'I remembered your face . . . I remembered your face and I had to tell you.'

'Tell me what?'

'That I . . .' His voice altered, became clearer and harder. 'They killed Aenid. They killed my beautiful wife. A centurion ran her through with a sword. When I tried to protect her, this was my reward.' His hand reached up to touch his scars and a tear ran down his cheek from the single eye. 'Then they scourged Boudicca, till the bone of her spine shone through the tattered flesh of her back, and violated her daughters, Banna and Rosmerta. Yet even a man without a face can ride and carry a sword and she took me into her company; me, the man who had trusted and befriended the Romans. I exulted when they burned and butchered and impaled and when the wrath of Andraste consumed Colonia. I saw you among the defenders of the temple and thought to kill you. But, when it came to it, something stayed my sword.'

'I owe you my life,' Valerius conceded.

'No,' Cearan hissed and the single eye flared like a glowing coal. 'You owe me a life. That is what I came to tell you.'

Valerius stared at him. 'I don't understand. I saved your grandson.'

'But you did not save Aenid, or Boudicca, or Banna or Rosmerta.'

Another long, unnerving silence that stretched out until Valerius felt compelled to break it.

'I need to know what happened after you left me.'

Cearan closed his eye and drew a long breath as if trying to conjure the answer from within, but reluctant to find it because of the pain it might cause.

'We reached Boudicca's camp before dawn the next day along an avenue of captives screaming in torment and lit by the fires that consumed Londinium. Word had just reached the queen of a great victory in the north, a legion wiped from the earth and its standards taken. Volisios, chief of her advisers, urged her to march north-east, to join forces with Mab, who had commanded the ambush, but the blood-lust of Londinium was still on her. She ordained that she would only take counsel from Andraste. The way to Verulamium lay open and the goddess commanded that it be destroyed.'

A servant entered with a jug of wine. Valerius poured two cups, but Cearan ignored the one offered to him.

'You think kindness can overcome seventeen years of hatred, contempt and suffering?' The single eye glared. 'You think you are doing me a service by placing me in these fine clothes and food in my belly? Do you believe any man will give bread to a well-dressed beggar? All the food will do is make my hunger harder to bear. You have always been weak. A strong man would have persuaded Paulinus of my case to become king when Prasutagus died. You did not have the courage. You as much as any of them are responsible for what came after, Gaius Valerius Verrens. Maeve saw it.' Valerius flinched, knowing what was to come. 'You could not protect her, so she came to me. Does your wife know about her? Are you too frightened to mention her name?'

Valerius shook his head. 'She did not want my protection. Her people appointed you her guardian and you taught her to hate me.'

'No,' Cearan rasped. 'You are wrong. That was the Romans who killed her father.'

'So you followed Boudicca to Verulamium?'

The slurred voice took on a note of triumph. 'We stood at Boudicca's side as Verulamium burned and listened to the screams as she showed the Roman-lovers the true meaning of the wrath of Andraste.'

'And Maeve endured this?'

'Maeve gloried in the slaughter.' The Briton's right cheek developed a spasmodic twitch and Valerius knew he was lying. Suddenly he felt nothing but contempt for this loathsome barbarian, so consumed by hate that no man must be left with even the illusion of love.

'You took my hand.' He shook the battered wooden fist on a leather stock that fitted over his right wrist. 'Is that not enough for you?'

'What is a hand?' Cearan leaned across the table so the spittle from his ruined lips spattered Valerius's cheek. 'If I can live without a face you can live without a hand.' The growing force of his hatred seemed to make the single eye glow all the brighter as he continued his story. 'We rested for a day as the ashes of Verulamium cooled. The queen's spies reported that the nearest Roman force was more than a day's march away, but within hours we were in contact with auxiliary scouts. Again, Volisios urged a link with Mab, but the druid Gwlym mocked his timidity. Boudicca was so thirsty for Roman blood that even double the lake she had spilled would not have satisfied her. She knew she outnumbered the Romans by ten to one, so she ordered her scouts to harry them and force a battle.'

'You walked into a trap.'

Cearan's head snapped up and the eye glared. 'We were betrayed.'

'Boudicca may have been a leader,' Valerius heard the scorn in his voice as the glow of his anger expanded inside him, 'but she was no warrior queen. She should have listened to her counsellors. Only a fool would have sent her warriors up that slope with nowhere to manoeuvre on either flank. Only a commander who had lost control would have allowed her baggage to block her only line of retreat. Paulinus played with her as a cat plays with a mouse. He goaded your rebels into attacking him and his legionaries slaughtered them like sheep.'

'You were there,' Cearan hissed.

Valerius leaned across the table so he was staring directly into the ruined face. 'You should have killed me, old man. I set the trap.'

Cearan leapt out of his seat and his hand snatched up the cup to smash it into Valerius's face, but the fingers of the Roman's left hand clamped on the bony wrist and twisted until the cup fell free. Cearan subsided back into his seat, but Valerius was not finished with him. 'I set the trap with the information Maeve gave me when we parted. *Avoid Verulamium for your life*, she said. So of course I knew where Boudicca would go.'

'She died hating you with a Roman sword in her guts,' Cearan sneered.

'No.' Valerius's voice was as bleak as a northern ice field. 'She cut her wrists with the knife I gave her.'

241

'How do you know?'

'Because I buried her.'

The anger seemed to have drained all the strength from the Iceni. As he pushed himself to his feet he seemed to have aged ten years in as many minutes.

'There is no more to say.' The rasping voice was empty of feeling. 'I will leave now. Have your mercenaries return my clothes. Better Celtic rags than Roman silk.' But Valerius noticed he picked up the cloak Shabolz had provided.

He followed the old man through the house to the street door, calling on a servant to bring the verminous, stinking rags. Cearan snatched them up without thanks and stepped into the street. When he'd trudged a few paces he turned, and the expression on his shattered features sent a shudder through Valerius. It was the broken, jagged-toothed caricature of a smile.

'Know this, Gaius Valerius Verrens,' he called out. 'In the name of Taranis I will take from you that which you most hold dear, dearer even than the hand I left you. This I swear.' He shook his head, but the single eye never left Valerius. 'You should have killed me, but you were always too weak.'

He turned away, leaving Valerius frozen in place and feeling as if someone had run an ice spear down his spine. Cearan's threat had been almost a perfect echo of the witch's curse . . . from an old friend and an old enemy.

XXX

There was no sign of either Iceni or threat when Valerius returned to the *basilica* the next day at the centre of his escort. Yet the feeling that his life was being disturbed by forces beyond his control or comprehension remained. Fear was too strong a word for what he felt. Why fear the threat of an aged beggar so weakened by privation he could hardly stand?

The inheritance dispute took less time than expected as one party said he had lost the papers he claimed entitled him to a share of a prime housing site. Valerius suspected its absence had more to do with the fifty *aurei* fine imposed on Priscus over the forgery claim than any carelessness. He was prepared to give more time to the case of the missing wife, but the evidence was almost non-existent. A woman had gone to the river to fetch water and not returned. Her husband, another former legionary, claimed his neighbour's son had either abducted or killed her, on no other evidence than that she was comely and he'd seen the boy looking at her. Valerius listened to his pleas for as long as was polite before dismissing the case for lack of evidence.

It meant they were ready to leave for Lindum at the second hour the next morning. The north road from Colonia only travelled as far as Venta Icenorum, which meant a long detour back to Londinium.

Valerius suggested Tabitha and Lucius might wish to remain there while he prepared the ground for a new veterans' colony, but Tabitha wanted to explore more of the country and, in any case, Lucius was inseparable from Didius.

They rode out from the west gate the next morning after a farewell ceremony from the *ordo*. Unseen by the escort, a shadowy figure watched the procession of riders and wagons out of sight from amongst the huts of the industrial area. When they were gone, Cearan led his horse a little way from the settlement into the trees before mounting and cutting a path parallel to the road. Valerius would have been surprised to see that he wore the new tunic and cloak provided by Shabolz, and by the quality of the gelding, on loan from a sympathizer of the anti-Roman cause. There were many such men among the native tribesmen, many more than the Romans would have suspected, and from all classes. Cearan kept his horse to a walk. He was in no hurry. He had business in the west and it pleased him to stay close to Valerius. He knew that his curse would have unsettled the Roman and who knew what opportunities the journey might bring? He'd already made one contribution to Gwlym's conspiracy, and he intended to make at least one more.

Valerius only rode a few miles before joining Tabitha and Ceris in the carriage. It came as a relief to put Colonia, and more especially Cearan, behind him. It was an ordeal which had had to be faced, but once was enough. Now he could truly forget the past and continue with his life. With the first court in Britannia behind him he felt as if an enormous weight had been lifted from his shoulders. There would be more, probably many more, challenges ahead, but he felt he had a certain measure of the province and its people. Or peoples.

For there were two Britannias.

'What are you thinking, husband?' Tabitha smiled drowsily.

Valerius glanced at Ceris, sleeping in the corner of the opposite bench seat, with her arms folded and her head nodding to the bounce of the wheels. He kept his voice low, so Tabitha had to lean towards him to share it. 'Oh, I was pondering on the changes here since my last visit. Colonia is much less of a frontier outpost than it was in Nero's day. You might call it an entirely Roman town, with all the institutions you would expect of a similar sized place in Latium or Etruria.'

'That was my impression,' she agreed.

'Even the villages we pass appear Roman, with main streets and shops and workshops, when once the people in them would have lived in scattered roundhouses.' He paused, trying to marshal his thoughts. 'Yet for all they *look* Roman, they're not. The reality is that places like Londinium and Colonia are islands in a sea of Celts, just as they were eighteen years ago before Boudicca.'

'You're not saying it could happen again, surely, Valerius?' She frowned. 'The people treat us well everywhere we go.'

He smiled. 'No. The day of the warrior is past, at least in the south. They no longer have the weapons, the armour or the will to do what they did. Paulinus, for all his faults, literally put the fear of death into them.'

'Then why so serious?'

'Because the weapons may not be there, but the resentment remains. All the tiny irritations that combined to create Boudicca – the taxes, the surveillance, the overbearing military presence and the arrogance of conquerors over conquered – still exist.' He looked towards Ceris again, but she showed no signs of waking. 'The seed corn of rebellion, should someone care to nurture it. Think, if I'd found against Tasciovanus the news of his humiliation would have spread among the native tribes like ripples from the stone you throw into a pond. All it would take would be one tribal leader to say "Enough". In the old days a man like that could command the loyalty of thirty thousand warriors from the sub-tribes and clans of his confederation.'

'But, as you said, there are no warriors.'

He laughed. 'You're right. I worry too much. It comes with the passing years. Do you know I am the same age now as my father was when he saw me off to Britannia, full of dreams of glory and all shiny in my new armour. I thought him very ancient then.'

She leaned closer and whispered in his ear. 'You did not seem at all ancient last night.'

'That's because I have you to keep me young,' he grinned. Ceris stirred and yawned and opened her eyes, blinking. 'And the baby?' His eyes drifted to the swelling beneath Tabitha's dress.

'The lady is past the time of the first threat,' the Corieltauvi girl informed him with all the authority of a legionary *medicus*. 'I think she may be allowed to eat meat today. But if she is sick again we will return to soft eggs and porridge. I have also put together a balm of oil, quince and roses which we will apply every night.'

'Ceris says it keeps the skin supple,' Tabitha laughed. 'When she's not looking I rub it on my face.'

'This is no laughing matter, mistress,' Ceris said sternly. 'We must take every sensible precaution.' The coach bumped over a large rut and all three were momentarily lifted into the air. 'Including spending much less time on the road in bumpy carriages. Can you not persuade her to stay in Londinium, lord?'

Valerius shook his head. 'She will not be moved, Ceris, but perhaps you can persuade her it would be in the best interests of the child.'

Tabitha's eyes narrowed dangerously, so he did the sensible thing and settled back into the cushioned seat and closed his eyes.

Lucius wove his pony through the trees with the gentlest touch on the reins, the animal's flank brushing bark at a pace Didius struggled to match on his sturdier mount.

'Slow down, you little . . .' The cavalryman let out a roar of frustration as a patch of bog slowed him again. Didius loved the boy as if he were his own son, but he struggled to deal with his growing confidence in the saddle and the fearless sense of adventure of which the legate had warned him. He caught a fleeting flash of pale flank off to his right and hauled his horse in that direction, ducking to avoid low branches.

'Lucius, get your arse back here.' If he had his way he would have tanned that arse, but he didn't dare risk the mother's wrath even though he knew Valerius would heartily approve. All the beauty and grace of a Greek goddess, but those dark eyes saw too much for Didius's liking.

Lucius grinned as he heard the shouts and dug his heels into the little mare's flanks, urging her on. He loved the freedom of the saddle, the breeze in his face and the feel of a glorious, biddable animal under his control. He felt a little sorry for old Didius, but the feeling was overcome by a wildness that sometimes filled his head.

'Come on,' he encouraged her, reckoning that the cavalryman would be able to hear them even if he couldn't see them in this thick forest undergrowth. A fallen branch blocked his path and he sucked in his breath and gave the horse her head. Three strides later he was flying, half out of the saddle and shrieking with delight, before they were over. On and on, the madness fading as he reached a stream and brought the mare to a stop. She snickered, breathing hard, and he patted her on the shoulder.

'I beg your pardon, Khamsin,' he said gravely. 'I promise you an apple when we get back to the others.' He dismounted and led her down to the water's edge, allowing her to drink from the clear waters. He crouched to dip his hand into the river. It was only then he sensed the other presence.

He looked up to see a cloaked and hooded man on a pale horse on the other side of the stream. His hand flew to the little knife at his belt, and he stood, shaking, but resolute. He thought he recognized the cloak and for a moment he wondered if one of the escort was playing a trick on him. Then the man spoke.

'You needn't be frightened of me, boy.' The words came out in a strangely slurred, sing-song Latin. 'But you're right to be wary. These woods can be dangerous.' He moved his horse a little closer to the stream edge. 'Bandits, wolves.'

'Stay where you are,' Lucius warned him in a voice he hoped carried his father's authority, but was in reality a nervous squeak. 'I'm not afraid of bandits or wolves. I'm not alone. Didius isn't far behind me.'

He sensed the man smiling behind the hood and he felt a red surge of anger. No man mocked a Verrens. 'Who are you? Take off your hood so I can see your face. An honourable man does not hide his features.'

In that moment the atmosphere changed and Lucius almost dropped the knife. The horse moved a step into the river before a crashing sound from the forest made the man draw it back.

'Lucius, where in all the gods' names are you,' Didius called.

Lucius looked over his shoulder. 'Here, Didius,' he cried.

When he looked back the other bank was empty.

'Tell me what happened.' Valerius tried to keep the relief from his voice as he crouched in front of his son. Didius stood at the boy's side, unable to meet Tabitha's eyes.

'It was my—'

'I am asking Lucius, trooper.'

'Yes, lord.'

'I slipped away from Didius, Father.' Lucius kept his eyes down. 'I'm sorry, but Khamsin was hard to control.'

'All right,' Valerius said. 'What then?'

'We stopped to let her drink in the river. That was when I saw him.'

'Description?'

Lucius's face screwed up in concentration. 'As tall as you, Father, I think. On a pale horse. But he didn't show his face. He wore a hooded cloak. And . . .'

'Yes?'

'He had a strange voice. Like Marius when he's really, really drunk.' He raised his eyes to look into Valerius's face. 'I'm sorry, Father.'

Valerius could have hugged him, but he kept his voice stern. 'No harm done.'

'I'm sorry, lord,' Didius said. 'I should have kept up with him.'

'I said no harm done, Didius. I know what the little . . .' Valerius sensed Tabitha stiffen. 'Well, we've had our lesson. Lucius, you're not to go out of sight of the carriage unless I give my permission, understand?'

'Yes, Father.'

'Didius, tell Felix I want flank guards and scouts. From now on we act as if we're in enemy territory. There's no reason to think there's only one of them, so I want complete vigilance at all times. Carry on.'

Didius saluted and went to where the officers waited.

'Our friend Cearan?' Tabitha asked.

'It sounds like it.' Valerius reached down and unconsciously ruffled his son's hair.

'What does he want?'

'I wish I knew.'

They reached the top of the ridge overlooking Londinium without further alarm, the escort worn to a shadow by constant vigilance and the savage driving of Felix, who felt responsible for allowing Lucius to leave the convoy.

'Thank the gods for that,' Didius said to Shabolz as they looked down the long, shallow slope. 'A warm bath, a decent rest, a cold cup of wine . . .'

'You'll be lucky if the legate doesn't throw you in the cells,' Shabolz said with unusual force.

'All I did . . .'

'What's that?'

'Where?'

'See, the dust?' The Pannonian pointed. 'A rider coming up fast.'

Didius caught a flash of colour among the trees below and a horseman appeared on the road. 'An Imperial courier?'

'Stay here,' Shabolz ordered. 'I'll alert the legate.'

Valerius was waiting beside the carriage with Tabitha when Didius rode in with another rider, identified by the yellow cloak which gave him priority on any road and at any way station. His horse had been ridden hard and Valerius guessed the man had word of their coming.

The courier confirmed it after gratefully gulping down the contents of a jug of water. 'The patrol from Durolitum came in at last light and said they'd passed you on the road. I've been riding since dawn to bring you this, lord.' He passed over a leather scroll case with a red seal. 'From the governor.'

'The governor is in Londinium?' Valerius didn't hide his surprise.

'No, lord. Another courier brought it in from the west yesterday.'

'Please excuse me.' Valerius motioned Tabitha to join him and they walked a little way from the group around the carriage. He handed her the scroll case and she broke the seal and deftly opened the straps to reveal a single sheet of parchment. She offered it to Valerius, but he shook his head. 'You can read as well as I can.'

'To the *legatus iuridicus* Gaius Valerius Verrens,' she read. 'If you are my friend, Valerius, you will join me at your earliest convenience at Viroconium. A situation has developed which requires your presence here. It may take some time, so be prepared to stay the winter. Your friend, Gaius Julius Agricola, proconsul.'

Tabitha looked up and met Valerius's eyes. 'Not Lindum, then?'

'You wanted to see the country,' he said. 'The west is as good as the north.'

She laughed, pleased that he accepted without argument that she and Lucius would accompany him despite the changed circumstances.

'This message mentions a situation,' Valerius called to the courier. 'Did your comrade talk of anything that would explain it?'

'Only that a rider had arrived at the camp, lord, and the governor's aides called all his senior commanders to his tent.'

'Felix? Take five men and ride ahead to Londinium. Start preparing everything we need for a prolonged absence. I plan to stay for only three days to deal with anything urgent that's arisen while we've been in Colonia.'

'Yes, lord,' the young decurion called over his shoulder, already walking to his horse and shouting out the names of the men who'd accompany him.

'And Felix . . .'

'Lord?'

'Equip us as if we're going on campaign.'

XXXI

On the far horizon smoke rose in lazy grey pillars from hundreds of cooking fires and forges, the unmistakable mark of a legion in camp. It had taken Valerius and ten of his cavalrymen three days of hard riding and little sleep to reach the ridge overlooking the valley of the River Severn. Tabitha, Lucius and the rest of the escort were a few days behind, travelling at a more leisurely pace. Valerius had decided to hurry west because he sensed an urgency in Agricola's message that was impossible to ignore. He'd long since given up wondering what 'situation' could be significant enough to drag the new *legatus iuridicus* a hundred and fifty miles and more away from a task that, less than a week ago, had seemed crucial. He gave the smoke a last look and nudged his horse forward. He would know soon enough.

The road approached Viroconium from the east, sloping gently down to the plateau above the river where the fort squatted behind stout walls and deep double ditches against a distant backdrop of sawtoothed mountains. They could make out individual legionaries moving between the wooden barracks and the administrative buildings. From what he could see, Valerius guessed it held only a single legion, presumably the Twentieth, and that the cohorts of the Ninth Agricola had counted upon were already on the march, or yet to arrive.

On the grassy flatlands by the river he made out the individual camps of at least three auxiliary cavalry wings and perhaps five infantry cohorts, their standards flapping in a north wind that had suddenly grown appreciably chillier.

A small group of horsemen emerged from the gate and Valerius recognized Agricola at their head, the scarlet cloak that identified his high status billowing behind him. Beneath the cloak all he wore was an ordinary workaday tunic despite the cold.

'You're a welcome sight, Valerius,' Agricola called out in welcome as he approached. 'We hadn't thought to see you for another two days at the earliest. Those horses of yours must have wings.'

'Governor.' Valerius rapped his fist to his chest in salute. 'It is good of you to meet us.'

'I'd thought to show you something of our dispositions,' Agricola said. 'You get a much better view from up here. Sextus,' he called out to the officer commanding his escort, 'show Legate Verrens' troopers to their quarters.'

'Get what rest you can,' Valerius called to the departing riders. 'You'll be on the road tomorrow to reinforce the lady's escort.'

They watched as the men rode away towards the fort. 'What's all this about dispositions?' Valerius smiled. 'I can see them perfectly well for myself.'

'Am I so transparent? Even a governor's *principia* isn't immune to flapping ears and there are things I have to tell you I'd prefer to keep entirely between ourselves.'

'This *situation* you mentioned in your message?'

Agricola nodded. 'Come, we'll take a look at the auxiliary camps.' He turned his horse north and Valerius fell in by his side. 'The first thing you should know is that the legate of the Ninth is dead.'

Valerius turned to stare at him. 'Fronto?'

Agricola nodded.

'Perhaps,' Valerius chose his words with care, 'he wasn't suited to an arduous campaign.'

'There's no need to be diplomatic with me, Valerius. In this matter

I think we have to be perfectly frank with each other. The man was an ignorant brute, and worse, no soldier. He should never have been given command of a legion. Unfortunately, he had the support of certain members of the Senate whose votes the Emperor depends upon. That makes his death a delicate matter. And it's made more delicate by the fact the manner of it raises a number of questions.'

They came to a halt at the top of the slope overlooking the camps by the river. Valerius took a few moments to digest what Agricola was telling him, and more important what he was not.

'You're saying his death was suspicious?'

'I'll let you make up your own mind as to that.'

'Of course.'

'Two days ago I ordered Fronto to take six cohorts of the Ninth two days' march into the hills to the west and set up camp there. The intention was to establish a base and send out cavalry patrols to explore potential routes into the interior and assess the strength of any Ordovice forces in the area. It was as much a test of their ability and morale as a military exercise. I sent two of my aides with him, which displeased him even more than usual.'

'No commander enjoys being . . .'

'Spied upon?' A bitter, fleeting smile from Agricola. 'He is under my command. He must accede to my authority. I suspected that, true to what I believed of his character, he would send his legion blundering into the mountains, with little advance preparation and smashing and slaughtering everything in his way. As it happened I was wrong. Our bold Fronto turned out to be as timid as a dormouse. The Ninth advanced barely twenty miles in two days. He wouldn't turn a corner without sending an auxiliary cavalry wing to scout the position first.'

'Some people would call it prudence,' Valerius pointed out.

'And others would use a harder word.' Agricola's eyes focused on the distant mountains. 'If I am to advance on the northern tribes next year it is vital I destroy the power of the druids before winter takes a grip. At Fronto's pace we wouldn't reach Mona before next summer. But that is of no matter now, because he's dead. He'd been drinking with his officers and went to bed at his normal time. At some point during the night he decided to take the air. Yes, I know,' he said, acknowledging Valerius's disbelieving grunt. 'The next morning a scout discovered him at the foot of a cliff with his neck broken.'

'An unfortunate accident.'

'Indeed, and there I would have left it had this not been found among his possessions.' The governor handed Valerius a wooden shaving of the type the clerks used to copy out draft orders before writing them fine. Valerius studied the precise Latin characters. *Marcus Caristanius Fronto is a dead man.*

'I see.'

'The fool who found this handed it to his centurion.' Agricola took the note back and tucked it into the pouch at his belt. 'The contents are not widely known, but enough to mean I can't do what I'm minded to and use it for kindling. Fronto's death must be investigated, and what's more it must be *seen* to be *properly* investigated. So what is more appropriate than that I send for my esteemed *legatus iuridicus*, a man trusted by emperors and versed in the darker arts of politics . . .'

'I think you exaggerate my talents, governor,' Valerius observed wryly.

'. . . whose arrival – how did Ovid put it? Yes – whose arrival kills two birds with a single stone. You will investigate Legate Fronto's death, Valerius, and with Fortuna's favour you will indeed discover that his fall was an unfortunate accident brought on by drink and foolishness. If not, I have no doubt you will find a murderer. You will note I do not say *the* murderer, for I believe you will not want for suspects. It will be up to you to choose the most expendable.'

Now Valerius was genuinely puzzled. 'Surely that would be up to the new legate?'

'You have not been listening, Valerius, or perhaps I have expressed myself badly. Two birds with a single stone. As well as investigating Fronto's death I am using my *imperium* to appoint you to command of the Ninth legion.'

'But the Emperor . . .'

'Will undoubtedly ratify my decision. My need is urgent, Valerius, and there are plenty of precedents for special appointments to legionary commands. Claudius appointed Julius Romulus legate of the Fifteenth Apollinaris in Pannonia long before he was of age, because he knew he was the right man to put down the Suebi, and the Danuvius had been stripped of legions for the invasion of Britannia. You are the only candidate of suitable rank in the province. You have experience of high command. Didn't Primus give you temporary charge of the Seventh at Cremona?' Valerius couldn't deny it. 'Good. Then it's settled. I need a strong hand at the reins of the Ninth, Valerius, and a steady one. A man who isn't afraid to take risks and who won't panic.'

Valerius tried to force his reeling mind to focus. Of course, that was it. 'Fronto's lack of enterprise would have been of no consequence if the Ninth were to march with the Twentieth. It would only be a problem if they were to serve as a detached force.'

'Precisely.' Agricola smiled. 'Which proves you are the right man for this post. Come, it will be easier to explain at my headquarters.'

They rode back to the fort and entered through the Porta Practoria. A groom waited to take their horses when they reined in outside the *principia*. Agricola led Valerius inside and along a corridor to a room with a large sand table at its centre. The scene was all so familiar it sent a shiver of anticipation through Valerius. Agricola had deluged him with so much information, changes and challenges and numbers, it had been like crouching behind a shield during an arrow storm. Now his mind cleared. If he had any doubts they could wait. He was a soldier again. He remembered the sand map Corbulo had created for his campaign against Vologases, the Parthian king of kings, a dozen officers listening intently as the general issued the orders that would determine whether they would live or die. It had shown a great swathe of desert, a few hills and the Cepha gap – the bane of Vologases' army. This was different.

'Viroconium.' Agricola pointed to a wooden block at the near side of the table. 'The Twentieth and six cohorts of the Ninth, plus four of aux-iliary cavalry and another eight infantry. Close to fourteen thousand

255

men. On the far side, Mona, the island of the druids, strength of the defenders unknown. Between, what looks like an impenetrable mountain range, but we know it isn't because Suetonius Paulinus fought his way through them before Boudicca gave him something else to think about.' He bent low to study the contours of the hills and for the first time Valerius heard doubt in his voice. 'Of course, those mountains will be filled with Ordovice warriors, with perhaps help from the other hill tribes. I had intended to attack them head on with all my forces, but my greatest fear is that they will melt away into the hills. Mona is not my only objective. It is imperative I destroy the power of the Ordovices and any threat to my rear while we're in the north. That is why I have developed a new strategy for this campaign, and why Fronto and the Ninth were so important.'

Valerius studied the map table. 'Where is the Ninth now?'

Agricola looked up. 'Your legion is here, legate.' He drew a line from Viroconium a short way west along a clearly defined valley which, according to the map table, ran straight as an arrow towards Mona. 'Depending on the opposition, it is around four or five days' march through difficult terrain to the coast opposite Mona.'

'Supplies?'

'Each man will carry food for three days. No carts, so everything else and a further week's supply will be carried on mules. My experience with Paulinus tells me there will be no shortage of watering places.'

The hills looked innocent enough on the sand table, but Valerius knew he must expect an ambush from every height, and every bend in the road to be contested. 'So the Ninth is to be the bait in the trap.'

Agricola nodded, a sharp movement like a starling pecking at spilled corn. 'In four days' time I will take the Twentieth and all our auxiliaries on a night march north. We will leave a token force in the fort to create the illusion of occupation. Trumpet calls, cooking fires, and movement between the barracks and headquarters buildings as normal.' He turned back to the table. 'This valley was surveyed by Paulinus's *exploratores* and found suitable, but he preferred the northern coastal route. See how it brings us to this river line, here,' he pointed to a place perhaps three quarters of the way to Mona, 'where we can wheel south and cut across your line of march. Your task, legate, is to wait until the morning after I march and advance towards Mona. If I'm right they will contest your progress, but only to draw you onwards. You will allow yourself to be drawn, and the small size of the force will make the Ordovice chiefs overconfident. My plan is to make them believe you are nothing but a relatively strong punishment operation to burn a few settlements and take a few hundred slaves in return for what they did at Canovium. If you look as if you have overstretched yourself I believe they will concentrate all their forces to destroy you.'

'And then you hit them in the flank,' Valerius said. It wasn't a bad plan, such as it was. He looked at the map, imagining a full legion marching through the narrow valley Agricola indicated. Timing was everything. So many things could go wrong. All it would take was one scout, or even a shepherd boy, to find their way to the main Ordovice force. 'What happens if the enemy discovers the Twentieth is gone and blocks your line of march while he deals with me? Thirty thousand warriors, I think you said.'

'Why then we'll find out just how good soldiers the Ninth really are,' Agricola said in an indifferent tone that irritated Valerius. 'Because you'll have to hold on until we've fought our way through to you.'

Valerius looked at the hills again. The narrow valleys and flanking heights. So many opportunities for ambush. By the time the Twentieth had extricated themselves Valerius and all his men were likely to be dead and they both knew it.

But he was a soldier again. He commanded a legion. And that was enough.

It was only then he remembered Domitia Longina Corbulo's letter. Fronto had been one of the four potential candidates for Domitian's high-level contact in Britannia. If he'd been murdered, as Agricola seemed to suspect, had that been the reason? Or were there other, more sinister, forces at work?

257

XXXII

'Crescens!' Valerius called. 'To me!'

Julius Crescens trotted up from his position a few ranks behind in the long column of riders. He wore a worried frown because he still wasn't certain why Valerius had detached him from the escort. They were at the centre of the First Ala Indiana, a five hundred strong unit of Gallic cavalrymen normally stationed at Isca, to the south. Agricola had grudgingly agreed to transfer the unit to the Ninth after Valerius pointed out he would need as much mobility as he could get in the mountains.

'Yes, lord?' the young cavalryman said with a deference that would have surprised his comrades.

'What can you tell me about Legate Fronto?'

Valerius was watching his face when he asked the question and he saw the instant Crescens's eyes took on that look of blank incomprehension so often the trooper's first line of defence.

'Sir?'

'Don't come the old soldier with me, Julius,' Valerius said without rancour. 'Whatever he's done in the past can't harm him in the grave. And he certainly can't harm you. I need to know what's been going on so I can put it right.' Crescens stared at him, the implications of

Valerius's words taking time to register. It was common knowledge the Ninth's legate had met an unhappy accident, but Agricola had left it to Valerius when to announce his appointment. 'That's right. The governor has given me temporary command of the legion.'

'Then may Fortuna aid you, if you don't mind my saying so, lord, because you'll need all the help you can get.'

'Let's start with Fronto.'

'Am I to be perfectly frank, lord?'

'Yes.'

'A proper bastard, lord. One of the worst.'

'And what makes him the worst? I need details.'

Crescens looked thoughtful. 'My father told me that in every legion centurions use their position to squeeze money from the men under their authority.'

'That's true enough.' Valerius knew a unit's senior centurions would often demand bribes from the legionaries in their century to award them leave they'd earned by right. If a man lost a piece of equipment in battle he was entitled to have it replaced, but often a superior required a little encouragement before he authorized the transaction.

'The Ninth's centurions were up to all the usual tricks. Letting it be known that men could buy their way out of fatigues, that type of thing. Only this was organized.'

'Organized?'

'Yes, lord. The senior centurion of every cohort was up to his neck in it, and they put pressure on the more junior ones. It was common knowledge that all the money went upwards. The legate was milking his legion dry. If anyone complained or refused to pay they'd have their backs stripped by the centurions' vine sticks.'

'Thank you, Crescens.' Valerius's throat felt ragged with the force of his anger. Corruption he understood, and sometimes a wise legate only saw what he needed to see, but this? 'I think we can safely say it will stop.'

'There's more, lord. Much more.'

Valerius sighed. 'Tell me.'

'At Lindum he'd get drunk and call for the best-looking boys to be sent to his rooms and the *primus pilus* would organize it, putting the fear of death into some recruit. I've seen lads who would single-handedly charge a Celtic battle line crying like babies when they got back to the barracks. One fellow Fronto took a shine to couldn't take it and cut his own throat. Blood everywhere.'

Valerius felt the bile rise in his chest. This explained why the legion was falling apart. The only real wonder was that there hadn't been a mutiny. 'Didn't the senior officers do anything about it?'

'The way I heard it the legate had his hooks in the officers too, sir. He'd ask them for a loan and if they didn't come up with the gold they'd end up patrolling the mud flats and the swamps in a thunderstorm on a lame horse and with a couple of the *primus pilus*'s thugs for company.'

'Tribunes don't lead patrols.'

'They do in the Ninth, lord.'

'Very well,' Valerius said. 'You've given me much to think on.' A thought struck him. 'Do you remember which century the boy who killed himself was with?'

Crescens gave him an odd look. 'No, lord.'

'And Crescens?'

'Lord?'

'This conversation never took place.'

As they twisted through the mountain valley Valerius began to understand the true scale of the task facing him. He knew these hills of old from his time with the Twentieth legion a lifetime ago, but his memory had dulled the gloomy, claustrophobic depths and the dangerous tree-choked gullies, any of which could hide a band of Ordovice warriors. Riding two abreast the column of riders and their baggage animals took up almost two miles of the rutted native track that split the hills. That could have made them vulnerable, but the prefect in command of the cavalry wing knew his business. Scouts ranged ahead, always within sight of each other and the column. Strong flank guards waited, ready to cut down any sortie. A full squadron guarded the rear.

The column reached the Ninth's temporary camp on a height overlooking a large lake just as darkness began to fall. The beasts of the quartermaster's cattle herd bellowed annoyance as the riders forced their way through the grazing animals and past stockades filled with the thousands of mules that would make up the legion's baggage train. Valerius had sent a courier ahead to announce his arrival and an honour guard of a full century turned out, armour glittering and swords unsheathed to welcome him with proper ceremony. The legion's camp prefect, its second in command, a taciturn, silver-haired veteran with a look of grim foreboding, slammed his fist into his chest armour in salute.

'Gaius Quintus Naso, *praefectus castrorum*, welcomes you and places himself at your service. I only wish the circumstances were different. The tragic death of our—'

Valerius silenced him brusquely. 'This isn't the time for speeches, prefect. It's been a long day. A little food, a cup of well-watered wine and a brief report of your situation and readiness will suffice.'

Naso flinched at the implied rebuke and his cheeks coloured, but he bowed his head. 'If you will follow me, lord, I will direct you to your quarters.' He led the way to the *praetorium*, the tented pavilion that doubled as the legate's home and office on campaign. 'We have left it precisely as it was when Legate Fronto had it.' The words held a note of apology and Naso watched Valerius's expression as the new legate's eyes wandered over the erotic wall hangings of golden-skinned youths performing acrobatic sex acts. Four padded couches surrounded a low table with a silver gilt top. The only other furniture was a battered campaign table Valerius suspected Fronto had inherited from his predecessor. A sweet, musky scent hung in the air and the whole atmosphere felt unwholesome. Valerius pulled back the curtain that led to his sleeping quarters. Here the smell was even stronger. The room held an intricately carved wooden bed the breadth of a Tiber barge and piled high with quilted trappings. 'Have that chopped up for firewood

261

and get the carpenter to knock me up a simple double cot that can be constructed and dismantled in a few moments. Burn the bedding.'

'Now, sir?'

'Do you expect me to sleep on the floor?'

When they returned to the main room a slave was setting a jug of wine and a plate of food at the campaign table. Valerius suddenly remembered that all he'd eaten since he broke his fast was a piece of dried bread and a handful of olives. He dragged a bench across to the table, poured a cup of wine and picked up a whole chicken. 'The dirty pictures can go, too,' he told Naso, ripping off one of the bird's legs.

The camp prefect bowed and left the tent. A few moments later six legionaries entered, led by a *duplicarius* and casting wary glances at Valerius. He waved them through to the bedroom and a muttered conversation followed before the *duplicarius* reappeared with a look of perplexed bemusement.

'Firewood, lord?'

'Yes and burn the bedding. And those.' He waved the chicken's thigh bone at the wall hangings. 'Unless you'd like to keep them for yourself.'

'Mars' arse, no, sir.' The man straightened. 'Begging your lordship's pardon. They're not to my taste at all.'

He disappeared into the room again, reappearing a moment later whispering instructions to his men as they manoeuvred the big bed through the narrow doorway.

'And *duplicarius*?'

'Lord?'

Valerius nodded at the soldiers, who wore simple short-sleeved tunics. 'Pass the word that while we're on campaign I expect every man to wear his sword belt and *pugio* unless he's sleeping or on the latrine.'

A moment of stunned silence followed before they marched the bed across to the entrance and pushed and pulled until they got it through. Naso returned as soon as the room was cleared. Valerius told him what he'd ordered. Naso looked uncertain.

'Corbulo insisted on it,' Valerius told him. 'And if it was good enough for Corbulo, it's good enough for me. Just because we're in camp behind defensive walls doesn't mean they won't attack us. Now, tell me our status.'

'Six cohorts of the Ninth,' the camp prefect rapped out the figures, 'nominally two thousand eight hundred and eighty heavy infantry, but with twelve men in hospital suffering ailments that keep them off duty, eight on leave, and twenty detached to guard the supply convoy that's due in two days. It will bring us up to a twelve-day ration strength. Fifteen hundred auxiliary infantry and fifteen hundred cavalry, counting the ala you brought in tonight, but we're short of remounts.'

'I'll try to change that. Did Legate Fronto brief you on the detail of our mission?'

'The legate was of the opinion that not knowing what lay ahead kept you alert and wary, sir. I gathered that we were marching into the interior, presumably to pay the Celts back for wiping out the garrison at Canovium, but I was a bit surprised we didn't have the Twentieth for company.'

Valerius shook his head. How could officers prepare a legion if they didn't know what they were preparing it for? 'You're right. We march at dawn in four days, so spread the word and make sure every unit is prepared. I'll give you the details tomorrow before I meet the officers. Join me to break fast at dawn. And arrange an interview with the *primus pilus* afterwards. What's his name?'

'Tertius.' Naso almost spat the word. He hesitated. 'As it happens he has already petitioned the new legate for a meeting. Legate Fronto . . .'

'We have much to discuss tomorrow, prefect,' Valerius confirmed with a grim smile. 'It can wait till then. You can tell me when we inspect the defences at dawn. I'll also want to see where the legate was found. And I'll look over the legion's accounts. Perhaps we should bring in my clerk to organize it all.'

'Of course, sir.' Naso's relief was written plain on his stolid face. He'd clearly expected to be relieved of his position or demoted.

'I have a question. Normally the legate would leave his *praefectus castrorum* in charge of the main camp. Why did he bring you with him?'

Naso hesitated before he replied. 'Because he wanted me where he could keep an eye on me.'

Valerius nodded thoughtfully. 'One more thing,' he said. 'Have we any idea what happened to the money? Over the years Fronto must have stolen a small fortune.'

'We don't know for certain, sir, but we found those.' He pointed to a pair of stout chests behind one of the couches. 'They were hidden under his bed, but I thought it best not to open them until word came back from the governor.'

'You did right, Naso.' Valerius smiled. 'That will be all.'

He watched the camp prefect go and took another sip of wine. A divided legion, a dead legate. And they weren't even his biggest problem. Tabitha would arrive tomorrow.

Valerius began working through the sheets of parchment on his desk. Ration returns, supply dockets, they were short of at least a hundred mules, signatures were required for the pay lists. All written by clerks and centurions, but all the legate's ultimate responsibility. A request to set up a temple to Mithras when they returned to Lindum, which Fronto, the fool, had turned down. The chief *medicus* was demanding another hundred water skins that didn't exist. He sighed. Perhaps Tabitha wasn't his biggest problem after all.

XXXIII

'Tiberius Gabinius Tertius?' Valerius kept his voice so cold it might have emerged from an open grave and Tertius, for all his twenty years' service experience, had to clench his hands to stop them shaking.

'*Primus Pilus* Tiberius . . .'

'Just confirm your name, Tertius,' Naso growled. 'We will discuss your rank later.'

Valerius had chosen to deny Tertius the dignity of an interview in the headquarters pavilion. Instead Naso had summoned the senior centurion to a tent normally occupied by the legion's ration clerks, close to the pig pens where the butchers were slaughtering hogs to be smoked or salted for the expedition. Tertius winced as the scream of another dying pig punctuated the conversation.

'You are Tiberius Gabinius Tertius?' Valerius repeated.

'Yes, lord.'

'I'm told you sought an interview with me. Why?'

'I'd like to apply for a transfer, lord.'

Valerius picked up a stylus. 'And your reasons?'

'I'd rather not say, sir.'

'Don't waste my time, soldier,' Valerius snapped. 'Let me answer for you. Because if you stay here some legionary you've fleeced or beaten will cut out your liver one dark night.'

'I only did—'

'You'll speak when I tell you to.' Tertius's mouth shut like a trap. 'Do you want me to read the list of charges we already have against you? Extortion, bribery, fraud, assault, misuse of office, illegal disposal of military property . . .'

'And we haven't really got into our stride,' Naso assured him.

'By rights I should drag you before a military court and have you run the gauntlet of your comrades,' Valerius continued. Tertius quailed at what was a certain death sentence. 'But I don't have time for that. Instead, you will provide me with a full account of your criminal activities in collusion with the late Legate Caristanius Fronto. I want the names of your accomplices and how much they were paid. Any man who was singled out for particular treatment and why. If you do so I will reluctantly put you on a horse back to Viroconium with a letter to Governor Agricola advising him to transfer you to the most remote legionary outpost he can think of. The Dacian frontier should do nicely.'

'Not a name out of place,' Naso added the warning. 'Remember, we have most of it already. Begin.'

It came out in all its sordid detail, every little rotten trick in the corrupt centurions' manual, and a few more besides: men fleeced for the slightest infraction, beaten if they complained, destroyed in mind or body by the men of the legate's personal bodyguard if they persisted. The young soldiers dragged terrified to share the legate's bed, sobbing like children when they emerged. As he spoke Tertius's voice became increasingly brittle, as if he could feel the noose tightening around his neck. Valerius listened to the systematic destruction of his legion's morale and would cheerfully have strangled Tertius with it.

'I have two questions,' Valerius said when the litany of shame ended. 'Were any other senior officers involved in this dishonour?'

Tertius shot a desperate glance at Naso and a nerve in his cheek twitched. 'No, lord.'

'And I need the name, cohort and century of the boy who killed himself at Lindum.'

'He was from the fourth century, Second cohort. His name was Julius something . . . Julius Noricus.'

'All right.' Valerius glanced at Naso, who nodded. 'Wait outside, but don't think of leaving the camp until you have my warrant for the governor.'

'Well?' he said when the centurion was gone.

'I think he was telling the truth. What he said fits with what I know and what I've heard whispered. I'd like to see the bastard at the end of a rope.'

'So would I, but I don't want my command of this legion to begin with an execution.'

'What will you do?'

'About replacing him?' Valerius tapped the table with the stylus. 'I can't promote any of the other cohort commanders; they're up to their necks in it. I'll ask Agricola to send us an experienced centurion. Fronto's bodyguard I'll transfer to the Twentieth with instructions to put them back in the ranks and in the front line when we cross to Mona. I'd like to get rid of the cohort commanders too, but I don't see how we can do without them.' He saw a shadow pass across the prefect's face. 'You disagree?'

'I would advise you to cut out the rot completely, legate. Fronto may have been the instigator, but these are the officers who did the damage among the men. To the legionaries they are the physical manifestation of their troubles. Leave them where they are and they will think it's business as usual.'

'What would you advise?'

'Demote every last one to the ranks and put them in different cohorts. The centurial ranks below them include some able men who tried to protect their legionaries and suffered for it. I can give you the names of suitable replacements and we can promote from below as necessary.'

'Very well,' Valerius said after a moment's consideration. 'Make it so.' Naso rose from his seat, but hesitated in the doorway of the tent.

'You have something you want to ask me, legate.'

'Do I, Naso?'

'Yes. You want to know how a man like me could stand by and let this happen. It seems so easy to say we should have done something, but at the time . . . I rose from the ranks. I don't have wealth. I don't have powerful friends. My whole life is invested in the uniform I wear and the bounty I will collect at the end of my service. I tried, truly I did, but he threatened to destroy my career. When I persisted he sent me on patrol into Brigante country with six of his escort. Lonely places. Gullies and crags just like this. They didn't say anything. They didn't have to. But the message was clear. If we do this again, you won't be coming back. Still,' he sighed. 'I should have done more.'

'Yes, you should,' Valerius said. 'Have the tribunes assemble and we'll go over the details of the campaign.'

He spent two hours explaining Agricola's plan to the three tribunes, outlining the line of march and the tactics he intended to use. They seemed very young – the senior military tribune had remained at Lindum – and they listened attentively, but they were understandably wary of their new commander. None had done enough to stop Tertius or protest to the legate and they knew it. Valerius could break any one of them with a single-line note to Agricola, but he let them know, without saying it outright, that they could redeem themselves by their endeavours on the march, and, hopefully, by their valour in the battle that would follow.

They thanked him as they left and he wondered if he should have been harder on them. Cearan had called him soft: weak. Did he still have the iron core it took to command a legion? Marriage and father-hood subtly changed a man. He became less angry at the world and at himself. Perhaps a commander needed that anger. The legate of his first legion had once told him that a legion commanded by officers who wanted to be liked by their men was a legion ripe for defeat. Yet the Ninth was a wounded legion that needed time to heal. You didn't heal wounds by wielding the whip. He remembered something else the man had said: 'There will be a day when your soldiers are mere coins to be spent. What will you do then, when you know you must order them into the abyss?'

Before he had time to come up with an answer he heard a commotion outside the tent and a familiar voice shrill with excitement. Tabitha walked in, smiling and pulling at the pins holding her shawl in place. 'This fashion for respectable married women to always have their heads covered is so annoying I may decide not to be respectable any longer.' Her lips twitched. 'Or perhaps not married. What kind of man makes his wife travel a hundred miles to Viroconium and then a dozen more on a farm track to camp in a muddy field?'

'A man who didn't have any choice in the matter.' He took her in his arms and kissed her, feeling the telltale bump against his lower stomach. 'Are you well, lady?'

'Ceris says I am built for childbirth,' she said with airy self-mockery, 'but I'm not sure whether that is a compliment or an insult. My breath is fresh, my skin is soft as rose petals and . . . well, that is something we ladies do not discuss.'

Valerius grinned. 'A compliment, then. In any case, what would you have done if I'd left orders for you to stay in Viroconium?'

'I would have smiled at Governor Agricola in a certain way, suggested that a woman's place was with her husband and be standing here now, of course. Is it true there is no bathhouse?'

'This is a temporary camp, not a military rest home. We bathe in the lake at the bottom of the hill, though it can be crowded.'

'A pity,' she sighed. 'I'd hoped to smell a little sweeter tonight. It is good to see you, husband.'

'And you, my love,' he whispered.

'It is permitted to stay the night?'

'Of course.'

'Only the governor suggested we may be parted for some time.'

He raised her chin and saw the glint of tears in the corners of her eyes. 'You don't insist on coming with us?'

'That would be irresponsible. Agricola said it could be dangerous and I know you would never place your family in danger.'

'Your beauty is only outshone by your judgement.'

'Agricola tells me—'

'I hope I see you well, Father.' They turned to see Lucius standing in the doorway holding the hand of Didius Gallus.

'Very well, Lucius. I do believe you have grown an inch since I last saw you.'

The boy grinned and broke away from his friend to inspect the room, studying the replacement wall hangings – pastoral scenes – and a painted marble bust of Vespasian. Valerius thanked the gods he'd had the sense to have the originals removed. He doubted Tabitha's greeting would have been as warm if she'd seen them.

'Didius, tell the kitchens to prepare a meal for us, but check with Ceris first to find out what is suitable for the lady.' He waited until Didius and Lucius had left the room before he turned back to Tabitha. 'You were talking of Agricola?'

'Before I left he hinted at some great mystery.' The statement held a question and her eyes told him she wouldn't take no for an answer. It struck him that Tabitha's quick mind and her experience as a special agent of Queen Berenice of Silicia might be useful in the next few hours. She had tracked down the fabled Book of Enoch to the Great Temple in Jerusalem and thwarted the turncoat Judaean general Josephus to take ownership of it.

'It involves the death of my predecessor,' he admitted. 'A man with many enemies who had an unfortunate accident. My second in command will join me soon to discuss it.'

'I'm intrigued,' she said. 'Would it be improper of me to sit somewhere close by and listen to what is said?'

Valerius knew Naso was a proud man who would be uneasy and less forthcoming if the legate's lady was in the room with them. But if he didn't know . . . 'Terribly improper.' He smiled. 'But I would be grateful if you'd give me your impression of what he says.'

Valerius's clerk announced Gaius Quintus Naso and Valerius rose from the campaign table to meet him.

'Please sit.' Valerius waited until the camp prefect took his place. 'We talked of my late predecessor earlier. A man with powerful friends.' Naso nodded. 'I'm sure you have done everything possible to investigate the circumstances of his death, but the governor has asked me to go over the details with you.' The natural question to ask was if Naso thought there was anything suspicious about Fronto's accident, but that might channel his train of thought a certain way. The lawyer in Valerius preferred to hear what happened untainted by any hint of suggestion. 'Tell me in as much detail as possible what you have managed to piece together about that night.'

Naso ran the back of his hand over his lips in a nervous gesture, but once he'd gathered his thoughts his voice was steady enough.

'It started as a normal day, but Agricola's aides had been out on patrol with one of our cavalry squadrons and the legate fretted that they might have noticed some imperfection. The concern made him more irascible than usual and he had the cavalry commander in his office threatening to have him whipped if he could not repeat every word they had said. He became obsessed with discovering what they thought. He decided the best way to do it was to hold a dinner for all the officers, get the men from the Twentieth drunk and charm it out of them.' A weary smile greeted Valerius's raised eyebrows. 'Yes, I know, but he could be like that. One minute purring like a cat, the next roaring like a lion. It was one of the things that made him so difficult.'

'And did this plan work?'

Naso shook his head. 'We all got fairly drunk, but the legate more than anyone. His attempts to squeeze information from Agricola's aides became increasingly embarrassing.' He frowned at the memory. 'I regret to say that he became quite amorous with one of them. Oddly, the aide didn't seem to take offence, but the second man pleaded he needed to start his report for the governor and left early, accompanied by Tribune Martialis who had early duty the following day. I stayed another hour before making my excuses, and the first aide and my other two tribunes left perhaps an hour later.'

'So Fronto was alone?'

'Apart from his servants. A guard on the west rampart saw the legate a short time before his relief came along. Fronto was disorientated and staggering and the man left his post to offer help. The legate charged him with deserting his post and said he'd have him crucified. That was the last time anyone saw him alive.'

'And someone discovered his corpse the next day?'

'The next morning. A standing patrol of auxiliary cavalry check the immediate surroundings of the camp at first light every day. There's a sharp drop to the south of the complex, hidden by the shoulder of the hill. The body was found lying at the bottom of the slope.'

'And where is the body now?'

'We cremated the remains with due ceremony the next day, as is the custom.' Naso's voice took on a defensive note. 'We dispatched his ashes to Governor Agricola as soon as they were cold.' Valerius stared at him, wondering why Agricola hadn't thought to mention Fronto's ashes during their conversation. 'Our chief *medicus* and two of his assistants examined the body and all three confirmed the cause of death as a broken neck.'

Valerius sat back for a moment, trying to picture the scene and what had preceded it. The drunken Fronto staggering through the camp, out of the gate and into the darkness. Why? Something wasn't right here. A slip, a stumble, the plunge into the void.

'How steep is the cliff?'

'Steep, but I wouldn't quite call it a cliff. A man could climb down it relatively easily in daylight.'

'And a broken neck was his only injury.'

'Apart from a few bruises, yes.'

'I'd like to visit the scene.'

'Of course.' Naso rose, clearly relieved. 'I'll put together an escort right away. They'll be waiting by the gate.'

Idiot! 'Wait. You said the guard on the rampart was the last man to see the legate alive?'

'Yes, sir.'

'Then how did he get out of the fort? Only the main gate is open after dark. Surely it was guarded?'

'Of course, sir. Four men at all times, day and night. That's the mystery. None of them saw him go and we have no idea how he left.'

XXXIV

'What did you think of Naso's story?' Valerius helped Tabitha into her cloak when she emerged, looking thoughtful, from behind the curtain into the bedroom.

'He was telling the truth, I think, at least as far as the facts were concerned, but I sensed he was trying to hide his own doubts.' Valerius nodded. The same thought had occurred to him. 'What I would really like to know is how the legate of a Roman legion could walk out of his own fort without a single one of his men seeing him. Is there a way other than the main gate?'

'I inspected the defences with Naso when I arrived. They are just as you'd expect in enemy country, even in a temporary camp. A stray mouse couldn't cross the rampart without being challenged.'

'The other gates?'

'I'm assured they were all closed.'

'You must talk to the guards on the main gate, then.'

'I intend to.' They emerged from the *praetorium* into the anaemic sunshine of a day neither autumn nor winter, but caught somewhere between. The first true frost had coated the earth a hoary white that morning, enough to leave any basin left out overnight with a skin of ice, and the east wind whipped down the valley in short, chilling bursts.

'But first I think we should see where he died. I have some thoughts about that.'

Felix, Hilario, Shabolz and Crescens, fully armoured and with hands on sword hilts, formed a protective shield around them and Naso led the way to the main gate. Valerius studied the stolid, impassive faces of the gate guards and wondered if these were the same men who'd been on duty the night Fronto died. Probably not, but he'd find out.

He greeted the men of the escort and thanked them for their devotion to Tabitha. 'Everything went well, decurion?'

'By your leave, lord.' Felix dropped back to take step beside him. 'Well enough. We had no problems,' he hesitated and glanced at Shabolz, 'but there was a suggestion someone might have been watching us. We saw movement in the hills two or three times, but could never pin down the culprit.'

'Most of the way, on and off,' Shabolz confirmed. 'He was there, but we could never quite get close to him. Like a fox, that one.'

'But we're secure enough now.' Tabitha squeezed his hand. 'At the heart of your legion.'

'Perhaps, but why take chances? When you leave here tomorrow I'll provide a squadron of Thracian cavalry who are due to return to Viroconium. And Felix?'

'Lord?'

'While the lady is staying at the Twentieth's fort, I want two of our men with her at all times.'

The sound of horses interrupted them as a group of riders forced their way up the slope from the lake. At their head Valerius was surprised to see the governor's diligent young aide who had welcomed them to Londinium. He reined in, slipped from his horse and approached with a broad smile to give Valerius the customary salute.

'Metilius Aprilis, at your service. I apologize for not being here to welcome you on behalf of the governor, legate,' he doubled in an elegant bow, 'and lady. He asked us to bring back a comprehensive plan of the surrounding area and I've been in the saddle for three days.'

'So he sent you to report on the qualities of the Ninth.' Valerius returned his smile. 'And what have you learned?'

Aprilis sent a wary glance in Naso's direction and leaned closer. 'I would say there is room for improvement, lord, but from what I understand there is no better qualified commander to bring out the best in them.'

Valerius ignored the flattery. 'And my predecessor?'

Aprilis handed his reins to a groom who had run from the fort, and joined the little procession under the suspicious eyes of Valerius's escort. 'In all conscience I do not like to criticize someone so recently dead, but he was a difficult man to respect, never mind like. I dined with him the night before his accident and had to leave early because of a prior commitment, but I confess I had tired of his ill-bred and inappropriate behaviour.'

'May I ask the nature of your commitment?'

Aprilis showed no surprise at the question. 'My colleague and I had agreed I should make a snap inspection of the guards that night, specifically the gate guards. I went back to my quarters and changed into uniform. Later, when I was carrying out my inspection, I heard Legate Fronto threatening to crucify some poor fellow.'

'At what time would that be, approximately?'

'Shortly before the second change of guard. I had timed my inspection for the period when the guards were most likely to be relaxed, but I was perfectly satisfied with their conduct and I intended to transmit that to the legate the following day.'

By now they were breasting the shoulder of a hill about two hundred paces from the fort's main gate.

'Thank you, tribune,' Valerius said. 'My lady.' He ushered Tabitha through the escort and increased his pace until they caught up with Naso. At the top of the rise they could see down to a crumbling edge where the side of the hill had fallen away, leaving an almost vertical, boulder-strewn slope.

Naso pointed to a spot about ten paces ahead and five paces below. 'We believe Legate Fronto fell from here. I ordered a sack of grain to be left to mark the position of the body.'

'If you will excuse us, prefect. The lady also has some experience in these situations and I would like her to view the scene. ' Valerius took Tabitha's hand and they picked their way through the tussock grass down to the edge of the slope under the curious eyes of the escort and the two officers.

When they reached the lip, Valerius looked down to where a sack lay on a patch of nettles just beyond the lowest boulders of the landslip. 'Not a long way to fall,' he said quietly to Tabitha.

'Far enough to kill him.'

Valerius looked at his feet and the line between them and the sack. 'Perhaps.' He knelt on the crumbling edge and studied the turf. 'He must have walked along here, but there's nothing to show that he slipped.' He straightened and stared at the slope again.

'That means nothing. He was drunk. All he needed to do was lose his balance, but . . .'

'Yes,' he agreed. 'There are his injuries.'

'Or lack of them. That sack seems a long way out. Is it as far as it looks?'

'There's only one way to find out.' Valerius crouched so he could sit on the very lip of the slope and then lowered himself until his feet found solid ground. He looked up at his wife and grinned. 'There are only two situations when I really regret only having one hand. This is one of them.'

He turned and half climbed, half slid down the incline, using his left hand to anchor himself as he moved from boulder to boulder. As he went he checked the surfaces of the stones for blood or anything that would mark the progress of a tumbling body, but he saw nothing. When he reached the bottom, the sack was perhaps a single pace away, about the length of a cavalry *spatha*. 'And this is exactly where Fronto's body lay?' he called up to Naso.

'It marks the position of his chest. The body lay north–south.'

Valerius stared up to where Tabitha stood and he saw her slowly nod. He made his way back up the slope and dusted off his hands and clothing before they returned to the others.

'Well?' Naso said as they approached. 'Are you satisfied?'

'Yes, prefect,' Valerius assured him. 'I'm perfectly satisfied that Legate

Caristanius Fronto, commander of the Ninth legion, was murdered.'

Naso's eyes widened. Aprilis gave Valerius an appraising look. The escort tried to look as if this was something that happened every day when you were the legate's bodyguard, and Felix muttered: 'Shit.'

'But how?' Naso spluttered. 'He was drunk and he fell.'

'He was also hated by almost every man in the camp,' Valerius said. 'Including you. But that is not what makes me believe he was murdered.'

'I will have to report this to the governor, legate,' Aprilis said in a tone that suggested he carried his commander's authority. 'I would be interested to hear your reasoning.'

'It is true that he was drunk,' Valerius acknowledged. 'But you'll agree that no matter whether drunk or sober it is difficult to believe he could have walked out of the fort without being seen. One gate, four guards, another twenty watchful eyes on the walls.' He waited until Naso had nodded his agreement. 'That means he must have had help . . . or someone drugged or bludgeoned him and smuggled the body out.'

'Body? Surely the fall killed him?' Aprilis directed the question to Tabitha.

'He fell, yes,' she agreed. 'Or more likely he was thrown.' She was careful to include Naso in the exchange. 'It would have been helpful to see the body, but I understand your *medicus* suggested a broken neck and a few minor bruises were the legate's only injuries.'

'Yes.' Naso looked as if he could barely believe what was happening.

'A man who slipped and fell would have carried the marks of his fall,' she continued. 'The slope is strewn with boulders and sharp rocks. If he fell, Legate Fronto would have tumbled over them and had any number of scrapes, cuts and even one or two broken bones. Yes, he could have broken his neck in the fall, but his body was also too far from the slope. His momentum could never have carried him so far.'

'Which allows us to conclude that he didn't fall.' Valerius took up the story. 'He was thrown. Picked up bodily by two or more men and hurled from the top to make it appear as if he'd fallen. If that's the case his neck was certainly broken before he fell. Why take a chance that

278

the plunge wouldn't kill him? So Fronto was murdered. It's the only explanation.'

'But what will we do?' Naso protested. 'The campaign . . .'

'The campaign will proceed as if this never happened,' Valerius told him. His voice took on a new hardness as he turned his gaze on the escort. 'And no man here will speak of this. As far as your comrades are concerned the legate died in an accident. Do I make myself clear?'

'Clear, lord.' Hilario glared at his comrades.

'Felix?'

'Of course, lord.'

'So we will go to war,' Valerius said. 'And you and I, Naso, will find the murderer.'

'You make it all sound easy.' The comment came from Aprilis as he accompanied Valerius back to camp.

'Whoever killed him is part of this legion,' Valerius said. 'It's just a question of finding who was where and when at the approximate time of his death. We'll start with the gate guards, and work our way through the men who had the most reason to get rid of him. You don't kill someone because he denied you leave or stole the cost of a new *gladius.*'

'The men he forced into his bed.' Aprilis let his disgust show.

'Not a pleasant thought, I know,' Valerius admitted. 'But I will find the killer. Of course, it would be easier if I'd had a chance to inspect the body.'

'Yes,' the young tribune agreed. 'The officers did appear to be in an unseemly hurry to have him cremated.'

Valerius turned to study him. 'Are you suggesting something?'

'Not at all.' Aprilis smiled. 'All I'm saying is that they wanted all this – and I don't just mean the murder – put behind them. A perfectly valid aspiration, you'd admit, for the good of the legion. On a different subject, I am leaving tomorrow and I'd hoped to be able to take the governor a summary of your findings. If that's not possible,' he continued hurriedly, 'I can give him my own . . .'

'No,' Valerius said. 'You'll have it.'

'Thank you, sir. I also understand that the lady Tabitha and your son

279

are to accompany the troop returning to Viroconium. I'd consider it an honour if you'd allow me to offer them my personal protection.'

'Of course, Melanius. But don't be surprised if she turns you down. Four of my men will be looking after her for me, and they're good.'

'All the better, legate,' Aprilis said seriously as they approached the fort. 'As your esteemed predecessor discovered, you can't be too careful in this gods-benighted country.'

XXXV

Cearan fought the urge to coax the gelding to a faster pace through the mountain mists and risk laming the animal or exhausting him. He could feel time running out, but the information he carried would be of little use if he didn't reach his destination. Roman patrols salted these mountains and in their present mood they would show him no mercy. He had stalked the convoy carrying Valerius's wife and son until they reached Viroconium. The amount of baggage unloaded told him the pair were likely to stay for some weeks, perhaps even the whole winter. He rubbed his aching back. He was much too old to be spending eight hours a day in the saddle, sleeping on the hard, unyielding earth to wake covered in frost. But if the recurring dream was right this would be the last trip. The track he followed was perfectly familiar despite the fog. He'd used it many times in the past ten years, since his wounds had recovered sufficiently for him to be of use. The druid's words as Boudicca's horde disintegrated in a welter of blood remained as clear in his head as if they had been carved in stone. 'Never forget that the gods have a use for you. Every warrior who dies here is but a seed planted for the future. Seek me out when you are ready.'

'But how will I find you?'

'I am everywhere.' The words had sent a shiver through Cearan that had nothing to do with the cold. 'I am legion. But if you are lost, mention the name Gwlym in the places where they are still true to the old gods.'

It had taken a year of searching, but eventually his enquiries had drawn him west to the Druids' Isle. In those days men believed it was inhabited only by the ghosts of those who had worshipped there. Sailors stayed well away from the haunted, blood-soaked shore and only the bravest chose to cross the treacherous narrow strait. Some came to seek out the past, some for treasure. None of the latter ever returned.

Cearan understood he'd been driven mad the day the Romans had stolen his reason for living. As he'd lain in Aenid's blood choking on his own, his heart had shattered and grief tore his mind apart as a wolf sunders a dying lamb. The mental wounds had taken longer to heal than the physical, if they truly ever had. Perhaps he was still mad, because how would a madman know? A savage, visceral hatred for all things Roman and a desperate, all-encompassing need to avenge his wife were all that sustained him.

At first what he discovered on Mona had shaken his faith, but slowly he'd begun to understand. When he'd looked upon Gwlym it had been like staring into a copper mirror. The wounds and disfigurements were different, but their effects were the same, sharpening the focus of the hatred, channelling the mind to a single aim. What kind of strength did it take for a man to pluck out his own eyes? And what could a man not achieve with that strength?

'Do you still believe?'

'Yes.'

'Then the gods have sent you.'

'What can I do?'

'You have sacrificed everything except your honour.'

Cearan had bowed his head and wept.

'Are you prepared to sacrifice that honour?'

'I am your man,' he had sobbed.

'We are weak . . .'

'I see no weakness.'

'But we will be strong again. Strong enough to do what would have been done if she had not been betrayed.'

'What would you have me do?'

'Debase yourself. Dress in rags and roll in filth. Starve. Seek out the Romans and the Roman lovers. Go among them as the lowest of the low. Beg food and shelter. Most will abuse you, beat you and spit on you. Those who do not will make you sleep with their pigs and share the food of their dogs. Persist. And learn. You will be my eyes and ears. You and a hundred others. Bring me news of Roman troop movements and strengths. Their suppliers among our people and the routes they use. And the names of those who work with them, profit from them or succour them.'

For seven years he had *rolled in filth* gathering the information Gwlym sought, risking perilous journeys to Mona to pass news to the druid. Those who supplied the Romans knew about their movements even before the legionaries themselves, because the farriers and armourers had to make preparations in advance. And if the merchants and farmers did not deign to talk to a disfigured beggar their slaves often would, thereby adding their masters' names to the long list of Roman lovers who would fuel the funeral pyre of Roman Britannia.

He had witnessed a Mona reborn, the ancient groves reconsecrated, the sacred treasures disinterred, the support of the gods secured with the flesh of a thousand sacrifices. And with Mona's rise, Gwlym's power grew. A trickle at first: farmers with donations of food, seeking the gods' blessing; peasants with rusted pieces of iron to be thrown into the sacred pool; a local clan chief with a dozen retainers and a slave to be offered for sacrifice. Druids who had burned or buried their robes and regalia to avoid execution began to reappear, and soon they were joined by the representatives of tribal leaders and kings, warily testing the strength of this new power in the land.

Two years earlier the druid had made a new request. As well as seeking information, Cearan was to spread word among the villages and farmsteads. The druids are returning. Make room for them around the communal pot and the council fire. Taranis and Andraste have regained their power and it is growing even as that of the Roman gods weakens. Sharpen your swords and spear points and paint your shields. Wait for the word.'

As he rode, the hatred and self-loathing that had consumed him since his encounter with Valerius had grown like a fire within him. All these long years he'd been tortured by the knowledge that Boudicca had been betrayed or deserted by the gods. There was no other explanation for the way Paulinus's army had appeared at the only time and in the only place that guaranteed the defeat of her enormous army of Celtic warriors. To discover that Valerius had been the instrument of her downfall and that *his* mercy had been the ultimate cause of it brought him once more to the brink of that seething pit of madness from which there would be no return. It was only by sheer force of will he survived. There would be no more mercy.

The gelding stopped of his own choice and chewed at a tuft of grass by the path. Suddenly the mist cleared as if it were a curtain drawn back by the gods. Cearan stiffened and felt a surge of what might once have been joy, but now was merely a savage pleasure. The mountain slope fell away before him with the track a pale snake winding through it. Beyond the slope lay a flat plain chequered with fields and farmsteads, and a hilly peninsula that jutted out into the ocean. But Cearan knew the peninsula wasn't what it seemed. It was an island.

Mona.

An hour later he approached the boatman waiting at the jetty. The man didn't raise his eyes from the fishing net he was repairing. 'Two hours till the tide is right.'

Cearan knew all he could do was wait. Nothing he said would change the man's mind or make him sail a moment earlier. Riptides and surging currents combined to turn the narrow strait into a deadly barrier as effective as any palisade. He tethered his horse to a nearby bush, with enough freedom to reach the narrow stream that ran nearby, found a sandy bank and lay back and closed his eye.

Later, he sensed a shadow blocking the sun and woke to find the boatman looming over him.

'It is time.'

He followed the ferryman to the narrow wooden boat and climbed in to take his place on a wooden bench worn smooth by the seats of a thousand others. The craft was built to carry six, but he was the only passenger. Another crossing existed further north where the strait narrowed still further, but this would bring him ashore closer to his destination. The boatman propelled the vessel with smooth easy strokes of the oars, a lifetime of experience keeping him on course. Cearan sat facing the far shore and as they came nearer he noticed men working with spades and mattocks just above the tideline. Another difference from his previous visits were the large heaps of wood piled on the sand at regular intervals. They might have been signal fires but for the upright wooden stake at their centre. The boatman stowed his oars as his craft beached on the shingle with a prolonged crunch. He leapt out and dragged it a few feet further to allow Cearan to land dry-shod. Cearan retrieved half a link from a copper chain from a pouch under his cloak and handed it to the man, who studied it for a moment before nodding agreement.

He walked up the beach past the line of pyres. Now he could see that the men were digging a deep trench. The nearest group studied him with wary eyes as he approached, suspicious of the Roman clothing he wore. They were seasoned warriors wearing only cloth *bracae*, their chests and backs covered in tattoos that told others their clan and status and the number of men they'd killed in battle. Cearan mentally compared them to similarly aged men of the eastern tribes, softened by years of bending to Roman will, their fathers' swords left rusting in the thatch and bronze shield covers used to water the cattle. It was the contrast between dusty sparrows with stooping hawks.

A big man with suspicious eyes, a hook nose and dark moustaches drooping below his chin laid aside his mattock and picked up a spear. Cearan raised his hands to show they were empty, but the warrior held the spear steady and aimed directly at his heart, the stolid face hardening as he noticed Cearan's terrible disfigurement.

'I seek the arch-druid Gwlym, and the spirit of the hare and the wolf ride with me.'

The spear point dropped. The hare and the wolf were the creatures of Andraste and her followers used the phrase to identify one another.

'Then you are welcome,' the man said. He pointed to a path that wound its way west through a bleak landscape of low, windswept dunes covered with a patchwork of sea grass and sparse scrub. 'If you follow that track for an hour, you will reach a farmstead. They will be able to tell you where the druids gather. Have you travelled far?'

'From the country of the Iceni.'

The warrior nodded. 'Far enough, then, to be thirsty.' He stooped and picked up a red clay pot and handed it to Cearan. The Iceni drank – a warm, thin beer that tasted of pine needles – and handed back the pot with his thanks.

They stood together for a moment looking out over the strait to the mountains beyond. 'Will they come soon, do you think?'

'Soon enough,' Cearan answered.

'Good. We are ready for them.'

A mile or so inland the ground changed to grassy sward, with cultivated fields and patches of forest. In one wooded area a stockade had been built, with high timber walls. Hard-eyed guards flanked the gate and from within came the chilling sound of women's screams. Cearan knew the source of that sound; indeed, he had contributed to it. One of the prisoners was the woman he'd ordered taken from the farm near Colonia. It gave him no pleasure to be reminded of their fate, but he closed his ears and hardened his heart and continued onwards. Smoke from scattered encampments along the coastline marked the locations of hundreds, perhaps thousands of warriors who had answered Gwlym's call to defend Mona. He passed the low mounds that were the resting places of the ancients. Most showed signs of having been searched for treasure even in this holiest of holy places, proving that even the Druids' Isle was not safe from those possessed by gold fever. In the distance a circle of enigmatic standing stones were silhouetted against the horizon like revellers caught dancing round a Samhain fire.

A small group of roundhouses marked the position of the farm and he found an old woman with lank grey hair and a toothless smile of welcome milking a goat outside the palisade. He enquired politely where he could find the arch-druid Gwlym, but her answer in the local dialect was so garbled as to be unintelligible. All he caught was the repeated word *nemeth*, which was similar to the term the Ordovices used to describe an oak grove. Eventually, she tired of his presence and threw out a hand towards the rising ground to the west. He thanked her, but she had already returned to extracting what she could from the goat's swollen teats.

A copse of trees stood out on the crest of the hill and instinct drew him towards it. He followed a direct line, having to scramble occasionally and stopping at intervals to regather his strength.

Just one more rocky crest stood between him and the trees. As he topped the brow of the hill he saw it had a broad rounded top with a dozen thatched mud and wattle roundhouses away to his left. The trees, a much broader band of oaks than he had imagined, filled the rest of the hill and spilled down the reverse slope. He turned to look back the way he'd come. From here he could see across the strait to the mountains of Ordovice country, where Agricola's legions might already be on the march. His mind flitted back to the confidence of the warriors guarding the shore, the trenches, the pyres and the tide race that swept through the strait at the speed of a galloping horse. All barriers of different types, the human, the physical, the mental and the natural. Yet a younger Cearan had once stood with a great Celtic leader on one side of a formidable river, backed by just such obstacles, while the legions of Rome formed up on the other. Despite all the Celts' precautions, the legions had crossed and Caratacus was forced to flee in defeat.

A shout interrupted his thoughts and a dozen armed men emerged from among the houses to surround him. Again he repeated the mantra of the hare and the wolf. 'I have news of great importance for the arch-druid,' he told the leader.

'Then you will have to wait here,' the man said with a wary glance at the ranks of oak trees. 'Only a madman would interrupt their ceremonies.'

Cearan sat against a grass bank, taking the last of his dry bread from the leather pouch looped across his shoulder and chewing pensively. It was colder up here and he pulled his cloak tighter about him. Or perhaps not cold. Something about this hill made him think of blood and death. He wondered about the lack of defences. But the druids had their own ways of striking terror into attackers. He had heard tales of ghost warriors and fences of skulls. What had he been thinking of, striking away from the path? The wind whispered through the tree canopy, but another sound caught his ear and he recognized the drone of men chanting. What horrors were being perpetrated behind that wall of trees?

At last, movement. Cearan rose to his feet as a procession of men in homespun cloth robes emerged from the oaks. At their head, flanked by two acolytes, walked the man he had come to meet, a diminutive, almost feeble figure with a weary ancient's stiff-legged gait. But Cearan knew how volatile Gwlym could be and the horrors he could bring down on any who failed or displeased him. He watched as the guard approached the column and relayed his message from a respectful distance. One of the acolytes raised his hand and the procession halted. After a moment the leaders stepped aside and the other druids continued towards the roundhouses. Three heads turned towards him and Cearan felt himself the focus of those pus-filled eye sockets.

'Approach.' The taller of the two acolytes waved him forward.

Cearan did as he was ordered, stopping three paces short of the little group of priests.

'Closer,' Gwlym rasped. Cearan advanced two steps until he was staring directly into the other man's face and the twin white craters seemed to be looking inside his soul. Two skeletal arms extended towards him and he cringed as the bony fingers ran over his face, probing the wounds and caressing the scar tissue. No other human being had touched his face since this man had used the healing powers of his order to save Cearan's life in a stinking fisherman's hut east of Venta

Icenorum. Cearan knew the action was designed to humiliate, to remind him of his disfigurement and the debt he owed the druid.

'Yes, this is the Iceni prince,' Gwlym confirmed. 'Once so proud of his beauty and arrogant enough to believe he could ignore the power of the old gods and even bend the great beast of Rome to his will.' Cearan froze. He'd thought the only man who knew of his negotiations to replace Boudicca as the ruler of the Iceni was Valerius. 'Not so proud now, my handsome prince. Dead inside all these years.' The thin lips curled in an amused sneer. 'But your suffering will soon be over.'

Cearan stared at him with his single eye. 'What have you seen?'

'It is not what I have seen, but what I can smell. Something is growing inside you. Already you can feel its effects. A dull ache at the base of your spine. A change in the consistency of your night soil.' Cearan's knees buckled and one of the acolytes stepped forward to hold him upright. The harsh voice softened a little. 'Soon you will no longer be able to be of service to me. But I have one last task for you, Cearan of the Iceni.'

The knowledge that he was dying – he had no doubt Gwlym was telling the truth, the signs were there – felt like a punch that knocked the breath from him. Odd that the reality of his mortality should have such an effect on him. He had thought he would welcome death, but the eternal darkness had no allure for him. It turned out he had many more things he wanted to do and to see. He drew himself up to his full height. 'Name it, lord.'

'First tell me what you have learned. Who will support us when the time comes?'

Cearan searched his memory and recited the long list of southern tribes, the Dobunni, the Corieltauvi, the Deceangli and the Cornovii, the Iceni, the Catuvellauni and the Atrebates, their sub-tribes and their clans. The chiefs who bent the knee to Rome, but secretly longed for the return of the old religion. Those who were fearful, but would be driven by the bloodlust of their young warriors. How many warriors each would field when the time came. 'When the Ninth and Twentieth legions are trapped in the valleys, the Deceangli and the Cornovii will combine to attack Deva, while the Dobunni and the Durotriges burn Isca.'

'So many?' Gwlym's bony fingers gripped his wrist. 'You are certain of the numbers?'

Of course he was certain of the numbers. How could he not be? He had created each and every one from his own imagination. It was all a lie. The druid believed he was all-seeing, but Cearan had been telling him what he wanted to hear for years, and he suspected others had done the same. Many would have done so through fear of the consequences had they not, but Cearan's reasons were different. Gwlym was the keeper of the flame of resistance, and without that flame Cearan's visions of revenge would have died long ago. The flame had to be fanned by dreams and optimism, and Cearan had fed Gwlym enough dreams and optimism to conjure up the balefire of Roman Britannia, if only it was true. The butchery of the Roman cavalrymen at Canovium would have been enough for now, but Gwlym had much grander ideas. Cearan saw the druid's ambitions as an opportunity to wreak the terrible revenge he sought on the man he hated more than any other.

'I have other information, lord. I believe it will please you equally.'

'What is it?'

'Many years ago you convinced me that Queen Boudicca was not defeated, but betrayed. You urged me to listen for any word that might identify the betrayers so they could be hunted down and subjected to your vengeance. I believe I have found the source of her downfall.'

Gwlym spat like an angry cat. 'Then they will suffer an eternity of agony before they are consumed by the slow fire of Beli Mawr.'

'It will be difficult, lord.' Cearan ignored the hiss of anger. 'The man is now a high-ranking Roman officer. He served with the beast Paulinus and seduced a Trinovante maiden into revealing Boudicca's line of march.'

'Then she too must die.'

'When she understood the scale of her betrayal she threw herself on the swords of the invaders.'

'Justly so.' Gwlym nodded gravely. 'This officer, we must find a way to him.'

'He is guarded night and day,' Cearan said. 'But there is another way.' He revealed the information his investigation had uncovered in Colonia and how he believed it might be used.

'Yes.' A sightless smile flickered on Gwlym's haggard features. 'I see it now.'

Cearan felt a gripe in his guts that reminded him of something the druid had said earlier. 'You mentioned a last service.'

Those empty eye sockets again, searching his soul.

'I want you to kill Julius Agricola.'

XXXVI

Valerius saw Tabitha and Lucius to the carriage next day, cheeks pink from the cold and wrapped in thick cloaks against the biting wind. Ceris waited to help them inside as the Thracian cavalry escort gentled their eager mounts and wisps of steam smoked the chill air above the horses. Their goodbyes had already been said and he and Tabitha parted with a chaste kiss and a whispered assurance of mutual love.

As they settled into the coach, Valerius approached the Corieltauvi girl. 'I ask you to take the greatest care of the lady Tabitha,' he said. 'And I grant you authority to take what decisions are in her best interests.'

Ceris speared him with a glance that suggested she needed no man to give her authority. 'The lady Tabitha is perfectly capable of making her own decisions,' she said. 'But she knows I would never suggest anything that would harm her and the child.' She took a last look around the temporary camp and its backdrop of grey, scree-scarred mountains. 'I am glad we are leaving this place. There is something unwholesome about it.' She turned to enter the carriage, but hesitated for a moment. 'I wish you had inherited a better legion.' Valerius stared at her until he remembered she'd been with the Ninth at Lindum and would have heard all the stories about Legate Fronto. 'But you are a soldier and you will make the best of what you have.' Her eyes took on a faraway look and her voice faltered. 'You are not infallible, Gaius Valerius Verrens. You should have killed the one-eyed man.'

Before Valerius could reply she was inside the wagon. He called Marius who would command the bodyguards, including Florus and Serenus. 'Stay close, Marius. The Thracians are capable enough, but beware the man with the scarred face. I may have underestimated him.'

'You may count on us, sir.' Marius nodded. 'And may Fortuna favour your honour. I wish . . .'

Valerius smiled. 'I know, but I need someone I trust in charge of protecting my wife and son.'

He saw Aprilis staring at him and remembered he'd forgotten the report for Agricola. 'My apologies, tribune.' He handed over the leather scroll case. 'All my findings so far in the matter concerning Fronto. If I discover anything else I'll send word by courier.'

'Thank you, sir. I'll make certain he gets it the moment we return.'

Valerius smiled. 'I think he may have other things on his mind.'

'I'm sure you're right. This will be my first campaign – I missed the Brigante business – and I'm not sure what to expect.'

Valerius patted his horse's flank. 'Just stay close to the governor,' he advised. 'You're his aide; it's not your job to get killed. But if you do get into a fight, keep moving, remember the edge always beats the point, and if you're inside the point your opponent is a dead man.'

'Thank you for your advice, sir. Be sure I'll take it.'

Aprilis's grin made him look almost boyish, and for a moment Valerius felt old. 'And while I'm handing out advice, keep one eye out for our former *primus pilus* Tertius. He has a lot to answer for. It grieves me to let him go unpunished, but Agricola may have a different view. I wouldn't want him slipping away.'

'I'll make sure he's looked after,' Aprilis assured him. He slapped his fist against his chest armour in salute. 'By your leave, legate.'

Valerius nodded. A trumpet call rang out and the Thracians nudged their horses forward, but he only had eyes for the carriage. The curtain drew back and he saw Tabitha's face, her expression solemn, with Lucius squeezed in close. He waved and they waved back, and then they were gone, leaving him with an immense sense of loss.

Next morning he formed the legion up on the grassy plain beside the lake. Not a full legion, of course. Six cohorts of legionaries with their supporting auxiliary light infantry and cavalry. Five thousand men, plus the fully loaded mules of the baggage train. No heavy weapons, because they would be moving fast through difficult terrain and against an enemy unlikely to mass against them. Still, Valerius felt a pang of doubt at the missing *ballistae* and *onager*. He'd seen the effect of the dreaded shield-splitters, five foot long bolts launched from massive wooden bows, and the damage they could do to an enemy's morale. Impressive enough, though. This, Agricola would tell you, was the true glory of Rome, this massed array of disciplined legionaries standing in their packed squares, armour glittering in the low morning sun, the points of their heavy *pila* twinkling, and their brightly painted shields a wall of colour. Six cohort standards, plus thirty-six *signa*, the spears that carried the unit citations of each century.

But no eagle.

Agricola had assured Valerius that he would be no Varus. The Roman general Publius Quinctilius Varus had lost three legions and their eagles in the forests and swamps of northern Germania, ambushed by the forces of a man who had once fought for Rome. An eagle was more than a legion's symbol, it was the unit's soul, for which every man must be prepared to die. A legion that lost its eagle lost its honour and sometimes its name, the survivors being broken up among other formations. The fact that Agricola wanted to send the majority of the Ninth's legionaries into battle without their eagle carried its own message.

Valerius stood on a hillside overlooking the still formations in the full panoply of a Roman commander. He wore a sculpted leather breastplate covered in gold leaf and his legate's sash knotted at his waist. His helmet was as magnificent as his chest armour, with a gilded rim and a stylized griffon's head below the scarlet horsehair crest. A scarlet cloak covered his shoulders held by a golden brooch on his left breast.

He'd known generals to send their legionaries into battle without a word, depending on experience and discipline to carry them forward to overwhelm the enemy. Corbulo had been one. But Corbulo's legions had loved him. The soldiers of the Ninth despised their senior officers, had no reason to love their centurions, and little faith in their comrades. Take them into battle like this and Valerius had no way of knowing how they would react when the Ordovices fell like eagles from the mountain heights or the very grass at their feet, the trees and the bushes erupted with flights of spears and slingstones. He had to do something, so he'd done the only thing he could think of.

'Legionaries of the Ninth legion Hispana,' he roared. 'Men call you unlucky.' He paused, and in the silence he could hear a wave of angry muttering as they reacted to the words, relayed to them by centurions stationed for that purpose in every cohort. 'But I am your new legate and I say you have been unlucky only in the men who led you.' A few shouts of 'Aye' swiftly silenced by the curses of the officers. Those who abused their authority have been dismissed or demoted. From this day forward the Ninth is a legion in which every man looks out for every other and fights for every other. As an example of this, there will be no retaliation against the centurions who have been reduced to the ranks or have lost seniority. All that is in the past. You have heard what happened at Canovium. Today the Ninth Hispana marches west to avenge their comrades who died. For that we will need every man. The Ordovice warriors we face are a hard and implacable enemy. They proved at Canovium that they will show you no mercy. You will show them none.' A great rumble of approval. 'We will march fast, maintaining the pressure on our foes and hoping to bring them to battle. That means every man must be vigilant for ambush. Every man must be instantly ready for battle. When the time comes and the enemy closes, your life will depend on the man next to you, and his on you. You are brothers in arms. Remember that when you argue over the last spoonful in the pot or whose turn it is to dig the shit pit.' They liked that and showed it, so he gave them a few moments to think about it. 'You, every last one of you, are the beating hearts of the Ninth Hispana, and between us we will make it a legion that will be remembered through-out history and strike fear in the Empire's enemies.' His words inspired a single cheer that swiftly multiplied to a roar from five thousand throats. Valerius raised his hand and the sound gradually faded. 'You march behind an eagle . . .'

He greeted the consternation on their faces with a grim smile.

'A legion without its eagle is not a legion. Hilario!' he called. The big man stepped out from where he'd been concealed in the ranks of Valerius's personal bodyguard. He was holding a lengthy object wrapped in a cloth bag. Valerius nodded and he pulled the cloth free. The idea had come to him three nights earlier and a relay of couriers had ridden for forty-eight hours to bring it here from Lindum. A legion without its eagle is not a legion. Hilario raised the object high and the roar that greeted it might have flattened the surrounding mountains. The eagle of the Ninth. Cast in brass and covered in gold leaf, wings flared and beak gaping in defiance. A legion's spirit. A legion's soul.

'This is your eagle,' Valerius continued as the roar subsided. 'This is what you fight for. Your former legate didn't bring it because he feared you wouldn't be able to protect it.' Cries of 'No!' and 'Never'. 'He didn't think you were worthy of it.' Valerius took the eagle from Hilario's hands and raised it high. 'Are you worthy of it?'

'Yes!' five thousand throats roared as one.

'Then get down on your knees and let me hear you give your oath to protect it.'

They knelt and in the silence that followed Valerius led them through the words. 'In the name of Jupiter Optimus Maximus we swear to protect this eagle, this symbol of our emperor's faith, to defend it to our last spear and our last breath, or may the gods strike us down. For Rome.'

'Rise.' Valerius handed the eagle to Gaius Quintus Naso as the acknowledgement echoed in the still air. 'Choose a man worthy of carrying it and a *contubernium* for close protection. We march in an hour.'

He turned away with a long sigh of relief. It had gone better than he expected. They still weren't the legion he wanted them to be. The divisions caused by years of abuse and the slackness and resentment that resulted from it couldn't be repaired by a few stirring words and the sight of an eagle. But it was a start.

The unit's Celtic scouts had selected the first day's camp site. They reached the place around mid-afternoon and as he waited for the legate's pavilion to be erected Valerius inspected the defences. Soldiers toiled like worker ants all around the perimeter digging ditches and building earth banks that would be topped by the palisade stakes each man had carried on the march. Four men from one *contubernium* of eight worked on each six-foot section of ditch, while the others raised their tent, replenished their water, built a fire to cook the evening's meal of sweetened porridge and helped dig a latrine. Valerius was pleased to see every legionary, whether working or not, wore his sword belt, even though the cavalry provided an outer defensive screen for the camp. The only sign they'd had of the enemy were a few scouts who'd disappeared at the first sign of pursuit, but Valerius was taking no chances. He watched for a few moments as the men worked, monitoring the depth of the ditch and the angle of the slope. Two laboured with mattock and pickaxe in the ditch, one shovelled the loose spoil into a basket and dragged it up the bank and the fourth spread the earth and tamped the spoil firm. It was all done with admirable efficiency and he praised the *duplicarius* in charge.

'Your tent is ready, sir,' Felix reported.

'Thank you, decurion,' Valerius acknowledged with a weary smile. 'A good start, I think. Fifteen miles and not too many stragglers. Tell the acting *primus pilus* I want every man to check his sandals at first light. One loose nail can lose us a man, and we can't afford to lose men. The quartermaster clerk can bring me the day's ration returns once I've eaten.'

'Yes, sir.'

'And Felix . . . Once the men are settled I'd like to speak to the soldiers who were on guard duty at the main gate the night the legate died. The camp prefect will have their names and their centuries. No formalities, they can come in their work clothes.'

'Sir.'

In due course the four men filed in, each looking wary in his own way, darting eyes and chewed lips, fists clenching and unclenching, as if wondering which direction the blow was coming from. Valerius's frown deepened at the sight. These were legionaries in the habit of being misused. The signs were a symptom of what had gone before and one which he must quickly reverse. Naso stood to one side of Valerius's campaign desk and the four men formed a rough line in front of them, staring at the tent wall between Valerius and his camp prefect.

'You can relax,' Valerius told them. 'You've done nothing wrong. All I want to do is talk to you. You've eaten?' An indistinct murmur of assent. 'Didius,' he called. Gallus had drawn duty as his servant. 'Bring these men a cup of wine.'

Wariness was replaced by consternation. They'd learned to fear their former legate. The best they could expect was to be flayed by his tongue, not handed a cup of wine.

'You're here because you were on duty the night Legate Fronto died,' Naso told them when they'd accepted their cups. 'As the legate said, you have done nothing wrong, but we need to know exactly what happened that night. Choose one man to speak for you, but if any of the others feels a point needs to be made, or something has been missed, do not be afraid to say so. It is your duty to speak out. Is that understood?'

A chorus of 'Yes, sir'.

'So who is your spokesman?' Three pairs of eyes darted to the left at Valerius's question, and the tallest of the four, a tanned, spare veteran with a long neck and a worried expression, stepped forward.

'Avidius, front rank, fourth century, Second cohort, sir.'

'Well, Avidius?'

'We were called by the duty centurion as usual that night, sir. Antonius, one of our tentmates, looked us over. We filed out of the tent and the centurion inspected us again and had no complaints.'

'I'm glad to hear it. So, the centurion marched you to your station?'

'Yes, sir.'

'Did you notice anything unusual on the way?'

Avidius looked at the others and licked his lips. 'Not unusual sir, but there was a commotion in the legate's quarters.'

'What kind of commotion?'

'Just shouting and laughing, sir.'

'No arguments?'

'No, sir. It all seemed quite cheerful.' Avidius gave an ironic snort, but stiffened at a glare from Naso, who Valerius doubted enjoyed being reminded of his part in the revels. 'We relieved the guard and took our positions. Two inside the gate and two out. It was a quiet night, sir. No late arrivals or leavers. Near the end of our watch I was inside with Pompeius here when we heard shouting from near the west wall. From what I heard I understood the legate was taking somebody to task, sir.'

'A gentle dressing down?'

'Well, no sir. He was threatening one of the wall guards with cruci-fixion.' He glanced at Naso. 'With respect to the dead, sir, when Legate Fronto made a threat he was perfectly capable of carrying it out.'

Valerius nodded. 'So you didn't think of intervening?'

'Not our job, sir. Not if we valued our heads.'

'And you didn't see Legate Fronto again?'

'No, sir.'

'The only thing that happened we didn't expect,' Pompeius, the youngest of the group, interjected, 'was the inspection. That's right, Avidius?'

'That's right, sir. Just after we heard the, er, altercation, one of the tribunes the governor sent to run an eye over the legion came to make a surprise inspection. He got us all together, looked over every inch of our equipment and asked us a lot of questions. Afterwards he was very complimentary, sir, about our turnout and our equipment.'

'Thank you.' Avidius's story confirmed what Aprilis had said two days earlier and Valerius had no doubt he was telling the truth. Which left one question.

'Do any of you have any idea how Legate Fronto could have left the camp?'

The men looked at each other. 'We've been asking ourselves the same question ever since that night, sir,' Avidius said. 'And we reckon the only way he could have done it is if he'd grown wings and flown.'

Valerius smiled. 'Given where he was found, soldier, I think that's the one talent the legate was lacking.'

He was about to let them go when he looked at something he'd written earlier. He exchanged a glance with Naso and addressed Avidius. 'If you're from the fourth century of the Second perhaps you can tell me the names of the tentmates of a former legionary named Julius Noricus?'

Four faces froze in the same instant, and it was the young soldier who replied. 'Beg to report, legate, that we *are* the tentmates of Julius Noricus.'

The silence seemed to last an eternity before Valerius drew in a long breath. 'Avidius, please fetch the rest of your *contubernium*. Don't stand on ceremony – this is urgent.'

Within a minute they'd been joined by four other men. Three older legionaries, obviously veterans, and one fresh-faced youngster.

'You are all the former tentmates of Julius Noricus?'

'All bar Antonius here,' the oldest of the men replied, automatically taking over the role of spokesman from Avidius. 'He joined us after . . .'

'After what?'

'After Julius left us,' the soldier replied. 'He was a gentle lad. Not really cut out for the legion.'

'I know what happened to him. What I want you to tell me is why.'

'I wouldn't rightly know, sir.' The words were accompanied by a blank stare as the man's eyes focussed on a point on the tent behind Valerius's back. Valerius let his eyes slide over the others, but all he read was the same look and he knew he would get nothing else.

'All right,' he conceded. 'I can understand that, but I command this legion and by the gods if you don't answer my next question you will no longer be part of it. Your tentmates were on guard duty on the night

Legate Fronto died. I want to know exactly where the rest of you were. And do not leave out a single detail.'

'We did what we always do before guard duty, sir.' The legionary's voice quivered with conviction. 'We played dice, but not for money, on my honour. We slept for a while, and then we were woken to relieve Avidius and the lads.'

Something about this information didn't fit. He turned to Naso. 'Is it normal for two watches to be drawn from the same tent on the same night?'

The camp prefect gave him a puzzled look. 'No, sir.'

'It puzzled us too,' the old soldier said. 'Because none of us was due to go on guard duty for another two days. Right piss— annoyed we were when we heard.'

'So it was out of the ordinary?'

'Completely, sir.'

Then why? Valerius's mind raced. No, not why: who? 'Which of your officers was responsible for the watch list?'

'The *primus pilus*, sir. And that was the other puzzling thing. He usually left it to his deputy.'

Tertius.

Fool that he was, he'd sent the man who could hold the key to Fronto's murder entirely beyond his reach.

'What do you think?' Valerius asked Naso when they were gone.

'You can't deny they had the motive and the opportunity to kill Fronto. We only have their word for it that four of them stayed in the tent. It's not too far from where the legate was last seen. Three to overcome him, one to put a blanket over his head. A neck lock and a quick twist. The gods know the bastard deserved it.' He shrugged. 'After the dressing down he'd had the wall guard wasn't going to react to any strange sounds. Then past their tentmates on the gate who are conveniently looking the other way. Yes, they could have done it.'

'But?'

'A veteran legionary's face is like a newly plastered wall. It could be hiding anything. I know,' he gave Valerius a wry smile, 'I've been one of them. If it was just the old soldiers I'd say get them in one at a time and sweat them. Really sweat them. But eight men, including a couple of new recruits? They're terrified of you, legate. Oh yes,' he saw Valerius's look of disbelief, 'that speech you gave them put the hairs up on the back of their necks, just like it did mine, but it also sent a *ballista* bolt up their collective arse and that look in your eyes scared them. They know when it comes to it you'll march them into the jaws of Hades without a thought. One of those men should have blinked, but they didn't, not even the young ones. Still, it might be worth . . .'

'I'd agree with you, but for one thing.'

'And that is?'

'If Fronto had done to one of my friends what he did to Julius Noricus I wouldn't have snapped his neck. I'd have burned the bastard alive.'

Naso nodded, thoughtfully. 'And then there's Tertius. A coincidence, surely?'

Valerius met his eyes. 'The one thing I've learned, prefect, is that when you're looking for a murderer there is no such thing as a coincidence.' He felt an itch that told him he could be missing something. He went over Avidius's testimony in his mind. 'What do you know of Metilius Aprilis, the governor's aide?'

A hunted expression flickered across Naso's lined features, but eventually he said: 'I think he would have had me removed, but for your presence.'

'Possibly,' Valerius agreed, to the camp prefect's consternation. 'I was thinking more of his background. He told me he'd never seen active service, but there was something about him that didn't seem consistent with what he said.'

'I know nothing about his soldiering, but I remember he boasted about having friends on the Palatine with the ear of the Emperor's inner circle. A brother or a cousin.'

Valerius felt a sudden chill that had nothing to do with the draughty tent. Could it be? It was the eyes that made him wonder. Yes, those eyes. He shook his head, but . . . There were no coincidences when you were looking for a murderer.

XXXVII

Tiberius Gabinius Tertius lifted his tunic and let out a sigh of contentment as he pissed copiously against the oak tree. When he'd finished he wiped his cock dry on the cloth hem and contemplated his future, which didn't look too bright. Oh, he had plenty of money stashed away from his little enterprises, but it was in Lindum, and it didn't look as though he'd be back in Lindum any time soon. An involuntary groan accompanied the thought. Normally he wouldn't have wandered this far from the camp, but he needed time to think. And then there was the other reason. His hand swooped to his knife hilt at a rustle among the nearby bushes, only to relax at the sight of the familiar face.

'It's you.' He let out a sigh of relief. 'Good, I hoped you'd happen along. I wanted to speak to you. You said I'd be rewarded if I did what you asked, but what's happened? I've been kicked out.'

The other man's smile didn't falter. 'From what I hear, you might have been dangling at the end of a rope. Maybe you should consider yourself fortunate.'

'That's what I mean,' Tertius spat. 'I could still end up at the end of a rope. I only have that one-handed bastard's word for it he's recommended a posting. What if he's told the governor what I told him? I'm a dead man.'

'Don't worry, Gabinius,' his companion said. 'It's all agreed. Look.' He showed the former *primus pilus* a scroll case. 'I've written the orders myself. It's back to civilization for you, my lad. No more muddy swamps, cold and rain. Rome and a nice comfortable berth at the Castra Praetoria.'

'The Praetorian Guard.' Tertius didn't bother to hide his scepticism. The Praetorians were the Emperor's personal protection force. If it was true he could look forward to an easy life of guard duty and lording it over the plebs, and get double the pay into the bargain.

'Take a look,' the other man grinned as he handed over the case. 'It's all there.'

Tertius did as he was urged. He opened the case and took out a single sheet of parchment. His eyes drifted down as he read the words and a broad grin appeared on his face. He lifted his head and the grin froze as a long-bladed knife slid into the base of his throat, piercing flesh and sinew until the needle point scraped against his spine. A soft gurgling noise emerged from his gaping mouth and he stood, shuddering like a stunned ox as he stared into his killer's emotionless eyes. The knife twisted and the assassin stepped back to avoid the enormous gout of dark blood that arced on to the leaf mould. At last Tertius's knees gave way and he crumpled to the ground. Surprisingly, a spark of life remained in the disbelieving eyes as the killer wiped the blade on his victim's tunic.

'Idiot,' he addressed the dying man cheerfully. 'Did you really think we could leave you alive?'

XXXVIII

Valerius walked through the camp accompanied by Shabolz and Crescens, trying to judge the mood of his legion by the sounds he could hear. In the past it had been simple enough. Corbulo's legions on the way to the Cepha gap had been confident in their ability to win whatever the odds, because their general had always proved that was the case. At Bedriacum men of the First Adiutrix were determined to show that a hastily thrown together mix of sailors and marines was as good as the older legions they marched with. And at Cremona the Seventh marched all the faster because Marcus Antonius Primus had foolishly offered his legions the possibility of endless plunder.

Here, as far as he could tell, there was no single mood. Laughter emanated from some tents, and music from others, but mainly they were quiet, the men sitting in darkness contemplating the days ahead, the possibility of battle, mutilation and violent death. The atmosphere reminded Valerius that Agricola hadn't deemed the Ninth fit to take part in his campaigns against the Brigantes. The last proper fight the legion took part in had been against an offshoot of Boudicca's horde and it had ended in slaughter when a detached group of precisely this strength had been massacred in an ambush. Most of these men had never experienced a major conflict. He tried to recall his own first experience of combat. A Celtic hill fort crammed with warriors and refugees. Climbing the slope shoulder to shoulder with sweating, frightened men as boulders and arrows clattered against the overlapping shields that were the only thing between them and a painful, bloody end. The explosion of euphoria and hatred as they'd broken through the gate and the slaughter that followed. He saw Shabolz staring at him and he realized his face had been reliving the experience. He replaced the savage expression with a sheepish grin and the Pannonian smiled.

They were approaching a fire where a group of legionaries had gathered, laughing with two of Agricola's Celtic scouts and a small boy.

'Tell us the story again, Arafa.'

'But you have heard it many times before, Zander.' Oddly, it was the boy who spoke, and in perfect Latin, but the voice was the throaty growl of a full-grown man. When they were within the light from the flames Valerius saw that the diminutive figure had a full copper beard and the reddened, grizzled features of someone who spent most of his life in the open air.

'Tell us the story of the Emperor's elephant,' another man pleaded.

The scout shrugged and rose to his feet, as one about to deliver a speech. Valerius saw that he was a midget, four feet tall at most, but also that he had the respect of these hardened soldiers. He smiled. Arafa was obviously a nickname. It meant 'giant'. The little man's head came up and his face twisted in a scowl of concentration.

'My father was a great man,' he began in the sonorous tones of a seasoned orator. 'He tamed the wild beasts and made them do his bidding.'

Valerius stood in the shadow of a tent, and motioned that Shabolz and Crescens could go. Crescens was reluctant, but the Pannonian pulled him away.

The midget's story held Valerius spellbound as he waited in the darkness. How a lowly slave became the keeper of the Emperor Caligula's elephant, befriended Rome's greatest gladiator and survived plots and conspiracies and the Emperor's often fatal whims, before being swept up in the convulsions that followed his assassination.

The small man sat down. Valerius suppressed his disappointment and was about to leave when one of the speaker's companions said: 'You can't stop there, Arafa. What about Colonia and Boudicca and the Temple of Claudius?'

For a moment the words froze Valerius to the spot. 'They'll keep for another night,' the midget laughed. 'My throat is dry and all I see around this fire are jugs of water, which is fit only for my pony.'

The voices faded as Valerius walked off towards the command tent, his thoughts two hundred miles and seventeen years away. He remembered the feeling in the veterans' banqueting hall that something was missing from one of the frescoes. Now it came to him. Before Boudicca had burned it to the ground there had been one similar in the outbuildings of the temple complex. Only on that depiction the Emperor Claudius wasn't standing on a dais. He had been seated on a ceremonial elephant.

Crescens and Shabolz stood guard at the doorway and saluted smartly when he approached. 'Julius,' Valerius said. 'Go back to the scouts and tell the small man I'd like to talk to him about tomorrow's march.'

When he entered, Didius Gallus was waiting with a basin filled with water. Valerius washed his hands and soused his face and dried himself off with a towel the cavalryman handed him. 'Bring me a jug of our best wine and two cups, please, Didius. That will be all for the night.'

'Are you sure, sir?'

'Sure.' Valerius smiled at the young man's devotion. 'And take a jug yourself to share with your tentmates.'

'Thank you, sir.' Gallus bowed.

Valerius arranged two couches on either side of his campaign desk. By the time Crescens walked in with the tiny Celtic scout he lay back with a cup of wine in his hand. 'Arafa' looked around the tented room with obvious interest, but he appeared completely at ease. Valerius waved him to the other couch. 'You can leave us now, Julius.'

He waited until the little man took his place. 'They tell me you identified the camp site. I applaud your choice.'

The scout picked up his cup and sniffed the contents. 'It wasn't difficult, lord. It's probably the only suitable place for ten miles.' He took a long pull of the wine and his grizzled features broke into a grin. Behind the beard his face had an ageless quality. He might have been anything between his late twenties and early fifties.

'You speak Latin well,' Valerius complimented him.

'You mean for a Celt.'

Valerius smiled. 'For a Celt, then.'

'That's because I'm not a Celt. I'm a Roman. Gaius Rufus. Born on the Capitoline Hill and come to Britannia with the forces of Divine Claudius.'

'You must have been young to be in the legions?'

That grin again, just the right side of insolence. 'I was an infant, the son of a slave.'

'I heard you tell an unlikely story a little earlier, about an elephant.'

Gaius didn't react to the suggestion he might have been lying. 'Every word, the honest truth,' he said. 'Bar a little exaggeration for effect. My father was the keeper of the Emperor's elephant, Bersheba, first under Divine Gaius, known as Caligula, for whom I'm named, then Claudius.'

'And where is your father now?'

'He died.' The dark eyes fixed on Valerius's. 'In the Temple of Claudius. Fighting beside you.' Valerius's cup froze on his lips. 'You wouldn't remember me, lord, but I remember you.'

'Impossible.' Valerius laughed, but there was little humour in it. 'Nobody got out of the Temple of Claudius alive.'

'You did.' The little man's eyes glittered. 'So why not me?'

Valerius was torn between disbelief and curiosity, but in the end curiosity won. How could it not? If it was true this little man knew more about him than he did himself. He lifted the jug and filled Rufus's cup.

'Tell me about it, from the point where you left off.'

Gaius took a long swallow. 'As my father told it, old Claudius was a bit of a rogue . . .' The little man related how his father and the Emperor's ceremonial elephant had been sent ahead with the legions, but Claudius had waited until they'd broken the military strength of the Britons before he landed. 'They fought six more battles, but they'd already decided who'd won before the first arrow was loosed. Claudius needed a military reputation to keep the purple, and my father's friend Narcissus, the Emperor's secretary, gave him it. Bloodless victories he called them, but the Celts had been paid to run away.'

Gaius told how, after the final victory and the surrender ceremony when the Emperor rode in triumph on Bersheba, Claudius and Narcissus decided his father knew too much. Fortunately, Narcissus had persuaded the Emperor just to leave Rufus behind rather than killing him.

'Bersheba reminded the Emperor of his mortality – he'd ridden her into battle and he didn't care to remember the experience – so she stayed too. My father received his freedom and Roman citizenship, and there we were in newly conquered Britannia, with no friends, enemies on every side and little hope of staying alive.'

'But you did,' Valerius said.

'Yes.' Gaius nodded. 'We survived thanks to Bersheba, who was as strong as ten oxen and as clever as any man. She could pull enormous loads and the fort at what became Colonia was built in half the time as a result. Eventually we prospered, thanks to Narcissus who made sure that when the veterans were granted land my father received his twenty-five *iugera* along with the rest. My father and Bersheba helped build the Temple of Claudius.'

The little man told his story without hesitation or variation. It was all so unlikely, yet every word rang true. Valerius wasn't sure whether to welcome what was to come or dread it. One thing puzzled him, though.

'I was in Colonia for months with my cohort. Surely I would have heard about this elephant?'

'In the years after the invasion Bersheba was a great wonder to the people around what was then Camulodunum,' Gaius said. 'But you would be surprised how quickly people become used to even the most exotic creature. Gradually the mood changed. The druids were rousing the Celts to take arms against the invader and she was seen as something Roman, one of the conquerors. People began to throw stones at her when we passed. One day somebody hit her with an arrow and my father decided it would be best to keep her on the farm.'

'You speak of her with great affection,' Valerius suggested.

A sad smile flickered on the scout's grizzled features. 'She was huge and clever and gentle. It sounds odd to say that she was more member of the family than beast of burden, but it is true.'

'What happened to her?'

'She was in her barn the night they came.' Something changed in the little man's voice. 'The night before they destroyed Colonia. We heard her distress cry and went out to find the barn alight. Bersheba was trapped inside. When we went to free her the Celts ambushed us from the darkness. She saved my father's life when she broke out, but she was frightened and terribly burned and she ran off into the night. We found her in a bog the next morning, the flesh hanging from her in strips and too weak to free herself. We watched her die.'

Rufus stared into his cup and Valerius relived the same night in the long silence that followed. The tiny pinpricks of flame that advanced like a tide over the darkened slope opposite Colonia. Rufus's barn would have been one of them, but something still troubled him. 'I don't understand how you could have reached the temple if you were on the hill north of Colonia at sunrise. The rebels would have surrounded the city by then.'

'Not quite surrounded,' the scout corrected him. 'From the hillside, my father, my stepmother and I could see the little lines of soldiers on the far side of the river. Boudicca and her warriors were attracted to them like moths to a flame. My father understood the militia would eventually be overwhelmed and he predicted any survivors would retreat to the Temple of Claudius. We knew of a ford upstream from the city and crossed there. You remember how the walls were

310

demolished in many places to make way for gardens and new houses?'

'Yes, it was the reason we decided to fight them on the meadow by the river.'

Gaius's eyes glittered in the flickering light of the oil lamps. 'We were able to slip inside unnoticed. The sounds of a terrible battle came from the direction of the river. There were Celts everywhere, but we were dressed little differently from them – my stepmother Maeve was a Celt – and they were too busy looting.' Valerius felt a shiver at the coincidence of the woman's name. He stared at the little man as he continued. 'But the deeper we went into the city the more numerous they became. The road to the temple was blocked and it was only a matter of time before we would have been discovered and killed. Then we saw the *testudo*.'

'You saw the *testudo*?' Barely a century of legionaries had survived to lock *scuta* and create the mobile, defensive carapace. Valerius remembered the stink of fear and sweat and soiled clothing, the agony in his legs and back, the sound of a hundred shields being battered against a hundred trees.

'We were in a garden close by the road when it came, smashing through the ranks of the Celts.' Gaius Rufus laughed at the memory. 'It was the work of a moment to step into the *testudo*'s wake of dead and dying and follow it close until we reached the temple complex. You know what happened next. They came wave after wave and eventually forced us back into the temple. Despair and heat, air thick enough to chew on, and a terrible, unbearable thirst.'

'We needed the water to cool the doors,' Valerius heard himself say. 'They set them on fire.'

'Yes. And there were too many of us.'

'I failed you all.'

'No, you did your best. You could have done nothing more.'

'And you survived?' Of all the fantastic, unlikely elements of the scout's story this was the most improbable.

'My father was dying, pierced through the side as he fought his way from the gate to the temple. Remember, he had helped build it. He told you about the tile. The loose tile you broke free to give access to the hypocaust.'

Valerius searched his memory. 'I thought it was Numidius.'

'No,' Gaius insisted. 'Rufus. You chipped at it till it was free and sent the young soldier . . .'

'Messor. They called him Pipefish. He died.'

'My mother was a midget. A dancer at the court of Caligula. I was eighteen then, but I looked like a skinny ten-year-old. My father urged me to strip, and as the doors burst open he thrust me into the hypocaust and replaced the tile after me. I was terrified, but I endured. For five days I lay in the darkness as they tried to burn the temple and tear it down. Every moment spent in the certainty of a terrible end.'

He waited for some kind of response, but Valerius was still reliving those final seconds. The boom of the battering ram. The door bursting asunder in a shower of sparks. Blood staining the air as Boudicca's warriors took their revenge. The blur of bright iron and the pain and the fear and the rage, and the fierce joy of having lived alongside warriors like Lunaris and Falco and Paulus. Death. But that had only been the gods' jest.

He could see the lightening sky through a chink in the curtained doorway. Night was fading, along with the past. Better to let it stay there.

'And now you're here, a Celt to anyone who didn't know better.'

The little man shrugged. 'I managed to reach the Twentieth. The legate thought I might be useful because I spoke the language and I can ride anything on four legs. It helped that the Celts think people like me have been touched by the gods. So, I became what I am. A scout. I live on the road and in the field. People talk to me. Every few months I return to the Twentieth with my report.'

'A spy then.' Valerius smiled to take the sting out of his words, but Gaius showed no offence.

'Where would a commander be without his spies?'

'And what will tomorrow bring?'

'They left you alone today so they could gauge your numbers and make you seem unthreatened. You can expect the same at the start of the day, but it won't last. Those sheep you see on the hills will turn into wolves.'

'Ambushes?'

'For now.'

'Agricola wants me to bring them to battle.'

'Then he'll likely get his wish, lord.' The little man's face split in a grim smile. 'Because for all the governor's clever schemes Owain Lawhir is no fool. I warned Agricola the Ordovices are not the Brigantes. Word that the Twentieth was taking another route would have reached Owain the day after they marched. He knows the only way to beat you is to defeat you while you're still divided and that's what he'll try to do. His warriors got a taste for killing Romans at Canovium and they want more.'

'You talk as if you think they can defeat us.'

'There'll be a lot more of them than there are of us, and their druids certainly have *them* thinking they can win. They're spreading word that Andraste, their most powerful female deity, is on the rise again, with Boudicca reincarnated at her shoulder. And there's something else.' One of the lamps spluttered out and a shadow fell across the bearded features, hiding his expression. 'Some story about the power of the Roman mother goddess that people speak about in whispers when they think I can't hear them. There's a feeling in the air I don't much like.'

'Then why don't you leave?'

'Because my father taught me that sometimes a man's honour and his loyalty to his friends is more important than life.' He laughed. 'Then again, if things go wrong I can always turn Celt and ride for the hills.' He got to his feet and stretched. 'I'd best be getting the scouts ready.'

'Thank you,' Valerius said. 'It was right that two survivors of Colonia should meet and talk together.' He yawned. 'I'm just sorry I cost you a night's sleep.'

'It won't be the last, lord,' Gaius assured him. As he was walking to the doorway Valerius called him back.

'Were you in camp when the legate had his accident?'

'I was,' the scout nodded. 'And we both know it was no accident, lord. Every man in this legion is aware someone murdered Fronto. But if anyone knows who was responsible they're not telling. One thing is puzzling people, though.'

'Yes?'

'There's not a soldier in this camp who wouldn't have cheerfully killed the legate if they thought they could get away with it, but not one of them would have given him the mercy of a quick death. Ask anyone and they would have made sure he suffered all the torments of Hades before he died.'

XXXIX

A screen of Gaius Rufus's Celtic scouts roamed the slopes of the wooded valley ahead of the marching column. The landscape became more bleak and forbidding with every step westward, towering grey mountains scarred by deep gullies and swirling with mists that could hide an army. Valerius had a sense that the very earth of this land hated them. Perhaps with reason. The primitive farms and settlements they'd passed had proved empty of people and stripped of anything of value. Agricola had given orders to raze every building they encountered. Valerius relayed the command with regret and now swirling pillars of smoke from their blazing timbers marked the advance of the Ninth legion and announced their presence to the Ordovice chiefs.

Valerius rode with Naso and a pair of aides at the centre of his bodyguard, behind a cohort of Asturian light infantry who made up the legion's vanguard. Troops of auxiliary cavalry acted as flank guards, forced closer than Valerius liked by the narrow contours of the valley. To his rear marched the newly appointed *aquilifer*, Claudius Honoratus, carrying the legion's eagle and accompanied by eight of the largest men in the legion armed with fearsome axes. Behind them came the six cohorts of the Ninth, six centuries of eighty men to each cohort. The legionaries marched six abreast with two paces between each rank, which meant close to two hundred paces for each cohort, so the men of the legion alone took up almost a mile of the winding track. They were followed by the long baggage train of more than a thousand mules carrying tents, rations, spare *pila* and swords, fodder for the cavalry horses and the mules themselves, a grinding mill and iron cooking pot for each tent of eight men. Lastly came the rearguard of more auxiliaries.

Every rank and file soldier carried half his own weight in armour, equipment, weapons and supplies. Mail covered his shoulders, chest and back or, if he was fortunate, the lighter *segmentata* plate armour: thirty-four iron plates and bands held together by straps, clips and laces. His big *scutum* – three layers of oak – hung by straps from his back in a leather cover. His day to day rations, water skin, cup and plate hung from a long pole over his left shoulder, and a *pilum* and a pair of palisade stakes over his right. Every man wore a *gladius* on his right hip and a *pugio* dagger at his belt. Valerius never ceased to wonder at the strength and stamina packed into those wiry bodies. As always he'd done his best to ensure they'd been well fed and watered on the march, with decent rest stops. The last thing he needed with such a small force was stragglers.

The enemy struck with a howl as the column had just entered a broader part of the valley where the densely wooded slopes spilled over on to the frozen sward. Thirty half-naked warriors hurled themselves from the trees against the nearest auxiliary cavalrymen. This was far from the first ambush. The results were always the same. One or two troopers hauled from the saddle and butchered before they could react, then the response as the cavalry recovered their wits and broke the heads of a few attackers. Valerius waited for the next act in the little drama, and the Celts didn't disappoint him. From the opposite side of the valley a much larger group, perhaps over a hundred men, erupted from the scrubby slopes and ran directly for the lightly defended mule train. Similar assaults had happened twice already that morning despite all his precautions. As he'd discovered before, men prepared to die were difficult to stop. This time he intended to give them their wish.

He'd deliberately left the flank open as an invitation to the Ordovice chief coordinating the assaults. The Celtic warriors sprinted across the frost-hardened turf carrying hooked reaping knives and big cleavers, intent on slaughtering or maiming as many of the pack animals as possible before making their escape. Valerius waited until they were halfway between the trees and the column.

'Now,' he said.

The mounted signaller at his side let out a long blast on his trumpet and the auxiliary infantry cohort stationed among the baggage threw off their cloaks and formed a double line between the attackers and the mule train. The unexpected sight checked the Ordovice warriors, but their leader screamed at them to keep going and they took up the cry, advancing again at a stumbling trot. In less time than it took to cover ten paces the thunder of hooves announced the arrival of the cavalry squadrons who'd been waiting for just such an attempt. They galloped along the treeline and wheeled to take the enemy in the rear as the auxiliary infantry moved forward at a steady walk, shields at shoulder height and *gladii* drawn. The Ordovices had believed they were wolves about to tear into the unprotected Roman baggage train. Instead, what followed was as simple as herding sheep to the slaughter. The charging troopers of the Ala Indiana smashed into the outer ranks of Ordovice warriors, swords hacking down on unprotected heads, their big cavalry-trained horses lashing out with their hooves and snapping at snarling bearded faces with their yellow teeth. As the shrieks of their dying comrades tore the air the men at the front of the attack sought sanctuary wherever they could, only to run on to the darting points of the auxiliary infantry.

They'd come to butcher mules, but the short scythes and heavy cleavers were as useful as spoons against the precision-made killing tools of their opponents. Now it was the Celts being butchered. The short swords flicked out as if the men were performing morning exercise, needle points piercing flesh and viscera to be ripped clear with that characteristic violent twist that left an enemy's guts trailing from his body. Valerius could have asked for prisoners, to be put to the question

317

or sold as slaves, but he wanted to send a message to whoever was facing him. Send as many as you like. I have an infinite capacity to provide more widows and orphans. This is the price of defying Rome.

One man tried to escape, feigning death then making a run for the trees. A shout alerted a cavalryman and the trooper swerved his horse and urged the animal after the fleeing Celt. Valerius watched as he closed, the heavy cavalry *spatha* held easily in his right hand, measuring the strides of his mount. The Ordovice felt his presence and jinked left, but the horseman had been expecting the move. He waited till the animal's right shoulder was level with the running man's head before chopping the blade down in a perfectly executed back cut that dropped the warrior like a sack of grain.

Valerius rode up as the auxiliaries finished off the wounded and stripped the dead of anything of value. He allowed his horse to walk to where the body of the fugitive lay just short of the trees. A *spatha*, longer and heavier than the infantry *gladius*, was as good a bludgeon as it was a blade. The warrior lay on his back staring at the sky, eyes already growing dull, but a scant hint of life remained judging by the pink bubbles frothing in what was left of his nose. The sword edge had split the front of his skull from crown to upper lip, leaving a ragged scarlet slash edged by slivers of white bone and a gaping crater in his forehead through which Valerius could clearly see brain tissue. His chest and upper arms were covered in blue ink tattoos: mesmeric, swirling patterns, vaguely discernible animals; wolf, boar, deer and odd snakelike creatures with diamond-shaped heads.

He felt a presence beside him and turned his head to find Gaius Rufus, looking almost childlike perched on his full-size horse. 'He was just a boy,' Valerius said. 'Not much more than fifteen or sixteen.'

'Don't waste your pity on him.' The little man slid from his mount, unsheathed his dagger and ran it across the young man's exposed neck. 'That double line of dots on his left arm marks the warriors he's killed. More than man enough to have cut your throat. Aye, and a few other things as well if the stories we heard about Canovium are true.'

Valerius looked to the hillside where the Britons had emerged. 'You were right. It was a good plan.'

'All I did was not see them like you told me to. Your Gauls did the rest.'

'Any news of their main force?'

'They're somewhere up ahead is all I know.' The scout spat to one side. 'There are plenty of others still out there on both flanks, but after seeing this I'd guess that the occasional sight of the cavalry will keep them honest.'

Valerius nodded. It was what he expected. 'Have you found somewhere suitable for tonight's camp?'

'There's a small lake with enough flat, reasonably dry ground to the west to build a fort. It's not ideal,' he acknowledged Valerius's look of distaste at siting the marching camp with the lake at his back, 'but the other options are worse. Of course, Owain knows what you're looking for, too, and just about where you need it to be.'

'You think he'll attack again after losing so many for nothing?'

'Killing a hundred of his warriors will make him think, but it won't stop him coming. More likely he'll keep backing off and hit us at the end of the march when the men are tired and off guard.'

An hour later, Valerius was watching the Ninth ford a small stream when a galloper came in from the scouts and reined in beside the command party. 'Gaius Rufus sends his compliments,' the man gasped, 'and asks you to join him up ahead urgently.'

Valerius called up the young decurion. 'Felix, we're crossing the river.' He turned to his camp prefect. 'We'll halt the column here for now, Quintus. Post a strong defensive perimeter and have men from each century fill up their water skins.'

'Sir.' Naso called an order to the signaller and a short blast rang out. The marching legionaries came to a grateful halt and rested on their palisade stakes, waiting for orders.

'How far?' Valerius asked the scout.

'A few hundred paces, no more, but the chief thought you should see for yourself, lord.'

The scout led as Valerius, his signaller and the men of his escort trotted through the auxiliaries of the vanguard. Out in open country Felix was wary as a cat and Valerius could hear Hilario muttering to himself in terms that weren't complimentary but which he chose to ignore. Shabolz and Crescens moved a little closer and he smiled to himself at the change in these men since that first day at Fidenae. If he could hone the Ninth to the same kind of weapon they would be a match for anyone.

The valley floor had been rising for the last mile, and now it flattened to a plateau. Gaius Rufus waited pensively astride his mount on a mound of tussock grass with two of his scouts at his side looking like giant protectors. In front of him a gentle slope rose to a low whaleback ridge perhaps a mile and a half distant, with mountains soaring to right and left like the walls of a cattle pen.

Valerius ordered the escort to remain and took Felix to join the small man. Gaius kept his eyes fixed on the far horizon. 'I fear we were both wrong, legate,' he said with a hint of self-mockery. 'There will be no ambush and no attack as we make camp. It appears Owain Lawhir intends to fight you here.'

Valerius scanned the rising ground again. Now he could make out the twinkle of the weak sun on polished metal and a deathly still mass of humanity covering the grassy banks and outcrops of grey stone like a rumpled blanket. They filled the valley from wall to wall, thousands of warriors, silent as the tomb, the only movement the distant flutter of banners in the centre of the ridge.

'Send for the camp prefect,' Valerius called over his shoulder. 'How many are they, scout?'

'Donal here has been closer than I, but between us we came to an estimate of about double our own numbers. Say ten thousand. Those are the ones we can see. Beyond the ridge, only the gods know.'

'Too soon,' Valerius whispered to himself. 'At least two days too soon. Agricola can't be here until the day after tomorrow at the earliest, perhaps not even then.'

His mount twitched nervously as Naso galloped up accompanied by an aide. Valerius reached down to pat its shoulder, as much to gain himself a little time as to calm it.

'We tried to—'

'At last.' Naso's jubilant shout cut Gaius Rufus off. 'Now we'll show the bastards what the Ninth can do. Shall I form them up, legate?' He studied the numbers and a grin twisted his handsome features. 'There'll be plenty for everyone, but they won't stand against legionaries. Canovium can be avenged within the hour. I believe the only question is whether we attack in column or in line. Sir,' he ended deferentially.

Naso's savage joy was greeted by murmurs of agreement from certain members of Valerius's escort. Their enthusiasm was reassuring and he had turned to give the order to form line when he caught Gaius Rufus's eye. A warning? Or had the scout become hesitant with the mass of the enemy in sight?

'There is plenty of time yet, Quintus,' he assured Naso. 'Let us consider a little further.'

He pulled his horse round and moved a little way ahead of the others, again studying the mass of men on the ridge and the banners fluttering in their midst. The banners! 'Ten thousand, you say, scout?'

'Yes, lord.'

'And do the banners tell you Owain is definitely here?'

'His symbol is a red fire worm against a green background,' Gaius confirmed. 'I believe you can see it in the centre.'

'And how many warriors would gather to the red fire worm in the search for plunder and the sight of Roman blood?'

'The Ordovices, with the tribes they hold in tribute, can put twenty thousand warriors in the field at need, but after Canovium Owain is a hero who will live for ever in myth and legend in these hills. With the druids' invocation of Andraste every young hothead in the surrounding tribes has been drawn to his banner. So let us say thirty thousand.'

Valerius nodded slowly, staring at the ridge as if trying to see through it. 'So the question is where are the others?'

'Does it matter?' Naso growled. 'Ten thousand or twenty, they are no match for Roman legionaries. I would advise you to attack, sir, while there is still light. The legion is ready.'

The final words were almost a plea, but a picture was forming in Valerius's mind. 'If Owain's other twenty thousand warriors are advancing to meet Agricola, he will be with them,' he said, almost to himself. 'This would be a feint, designed to pin us in place for as long as possible.'

'All the more reason to sweep them aside now,' Naso insisted.

'But would he abandon the banner that won him so much honour and fame? And if they are here, where?'

He aimed the question at Gaius and the little man returned his look with a humourless grin. 'We lost three men trying to get through those hills,' he pointed to the right flank, 'and another two on the left. Ambush parties as thick as fleas on a hedgepig's arse.'

'Which means there's something they don't want us to know.'

'That's what I've been trying to tell you,' the scout said.

Valerius made his decision. He nudged his horse towards Naso. 'I believe they want us to attack now, prefect, and that Owain Lawhir fancies he can annihilate us. But I will not oblige him. Instead, you will return and order camp to be set up on the far side of the river.' He could see the other man's jaw working with suppressed fury, but he continued relentlessly. 'We will need a strong line of pickets between ourselves and the enemy. Rufus's scouts will stay here to act as our early warning.'

'But if they attack? Canovium.'

'There will be no second Canovium. This is a legion, or close enough to it, on full alert. Owain's warriors have marched as far as we have, probably further, and I doubt they're as used to it. No, he's made his plan. He'll rest them and in the morning he'll tell them they'll soon be drinking Roman blood and presenting their wives with necklaces of Roman fingers. But while he's telling them that, we'll be attacking with the low winter sun at our back and shining directly in their faces.'

Naso knew better than to protest further. He saluted and set off back to the river.

Valerius called Gaius Rufus to him. 'Leave what men you think necessary here to make sure there are no surprises in the night, but I want you with me.'

'You want me to try to scout the hills tonight?' Gaius asked, his voice betraying that he knew it was a death sentence.

'No. I want you to find a way around the hills tonight for the auxiliary cavalry and get them there,' Valerius pointed to the centre of the ridge. 'An hour after dawn. Because that's where we'll be and if I know anything about soldiering we'll be fighting for our existence.'

'We hit them from the rear.' Gaius's face creased into a grin.

'Exactly.'

The little man sobered. 'Better if we go back a mile or two and take a wide loop outside their guard posts.' He rubbed his hand through his beard, his mind working through the pitfalls. 'We can move faster that way. It's all a matter of timing. I will do my best, lord.'

'That's all I ask.'

'May I make an observation, lord?'

'Of course.'

'At daylight, if Owain sees there are no horse lines he will be suspicious.'

'I will take care of that,' Valerius assured him. 'Your job is to get them into position and make sure those crazy Gauls charge in the right direction.'

Cadwal sat his horse and waited for the sun to rise. He'd chosen the east gate because his men would be silhouetted against the light with their faces in the shade. The druid had instructed him to attack at night, but unlike his patron, King Owain, Cadwal wasn't in thrall to Gwlym. He'd scouted the fort for three days counting the men on the walls, marking each one until he was certain the garrison couldn't number more than fifty men. He had fifty of his own, but he preferred better odds. Dried blood clotted the rings of the patched mail he wore and his helmet had a slingshot dent in it. He'd probably watched the man who wore it last being killed. The thought made him smile. Today he would kill Romans again. It was what he did best.

The darkness faded to a silvery gloom. Still not enough light to see and he wanted the Roman sentries to see him. But not too soon. Only ten men would accompany him to the gate because he didn't want to alarm the guards. 'Remember, you're exhausted and you're wounded. Hold each other up. Stagger, but don't overdo it. Keep your heads down.' Like him they were dressed in bloodstained tunics and armour stripped from the dead at Canovium, but they were on foot. 'Now.' He nudged his horse forward on to the roadway.

The sentry squinted his eyes against the low winter sun. Men, coming up the Venonis road. Were they expecting a shipment of supplies? But there were no wagons. He let them come closer, his hand edging towards the alarm bell. Roman uniforms, led by an officer on horseback. Still, there was something about them. The officer rode slumped in the saddle and his horse was clearly exhausted. As they approached he could see the bloodied bandages on the men behind the officer and the way they stumbled and had to support each other. He reached for the bell rope.

'Cocceidus said not to wake him unless there was a definite threat this time. He wasn't happy when we pulled him away from that little whore of his because of the dog barking.'

'But these . . .'

'Do they look like a threat?'

'Well . . .'

'Who goes, and what's the watchword,' the other man called as the ragged little column approached the gate.

'Survivors from Canovium,' the officer croaked in the guttural dog Latin the auxiliaries used. 'I don't know what day it is, never mind the watchword. Help us.' He slipped from the saddle and might have fallen, but he caught himself on the pommel. 'For pity's sake. We've been in hiding or running away from the Celts for a month. They killed half of us and Pastor is like to die if he doesn't see a *medicus* soon. We haven't eaten in a week or had a drink for three days. Please . . .'

He staggered towards the gateway. The two guards looked at each other before the more senior nodded. They ran down the stairs and unbarred the gateway. The officer stumbled inside, clutching at the youngest sentry, who'd barely been in the Twentieth a month. 'Thank you,' he whispered. He seemed to grow bigger and the young legionary felt a terrible burning sensation beneath his left arm. The world turned upside down and all the strength went out of his legs. As Cadwal laid him to the ground the boy saw the bloodied knife in his hand. A few feet away his comrade had grown a ragged smile beneath his chin.

Cadwal's other men sprinted for the fort as soon as the gate opened. 'Find them,' Cadwal hissed. 'Find the woman and the boy. But anyone who harms a hair on their heads will answer to me.'

XL

An hour of daylight remained, but Valerius had never felt so tired as he waited for his officers to gather in the command tent. Fool not to sleep the previous night, and no chance of getting any tonight the way things were going. A bowl of water appeared on the portable campaign desk in front of him. He looked up. Didius Gallus was fast becoming a mind-reader. 'Thank you.' Valerius sluiced the icy liquid over his face, gasping at the shock to his flesh but feeling much better for it. Didius handed him a towel and brought him a cup of wine while he was drying his face.

When Valerius was finished the young cavalryman picked up the basin and towel, but he hesitated before leaving the tent.

'Yes?' Valerius said.

'We are to do battle tomorrow, lord?'

'That is my hope, yes, Didius. Does the prospect concern you?'

'Oh no, lord.' The younger man grinned. 'I was with the governor on campaign against the Brigantes. He commended me for killing two of their warriors.' Yes, Valerius thought, war was a great adventure for the young, although he remembered his own first campaign as a combination of long periods of boredom and countless miles in the saddle, punctuated by islands of bloody action and mind-numbing fear.

'We will win a great victory, lord,' Didius added. 'Everyone says so. The lady Tabitha and Lucius will be proud.'

Valerius felt a tightness in his throat at the mention of their names. There had been so much to do that he'd barely thought of them in two days, but how he missed them. 'A campaign,' he said gruffly, 'especially one as hazardous as this might prove, is nowhere for a lady and a young boy. Better they are safe in Viroconium ready for the heroes' return, eh?'

He knew the glib dismissal made him sound pompous, but that was the thing about love. You didn't control it, it controlled you. Valerius only wished he was as confident of victory as his soldiers. Everything depended on the little man currently leading his entire cavalry force away from the chosen field of battle on a trek of unknown distance or duration. Naso's head appeared through the curtained doorway to announce that the officers were filing into the outer room.

Didius bowed and would have left, but Valerius called him back. 'I have a job for you and it may take all night, so best if you start now.' He explained what he wanted and the younger man's brow creased in a puzzled frown. 'Do you think you can do it?'

'Of course, lord.' Didius considered the potential complications. 'We can get them into position, but from my experience the problem is getting them to stay there.'

'You'll think of something,' Valerius assured him. 'Now send in the others.'

'You know what the situation is.' He addressed the cohort commanders of the Ninth Hispana and the prefects of the attached auxiliary units. 'The enemy is drawn up before us in a position of strength and in superior numbers.'

'Then we have them where we want them,' a voice laughed from the back, to murmurs of approval from the other centurions, young, confident replacements of the crooks now in the ranks.

'Yet they think they have us where they want us,' Valerius continued. 'And they may be right. It's my belief that the force that is blocking the ridge ahead may well be only half, or perhaps a third, of the true Ordovice strength.' They totted up the numbers in their heads and the atmosphere turned solemn. 'When we attack King Owain Lawhir he will allow himself to be pushed back on to the very crest of the ridge, but his retreat will be a feint. As the valley narrows our lines will lose their cohesion and become compressed. At the moment of greatest confusion perhaps twenty thousand of his best warriors will fall on us from the surrounding hills and swamp our flanks. Trapped between three superior forces, we will be overwhelmed. At least that is what King Owain hopes.'

'Then surely, sir, we should retreat and fight them on ground that suits us, sir?'

Valerius marked the speaker as one of the young centurions who would one day be a candidate for *primus pilus*. He smiled, but before he could reply another voice broke in.

'A Roman legion does not retreat from barbarians.' Naso repeated his mantra of a few hours earlier.

'If I had the choice, camp prefect,' Valerius told him, 'that is precisely what I would do. Centurion Candidus is right. The only prudent action when faced by overwhelming odds in a superior tactical position is to withdraw. Unfortunately, in this case it would cost me my head. This, gentlemen, is not a matter of tactics. It is a matter of strategy. I am under direct orders from the governor to fight the Ordovices wherever and whenever I find them. So we will attack, but not in the way King Owain expects.'

He rose from his seat and went to the spot he'd had roped off on the earth floor, picking up a lamp on the way. The flickering light illuminated lines he'd drawn on the ground earlier and the men crowded round and craned their necks to get a better view.

'We will attack with six cohorts, in line formation . . .'

'But you said . . .'

'Yes,' Valerius agreed. 'That is precisely what the Ordovices will expect. Three ordered lines of legionaries advancing across open ground to meet them, with cavalry protecting their flanks. The old way, as we have always done it. Except we have no cavalry.'

'They rode out to the rear an hour ago,' Candidus said. 'We thought they were exercising their horses.'

'I'm glad you noticed.' Valerius smiled. 'I hope the Ordovices did not. But don't worry. You will have horsemen on your flanks.' He lifted his eyes from the map and allowed them to drift over the assembled men. 'Our orders are to bring the enemy to battle and that is what we will do.'

'Even if we are walking into a trap?'

'Especially if we are walking into a trap. The attacking cohorts will be the Second, Third, Fourth and Fifth, plus the First Tungria and Second Pannonia, replacing the Sixth and Seventh cohorts. The actual Sixth and Seventh cohorts of the Ninth legion will remain in reserve,' he ignored the rumble of anger from the disappointed centurions, 'under the command of the camp prefect.' Naso shot him a glance of astonishment and despair, but he continued outlining his plan. 'The men of the Sixth and Seventh will exchange shields and cohort standards with their auxiliary counterparts.'

'This is an outrage,' the Seventh's cohort centurion cried.

'On the contrary.' Valerius turned to him, his voice cold. 'It is a ruse of war that could save many lives, perhaps your own. But if you wish to be relieved of your command all you have to do is say so.'

The man's eyes radiated fury, but his answer was an emphatic 'No, legate'.

'Then listen.' He crouched to scratch a line in the dirt. 'We will advance until we make contact with the enemy. If I am right they will retire rather than accept serious casualties. We will continue to press them as if we seek their destruction, but at our own pace. It is vital that our front ranks maintain discipline.' He looked up to meet each of their eyes once more. 'There can be no fever-crazed dash after the enemy. At that moment, if I am right, their reserves will fall on us from either flank.'

A murmur of dismay, because they could all envisage the panic and the carnage as the enemy poured from the hills and crashed into their unprotected flanks, smashing the defenceless lines into oblivion.

'But that will take time,' Valerius reassured them. 'Time enough for us to form square.' He saw the blank looks. 'We will form a single unit square of six cohorts, because if we do not we will all die, but that will be as nothing,' he turned to where a figure had appeared through the doors at the prearranged moment, 'when compared to losing this to the enemy.' Every eye went to the eagle carried aloft by the legion's *aquilifer*, his face a mask of resolve, eyes glittering like those of his gilded burden. 'You would tell me to send it back,' he challenged them. 'Because the enemy is too numerous and their position too strong. But that is to admit defeat before we begin. Your men will fight all the better for knowing the legion's eagle is in their midst. They will fight for it and they will die for it.' Men who had gladly faced death in battle took a step back at the savagery in his voice. 'I will not lose the eagle of the Ninth. Not as long as I have breath in my body. This is how it will be.'

They listened as he outlined his plan, nervous, but determined not to show it, each concentrating on his own part in the complex manoeuvre. When he finished the silence seemed to quiver like a taut bow string.

'Are your men capable of this?' he demanded.

'We've never practised creating a full legion square in battle conditions,' Naso said quietly. 'Legate Fronto believed it would never be used and thought it too much trouble.'

'Would cohort squares not be just as formidable, sir?'

Valerius shook his head. 'If the six squares operate in close formation we lose the advantage of seven hundred spears. Too far apart for mutual protection and the Celts will slaughter our cohorts one by one.'

'They can do it.' The hard voice came from a little apart, where a man stood with the *phalerae* of a *primus pilus* dangling from his chest armour. His intervention generated a murmur of disquiet because he'd only recently arrived from the Twentieth legion to replace the disgraced Tertius. 'Any soldier capable of finding his place in a cohort square can do the same in a full unit square . . . as long as their officers know their jobs.' Disquiet turned to anger as the centurions of the Ninth realized their competence was being challenged, but the *primus pilus* seemed to find their displeasure amusing. 'I'll make sure they know their jobs if it takes all night, legate.'

'Then we're agreed. Have the men ready an hour before dawn.' Valerius signalled the end of the conference and they began to file out. He exchanged a nod with the *primus pilus* and pulled Naso aside. He felt the other man stiffen.

'I know you want to be part of the attack, Quintus, but I need someone I can trust to lead the reserve. Do not let your disappointment cloud your judgement. This plan has three working elements and if any one of them fails we all die. The Celts will think we've left auxiliaries to guard the camp and the baggage train. You have two cohorts of heavy infantry.' He brought his face close to the other man and the power of his authority shone from his eyes. 'Think of it, Quintus. They believe they have us trapped in the narrow gap between the hills, but if you time your attack perfectly it is *they* who are trapped, between the anvil of the square and the hammer of your legionaries. But the decision must be yours. Too early and they will have time to turn and attack you. Too late and they may already have annihilated us.'

'How will I know?' The enormous responsibility had knocked all the anger out of Naso and replaced it with doubt.

'You're a good soldier, Quintus.' Valerius clapped him on the shoulder. 'You will know.'

XLI

Gaius Rufus gently reined in his mount and stared into the darkness. He could feel the mountains towering over the narrow gully, and eyes utterly attuned to the night picked out details in what would otherwise be a uniform black. The trees beside the narrowest of paths were rowan and scrub oak, because they lost their leaves not long after the first frost, unlike the birch which would keep hers for another month. Through the skeletal weave of branches and twigs he could see the stars, which told him he was going north: the right direction. From a few paces behind came the soft snort of a horse breathing through its nostrils and he winced at the sound. Nothing he could do about that, of course, the animals had to breathe, but he'd ordered the men to cover their horses's hooves in sacking to deaden the noise of their passage. This horse belonged to a scout stationed an agreed distance behind, and beyond him there was another, to relay his whispered instructions to the commander of the column.

The burden of the column felt like the weight of a full grown bull on Gaius Rufus's narrow shoulders. A thousand men on a thousand horses strung out in pairs for almost a mile, on a path barely wide enough to take a single animal. A thousand chances for a carelessly slung *spatha* to clatter against a rock outcrop. All it would take was one of the cavalry-trained horses to break the discipline of thousands of hours and let out a whinny and the entire country would rise against them. He could feel his heart pounding in his chest, every heartbeat another precious second wasted. But some instinct kept him frozen in position. The night was trying to tell him something, even though he couldn't understand what it was.

Gaius slipped out of the four-pronged cavalry saddle and dropped soundlessly to the ground. He moved forward up the rocky path at a crouch for another twenty paces, then sank on to all fours. Something inside his head screamed at him that danger was near. A sound. Just the merest whisper. His night owl's eyes picked out the track ahead, rising to cross a shoulder of rock. He moved left on to the rock slope and slithered his way upwards. When he reached the top he waited until the softest glow became apparent somewhere to the right, seeming to originate deep in the bowels of the earth. He crept forward until he had a view of a cave mouth. Inside, five warriors wrapped in cloaks crouched around the tiniest of fires trying to keep warm. The light from the fire destroyed his night vision and he backed away until he was in darkness again, waiting for it to return. There. To the right of the cave mouth a sixth warrior stood, merging with the rock and watching the track below.

His hand instinctively dropped to the cold hilt of his dagger, but his mind had already made the decision. Too many. Too well protected to be killed with any certainty of silence. And there would be more out there. You didn't place a guard post unless you had enough force to take on whatever it was guarding against. Reluctantly, he slipped backwards down the slope and ran to warn the second scout.

The man bent low out of the saddle so Gaius's lips were close to his ear. 'Tell the prefect we have to turn back again,' Gaius whispered. 'We'll try further east.'

A muffled curse that would be repeated a thousand times when word reached the column. Gaius returned to his horse and waited, imagining the chaos and confusion as a thousand men tried to turn their mounts in complete silence on that narrow path. He leaned against the animal's haunch and closed his eyes. 'Epona aid us,' he whispered. Gaius had forsaken Roman gods after his father's death in the temple. He'd chosen Epona, the Celtic horse goddess, as the most appropriate for his calling. She'd never actually been there when he'd needed her, but it made him feel better.

But time was running out.

Darkness covered the land like a blanket. Valerius stood on the rampart wall staring west, but even the glow of the Celts' campfires had faded. All around him he could sense movement as century after century poured from the gates to form up in their cohorts ready to march across the river. Engineers had worked through the night to construct three bridges that, along with the ford, would allow the legionaries to reach their assigned positions in a quarter of the time. The familiar clink of metal equipment accompanied the movement, along with whispered exhortations from centurions and decurions. He could hear the creak of the bridges as they took the weight of fully equipped soldiers crossing on planking deadened with pieces of felt. If the gods were kind, somewhere to the north little Gaius would be leading the horsemen of the Ala Indiana and the Ala Thracum through the hills to form up out of sight on the Ordovice flank. The knowledge that those same hills might be empty of any support sent a shiver through him. Could he win without them? Four thousand against thirty thousand? It was possible, if the four thousand were Roman soldiers whose fighting qualities and discipline had carried them to the very edges of the earth. But it was much less likely. Cavalry caused panic and he needed panic to ensure victory.

Enough reflection. He ran down the dirt embankment to join his escort. Didius Gallus held his horse and helped him into the saddle before mounting his own.

'I hope you slept well, Felix?' Valerius said to the escort commander.

'Very well, sir,' the decurion assured him, having spent the last six hours with his men helping Didius Gallus complete the near impossible task Valerius had assigned them.

'What's that strange smell?'

'I couldn't say, sir,' the other man replied. His nostrils had become so accustomed to the fierce stink that it no longer registered. 'Perhaps the latrines are upwind this morning.'

Valerius looked to the east. Did he see a thin line of something not quite black? 'Let's take our positions. Does the Second know we're coming? It would look careless if someone put one of my own *pila* through my liver.'

'Centurion Candidus knows and I waited while he issued his instructions, sir. They won't launch at any mounted men.'

'I'm glad to hear it.' Valerius pulled on the reins and steered his mount towards the west gate. Confidence. He must show confidence, because it had become apparent how little confidence the centurions had in their men, and the men in each other. Julius Ulpius Canalius, the *primus pilus* from the Twentieth, had visited him during the night to report his fellow centurions' doubts about their men's ability to carry out Valerius's instructions in the time allowed and during a battle.

'I thought you might like a last opportunity to consider cohort squares instead, sir,' he suggested.

Valerius had shaken his head. 'No, *primus*,' he replied lightly. 'The dice are thrown. We'll stay with what we have. It's amazing how it concentrates a man's mind when another fellow is trying to chop his head off.'

They were outside the fort now and passing through the shadowy rear ranks of Naso's reserve cohorts, identifiable by their oval auxiliary shields, and lack of treasured unit standards. For once he was glad his men couldn't recognize him because he doubted he was popular with the legionaries of the Sixth and Seventh. A small group stood a little way in front, close to the river's edge, and Valerius made his way towards them. The camp prefect saw him coming and met him a short way from his fellow officers.

'Your men look well, Quintus.'

'They're ready, sir.' Naso accepted the lie as the compliment it was intended to be and Valerius could hear a lightness in his voice that had been missing a few hours earlier. 'You could even say they were spoiling for a fight.'

Valerius laughed. 'I'm sure they are, and I can imagine who with.' Naso reached out and stroked the forehead of Valerius's mare, winning a soft 'hrrumph' of pleasure from the animal. 'I don't envy you, Quintus. You have the most difficult job of any of us. When you're in the middle of things you don't have time to worry. The waiting and watching and wondering are the worst of it.'

'We won't let you down, sir.'

'I know, Quintus.'

'About last night . . .'

Valerius cut off the apology. 'I would have felt the same. May Fortuna favour you today.'

'May Fortuna favour us all, sir, and I look forward to meeting you later.'

Across the ford, hooves clattering on the rocks and splashes of freezing water soaking those behind, accompanied by gasps and muffled curses. On the far side they advanced at a slow walk over turf made firm by the frost.

'Who goes?' a voice demanded from the gloom. 'And what is the watchword?'

'Legate's party,' Felix replied without hesitation. 'The watchword for the day is Vulcan.'

'Pass through the Fifth cohort, but be careful of those Gaulish madmen ahead of us in the second line. They're jumpy as cats and don't much mind whose head is hanging from their tent poles tonight.'

Felix thanked him and they advanced until they could see a line of dark shadows. 'Make way for the legate,' the decurion called softly. The line parted. The Fifth cohort provided the right side of the final rank of the attack, with a Pannonian auxiliary cohort on their left flank completing the line. The 'Gaulish madmen' were the Second Nervian cohort on the right of the second line, alongside the Fourth cohort. Two cohorts of legionaries, Second and Third, made up the front rank.

Each rank was composed of a solid line of nine hundred shields, backed by men armed with a pair of *pila* and twenty-two inches of tempered, needle-pointed iron as familiar in their hands as the spoons they ate with every day. A legionary fought beside the seven men he slept, ate and shared the latrine with. They were as close as any family, and, at their best, they would die for each other rather than abandon a tentmate. Some of them would undoubtedly be dead before sunset. If he was not one of them Valerius would walk among them in the aftermath of the fight, making himself look into the dead faces, and at the shattered skulls and spilled guts, and telling himself it had all been necessary. But was that true? Valerius was as certain as he could be that Agricola's strategy of dividing his force was a mistake. The Ninth and Twentieth legions combined would have brought Owain of the Ordovices to battle eventually. Honour and his Celtic pride would have ensured that. But the Ninth was here, and nothing would change that. So they would fight. The only difference between this and the previous battles Valerius had fought was that the outcome depended on the actions of men he barely knew. If Gaius Rufus failed to find a way through the hills with the auxiliary cavalry or Quintus Naso made the wrong decision there would be three or four thousand Roman corpses feeding the foxes and the crows by tomorrow's sunrise. Valerius had already decided that if the eagle was in danger he would have Felix and the escort break out and take it to safety. He knew they would be reluctant to leave him to die with his men. But they were soldiers. When it came to it they would obey orders. He smiled despite the nerves that had turned his stomach into a bellyful of mating toads. Well, perhaps not Hilario.

They passed through the Nervians without mishap and Valerius led his escort left until they reached the little huddle of men he had stationed between the first and second ranks. 'Nearly time, *aquila*,' he said to the hulking figure of Honoratus, who stood at the centre of his guards holding the raised staff. A leather hood covered the legion's spiritual symbol. 'I think we can do without that now.'

Honoratus undid the ties and removed the bag to reveal a dull gleam in the darkness. Valerius looked to the east. Yes, it was certainly getting, if not lighter, at least a little less dark. A drop of moisture fell from the brim of his helmet on to his nose. Rain? He touched his cloak and realized it was covered in minute droplets of water. Not rain, but the blanket of mist that occurred close to rivers on mornings like these in the north. He gave it a moment's thought. Why not? He called Felix to him. 'Pass the word to the *primus pilus* and senior centurions that the legion will advance one hundred and fifty paces. I want it done in complete silence.'

'Sir,' Felix saluted and disappeared back into the gloom.

Another glance at the eastern horizon where a line of jagged peaks was just visible against the dull, pre-dawn glow.

Not long now.

XLII

King Owain Lawhir watched the roseate light of dawn strengthen beyond the eastern mountains and felt for a moment as if he possessed an almost mystical power. Perhaps the arch-druid was correct and a new age beckoned, an age when men no longer need fear losing everything – possessions, liberty and life – to Roman greed and lust for power. He had not wanted this fight, but the gods had chosen him and it had been inevitable since that day among the great stones on Mona. Gwlym would be there now making his crazed plans for the great demonstration that would seal the power of Andraste and strike terror into the invaders. Owain had asked himself why, if the druid was so certain of the victory he had promised the warriors of the Ordovices, and the rebellion that would spread like a wildfire across the land, he would have diverted so many men to defend the island. The truth, of course, was that Gwlym was not confident. Yet Owain's own faith had grown with every new batch of warriors who had made their way to join him, warriors from every tribe in the south, he guessed: the disaffected and the dispossessed, the angry – and the fearful. Not for their lives, which they cherished but would be fulfilled if they died in battle against the invader, but of what the Romans would take from them next.

The moment he heard Agricola had split his forces he sensed a great opportunity. He led the greatest Celtic army since the time of Boudicca. If he could meet either part of the Roman force on his own ground and his own terms he could destroy it before turning on the second. When he'd been certain of the route the weaker portion would take he had rushed his warriors to meet it, with only the supplies a man could carry. Now they were footsore and hungry, but strengthened by the knowledge they would bathe in Roman blood before the sun set.

As if at his command the winter sun appeared over the horizon and lit the valley ahead. Owain felt a sudden stab of doubt when he saw the low carpet of mist that spread from wall to wall, hiding everything beneath. What if the Romans had escaped during the night? No. He knew the mettle of his opponent. He had watched the attack on the Roman baggage train from a mountain spur and seen the clinical efficiency with which the soldiers had slaughtered his young men. He'd advised against the assault, but sometimes young men had to make their own mistakes, and pay the price.

The man who planned that slaughter would not run. But would he take the bait? Owain had deliberately left his centre weak to invite an attack. The warriors who surrounded his banner in the middle of the saddlebacked ridge were less than a third of those he led. Twenty thousand others lay unseen behind the crest of the mountains on either flank. They would wait until the Roman advance reached a certain marked point and then fall on the vulnerable flanks. He'd spoken to old men who had fought with Caratacus and they assured him that the Roman legions always attacked in line. The mist began to shred in the warmth of the sun and his heart beat a little faster. He gripped his sword hilt and slid the blade in and out of the scabbard, an old habit he'd tried, without success, to break. He could see the walls of the fort now and the mist was thinning with every passing second.

His heart stopped.

'Teutates save us,' he heard someone whisper, and it took a moment before he understood that the words had emerged from his own lips.

Out of the mist, much closer than his mind could comprehend, appeared rank after rank of heavily armoured soldiers, standing silent and motionless in a display more daunting than if they'd rushed shrieking at the Celtic line. So close they were almost at the mark he'd placed to trigger the ambush. Panic threatened to consume him, but gradually he regained control of his racing mind. This was what he'd wanted. They were in the formation and numbers he expected. It was only the shock of their proximity that had made him anxious. They had fallen into his trap. He looked for the cavalry, whose mobility was the only threat to his success now. There they were on the flanks where they were meant to be. Stationary, but ready to react to any threat. Had he not prepared for their presence, he might have been worried, but his men had spent the night digging concealed pits the Romans called *lilia* in an almost unbroken bed between the cavalry positions and the vulnerable eastern edge of his flanking forces. Within moments of their charge the ground would be littered with fallen cavalrymen and injured horses.

A horn blew with startling clarity.

They were coming.

The mist vanished like a curtain being swept aside and Valerius was greeted with the sight of a hillside carpeted with thousands of bare-chested, tattooed warriors. A moment of shocked silence followed before a great roar rose up from the mass of Celtic spearmen, gaining in volume until it seemed to fill the entire valley.

'Sound the advance.'

Barely two hundred paces separated the three painfully thin lines of legionaries from the enemy. Valerius felt a moment of doubt as he considered his vulnerable flanks, naked without the usual protection of their auxiliary cavalry squadrons. The mules Didius Gallus and his comrades had positioned through the night stood where they were tethered with their confused and nervous handlers on their backs. From a distance they looked like cavalry formations, but they were as much use as a herd of cattle.

The Ordovice warriors continued their cacophony of sound, but they contented themselves with waving their spears and making occasional feint attacks, rushing forward, then retiring when the Romans failed to react. Valerius's greatest fear was that Owain would order an attack when he saw the true weakness of the forces against him, but the Celts remained in position. Should he have settled for cohort squares? When he looked at the numbers facing him and their proximity it seemed a more sensible position. Should he halt the attack short of the Ordovices to give his men more time to change formation? Or would that encourage the assault Owain seemed reluctant to make? And all the time his eyes flicked to the heights to right and left where he knew an even greater host waited to fall on the Roman flanks like a mountain avalanche.

The legionaries advanced at that disciplined, remorseless, steady pace that had given Rome control of the world from the bleak mountains of Brigantia to the deserts of Judaea. Valerius followed between the first and second lines, with his *aquilifer* at his side, holding the eagle raised for all to see, its beak gaping and the gilded wings flashing in the sunlight. He resisted the urge to reach out and touch the glittering symbol that was the heart and soul of the unit, experiencing a moment of superstitious dread that in a few hours it would lie in the grass with the blood of its legate tarnishing its golden feathers. The steadiness of the men around him stilled his fears. Rome paid them and fed them, but they did not fight for Rome. They fought for pride, pride and their tentmates. This was the Ninth legion. His legion. They would prevail.

Fifty paces. A hundred. With every pace the cacophony from the enemy grew, until the very air seemed to shudder at the sound. Slowly the mass of men transformed into individual snarling faces, the strange patterns and animal shapes of their tattoos clearly visible. Lank hair falling to their shoulders or dyed yellow and spiked into a crown of thorns. Young men, for the most part, with a scattering of elders identifiable by their silver hair or balding crowns. A few carried oval-shaped shields, but most were unprotected. Some meant to fight entirely naked, whirling and dancing and screaming their defiance at the Romans. The majority were armed with spears, but some held only axes or rusty farm implements. Valerius knew that only their chiefs and champions could afford the treasured and beautifully crafted Celtic swords worth more than the value of a heavy golden neck ring.

Closer and closer. Should he . . . ?

A sharp cry from one of the escort – Shabolz? – and he knew the Ordovices had made the decision for him.

'Sound form square,' Valerius ordered the signaller. A series of shrill, urgent blasts from the trumpeter was followed by the *primus pilus's* roared command.

Valerius looked up to the northern heights and his heart quailed at the great wave of bodies flooding over the crest and plunging down the slope. He knew the same scene would be mirrored to the south. Thousands upon thousands of warriors charging to smash into the Roman flanks.

But those flanks were changing with every passing second. Valerius sat motionless in the saddle barely daring to breathe as the formation shifted. If a single man panicked or a century didn't know its business they would all die. A ripple ran through the two cohorts in the front line as men performed the intricate, choreographed movements their officers had drummed into them the previous night. Their position in the line had been dictated by this moment. The men of two centuries in each cohort held firm, while those beside them took a step back and held, or stepped back again so they formed three lines. With a rattle of wood on wood the front rank closed up to form a solid wall of shields. The movement complete, the right hand cohort began to pivot back, the outer files forced to run to keep their positions while those at the hinge merely shuffled. In the same instant the left hand cohort of the second rank was trotting into position to form the left wall of the square. Meanwhile, the two auxiliary cohorts formed up in close order and marched into the arms created by their legionary comrades, the one to disappear as its members divided to create an inner fourth line of defence, the other to take its place beside Valerius and his escort, where it would provide a flexible reserve to meet any breakthrough.

If Owain had attacked with the men on the ridge while the manoeuvre was taking place the Romans might have been annihilated. Instead, the Ordovices stayed frozen in position, the nearest warriors fewer than seventy paces from their hated enemy. They had their orders to remain in position and their chiefs and clan elders had been snarling at them every time they threatened to move. First Owain had looked for a threat as the front line's shape transformed, then he'd puzzled as to its purpose. By the time the Fifth cohort trotted forward to fit into place as the rear wall of the formation it was too late.

The great twin walls of Ordovice warriors reached the valley bottom and swarmed over the wiry turf towards the Roman square and simultaneously the force surrounding Owain launched itself forward with a great roar.

'Spears,' Valerius called. His order was echoed by the Ninth's centurions and two and a half thousand fists closed on the wooden shafts of weighted *pila* and brought them to shoulder height. 'You will throw by ranks. Wait for the command of your centurions.'

A hundred and sixty men on each flank of the square had direct contact with the enemy and the width of their shields dictated that the sides measured something like a hundred and eighty paces. Behind them three more ranks pressed close enough for the man in front to feel the heat of the soldier behind's body. The area they encompassed was so compact Valerius had a sense of being within touching distance of everything around him. There would only be time for each rank to make a single cast. The distance had to be right. Normally Valerius would have preferred every legionary and auxiliary to launch his weapon simultaneously. But the force on the ridge led by Owain was already much closer than the warriors on the flanks, and there was no point in the rear rank launching their *pila* until they had targets. So he would leave it to his officers. The most experienced centurion in each wall would give the command to throw.

By now the enemy was converging on three sides, but the imminent danger came from the west where they were closest and King Owain's champions led the charge. Valerius heard the clear voice of Julius Ulpius Canalius reminding his men to throw in ranks. 'Throw,' he called. An audible grunt as one hundred and sixty weighted *pila* flew from the hands of men expert in their use in a flat trajectory that took the body of charging warriors at chest height. 'Throw.' Shrieks of agony and the sickening thud of metal tearing into human flesh and sinew blended with the second order to launch. Another flight of javelins arced out from the second row and sailed into the packed ranks of men jostling to get at the hated Romans. 'Throw.' A new voice from the south flank. Screams and howls from a different direction, and now a new sound joined the symphony of battle, a prolonged rippling crash as the charging men launched themselves at the wooden shields defending the Roman square.

This was the time of crisis and Valerius concentrated on the north face where the Ordovices struck with enough force for men as far back as the fourth rank to recoil from the impact. As soon as they had launched their spears the legionaries in the front rank brought their curved rectangular *scuta* up to shoulder height, so only their eyes were visible between shield edge and helmet rim. Those in the second rank used their *scuta* to shelter the heads of those in the first. Both were able to use their remaining seven foot javelins to lunge forward at their enemies' eyes, chests and throats. The Ordovice warriors who faced them carried longer spears designed specifically for thrusting, but no spear could pierce three layers of seasoned oak or the iron of a legionary helmet. For the men of the Second cohort of the Ninth every thrust counted and the tattooed men reeled away, blinded, or with blood spurting from a torn throat or pierced chest, collapsing to their knees as the life drained from them. Every man who fell acted as a bulwark against those behind. Some of the Ordovice champions became so enraged they used their own dead and injured as a platform to throw themselves on to the second and even third rows of the defence, there to be impaled by the nearest spear. The line bent and buckled, but Valerius could see the Celts didn't have the strength to break through. Slingshot pellets of lead and stone cracked into the raised shields and Valerius heard the whirr of several passing close by his head, accompanied by the occasional arrow. The Celts didn't have units of archers, but enough of them could use hunting bows to be a nuisance. He would inevitably lose men as time passed – already a slow stream of casualties were limping into the centre to be treated by the *medici* – but the defence was designed so they could be replaced from the rear ranks without breaking the integrity of the square. What worried him was the strength of the *pila* they used. The javelins were lethally effective as throwing weapons, especially against an enemy who didn't wear armour, but for close work they had a major flaw. The iron shaft connecting the pyramid point to the wooden spear was made of softer metal. When thrown, the point would pierce an enemy shield or body but then the weight of the spear would bend the iron, ensuring it couldn't be instantly returned. Used as a stabbing weapon against the naked warriors the shafts would last longer, but from experience he knew they would eventually give. He'd tried to mitigate that weakness by ordering the third and fourth ranks to alternate unused javelins with those in front. The pattern of fighting was replicated on the east and south faces. In the south the Ordovices had been forced to race almost a mile from their concealed positions and their momentum was spent by the time they reached the Roman shields. To the east there had been no great collision as the great hosts to north and south flowed round to envelop the Roman formation.

Valerius's greatest concern was the north flank, where the Ordovice avalanche had struck with enough force to knock the square out of shape and where most of the injuries were being inflicted. Whole sections of the reserve cohort of auxiliaries were being called forward to replace wounded and dying legionaries and Valerius guessed that the combined impact of so many warriors had torn gaps in the first two lines. He'd seen it happen before. Some of his men would have been ripped from the safety of their positions in the line and thrown to the attackers as lambs are thrown to wolves, and with much the same result. A soldier's instinct made him want to rush to the endangered flank and advise the centurions, even to join in the defence. But a legate's duty was to stay in the saddle surveying his command with what he hoped was a look of stern confidence on his scarred features. As much a symbol of his legion's invincibility as the eagle guarded by the men at his side.

A cry of dismay drew his attention, followed instantly by a chilling bay of triumph. The angles of the square where the different units met were its weakest points. This, combined with the pressure being applied on the defenders of the northern flank, had forced an opening in the north-east corner and already Celtic warriors were streaming inside to attack the rear defenders.

'Shabolz,' Valerius called, but the Pannonian and three of his mess-mates were already urging their horses towards the gap, hacking at the Ordovice intruders as they rode. A century of their fellow Pannonians from the reserve followed and as Shabolz and his troopers used their horses to plug the opening they hacked the infiltrators into bloody scraps. Valerius saw one horse fall, the rider vanishing into a seething pool of enemy warriors, but the swift intervention had prevented disaster.

For now.

'You did well,' he said as the three riders returned. 'Who . . . ?'

Shabolz met his gaze with solemn grey eyes. 'Licco rides among the stars,' the Pannonian said. 'He is a soldier. A good death and a quick one was the best he could hope for and the gods gave him both.'

Valerius nodded. To show emotion would be to cheapen Licco's death, but he had to bite his lip to ensure he displayed none.

He turned away and inspected each flank of the square in turn. They seemed stable enough, but the stream of casualties continued to increase. The bloody ground where the *medici* worked was littered with men awaiting treatment or bandaging their own wounds. He could hear the increasingly urgent requests of the centurions for replacements, or tiring men being ordered out of the front line. In camp a soldier might spend hours every day exercising with a heavy *scutum*, but no man could hold one shoulder high for ever. And there was something about battle that drained the strength more quickly than any training session.

Time. Time was his enemy. The attackers too would tire, but there were so many more of them. When one collapsed or became sickened by the slaughter ten would fight to take his place. As long as the square held it would cause Owain's men casualties, but it could never defeat them. Everything depended on Naso and Gaius Rufus, but Valerius doubted the one without the other would be strong enough. They must act in concert.

Until they did, the men of the Ninth must survive. And endure.

As time passed and the casualties continued to mount, the pressure on the square increased from all sides. The Celts still threw themselves at the Roman spears over a wall of dead and dying. Valerius's legionaries fought with a quiet, deadly intent, their only sounds the grunt as they thrust the *pilum* point home into Ordovice flesh, or the cry as they took a wound. The Pannonian replacements had long since been used up, their place taken by exhausted legionaries who had been in and out of the front rank three or four times and who struggled to stay upright as they leaned panting on their shields or sucked greedily from water skins.

Valerius was reluctant to move from the saddle where his men could see him, but the groans and cries of the wounded reminded him of another responsibility. Handing the reins to Felix he slipped to the ground and, accompanied by Hilario, walked stiff-legged to the area where the *medici* worked with silent concentration. As he approached, Julius Hellenicus, the chief *medicus*, looked up with a grimace of annoyance, his arms bloody to the elbow and his face spattered with gore.

'No one considers the wounded when they plan these things,' Hellenicus spat. 'Look at them. If this square gets any smaller I'll be stacking them on top of each other.' Valerius looked around and saw that Hellenicus was right: the area the square encompassed seemed to have shrunk without his being aware of it. The ground he stood on was slick with the lifeblood of the men lying on it, churned to mud by the passage of hundreds of hobnailed boots and littered with nameless scraps of flesh. 'Leave him,' the *medicus* grunted at one of his men treating a legionary with a red pit where his right eye had been. 'Can't you see he's dead?' They were interrupted by a shriek and the stink of burning flesh as another *medicus* cauterized a spurting wound with the point of a white hot poker from one of the medical unit's braziers. Hellenicus ignored the noise. 'We're down to a cup of water a man. And if this goes on much longer we're going to run out of bandages.'

'I'll see what I can do.'

'Water,' the *medicus* repeated mechanically. 'We can cut bandages from the tunics of the dead, but we need water.'

'Anything else?' Valerius asked.

'It won't help much,' Hellenicus waved a weary hand at the lines of wounded men, 'but you could speak to them.'

Valerius eased past him and worked his way through the casualties. He spoke to those who seemed lucid enough to understand, assuring them he'd make sure they were looked after. Many were so locked away in their own agony they were somewhere between this world and the next. Others stared at the grey sky with eyes that would never see again. One man, spitting teeth where a slingshot had broken his jaw, ignored Valerius's protests, got to his feet, and made his way back towards the ranks. Valerius watched him go, teeth clenched to still the emotions that filled him like the churning pool below a waterfall. He had brought them to this. He alone was responsible for every man dead and maimed. A face he recognized, twisted with pain, a bloody rag stuffed beneath his armpit where he'd been pinned by a spear, armour and tunic stained red. Valerius knelt beside the man.

'Avidius?'

The eyes flickered open, but it took a moment before the soldier focused on him.

'Legate.' Avidius's voice emerged as the merest whisper, ragged with the agony of his suffering.

'You fought well,' Valerius assured him. 'You and all your comrades of the Second cohort.'

Avidius's eyes closed again and he whispered something unintelligible that might be a prayer. 'Antonius and Claudius are dead.'

'I'm sorry.'

The eyes opened. 'We will beat them, sir?'

It was half question and half statement, but Valerius chose to answer. 'We'll beat them.' He rose to his feet.

'That night . . .'

'Yes?' Valerius crouched again. 'You've thought about it further? The night your legate died?'

'I wish I'd killed him.'

'I can understand that, Avidius, I truly can. But you didn't. You were on guard. Is there something else you've remembered?'

'Ask . . .' The voice almost faded entirely and Valerius had to put his ear to the dying man's mouth. 'Ask the tribune who inspe . . .'

'He's gone, lord.' Hilario reached past Valerius to close the fading eyes.

Valerius looked to the skies and tried to still the contradictions whirring through his mind. He had no time for this. He must concentrate on the battle. He looked to the north-west. Where were the cavalry?

'Sir, you should see this,' Felix shouted.

XLIII

Gaius Quintus Naso looked to the hills to the north-west for the hundredth time and muttered a soft curse. Where were the cavalry?

He'd witnessed the moment the mist cleared to show the men of the Ninth legion perched almost on the lion's lip, within bowshot of the main Ordovice host, and their slow march to victory or death. His heart had stopped when the great wave of howling warriors fell from the flanks and he'd been certain Valerius's three fragile lines must be swept away in a maelstrom of horror, with his own end not far behind.

The speed of the transition from line to square astonished him. Even so, he'd been certain the six cohorts would be smashed to pieces or swamped in that great mass. Yet they'd held out, and they held out still. But for how much longer? He'd watched the square compress foot by relentless foot until, from less than a mile away, it appeared a man might launch a *pilum* from one side to the other. It must have been thirty minutes now and the men behind him knew what that meant. There would not be a man in the square whose strength wasn't sapped. The growls and mutters had started long before, and the rap of the centurions' vine sticks and demands for silence had done little to still it. Quintus Naso understood why. Out there, men – their comrades – were fighting and dying while they were forced to watch. But again there was that question: for how long?

Valerius had planned for Naso to attack with his infantry cohorts when he saw the two cavalry wings breasting the northern rise. But he had left the final decision up to the camp prefect. Now there was no sign of the scout Rufus or the cavalry, and every military instinct told Naso that Valerius and the Ninth were on the brink of annihilation.

He called an aide to his side. 'Gather up every man in the fort and tell them to arm themselves with anything they can get hold of. Empty the armourer's cart of everything with an edge.'

'The baggage detail and the camp guard, prefect?'

'Everybody,' Naso snapped. 'If we can't find a way to win there won't be a camp and we won't need the baggage. Personal slaves, too. They'll be as dead as the rest of us, so they might as well get the chance to die fighting. That should give us a second line and a small reserve.'

He waited impatiently while muster parties were organized to bring the non-combatants and camp followers forward. 'Cohorts will form line,' he told the senior centurion, 'but no trumpets. They've ignored us so far so let's keep it that way.'

Eventually, the centurions bullied a mob of confused, frightened muleteers, labourers, baggage handlers and cattle herders into forming a second line of close to nine hundred men. Fewer than half of them had helmets or shields and he had no idea how many would fight, but they made his pathetic little force appear twice as strong as it was in reality and that might make a difference. If they'd been trained soldiers he would have considered attacking in a wedge formation and simply lancing his way through to reinforce Valerius, but all that would do was leave them trapped anyway.

He rode out in front of the long lines of men. 'Our comrades are fighting and dying less than half a mile away,' he roared. 'Your legion's eagle is in danger of being lost. Help is on the way,' he continued, knowing it was probably a lie. 'We will march at double pace until we are halfway and at the trot on my order. If any kind of sizeable force attacks us, you know what to do. If they don't we will attack them.' He raised his sword and pointed it in the direction of the vast host of Ordovice warriors. 'There is your enemy. Slaughter the bastards. Advance. Double pace.'

Valerius remounted and rode to the centre of the square where Felix was pointing east. In the low ground towards the river two lines of legionaries were marching towards the battle. Two lines? Where did he get the men? That didn't matter. What did was that Naso had felt the need to attack before the cavalry reached them. Or possibly, he reflected, because he knew they weren't coming. Valerius understood why the *praefectus castrorum* had made the decision; he would probably have done it himself. Naso believed the square was about to be destroyed and he might be right. It was a square in name only, a crumpled misshapen thing that had been under relentless pressure for over forty minutes now from tens of thousands of Ordovice warriors. A mixture of discipline, pride and self-preservation was all that kept these men fighting with the last of their strength. He rode towards the battered eastern wall in an attempt to form a better impression of Naso's intentions. From a point just behind the fourth rank he could see what should have been clear earlier: the ragged state of the second line. Now he understood where Naso had found his 'troops'. He was mentally congratulating his deputy when a lead slingshot pellet smashed off the crown of his helmet leaving him reeling in the saddle with his ears ringing. Felix took the reins of his horse and dragged him back to the reserve position.

'For all the gods' sakes, lord, you'll get yourself killed if you expose yourself like a raw recruit,' the young decurion rebuked him.

Valerius muttered an apology, but his mind was already working on the implications of Naso's attack. They were still invisible to the Celts attacking the square from the east, but that couldn't last. He must take advantage of it while he could.

'Hilario, find a spare horse.' He nodded towards the *aquilifer's* party.

The big cavalryman caught his meaning immediately. 'He can have mine,' he said, dropping from the saddle. 'I'm not going anywhere.'

Hilario led his horse close to where Honoratus stood at the centre of his axe men. The standard-bearer must have sensed his presence because his head turned and Valerius saw a momentary look of puzzlement on his blunt features. Slowly Honoratus realized the implications of Hilario's presence and he shot a glance of pure hatred at Valerius. He must have given an order to his bodyguard because they moved forward as a unit close to the rear of the fighting line and planted the staff of the eagle deep in the bloody turf. The defiant gesture brought a weak cheer from the wounded lying nearby and Valerius called Hilario back.

'We can wait,' he said.

But he'd made up his mind.

'Felix,' he said quietly to the escort commander. 'When Naso's cohorts begin their attack you will take Honoratus and the eagle and break out with the escort from the south-east corner.'

Felix opened his mouth to protest, but he saw the look on Valerius's face and shut it again like a trap. 'Sir.'

'I will not lose my eagle.'

'No, sir, but you—'

'A legate has a duty to stay with his men. Just save the eagle and my name, Cornelius.'

Felix brought his fist to his chest in salute. Valerius nodded. They both knew he was sending most of the escort to their deaths. Naso's attack might distract some of the Celts, but the cavalrymen would have to sacrifice themselves to clear a path for the eagle.

He heard a roar from behind as the warriors on the east side at last saw the attacking formation. '*Aquilifer* Honoratus, to me,' Valerius roared.

Honoratus turned with a look of anguish. Valerius saw the temptation to ignore the order cross his face before the discipline of a lifetime overcame it. The eagle-bearer marched to Valerius at the centre of his eight-man bodyguard. Their faces mirrored their commander's consternation and anger. Valerius steeled himself to meet their gaze. These men had given their oath to protect their eagle to their last breath and last drop of blood. They were the elite of the legion. The best of the best. What he was about to do would tarnish their honour, but he had no—

The eagle party seemed to freeze in mid-step and an illusion of stillness filled the battlefield as thirty thousand ears picked up a rumble of thunder above the sounds of men fighting and killing and dying. Valerius looked to the sky, but all it promised was snow.

'Lord.' Felix pulled his arm. 'Look.'

A great wave of horsemen rolled over the crest to the north-west of the swarm of Ordovice attackers and flooded the hillside. Valerius experienced a flash of puzzlement at the number of standards he saw, but he had no time to dwell on it. Suddenly everything was happening at once. A cheer went up from those legionaries who could see the men riding to their salvation, taken up all along the Roman lines as word spread. An echoing cheer came from beyond the east flank as Naso saw his opportunity and launched his attack on warriors who still had formed no coherent defence.

'Second and third ranks, launch spears,' Valerius roared. Anything that would add to the Ordovice confusion. Felix rode off to pass on the order and he heard the echoing cries of 'Throw', 'Throw', 'Throw' from the surviving centurions and decurions before a pitifully weak shower of *pila* soared out to be absorbed by the seething mass of Ordovices.

A helmetless figure with a bloody face ran up and Valerius recognized his *primus pilus*. 'Orders, sir?' Julius Ulpius Canalius brought his arm to his chest in salute.

For the first time Valerius felt the true fire of battle swelling inside him. With men like these how could he ever have considered defeat? 'First, second and third ranks hold firm. Fourth rank to form up with the reserve in column formation.' He guessed it would give him something like eight hundred men. A mix of legionaries and auxiliaries, and all close to exhaustion, but that couldn't be helped now. All that mattered was to take the fight to the enemy. A great howl in the middle distance and the hair on the back of his neck stood on end. The sound of cavalry charging home. 'Column of eight.' His weary mind dredged up the essential, but forgotten, detail. 'The escort will lead, *primus*, but we're going to need a way out.'

'May I suggest the south-west angle, legate, in two minutes.' The centurion returned his commander's savage grin. 'Still some steady lads there.'

'Make it so, *primus*. Cornelius.' He checked his helmet strap and his hand dropped to the hilt of his sword for the first time since the battle began. 'We're going to make room for the attack. Form fours and follow me.'

'The legate will naturally be in the middle rank,' Felix suggested with an exaggerated formality that almost made it an order.

'Not this time, Cornelius.' Valerius smiled. 'I'll join you in the front rank with Shabolz and Hilario.'

The delay while the column formed gave him time to draw breath and a last chance to take stock of their situation. He looked up in time to see the great swarm of cavalry – his disbelieving mind counted at least *four* wings of auxiliaries – smash deep into the northern flank of a Celtic army that had supposed itself on the cusp of the greatest victory since Boudicca's time. A victory that would make every warrior who fought in it the subject of song and story for a dozen generations. The shockwave of the impact rippled through the mass of the Ordovices like a summer storm whipping through a forest. Swords rose and fell on unprotected heads in the determined, relentless rhythm of men scything their way through a field of corn. From the rear of the cavalry formations the sky darkened as a vast shower of arrows rose, and rose, reached their limit, and fell to plummet into naked torsos packed so tight every one must have made its mark. A tremendous howl of consternation and pain accompanied their delivery.

Canalius reappeared, gasping for breath. 'Column formed and ready, sir. You'll get your opening on the signal.'

'Well done, *primus*. I leave the rest in your hands. If the pressure eases on the square push forward where you can. They're confused and they're frightened, ripe for defeat. All that matters is that we fight them where and when we can. Kill the bastards.'

The centurion's eyes lit up like twin fires. 'For Rome, sir.'

'For Rome,' Valerius echoed the traditional mantra. 'Signaller? Sound the charge.'

Valerius held his horse in check as the trumpet blast faded. He could feel the frustration of Felix and Hilario at the delay. Not yet. Fifty paces away the jaws of the south-west corner of the square began to ease apart, first the rear rank, then the third. It was a dangerous movement that could invite disaster if he mistimed his charge. 'Now!'

He dug in his heels and urged his mount forward as the legionaries in the second rank shuffled to left and right, slowly followed by those in the first. The final man on the left side must have felt the brush of the mare's mane as they passed, so swiftly did the charging horses fill the gap, smashing aside the Ordovice warriors who rushed to exploit it. Not one enemy entered the square. Suddenly all Valerius could see was snarling, hate-crazed faces and glittering spear heads as quickly brushed aside by the charging horses as they appeared. A spear darted at his mount's shoulder and Valerius flicked it away with the edge of his *spatha*, continuing the movement so his point carved a great rent across the bearer's tattooed chest. Four abreast they ploughed through the sea of enemies as easily as a galley with a following wind, scattering bodies aside and leaving terror and dismay in their wake. Behind them the remaining horsemen fanned out to clear new channels, hacking right and left at the exposed heads and bodies of any foolish enough to stand in their way. Valerius heard an equine scream of agony to his right and he twisted to see Hilario catapulted from his saddle. The big man's horse was down with a spear deep in its chest, already snorting blood from its nostrils. He half turned to go to the big trooper's aid, but Hilario was already on his feet, sword in hand and his flanks protected by Shabolz and Didius Gallus. At the same time the head of the legionary column emerged from the gap at the trot, shields up, *gladii* at the ready and their exhaustion forgotten in the desire to reach the enemy who had tormented them. Valerius had intended that the column, a compact mass of men eight shields wide, retain its integrity and smash deep into the heart of the enemy. Most did push on, directly in the wake of the charging horses, but those on the flanks ignored their officers and fanned out to seek the enemy where they found them. The indiscipline was a symptom of their lack of training under Fronto and a deep anger that had been building up in them for many months. It might have caused disaster. Instead, it acted like the first spark of a wildfire.

Valerius had seen it before, that moment when discipline broke down and a collective madness fuelled by bloodlust and suffering took over. Now he was only aware of a great cheer as he fought his way through the mob of his enemies. Behind him, the men guarding the edges of the gap advanced to the aid of their comrades in the column. First four or five, then ten, then fifty, and suddenly the whole side of the square, a cohort strong, was pushing forward over the piles of Ordovice dead. It was the same on the west side, where the men could see the cavalry revelling in the slaughter to their front and left. When Canalius, the *primus pilus*, understood the square was about to disintegrate he did the only thing he could. He sent runners to order the centurions in command of the north and east sides to advance in their turn.

Oblivious of what was happening behind him, Valerius searched for a cavalry unit within reach. The bravest of the Ordovices were still packed in front of the Romans they'd been fighting. But others, more timid or more prudent, were making their way resolutely towards the rear, a scattered, indisciplined mass streaming across the ridge towards home or some hoped-for sanctuary. For a trained cavalryman they were inviting prey, but, as he scanned the area for a suitable target, Valerius's eye chanced on an isolated group standing their ground by a fluttering banner on a small hummock in the centre of the ridge.

'Wheel right.' He emphasized the order by extending his arm in that direction. The survivors of his escort curved round in a perfect arc that brought them on a direct line to the banner. Half of the men surrounding it were spread out exhorting fleeing warriors to return to the attack. One or two others appeared to be remonstrating with each other. One man stood impassively beside the flag staring at the chaos before him.

Didius Gallus reappeared to take Hilario's place at Valerius's shoulder and the little column of Roman cavalrymen bludgeoned their way through the fleeing Ordovices. The big horses shouldered the unwary aside and the troopers cut down any who showed signs of resistance. Valerius became aware of another cavalry formation fighting their way towards him, but he only had eyes for the man beside the flag. At last the warriors beside him saw the danger to King Owain Lawhir. A shout of warning alerted the men of his bodyguard who had been attempting to turn the flood of demoralized Ordovice fighters and they ran to form a thin barrier between the attacking Romans and their king. Big, broad-chested spearmen, seasoned warriors all, arms and shoulders black with the tattoos that proclaimed their valour and their lineage.

'Form line,' Valerius called over his shoulder, slowing marginally to allow the following ranks to carry out his order. They outnumbered the defenders by two to one and they charged shoulder to shoulder, an unbroken line of thundering horses. A hundred paces passed in a dozen heartbeats. So close now Valerius could see the expressions on the enemy's faces, resolution, uncertainty, confusion, but never fear.

'Open order.' The cavalrymen nudged their horses to allow a blank file between each. The spears in front wavered, seeking individual targets. Valerius chose a man in the centre of the line: a bearded warrior with his hair dressed in spikes that made him seem a foot taller. The leaf-shaped point of his long spear centred on the chest of Valerius's mount. Valerius angled his charge to take him past the warrior's right shoulder as the man would expect and he saw the spear point twitch to follow him. A good soldier and a brave warrior. No thought of his own safety, every fibre of his being focused on bringing down the horse. What happened after could be left to the fates.

Within four strides Valerius nudged his mount so it swerved right across the warrior's front. Too late for the spearman to follow the horse, but there was always the man. Valerius had a glimpse of the spear point searching for his breast. Had the sword been in his right hand he would have been dead. But this was Gaius Valerius Verrens, who had held a sword in his left hand for the best part of two decades. He flicked the spear shaft aside with the edge of his *spatha* and in the same movement brought the blade round in an arc. The point of the heavy sword caught the warrior high in the stomach and the edge ripped upwards to shatter ribs and breastbone. A shriek of mortal agony, a face etched with horror, and scarlet misted the air.

Nothing stood between Valerius and the man on the hummock. Owain Lawhir, High King of the Ordovices, stood motionless by his dragon banner, his face set like stone and his eyes fixed on the fighting below. A golden circlet in his greying hair proclaimed his rank and he wore a mail vest selected from the booty of Canovium. His right hand rested on the hilt of his iron sword, but he made no attempt to draw it. As Valerius bore down on him he took a step away from the banner. Valerius raised the sword, still dripping gore from his last victim. In the final moment Owain looked up into his eyes, baring his throat. With a feeling almost of regret, Valerius swung the heavy blade. He felt the familiar hesitation as the edge cleaved living flesh and sinew, the momentary shock of solid bone, blood spurting high. So died Owain Lawhir, High King of the Ordovices.

'Lord.' A rasping voice broke the fleeting lethargy that had gripped Valerius. He looked round to find the diminutive figure of Gaius Rufus grinning from the saddle of a horse that looked three times too large for him. The scout held a long spear comfortably in his fist, with the butt settled in his right boot. Blood trickled down the shaft from the point on to his hand, and he flicked it away in an unconscious gesture. His eyes, red-rimmed and sunk deep, had the look of a man who hadn't slept for a week.

'I had expected you earlier, scout,' Valerius said.

'And so we would have been.' Gaius's grin didn't falter. 'But we picked up some slowbodies from Agricola's column along the way and it seemed best to adjust to their pace.'

'They made a difference,' Valerius conceded. He looked out across the field where the four cavalry wings continued to do terrible slaughter among the Celts who milled in confusion, trapped between the horsemen and three lines of legionaries, still unaware of their defeat. For every intuition told Valerius the battle was won. The fighting would go on for a while, but Naso's cohorts and the men of the east flank formation were driving an indisciplined host towards the hills to the south, where they joined thousands more fleeing from that flank.

'That they did,' Rufus agreed, shaking his head in wonder at the sheer number of Celts. 'It would have been like a flea attacking an elephant.'

Valerius wanted to ask him where he'd found the extra horsemen, but he had more important things to consider. 'Well, despite your tardiness, I'm appointing you commander of my cavalry.' Rufus's head came up in astonishment. 'Temporary and unpaid, naturally.'

'Naturally.' Rufus greeted his advancement with a wry smile.

'When I judge the time is right we'll withdraw the cavalry and leave the infantry to deal with what's left. All but two cohorts. Your men will have an hour to water their horses and get what rest they can. The important thing now is not to let them settle.' He nodded towards the fleeing Celts. 'In a couple of hours, if we leave them alone, they'll begin to wonder if they really were defeated. So pass on my orders to send two regiments to drive the main contingent west. Keep them moving, keep killing, push them into the sea.'

'There are still a lot of them.' Rufus frowned. 'What if they decide a few cavalrymen aren't frightening enough to be worth running from?'

'That's why I'm sending two legionary cohorts after you, with another cavalry wing for escort. Bypass any force that wants to make a fight of it. Keep the rest moving.' He held the little man's gaze. 'We don't have time for prisoners or slaves. Kill them all.'

A moment of doubt lingered on Rufus's grizzled features, but he nodded. 'And you, lord?'

'Me?' Valerius shook his head as if he hadn't considered the question. He looked back towards the mound where the men of his escort were stripping the dead of the Ordovice royal court. 'I'll be taking King Owain's head to Julius Agricola. We'll meet again on the shores opposite Mona.' He stifled a yawn that reminded him he hadn't slept for two nights. 'But first I will take what rest the shades of these brave soldiers will allow me.'

XLIV

The following day Valerius left Shabolz and his Pannonian comrades to tend Licco's funeral pyre. The other Roman dead would lie together till the end of time in a great burial pit dug by their tentmates, while the mouldering bodies of the Celts would feed the buzzards, ravens and foxes attracted by the growing scent of death.

With the remainder of the escort he crossed the ridge where Owain's banner still flew. On the far side lay a long slope down to the fertile plain that separated the mountains from the sea. He could see movement, but whether it was fleeing Ordovices or the Roman cavalrymen pursuing them it was impossible to tell. The only signs of the advance were the familiar pillars of smoke from burning houses and farms, and the pinpricks of flame that heralded another addition to their number. Beyond the plain, a thin strip of silver marked the strait that separated Mona from the mainland, which Agricola's army must cross if it was to take the island.

Dead and dying warriors lay scattered along the route. Twice they came across little groups of Celts dragging one of their injured into hiding. Felix and the others would have ridden after them, but Valerius insisted they continue without pause and hurry to meet Agricola. In truth he was sick of killing. The order he'd given Gaius Rufus had been the right one, and in line with Agricola's orders. The fewer Ordovices left to defend Mona or harass his rear the better, and word of the great slaughter would spread north, where minds would be focused on the consequences of resistance. But the very fact of the Ordovice rising was proof that such lessons never lasted long, and the hatred they provoked was like a seed planted in the spring that blossomed when least expected.

Their route took them diagonally across the plain towards the valley the Twentieth must negotiate to reach Mona. Here too bands of fleeing Celts streamed towards the sea and the possible sanctuary of the Druids' Isle. Despite Felix's protests it was too dangerous Valerius insisted on taking a closer look at what lay before them, and they turned west towards the shore. They reined in above a long, narrow beach and Valerius surveyed the placid waters that separated them from the tree-covered slopes a few hundred paces away. Valerius had seen wider rivers. The Tamesa, the Danuvius and the Rhenus all posed a greater obstacle than this.

'This won't stop Agricola for long,' Felix murmured.

'I doubt it will,' Valerius agreed. 'He's been here before, when Paulinus made the crossing. His engineers were working on boats before he left Viroconium. They'll carry them here in pieces and assemble them on the shore.' His nose twitched as the breeze wafted a familiar scent from the far shore. He frowned. 'I wonder . . .'

On the opposite bank a dozen Celts emerged from the trees and ran to the shoreline, shouting and cavorting. 'Laugh all you like, little Celts,' Hilario rumbled. 'Agricola is coming to get you.'

Valerius had seen enough, but as he was turning away he noticed movement to the north. A makeshift raft with five or six men crouched on its boards emerged from a hidden cove, followed by a second and a third. The occupants paddled frantically with pieces of timber and whatever they had to hand.

'We should have brought a few archers,' Felix complained. 'Then there'd have been twenty fewer to meet us on the other side.'

'Nothing we can do about it now.' The rafts had already reached the middle of the strait. On the far side the Celts continued to shout and gesticulate, but the tone had a new edge and the shouts were directed at the men in the rafts. As Valerius watched they became ever more voluble and animated. Valerius's mount shifted beneath him and he looked down to see water beneath her hooves where there had been none. A few moments before the strait had been mirror calm in the stillness. There still wasn't a breath of wind, but now the surface had turned choppy.

'Mars save us,' Felix whispered. He was staring to the left and Valerius followed his gaze to where a white-topped wave three feet high raced up the strait at the speed of a charging horse. They watched as it surged past, almost innocuous in appearance, but with a sense of immense power, followed by a whirling, surging mass of rough water. On the rafts the men paddled with a frantic intensity right up to the moment the wave struck. Valerius expected the surge to carry the rafts along, perhaps as far as the open sea, but the sheer power of it flipped the first over, sending men flying into the water. The wave struck the second and third rafts a heartbeat later and the fragile craft simply disintegrated. For a few moments they could see heads and waving hands in the rushing water, then they were gone, leaving a few bobbing timbers.

'If Agricola is expecting us to cross that,' Hilario growled, 'I hope he's going to make a very expensive sacrifice to Neptune.'

Valerius glanced to where the Celtic warriors had given up taunting the Romans and were now working to pile timber at the foot of a post set just above the tideline.

'It may not only be the sea we have to worry about.'

They met more of Agricola's cavalry when they turned east again over the plain. The decurion in command told Valerius the governor planned to set up camp with the Twentieth beside a river six or seven miles up the valley and make the final march the next day.

The camp was still under construction when they reached it, but they'd completed the governor's pavilion. Valerius told Felix to have the men fed and horses watered and took the leather sack that had been tied to his saddle pommel. Hilario and Gallus escorted him to the doorway of the pavilion and a guard went to announce him. 'The governor will see you now, legate,' he said when he returned.

Dressed in a simple tunic, Agricola sat at his campaign desk dictating to a young tribune who recorded his words with a stylus on a stack of waxed tablets. The governor waved Valerius to a couch in the corner of the tent which Valerius was surprised to see already occupied by Terentius Strabo, legate of the Second Augusta. By rights Strabo should have been with his legion at Isca. He made no attempt to welcome Valerius, which reminded the one-handed Roman that the sullen legate was one of three men left in Britannia who might be Domitian's creature and therefore Valerius's enemy. Agricola ignored them and continued with his dictation. 'And the Twentieth legion, which I had the privilege to command, overwhelmed the hill fort's defenders and thus destroyed the power of the Ordovices . . .' There were so many inaccuracies in the short statement that Valerius blinked. Agricola added a short list of awards he planned to confer. 'That will be all.'

He turned to Valerius as the young man left the room. 'My unit historian. One can't be too careful about posterity,' he said with a tight smile. 'Strabo is here to receive his final instructions and chooses to stay for the final operation.'

'It was my privilege to witness a great victory,' Strabo agreed in a voice that didn't sound in the least privileged or impressed.

Valerius had assumed word of the Ninth's victory would have reached Agricola by now and the lack of warmth in the governor's welcome surprised him. Perhaps the fragment of dictation heard went some way to explaining it. Or was there another possibility? Valerius studied Strabo for some indication that he might have poisoned Agricola's mind against him, but he found none.

'I didn't expect to see you here.' Agricola's voice matched his look. 'I thought you'd be finishing the job.'

Valerius placed the leather bag on the desk. It had a damp brown stain on the bottom. Agricola studied it with distaste. 'My Celtic scouts tell me this is the man who ordered the raid on Canovium.'

Strabo snorted disdainfully. 'Have we descended to the level of the barbarians?'

'Your job was not to kill Owain Lawhir.' Agricola ignored the other man. 'It was to hold his forces in place until I arrived with the Twentieth to annihilate them. Instead, they tell me you attacked and now thousands of Celtic warriors are rushing to defend the druids on Mona. Every Ordovice you allowed to escape makes the attack more difficult and puts my legionaries at greater risk. You allowed your lust for glory to blind you to my strategic aim.'

Valerius felt the heat of his anger growing with every word. He could have pointed out that Agricola's strategy depended on his approach remaining undiscovered, and that Owain had known of his route the moment he'd left Viroconium. He could have argued that attack had been his only option, and that if he'd stayed his hand Owain and his entire army would have escaped to Mona at the first sign of Agricola's approach. Instead, he said: 'I would commend the selfless conduct and bravery of Quintus Naso, camp prefect of the Ninth legion, whose supporting attack was crucial to the victory.' He put an emphasis on the word victory, clearly at odds with Agricola's view, making Strabo raise a cultured eyebrow, but the governor didn't react. 'Also my *primus pilus*, Julius Ulpius Canalius, for his unflinching courage in the first line of defence, and the scout, Gaius Rufus, who led my cavalry in the flanking movement crucial to the success of the mission.'

'*Our* cavalry,' Agricola corrected him. 'You would not deny the Twentieth's part in the battle, I'm sure.' Valerius nodded his head in acknowledgement, wondering what the governor's dispatch to the Palatium would say. 'But that is in the past. Now we must coordinate our assault on Mona. Despite the reinforcements they have received,' a tight smile of admonition, 'Between us we will make short work of these filthy druids and their supporters.'

Valerius mentioned the tidal surge he'd seen swamp the Ordovice rafts.

'Yes.' Agricola got to his feet, stretching to ease his back, and walked across to the sand table where a rough model of Mona and the shore of the mainland had been created. 'Our timing must be precise. I've ordered my cavalry to round up any boatmen or fishermen they find for questioning, but I have Paulinus's tables recording the tidal movements.

As I remember it there are several possible sites for the crossing, which suits us admirably. The Twentieth will make the main attack. I have two hundred assault boats in my baggage train. My Batavian water rats will provide the crews. They have more experience of river crossings than any other unit in Britannia. Each boat can carry ten men, so we can put up to two thousand fully armed legionaries on the beach in the first wave.'

Valerius imagined the short crossing. The Celts massed in the trees. 'They'll be waiting for you,' he pointed out. 'If they attack the boats in the shallows you could suffer heavy casualties.'

'I'm aware of that. But if my plan succeeds they won't know where the landing will happen. As I say, the Twentieth will carry out the main assault,' he pointed to a narrow part of the strait, 'here in the north. However, we will disguise all our preparations. In the meantime, the Ninth will have carried out a probing attack in the south to draw any reinforcements there. My cavalry and auxiliary infantry will mass here in the centre, disguised as legionaries, and make a demonstration which will hold the defenders in place while the real attack happens elsewhere. They'll also undoubtedly hold some kind of force in the west in case the attack is supported by a naval operation.'

'It would make sense.' Valerius pointed out the obvious.

'It would also have taken time I do not have.'

Valerius noted that once again Agricola was using the Ninth as bait. It was only now he remembered the witch's prophecy. *You will fight your battle and taste your victory*, Aurinia had said, *but it will turn to ashes in your mouth. You will have your legion. But it will be the legion of the damned.* Sometimes it seemed the governor was determined to destroy the Ninth Hispana. If that was the case, Valerius was equally determined not to let it happen. Yet he had no choice but to obey Agricola's orders. If he wished to sacrifice one element for the success of the overall operation the decision was his. Studying the sand table, Valerius noticed that the area where the governor planned to mass his cavalry was one of the least likely crossing places. The chances were that the Ordovices would see it for what it was, a feint, and hurry their defenders to where the crossing was already in progress.

'May I assume that at least half of the boats will be made available to the Ninth?'

'You may assume nothing of the sort.' Agricola leaned across the table. 'I'm prepared to allow you fifty of the craft, but otherwise you'll have to find another way to get your men across. You're a resourceful man, Valerius; I'm sure you'll come up with some stratagem. I don't have to tell an officer of your experience that it's essential the main crossing is carried out in overwhelming numbers.'

'When do we cross?'

'The tides are right in two days. We must take advantage or wait a week and more. I don't see any point in wasting time. As you said in Londinium, winter is fast approaching. Your boats will be with you before dusk. A day to prepare, then a dawn crossing. We'll give you till the end of the second hour to make a proper demonstration and pin them in place before the Twentieth makes the crossing.'

Valerius thought the timetable overhasty, but he could see that Agricola wouldn't be moved. 'In that case,' he replaced his helmet, 'I had best get back to my men.'

'I'm sorry, Valerius.' Agricola sounded more conciliatory as he walked him to the doorway. 'I understand your concerns, but my responsibility is to the Emperor and to ensure the success of this mission.'

When he was out in the open air, Valerius drew in a deep breath. The anger remained, but there was something else that puzzled him. Something in Agricola's tone he didn't understand. It was almost as if the man pitied him.

He walked back through the camp to where he'd left the escort. Tents were being erected all around him and legionaries continued to work on the bank and the ditch. On the way he remembered he'd promised Julius Hellenicus that he'd replace the medical supplies depleted in the battle. He changed course for the hospital tent, which was always the first to be set up along with the commander's. In the gloom he could see that only two or three of the low cots were occupied, the patients anonymous humps beneath the blankets. The chief *medicus* and his assistant were setting out their equipment beneath a lamp at the far end of the big leather tent. The man looked doubtful on hearing Valerius's request. 'I'll do what I can, but we expect to be busy ourselves in the next few days. Still, I should be able to put together a mule load if you can wait?'

Valerius said he'd return with some men. He was on his way to the exit when one of the few patients tried to raise himself up on his cot as he passed. Valerius called to the *medicus* and would have continued on his way, but the man threw back his blanket with a groan of agony. A large bandage covered most of his head, but beneath it Valerius recognized the haggard, pain-racked features of Rufius Florus.

'Bring this man water.' Valerius hurried to the cot and pushed the injured cavalryman back, his mind racing with the potential consequences of Florus's presence. A terrible paralysing fear threatened to overwhelm him. 'Stay, Rufius,' he said urgently. 'I'm here and your comrades are nearby. Tell me what happened.'

'Taken.' The young trooper's whisper was so faint Valerius had to bend over him to make it out.

'Who was taken?'

'Ceris,' Florus sobbed. 'They took Ceris.' Valerius felt a guilty surge of relief, instantly dashed by his next words. 'Ceris and the lady. Lucius too. Marius and the others are dead. Aaagh.' Florus cried out as Valerius's fingers dug into his flesh.

'Careful, legate.' The *medicus* put the nozzle of a water skin to Florus's lips. 'His ribs are cracked and he has a fractured skull.'

'I need to know what happened.' Valerius could hear the fear in his own voice.

'He's unconscious. He can't tell you anything else.'

'Then revive him.'

'That could kill him,' the *medicus* snapped.

Valerius fought waves of panic. 'Tell me how he got here.' He almost choked on the words.

'He rode into camp more dead than alive,' the *medicus* informed him. 'It must have been on the fourth day of the march, and he wouldn't be treated until he'd spoken to the governor.'

Valerius gaped. 'Agricola knows about this?'

'I don't know what was said, but they certainly spoke, and then he was sent here to be looked after.'

'Agricola knew,' Valerius whispered, almost to himself. 'But why . . . ?' He straightened. 'Look after the boy. I will be back for the supplies.'

He marched out of the medical tent and went straight back to Agricola's headquarters. The two guards saw the look on his face and stepped in front of him, but Valerius pushed them aside.

'The governor is not—'

'The governor will see me now,' Valerius snarled as he pulled back the curtain.

He heard two swords being drawn with that familiar musical hiss, but he ignored the sound and stepped inside. 'You knew.' The words emerged through clenched teeth.

Agricola looked up and dismissed the guards with a wave of his hand. 'I have men looking for them,' he said. 'There was nothing you could do about it and I deemed it important for the coming operations that you were not distracted.'

'My wife, my son and my unborn child?' Valerius felt like taking Agricola by the throat and shaking him the way a terrier shakes a rat. 'And you didn't want me *distracted*?'

'Four nights ago a substantial force of Celts raided the fort at Viroconium. They overcame the garrison and slaughtered most of them. The survivors, including one of your men, saw three prisoners being carried off by the raiders. As far as we know they have not been harmed. Four squadrons of cavalry are scouring the mountains for them. You were in the midst of your battle when they were taken, Valerius. What difference could you have made?'

It was true, but that did nothing to alter the terrible sense of watching his loved ones being swept down a swirling river and being incapable of doing anything to save them. 'At least I could have made my own decision,' he said, knowing how pathetic he sounded.

'I need you here,' Agricola snapped. 'No one else can take the Ninth across those straits and do what needs to be done.'

'You should have told me.'

'Perhaps that is true.' Agricola's voice softened. 'But it makes no difference now. You are here and here you must stay and trust in the Ala Indiana to find her. They are good men under a sensible commander. Young Aprilis is my best man. If anyone can find them he can. Where would you go, Valerius? What would you do? Ride back to Viroconium and try to follow the raiders' tracks? It would take you two days' hard riding to get there. And when you did you would find nothing. Go back to your men and prepare them for the attack. I will send word of any news.'

Valerius stood with his head bowed, all the anger drained from him and replaced by despair. Agricola called for his guard. 'The legate has been taken unwell. Send for the commander of his escort.' As they waited for Felix, he turned to Valerius. 'I take it you made no further progress in finding Fronto's killer. If indeed he was murdered at all.'

It took a few moments for the words to sink in, but when they did Valerius stared at the governor. He had respected this man, but now? 'Yes,' he said eventually. 'Fronto was certainly murdered. I think I know how and why, but I doubt I would ever be able to prove it.'

'So you have a suspect. May I ask who it is?'

'You.'

The silence stretched out for a dozen heartbeats before Agricola let out a bark of laughter. 'I believe your ordeal has deprived you of your senses.'

'It doesn't matter now, Julius.' Valerius shook his head. 'If any man deserved to die it was Fronto. You had your reasons. You would never have trusted a man like him to lead the Ninth into the Ordovice mountains, but you couldn't get rid of him by conventional means because of his friends in the Palatium. So he had to die. At first I thought the killer must be someone he'd hurt, perhaps an entire *contubernium*. Of course, you wanted me to think that. Yet the way he died was too quick and clean. His men would have made him suffer. The more I thought about it the more it became clear this was no murder, but an execution. I think Aprilis distracted the guard while your assassins, probably Aprilis's bodyguard, killed him and threw his body off the cliff. Tertius, the *primus pilus,* was the only other man aware of the plot, but he conveniently disappeared from the convoy Aprilis accompanied. A young officer with a bright future, Aprilis. Intelligent, ruthless, and with friends in high places, I hear.'

Agricola's eyes turned evasive. 'You're playing a very dangerous game making accusations of that nature, Valerius,' he said carefully.

'As I say, it doesn't matter. You will write the final report on Fronto's death. Perhaps you've done it already.' He heard Felix addressing the guard. 'Now, with your leave I will go and join my men.'

'Be very careful, Gaius Valerius Verrens,' the governor whispered. 'These are dangerous times. Don't get yourself killed.'

But Valerius was already gone and Agricola was far from his mind. Only one thing mattered now. How was he going to save his wife and son?

If he'd turned back he would have been surprised to find the governor in conversation with the young man they'd been discussing only moments earlier. 'He knows too much,' Metilius Aprilis insisted.

'The fact that you have a brother on the Palatine means nothing,' Agricola snapped.

'It gives me a direct link to Domitian. What if he makes the connection?'

'That is none of my concern.' Agricola looked pensive. 'There will be a battle in the next few days and I have placed the Ninth in the position of greatest peril. One thing we know about Gaius Valerius Verrens is that he will be at the forefront of the attack. Perhaps the problem will take care of itself? In the meantime I suggest you return to Viroconium and make sure no evidence exists to link you to the loathsome Tertius.'

Aprilis smiled. 'And if I happen to encounter the wife and boy on the way?'

Agricola looked up and held his gaze. 'I'm sure I can count on you to make the right decision.'

XLV

Gaius Rufus hadn't slept in three nights and he'd spent all day in the saddle. When he reported to Valerius at the Ninth's temporary camp opposite Mona he could barely stand and drank the cup of wine he was handed in a single draught. He wiped his lips with the back of his hand and let out a long sigh. 'By all the gods that was good,' he said. He studied the man opposite and decided that if one person in this army looked worse than he felt it was Valerius. 'We did as you ordered and kept pressing them. They didn't put up much fight, and those we caught we killed. The rest scattered into the mountains or crossed over to the Druids' Isle, but then you know that.'

Something in the scout's tone told Valerius Agricola's rebuke about his command of the Ninth had become general knowledge. He nodded. 'I mentioned your name in my report to the governor. I hope he makes his gratitude known in some tangible way.'

The little man shrugged. 'I have more gold than I can carry. We ran down some of Owain's court when they were burying the presents he planned to give out after his victory.' He reached into a leather pouch on his belt and drew out an object that sat in his palm glittering buttery yellow in the lamplight. It was a ring, a double circle of gold fashioned in the shape of a fire worm – a dragon – with a single faultless sapphire set in its mouth. 'I thought your wife might like this,' he said shyly. 'The stone matches her eyes.'

The reminder of Tabitha caused bile to rise in Valerius's stomach and he turned away, clutching his mouth. 'Lord,' Gaius pleaded, shocked at the reaction his gift had provoked. 'I meant no insult or harm. If I have caused any hurt I will repay it a hundred times. Please.'

Valerius fought to regain control of his emotions. The truth was that for the first time in his life he was utterly helpless. They might be dead already. 'The Celts raided Viroconium four nights ago. They killed the garrison and took my wife, Lucius and Ceris.' He shook his head, wiping his lips with his left hand, and his voice shook as he relayed Florus's words. 'I don't know whether they are alive or dead, but I will pay anything or do anything to get them back. The raiders struck like ghosts. No one knows where they came from before the attack, or where they went after it. Only one man has the knowledge, the skills and the experience to find them.'

Rufus dropped to his knees and bowed his head. 'I am your slave in this, lord.'

'No, Gaius Rufus.' Valerius drew him to his feet. 'You are my champion.'

'Viroconium?' The scout turned the matter over in his mind. 'No chance raid, then, not even against a reduced garrison. It was planned and carried out for a reason. King Owain seeking some leverage against the governor in case of defeat? Or,' he glanced towards the wall of the tent that hid Mona, 'those who persuaded him to attack Canovium parading their power to strike at Rome whenever they choose. In either case they will be coming in this direction. There are only three or four trails they could take. If I can cut their tracks or find someone they have spoken to I should be able to follow, or at least . . .'

His voice faded, but Valerius knew what had been left unsaid. *At least discover whether they're dead or alive.* 'It will be dangerous with so many defeated warriors wandering the hills.'

A tired laugh. 'Danger and death have ridden at my shoulder since the day I crawled out of the hypocaust in the Temple of Claudius. I can still smell the rotting flesh and taste the smoke.'

'What do you need?'

'A hot meal and a fresh horse and I will be in the saddle within the hour.'

'Thank you, Gaius.'

The scout clasped Valerius's left hand. 'I will find her for you, lord, if it takes all eternity.' He turned away, stoop-shouldered and shaggy, like a two-legged hound, but with a cavalryman's swagger that belied his exhaustion. Valerius looked down at the golden circle in the palm of his hand.

The next day passed in a frenzy of preparation as the Ninth's engineers assembled the assault boats and Valerius had them tested on a nearby river away from prying Ordovice eyes. With fifty boats the Ninth could only cross a cohort at a time, and each unit had to be assigned its place in the assault. Timing would be everything. The first wave would be exposed, but Valerius planned to order a cavalry wing to swim their horses across to protect each flank. Weariness overcame him soon after dusk, but his mind was too active to allow sleep. He lay restive in his cot listening to the changes of watch, his brain haunted by the faces of Tabitha and Lucius and the restless soul of the child he might never see. He could feel his son's ungovernable fear and, in turn, he feared the power of his wife's anger. Tabitha's instinct would be to protect her son like a mother wolf and lash out at Lucius's tormentors, but that could be fatal. Make them think you are cowed, his mind advised. Do not meet their eyes. Endure and survive for his sake and mine. The thought of what might be happening to her even as he lay there sickened him.

He tried to blank out the sights he'd seen in the burned-out lands ravaged by Boudicca. The Celts could be mercilessly cruel and end-lessly imaginative. Only Ceris's presence gave him any kind of hope. For all she was Corieltauvi and they Ordovices, they were still Celts and she would know their ways. Neither of them had shown it overtly, but Valerius sensed that a true bond of friendship and respect had grown between the two women. Ceris would try to guide Tabitha through her ordeal. Where Tabitha could be mercurial and would take any chance to escape that offered itself, Ceris would caution patience and await her opportunity. Their greatest hope would be that Gaius Valerius Verrens, Hero of Rome and holder of the Corona Aurea, would somehow reach them. Despair grabbed him like a clawed hand in the vitals as his true helplessness struck him. He couldn't help them unless he knew where they were in that vast mountain fastness to the east. Even then he was under Agricola's orders to lead the Ninth's assault on Mona the next day. For now, all he could do was place his trust in Gaius Rufus.

Sleep must have come, or he was so buried in the black tomb of his thoughts the effect was the same, because he wasn't prepared for the hand that touched his shoulder. 'Lord,' he heard in the whispered voice of Didius Gallus. 'I'm sorry to disturb you, but a man is here to see you. An informant who claims to have vital information about the enemy dispositions that must be conveyed to you personally.'

'Very well.' Valerius rolled from the cot and winced as his feet touched the freezing earth. He threw a cloak over his tunic, blinking as Gallus lit the oil lamp. His wooden fist with its leather stock lay on a chest by the side of the cot and he reached for it in an automatic movement, only to draw his hand away when he heard voices outside.

Hilario and Crescens hustled the prisoner into the tent between them. Valerius froze as he recognized the shattered face. They'd tied Cearan's hands behind his back and he stood with his head bowed. His skin had an unhealthy yellow pallor that had not been apparent in Colonia and his lank grey hair hung like a filthy curtain over the single eye.

'Untie him,' Valerius ordered. Crescens pulled at the knots binding the Iceni's wrists and stepped away. Cearan massaged the angry red weals on his translucent flesh. Eventually he looked up. They were a good six feet apart, but still Valerius had to steel himself not to flinch before the malevolence in his gaze.

'They say you have information for me?'

'What I have to say to you is for your ears only.' The Celt nodded in the direction of Hilario, who met his look with a stony glare.

'I trust these men with my life. I believe I can trust them with whatever information you have.'

'This is about your woman.'

For a moment Valerius's vision turned red. When it cleared Cearan was beneath him and his left hand was clamped around his throat. Hilario and Crescens dragged him away, leaving the Iceni lying gasping on the dirt floor.

'Give me ten minutes with him, lord,' Hilario said with a softness infinitely more chilling than his normal threatening demeanour. 'He'll soon tell everything he knows.'

'Leave us,' Valerius said, as Cearan raised himself painfully to his feet.

'Lord . . .'

'I said leave us.' Crescens flinched at the violence in Valerius's tone, and the two cavalrymen backed away to the door. Valerius's eyes never left Cearan as he picked up the rawhide stock of the wooden fist and placed it over the mottled purple stump of his right arm, tightening the leather laces with a deftness acquired by years of practice. Cearan watched with a look of contemptuous anticipation.

'Say what you have come to say,' Valerius told him.

'Your woman and your brat are on Mona, where Gwlym awaits your coming with pleasure, along with twenty thousand of his followers.'

A spark of hope flared in the cold emptiness of Valerius's heart at the knowledge that Tabitha and Lucius were only a few short miles away, but he kept his features emotionless. 'Who is Gwlym?'

'Gwlym is the arch-druid of Elfydd.' A cold smile flickered on the undamaged portion of Cearan's face. 'What you call Britannia. He has invoked the spirit of the hare and the horse and the wolf. Andraste rises again to sweep the Romans from the land.'

'What has this to do with my wife and son?'

The single eye glittered with a new fanaticism. 'Gwlym has decreed that Boudicca failed because the Roman Mother Goddess did not look kindly on her. This time he intends that she and Andraste are the twin spear points on which the Roman governor Agricola will be impaled.'

Your woman and fifty other Roman lovers will ensure the cooperation of the Mother Goddess.' Cearan's lip twisted in a sneer. 'The moment a single Roman craft sets off from the shore Gwlym's acolytes will light the fires, and you will watch as they tear the child from your woman's womb and burn it before your eyes. You will hear her screams as she burns and you will suffer the anguish Cearan of the Iceni suffered.' With his final words Cearan tore at his tunic until he had bared his skeletal breast. 'And now you will kill me.'

'No.' Valerius shook his head as he advanced on the Celt and kicked the legs from beneath him. Cearan landed flat on his back, all the breath knocked from his lungs. 'Not until you have told me precisely where they are being held and the positions of Gwlym's defences.'

Gwlym spat at his boots. 'I will tell you nothing and you will watch them burn. You cannot hurt a man who is dying.'

Valerius smashed him on the side of his head with the artificial hand to stun him and bent to kneel over him. Cearan heard a sharp click and the glittering blade of a small knife appeared from the centre knuckle of Valerius's wooden fist. When he spoke Valerius's voice was flat and emotionless, but there was a message in his eyes that made Cearan shudder. 'I think you will find you are mistaken.'

The first agonized shriek brought Hilario and Crescens to the tent doorway. 'Ready my escort with three days' rations.' Valerius didn't look up from the prone figure beneath him. 'And tell the camp prefect to await my orders within the hour.'

XLVI

Tabitha held Lucius closer to her breast to stifle his snuffling and her own agitation. They sat against the mud and wattle wall of a verminous Celtic hut which she guessed – from the sea journey they'd been forced to endure – was on the island Valerius and his legion had been sent to invade. That, at least, would partially explain why they were here. Ceris crouched a few feet away from them, conducting a hushed conversation with two of their fourteen or fifteen fellow occupants. Some kind of trade, the two women agreed, a bargaining piece to be exchanged for some favour or perhaps a high-ranking captive on the Roman side. Yet Tabitha had felt the Corieltauvi girl's unease and she suspected Ceris was keeping something from her. Their fellow captives, all women and all, more puzzlingly, at various stages of pregnancy, were plainly terrified.

She didn't know what she would have done without Ceris's commanding and comforting presence. Tabitha came from a background that had introduced her at an early stage to conspiracy, subterfuge and plots, and, occasionally, outright danger. But this strange, alien land, with its cold, damp mountains and their savage occupants, confused and frightened her. She had no way of communicating, except through Ceris, and it left her feeling helpless.

They'd come so close to escape at Viroconium. Marius had heard a commotion at the gate and taken Serenus to investigate. Moments later she'd heard screams and the clash of swords. Ceris had swiftly woken Lucius and dressed him, while Tabitha gathered together the sack of necessities they always kept to hand. Ceris's lover, the boy Rufius, had wanted to go to his comrades' aid, but she'd insisted he stay with them. It was Ceris who led them crouching through the darkness between the barrack blocks, hoping to find the west gate clear of the raiders, but they'd almost run into a group of Celtic warriors on the way and they'd been forced towards the outer walls. A guard hung upside down from the stairway with his throat cut and his belly open. Rufius told them to stay hidden beneath the stairs and ran off. Ceris cursed him, but a little later he'd returned with a length of rope and led them up to the walkway. Rufius had secured the rope to the wall. Ceris descended first, slipping down the rope with the agility of a squirrel. Rufius retrieved the rope and tied it around Lucius's waist, but they could hear more and more Celts moving about the barracks. Just as Tabitha was about to follow Lucius she'd heard a shout from her left.

'Go!' Rufius insisted. 'Get away while you can.' At the same time he was sprinting past her towards the band of Celts running towards them along the walkway. Tabitha slid down the rope so quickly she'd burned her hands and the last she'd heard of Rufius Florus was a cry of pain and the sharp thud of a falling body. Ceris hadn't even hesitated, hustling them away towards the slope that led to the river. Shouts from left and right. Branches whipping out of the darkness to tear at any bare flesh. Tripping and stumbling, Lucius's small hand tight in her grip. Her heart pounded with fear, offset by pride. She could feel him sobbing, but not a cry or a complaint left his lips.

Ceris must have been able to see in the dark, because when they reached the flat she managed to steer them between the ditches of the auxiliary marching camps. At last they heard the sound of the river. The raiders would have killed the bridge guards, but there were always small boats moored nearby. Tabitha recognized an expanse of moonlight-fractured water, but it was instantly blacked out by silhouettes that seemed to grow out of the earth. A massive hand gripped her throat before a torch flared to reveal the bearded giant who held her. Nearby, Ceris was pinned to the muddy earth by two other men.

'Run, Lucius,' Tabitha cried. Instead, Lucius flew at the man holding her, arms flailing and shrieking at him to let her go. The attack lasted for a dozen heartbeats before another Ordovice stepped out of the darkness and picked him up by the waist.

The Celts put them on horses and tied their hands to the saddles. Ceris attempted to remonstrate with the big man who led them, but his only reply was a heavy-handed slap that left her cheek bright red.

Tabitha saw a tear trickle down her cheek, but it was a tear of anger, not fear. 'We are not to speak.' Ceris glanced warily at the man. 'His name is Cadwal and he says it makes no difference to him whether we have tongues or not.'

For two days they travelled west by perilous mountain tracks and through sullen, doom-laden ravines. At first Tabitha had prayed a Roman cavalry patrol would stumble on them, but on the only occasion they saw the sunlight flashing on auxiliary spear points in a valley far below the leader spat an order and she'd felt the icy sting of a blade at her throat. There would be no rescue; the Celts would kill them first.

The morning of the third day brought the salt scent of the ocean and they reached a small settlement in a sheltered bay where a trading boat with a square sail waited just off shore. While his men set fires to cook the midday meal Cadwal had hailed the boat and within the hour Tabitha, Lucius and Ceris had been hustled aboard.

'I'm sorry, mistress,' Ceris whispered as the big man spoke to the boat's captain. 'There was nothing I could do.'

'There was nothing any of us could do,' Tabitha replied with a shaky smile. 'But as long as we still breathe there is hope. If there is a way,' her voice took on a fierce certainty, 'Valerius will find us.'

She saw Cadwal glowering menacingly at them from beside the steering oar and they hadn't exchanged another word until they'd arrived at the stockade.

Ceris slithered back towards them. Her face was deathly pale. 'We must find a way to get out of here. We can't wait for Valerius.'

'They'll kill us,' Tabitha objected. 'I can't risk Lucius being hurt.'

'That's why we must escape. They're going to kill us anyway.'

Before Tabitha could reply the curtained door whipped aside and a young guard appeared in the doorway, creating a wave of panic through the hut's occupants. He searched the gloomy interior of the hut until he found Tabitha and snapped what she took to be an order.

'He says you must go with him,' Ceris translated. She saw Tabitha's face pale and the instinctive movement towards Lucius. 'No,' she cautioned. 'I don't believe they mean to harm us yet.' She rose to her feet and spoke to the young man in a soft, almost caressing tone so different from her normal sullen monotone that Tabitha wondered if she were listening to the same woman. Whatever was said had an immediate effect on the young warrior and he answered in a more conciliatory voice, holding the curtain aside. 'He says you should be honoured to meet the arch-druid.' Ceris helped Tabitha to her feet. 'Lucius will be safe with these women.'

They followed the guard from the hut and out into the flat winter sunlight. Tabitha shuddered and wrapped her cloak tighter about her body. It was not just the cold that affected her, but the men who waited in the centre of the compound. Cadwal was one, massive and imposing in his polished iron mail and with a spear in his hand, a sword belted at his waist and four similarly armed warriors at his back. They hovered protectively beside two tall, clean-shaven men in what Tabitha took to be priestly robes, though like their owners the robes were matted with filth. But it was the shrunken, dried-out husk of a figure who stood between them who instilled true fear. White pus dripped like obscene tears from the raw scarlet flesh of his empty eye sockets, yet Tabitha had never felt such intense scrutiny. It was as if the druid could see inside her and her arms tightened protectively over her bulging midriff. One of his acolytes whispered something into his ear. He stepped forward and she would have reeled away from the stench he gave off had the guard not held her by the arm. The druid's hands came up and she felt a wave of revulsion as they touched her face, bony fingers with curling, inch-long nails searching out the contours of her features, the skin dry and made abrasive by ancient calluses.

A whisper escaped his thin lips, and they twitched in a smile that made her want to vomit. She struggled to understand what was happening. This revolting old man was nothing like the priests of her native Emesa, where they worshipped Elah Gebal, the black stone, messenger of the Sun God.

Yet he had power, and that power was clear in the harsh nasal bray that emerged from his lips. One of the other druids nodded to Ceris and she began to translate, every word uttered with obvious reluctance. 'You should know he is Gwlym, arch-druid of Elfydd, and that you will be his personal emissary to the Mother Goddess, along with the other Roman women and Roman lovers he has gathered here. The fires have been set and they will be lit the moment the first Roman boat sets off from the shore. Your husband, who betrayed mighty Boudicca . . .'

'My husband betrayed no one,' Tabitha spat back. 'Boudicca was his enemy and he was a soldier. Any man who uses war as an excuse to abuse and kill women and children is no man at all. Gwlym, arch-druid of Elfydd, is no warrior or leader, he is a coward, who will be reviled by history. The Mother Goddess will recoil in disgust at his gift and her wrath will fall upon him. I, Tabitha, princess of Emesa, place a curse on him and all who follow him. Tell him that.' Ceris hesitated, but Tabitha held her gaze. 'Tell him.'

Ceris translated the words. Tabitha saw Cadwal's grip tighten on his spear and his warriors shuffled uneasily. Gwlym's upper lip curled and the muscles in his cheeks twitched. When he spoke Ceris struggled to keep up with the avalanche of hatred that erupted from him.

'He says you know nothing of this island and its gods. Your words condemn you as a witch and a sorceress. His only regret is that he cannot send Valerius Verrens to Taranis at your side. Tomorrow as the sun breaks above you will watch your son die and he will personally light the fire that will consume you. He looks forward to tearing your

383

unborn from your womb and consigning it to the flames before your eyes.'

Tabitha felt a wave of nausea and her world seemed to spin, but somehow she kept upright. 'Whether we live or die, Gaius Valerius Verrens will be your bane, Gwlym, arch-druid of Elfydd, this I swear in the name of Elah Gebal.'

She spun and marched back to the hut. As Ceris took station by her side she whispered, 'You were right. We can't wait for Valerius. We must act now.'

'But how? The guards are all young, but they're strong and fully armed.'

'Strength is not everything.'

XLVII

Two slaves worked to clear the dirt floor of the tent of the last remaining signs of Cearan's ordeal while Hilario strapped Valerius into a simple auxiliary's leather jerkin and mail vest.

'You should have left him to me, lord.'

'You think a patrician shouldn't get his hands dirty?' Valerius tested the fit of his wrist stock until he was happy. It had taken the best part of the hour to prise the information he needed from Cearan. Whether it was accurate was another thing. The Iceni had breathed his last with a final curse for Valerius. How did he feel? He felt nothing. Later, perhaps, it would be different. The old Cearan had been a friend: a man to admire and respect. A man who could be forgiven, even, for the loss of a hand. But he had become corrupted by his disfigurement at the hands of the Romans and driven beyond sanity by the loss of his wife. The old Cearan no longer existed for Valerius. The man who had twisted and howled under his knife had placed Tabitha and Lucius in the hands of a monster. His conduct rendered him unfit for mercy or compassion. He was an instrument to a necessary end. All that mattered was that Valerius discover the precise whereabouts of Tabitha and Lucius. He felt certain Cearan had told the truth about their fate. The only question was the timing.

'It is not fitting,' Hilario complained. 'Such butchery is journeyman's work.'

'The squadron is ready?' Valerius dismissed the subject.

'Yes, lord. Crescens and Nilus just rode in with the little scout.'

'Good.' Valerius breathed a sigh of relief that the scout had been found. Without Gaius Rufus he would be like a blind man groping his way along a cliff path.

Felix appeared in the doorway and blinked at the latrine stench that filled the tent. 'The camp prefect to see you, sir.' He swallowed.

'Send him in,' Valerius said. 'And check that my instructions have been followed.'

'Of course, legate.' Felix gave him a look of puzzlement.

'I know you've done it already, Cornelius, just humour me.' Naso walked into the tent and Valerius waved him to a couch. 'I'm sorry to have disturbed your rest, Quintus, but I've little time and much to do. The Ordovices have taken Tabitha and Lucius and are holding them on the island. You will take command of the Ninth's preparations for the assault on Mona and lead the attack.'

'You're abandoning your legion?' Naso almost choked on the words. 'Agricola will have your head, Valerius. I can't—'

'You're the most experienced soldier in the Ninth Hispana, Quintus,' Valerius persisted relentlessly. 'You saved this unit when I got it trapped on the ridge and you kept the Ordovices off balance during the chase. But for your efforts Agricola might face another five or ten thousand defenders. I have no choice in the matter.' He pushed himself to his feet. 'If you don't think you're up to it you'll just have to choose someone else.' His voice softened. 'They're going to kill them, Quintus. Do you expect me to leave them to the Ordovices?'

'No, sir.'

'Then this is how it will be.' Valerius outlined Agricola's plan of campaign. The Ninth launching a probing attack in the south, the cavalry demonstration in the centre and the Twentieth's preparations concealed until the last minute at the northern narrows. 'You see his plan?'

'Yes.' Naso sounded dubious. 'He's using us as bait again. The Ninth puts its head in the lion's jaws and gets chewed on until the Twentieth sneaks up and kicks the beast on the arse. Not so bad for the Twentieth, but . . .'

'By the time you cross we should have created a diversion that will pull them away from the coast.' Naso produced a wry smile and Valerius shrugged. They both knew that even if the escort reached Mona unobserved their chances of surviving the night and rescuing Tabitha on an island swarming with Celtic warriors were minimal. In his heart Valerius had no greater hope than to reach his wife and son and give them a painless release from the world before dying at their side.

'The Ninth will do their duty, sir.'

'I never doubted it, Quintus.' Valerius slapped him on the shoulder with his left hand. 'My only regret is that I won't be there to lead them.'

Naso accompanied Valerius to where the escort waited, formed up in the torchlight on the parade square in front of the command tent. Two lines of indistinct figures hunched in the saddle with their cloaks wrapped tight against the raw chill and provisions hanging in bags from their saddle horns. The horses shuffled restlessly, steam snorting in clouds from their nostrils and drifting from their heaving flanks. Didius Gallus stood expectantly in front of them holding Valerius's mount, but the one-handed Roman ignored him for a moment, instead choosing to walk along the lines inspecting men and horses.

He stopped in front of Shabolz and patted his horse's neck. 'I cannot order you to accompany me on this mission.' He spoke loudly enough for every man to hear. 'What I am about to do is personal and unauthorized. Some of you will already know. Others will have heard rumours. The lady Tabitha and my son Lucius have been abducted by the Ordovices, along with our comrade Ceris, and are being held prisoner on Mona.' An angry murmur went up from the waiting men. 'I have information about their location and how they are guarded, but I don't know how we will get there. The Celts on the island know

387

Rome is coming, but not when. The likelihood is that any man who accompanies me will be dead by morning.' He let them think about that, but he saw a shadow of a smile cross Shabolz's lips. 'When you came to me you were more eager to fight each other than any enemy, but our service together has changed that. A bond has grown between you and between us that can never be broken. I trusted you with my life and I never had reason to regret that trust. Any man who decides to stay behind has nothing to be ashamed of. Whatever happens, you depart here with honour and my respect, but decide quickly because we don't have much time.'

'Then why are we farting about here?' Hilario was the end file and he turned his horse towards the gate. The others followed him in an unbroken double line.

Valerius felt his breath catch in his throat as Didius Gallus helped him into the saddle.

'May Fortuna favour you in the morning, prefect,' he called to Naso.

'One way or the other we will meet on the other side, legate.'

'Gaius Rufus.' Valerius shouted to disguise the break in his voice. 'I know you're hiding out there somewhere. Come here and make yourself useful.' A rider slid out of the shadows beyond the torchlight. 'I need you to get us on to the island tonight.'

'Yes, lord?' They rode towards the gate while Rufus considered the implications of Valerius's request.

'And it would be preferable if we stayed alive until an hour before dawn.'

'That might be more difficult, lord.'

'But not impossible, Gaius. Not impossible.'

'Who but the gods can decide that, lord?'

'But you and I are the last survivors of the Temple of Claudius and I say the gods are on our side.'

They reached the gate, where Felix and the escort were formed up waiting for them. Rufus nodded to himself. 'Then we should turn south.'

'South?' Valerius frowned as his men moved into position behind them. 'Surely the straits widen to the south.'

'They do, lord, but in certain places and at certain times the Shifting Sands reach out from east and west. They never meet, and the channel between is deep and treacherous, but . . .'

'I take it they call them Shifting Sands for a reason?'

'Indeed. A man never knows where they will be from one night to the next.'

'And no doubt the far shore will be watched?'

'Of course,' Valerius heard the hint of a smile in the little man's voice, 'but only during the day. Only a fool or a man bent on suicide would attempt the Shifting Sands in the dark just when the tide is about to turn. Or a man certain he had the gods on his side.'

'They are holding my wife and son in a place called Bryn Gafr, the Hill of Goats.'

'Then if we live you are fortunate among men, lord, because Bryn Gafr is only a little way to the north-west. If Neptune does not claim us a blind man could find his way from the Bachyn Pysgod on the far side to Bryn Gafr.'

'I am pleased to hear it,' Valerius said. 'Because as I understand it we will have to reach it in the dark.'

They rode south through the night, crossing the river at a ford east of where they'd tested the assault boats. Valerius felt a sharp pang of guilt at the responsibility he'd placed on Naso's shoulders, but quickly thrust it aside. There was no turning back now. The route Rufus chose took them in a wide arc away from the strait so there was no chance of a sharp eye on the far shore picking up even the slightest glint of metal in the hazy light of the crescent moon. Behind him, his escort rode in silence, with Felix and Shabolz in the lead. He ran them through his mind, testing their strengths and weaknesses. None of these men had to be here. For a moment pride took the edge off the dull ache of despair that filled his chest like cold stone. He had worked out a plan of sorts, based on the information he'd squeezed in blood from

389

Cearan, and he conjured up individual faces that would fit particular roles. The problem was they were so few. He sent up a brief prayer to Jupiter Optimus Maximus that she was still in the place Cearan had identified at the cost of so much pain. Would they move her closer to the place they intended to kill her? What would she be thinking now, trapped in the darkness like a caged falcon? Her first duty would be towards Lucius and he imagined her reassuring the boy to try to alleviate his fear. How much had they told her? The very thought of it had driven him to slaughter Cearan like a tethered beast. What would it do to her knowing what awaited her in the first light of dawn?

An involuntary groan escaped him and Gaius Rufus reached out to lay a hand on his arm in a motion that was almost fatherly. They were the last survivors of the Temple of Claudius. The gods would not forsake them. The little man picked up the pace and Valerius and the others automatically matched it.

'How long?' Valerius asked quietly.

'Less than an hour,' Rufus replied. 'We will have only one opportunity. If I miss my way on the Shifting Sands, the tide will catch us, and . . .'

'You will not miss your way,' Valerius assured him.

Because if Gaius Rufus missed his way they would all die and Tabitha and Lucius would be led to the place of sacrifice in the morning to suffer all the druids' malignant cruelty.

XLVIII

'Shall I have the prisoners brought forward into their positions?'

'The men you may have, but not the women.' Gwlym's reply held a note of rebuke that irritated Cadwal. 'If we stake them out now they will be half dead of cold by morning and I want them fully alive to experience their passing. Their screams will be a knife in Roman hearts and a torment to drive Agricola's legionaries beyond sense and on to our spears.'

'It will take time,' Cadwal persisted.

'Silence,' Aymer, the taller of Gwlym's acolytes, hissed. 'The archdruid has spoken. Your only answer is to obey.'

'Make sure everything is ready.' Gwlym adopted a more conciliatory tone. Cadwal had done well at Viroconium and the druid sensed potential there. The Ordovices needed a new king and it might suit Gwlym to have someone of less intellect than Owain Lawhir wearing the crown, someone more amenable to suggestion.

The druids stood on a promontory that looked out over the strait to the mainland and the camp where the men of Ninth Hispana worked frantically to complete their preparations. Of course, Gwlym's sightless eyes couldn't see the light from the armourers' forges and the torches of the quartermasters as they rushed about dealing with last minute crises. Yet they were clear in his head, as were the dispositions of all Agricola's forces. Thanks to his spies he knew the Ninth's undisguised preparations heralded a probing feint intended to draw some of his men to the south and keep them there. He knew five thousand dismounted cavalrymen waited in the darkness ready to appear on the beach further up the coast at first light in a demonstration designed to make him keep a substantial force here. That was why he'd positioned the bulk of his warriors in the north, just behind the only beach wide enough for a Roman landing.

Gwlym didn't need to see. He sensed everything in the world around him. A soft breeze stirring the skeletal twigs of a tree already stripped naked by winter. The almost imperceptible hiss as frost settled on the close-cropped grass at his feet. Warmth from a nearby fire and the unlikely waft from the wings of a bat drawn from its long sleep by the heat and the light. The pulsating nervousness of the Roman troops on the far side of the strait stirred his senses like a panicked heartbeat. The keening war songs of his warriors as they waited in the darkness finding solace and courage in millennia-gone victories. His own mind was at peace. He had foreseen this moment ever since they'd carried him from the field of Boudicca's last battle. Suetonius Paulinus had left unfinished business when Boudicca drew him away from his frenzy of slaughter and sacrilege. It was only a matter of time before the red scourge returned.

Gwlym understood the risks, but he'd fought this battle a hundred times in his head, refining his plan to meet every possible crisis. It was a pity Owain had failed to take advantage of his opportunity to annihilate the Ninth, but it made no difference to the overall concept. The Ordovices defending Mona were fighting not only for their lives and their religion, but for their families. Gwlym had insisted every warrior be accompanied by his wife and children and now they waited in a great camp in the centre of the island. Gwlym had never had a wife or a family, but he knew men fought all the better when they were at risk. He also had his secret weapon. Every expert bowman and slinger in the west had congregated on Mona weeks before and had spent their time fletching arrows and moulding lead slingshots by the thousands and the tens of thousands. Gwlym would pin the Romans on the narrow strip of sand and shingle between sea and forest and that sand would run slick with Roman blood. He imagined the hail of arrows and slingshots flaying the packed Roman ranks as they stood trapped on the beach. The first waves would be annihilated as their comrades floundered in the shallows. Then the might of the Ordovice's would swarm over the twitching corpses to drive the survivors back to the depths where the riptide would wipe Mona clean of Roman filth. It came to him that if Cearan had succeeded, Agricola might already be dead and the Romans in turmoil and headless. Yet that was a small thing in this great scheme involving the coordinated movement of tens of thousands. Better, perhaps, if his soldiers watched the Roman commander burn in the inferno of Hades that awaited them.

They crossed a narrow stream. Valerius heard Gaius Rufus murmur 'Carrog', perhaps reminding himself of a landmark. The men rode in silence, apart from the muffled breathing of the horses and the soft chink of horse brass. Not even the bark of a fox or the shriek of an owl to disturb the almost unnatural quiet. His nose told him they were close to the sea again, the bitter scent of rotting seaweed and salt hanging in the still air. Directly after the crossing they turned west into a flat landscape that alternated between salt marsh and sand dune. A feeling of emptiness within and without, each man alone and vulnerable even though he knew another rode at his side and at his back. Valerius's hand instinctively sought the security of his sword hilt. He stilled it with difficulty. 'Child,' he chided himself, 'to be frightened of the dark with the enemy a long, hard swim away.'

The slap of wet sand beneath the horses' hooves, then the splash of water, so not low tide, no, not by a long way. Rufus drew his mount to a halt and Valerius angled in behind him. He fumbled in his saddle bag and pulled out a white cloth and a long pin with which he attached it to the scout's cloak. He felt Felix performing the same operation on his own cloak.

'Not a foot from this beast's arse,' Rufus whispered. 'Not if you value your life.' Valerius passed the message to Felix and heard it fade down the line. The cloth was just a dull patch of contrast in the blackness, but enough to ensure no one would become detached if they kept their senses about them. They would ride single file because the Shifting Sands were fickle ribbons of more or less solid ground with hidden depths to either side. One step off the path and man and horse would be left floundering in the darkness, eventually to be dragged to the depths by the weight of their equipment when the horse tired. Valerius had considered ordering his men to dump everything but their swords, but the likelihood – the certainty – of combat and the weight of opposition they would face on the far shore persuaded him the risk was worth taking. He concentrated on the dull patch that identified Rufus and cursed as the little scout wound first one way, then the other, making it near impossible to stay within a horse-length, never mind a foot. His eyes struggled for focus in the darkness and his mouth felt as if it were filled with ashes. He blinked. And froze. Nothing. Rufus was gone. He waited, surrounded by emptiness, panic welling up inside. He heard Felix curse.

'This way, idiot.' A harsh whisper from his right and his bowels turned liquid with relief. 'But stay to the left of the path.'

Path? All Valerius could see beneath his horse was an expanse of glittering black. He followed the sound of the voice and a few strides brought him to the shadowy outline of horse and rider.

'Thank you,' he whispered.

'Don't thank me yet,' Rufus hissed. 'It's taken longer than I bargained for.' The little man studied the moon. 'Maybe too long.'

'We go on,' Valerius insisted.

'I know.' Rufus sounded interminably weary. 'This time stay close.'

They continued for what seemed like an age, but was probably less time than it took to saddle a horse, until Rufus said quietly, 'Stop where you are. This is where we swim.'

Valerius passed the order back down the line. He tried to remember who was at the rear of the column. Yes, Didius Gallus had volunteered along with Crescens. If Rufus was right . . .

'We go in twos,' Valerius whispered.

'It will waste time.'

'That wasn't a suggestion. It was an order.'

'All right.' Valerius could hear the urgency in Rufus's voice. 'When you're in the water turn north-west. Follow the line of the moon. Swim as if Taranis is on your tail.'

By the time Valerius had passed this second order back, Rufus had him by the reins and was hauling him forward. 'Column of twos,' he repeated to Felix.

Within two paces the sand disappeared beneath them and his horse was swimming. The weight took the beast down to the shoulders and she gave a soft panicked whinny. Valerius gasped as the freezing water closed over his thighs. For a moment he thought his mount would founder, but her head came up and he could feel her legs pumping. He directed the animal along the thin sliver of light from the moon, cutting a wake through the still water. He felt a moment of doubt. Surely a direct crossing would have been quicker? No point questioning Rufus. The little man had led them here without incident and he knew his business. The scout, lighter and less heavily equipped, forged ahead. Valerius imagined he could hear a rushing sound and he glanced south. All he could see was darkness, but somewhere out there the tide was undoubtedly building. On and on and still no sign of land. The horse began to struggle, gasping for breath and snorting from her nostrils. He could feel her heart pounding against her ribs. Behind him he knew the others would be experiencing the same sense of frustration and growing despair. Should he call out to them to abandon their mail if they could? Would it make any difference? A sudden tension in his ears. A shout from ahead, Gaius Rufus urging him forward. He clapped his heels into the horse's ribs. Yes, it was out there, a continuous rumble, growing like approaching thunder. He could feel the sweat running down his back, but his only thought was for Tabitha. If he died she died. A lurch and the horse almost threw him from the saddle. Another and she regained her feet. Land, or at least another sand spit. He pushed her on another few paces until he found Rufus. The scout stared into the darkness beyond him.

'Names,' Valerius hissed as a horse passed in the darkness.

'Felix.'

'Shabolz.'

'Hilario.'

'Nilus.'

He counted them off two by two, trying to put the growing rush of water out of his mind.

'Lord, we should go to higher ground,' Rufus urged.

'Not yet.'

'Metellus.'

'Aper.'

Bato, Sido, and two more Pannonians.

'Paulus.'

'Aurelius.'

His mount shifted beneath him as another four files of two men forced their horses out of the water in a flurry of spray. Valerius looked down. Seconds ago the glittering surface had just covered hooves; now it had reached the animals' fetlocks. Somewhere to the south the rush was building up to a roar. Two more files to go.

Two more riders emerged from the darkness. A whispered gasp, barely audible now. 'Candidus. Maternus.'

'Lord!'

'Go, all of you.'

'Mars' sacred arse.' The shout came from the darkness to his left.

'Get them out.' Valerius rode towards the origin of the cry. The surface of the sand spit curved west then south, creating a giant fish hook. Gallus and Crescens must have mistaken their angle and made the longer crossing. Crescens was floundering in the shallows beside his horse and Gallus had stayed with him.

'Ride.' Valerius grabbed Crescens's reins. Gallus hesitated for only a heartbeat before obeying the order. To the south the roar grew in volume and power and a glowing white line filled the entire horizon. The sight paralysed Crescens. 'The tail,' Valerius shouted. Cavalry troopers were proud of the long flowing tails on their horses, which they decorated with ribbons and bells for parades. Valerius was already kicking his horse into motion and dragging Crescens's mount with him. Crescens just had the presence of mind to snatch at the thick horse-hair, and he was almost jerked off his feet as the big animal hauled him bodily across the surface of the sand. Valerius didn't dare look as he leaned across his mount's neck and urged it into a gallop. Behind him Crescens was forced to take impossibly long strides, bounding like a frightened deer and trying to avoid flying hooves, whimpering in terror as the water grew deeper beneath his feet and the tidal surge sped closer, the thunder of its coming filling his ears. Valerius cursed as his horse began to struggle, then felt a jolt of exhilaration. It wasn't exhaustion that slowed the animal but the slope of the beach. Another dozen strides took them clear just as the great wave swept the sands behind them, consuming everything in its path. Crescens collapsed in the sandy grass above the tideline, clutching at the stems as if he thought he'd never feel them again. Valerius's horse stood on shaking legs and he squeezed at the reins until his left hand hurt.

Shadowy figures surrounded them. If they'd been enemy warriors the two men would have been slaughtered in a moment, but it was Rufus and the men of the escort. Hilario and another rider carried shapeless bundles across their mounts' withers. As Valerius watched they pitched the loads to the ground with a pair of audible thuds.

A hand reached up to take his reins and Didius Gallus helped him from the saddle. 'I'm sorry, lord. We lost touch with the men in front. If we'd been another . . .'

'All that matters is that you're here, Didius.' Valerius clapped him on the shoulder before he inspected the two still bundles.

'Lookouts,' Rufus said. 'Fools were sleeping beside a fire behind one of the dunes.' He turned one of the bodies over and in the gloom Valerius could just make out a pair of startled eyes and the dark slit beneath the chin. He couldn't have been more than twelve years old.

'Shabolz? Hilario? Crescens?' Valerius called softly. The three men came forward and knelt close enough for him to make out their individual shapes.

'You have your flints and iron and your tinder is dry?'

'Yes, lord,' Shabolz and Hilario said in unison. The men had carried their fire making equipment in leather bags tied beneath their chins.

Crescens's hand went to his throat where his leather bag dripped water. 'I can borrow dry tinder from Didius, lord,' he assured Valerius.

'You know what to look for?'

'Yes, lord.'

'They'll be directly opposite the Ninth and Twentieth and there may be a third in the centre. If you can't find it follow your nose. Choose a man each as back-up and make sure he's carrying spare tinder and iron.' He looked up at the moon. 'Give us an hour and half as much again.' He knew the timings would be vague, but there was nothing he could do about that. 'If we're not in position by then we never will be. We will regroup at the stone circle east of the Hill of Goats.'

They moved off, Shabolz calling softly for Bato, his fellow Pannonian. Hilario chose his tentmate Candidus, and Crescens paired up with Nilus. They would face a perilous mission to locate their targets in the dark in the midst of a host of enemies, but Valerius had faith in these men. If even one succeeded it would give him the chance he needed.

'Mount up,' he called. When they were all in the saddle he turned to the diminutive shadow that was Rufus. 'Take me to the Hill of Goats.'

XLIX

'The stockade is three hundred paces to the west, beyond that wood,' Rufus whispered. A smudge against the lighter darkness of the horizon seemed to indicate where Rufus meant. The twelve remaining riders sat their horses at the centre of a circle of eight great stones twice the height of a man. Rufus assured him no Ordovice would approach these ancient places because either the men believed them haunted or they were the province of the druids, who sometimes carried out their rituals amid the stones. Valerius sniffed. He fervently hoped it was the former, but the air had a taint that made him wonder.

So close. They were so close.

Since they'd left the sea he'd been assailed by a curious mixture of exhilaration and a feral savagery he'd never experienced before. Rufus guided them unerringly between the warrior camps that dotted Mona's coastal hills and valleys, marked by the unconcealed fires that were clear evidence of confidence in victory. They'd walked the horses much of the way, to rest them, but also to avoid the distinctive silhouette of Roman cavalry which would alert every sentry on the island. Valerius was conscious that each step they took and each moment they remained undiscovered brought him closer to Tabitha and Lucius. So close that he could almost taste their scent. They would not stop him now.

'We'll leave the horses here with one man to guard them,' Valerius told Felix. 'Rufus leads. When we reach the wood we'll split into two groups. You take Metellus, Paulus, Maternus and Aper and cover the north side of the compound. I'll take Gallus, Aurelius, and the Pannonians and cover the south. There should be a guard of ten men at most, all outside the walls. Once we get the signal from Shabolz and the others we'll take them.'

Rufus looked up to check the position of the moon. 'We should start now.'

A mile away, so close to the shore he could hear the waves hissing through the pebbles on the beach, Shabolz crouched in a dense clump of bushes and waited. The distinctive tang Valerius had spoken of was thick in his nostrils. He'd already visited his target to check and his fingers were still sticky from the residue of what he'd confirmed. Reaching his position had been one of the most difficult tasks he'd ever attempted. The Celts were thick as fleas on a dog's bedding this close to the shore. He'd been forced to squirm on his stomach only a few paces from them, his gut tight with the knowledge that a single sound would condemn him to a lingering and painful death. On the way he heard strange mutters and groans that puzzled him, but he couldn't allow himself to be distracted. The key to the island's defences had been the last thing Valerius had wrung from the Celt with the shattered face, but his suspicions had been alerted on the ride to see Agricola two days earlier. A great trench deep enough to swallow the tallest man and filled with layer upon layer of pitch soaked wood and hay. It was designed to be fired as the first Roman set foot on the beach, trapping the invaders where they could be slaughtered at leisure.

Shabolz smiled. A truly fiendish weapon. He hadn't thought the Celts were capable of such sophistication. Perhaps he'd underestimated them. Never again. If things had gone to plan Bato would be in a similar position at the far end of the beach opposite where Agricola's dismounted cavalry would make their demonstration in less than two hours' time. Only one of them needed to get it right. They'd left Crescens and Nilus where the Ninth would land. Hilario and Candidus had the furthest to travel, but they should have reached their position by the narrows now. In any case – he looked up at the moon – Valerius would be waiting. A shadow moved across his vision and he dropped down and froze. Not yet. He looked at the moon again. Did he have any choice? He slid through the undergrowth and slipped from cover to the edge of the trench.

It took seconds to retrieve flint and iron. He prayed his sweat hadn't made the tinder damp. He would have one chance. He placed the fluffy mass on the ground and took flint in his left hand and struck with the iron with his right. A glowing spark fell on to the tinder but didn't catch. He hissed and struck again. This time a glow appeared in the dried rush head and he blew gently on it. A tiny flame appeared and he took a deep breath and lowered the burning material cautiously into the trench, immediately slithering back into the bushes.

At first nothing happened, then he saw a soft orange glow above the trench and a billow of black smoke. Suddenly flames were leaping high and charging south, like a burning sword blade plunging into the heart of the enemy, consuming and feeding off what was below, uniting to climb to the height of a double-storey house. Shabolz saw a flicker at the far end of the beach followed a heartbeat later by a similar racing inferno. The roar of the flames dampened any noise and Celts were charging this way and that crying out in consternation and confusion. The Pannonian wrapped his cloak tight around his mail and simply walked away from the flames into the darkness.

Ceris crept close to Tabitha. 'I have a gift,' she whispered. The Corieltauvi girl had been gone for so long Tabitha wondered if she'd somehow found a way to escape. Now she understood why. Her fingers explored the slim contours of a small knife. Rough wooden hilt and a short but lethally sharp blade that tapered to a point.

'Where . . . ?'

'I heard a rumour that the Trinovante woman had one, but was too frightened to use it. I persuaded her our need was greater than hers. It's not much, but at least it gives us a choice.'

She was close enough for Tabitha to see the gleam of her eyes in the darkness of the hut. Valerius's wife reached out and ran her free hand through Lucius's hair, allowing her fingers to drift down to his neck and the life force pulsing just below the soft skin. A choice. A choice between a swift, clean death and the abomination the druid planned for them. Given the opportunity she doubted any woman in the compound would choose otherwise.

But it was also a surrender, and Tabitha was not prepared to admit defeat just yet. She released her son and ran her thumb along the edge of the blade. A good edge, and, she sensed, a good solid knife, made of decent iron. She sat with her back against the wall of the hut. It was constructed of hazel sticks woven around stout wooden posts and coated with mud on the outside to keep out draughts. Perhaps . . . 'Help me, Ceris,' she whispered.

Ceris didn't fully understand what was happening, but she heard Tabitha grunt and the sound of wood creaking. She moved in beside her mistress and realized the Emesan was hauling at one of the hazel branches. Ceris grasped the same branch and after a few minutes they managed to work it out of position and pull it clear. Still she was unsure of what was happening, but Tabitha ran her hands along the length of the branch until she found an end. 'Five feet,' she murmured, and began to work at the wood with her knife.

By now a restless murmur had rippled through the occupants of the hut. Not one of them had slept, their minds tormented by the thought of the agonies that awaited them. They knew something was happening, but not what, and the lack of knowledge provoked fear and alarm. Tabitha ignored them and sliced at the hazel until she was happy with the result. 'Here.' She handed the stick to Ceris and the Celtic girl felt a surge of hope as she tested the point. What she held in her hands was not just a slightly warped piece of ancient hazel. It was a weapon.

'If we work together we can arm every woman in the compound.'

402

Urgency gave Tabitha's voice a brittle edge. Ceris passed the hazel spear around the women.

'What good is a piece of wood against seasoned warriors?' one demanded. Tabitha ignored her, because for every dissenting voice there were ten growls of determination.

'Organize yourselves into pairs and tear two sticks from the walls. Bring them to me to be sharpened. Work as quietly as you can. Ceris, can you pass word to the other huts?'

'Yes, lady.' The guards never came into the compound at night. Gwlym had ordered that the prisoners should remain unviolated, on pain of death. She lowered her voice. 'But she has a point. Women with sticks against warriors armed with swords and spears?'

'You told me yourself that the original guards have been replaced with old men and boys.' Tabitha spoke so every woman in the hut could hear her. 'We are fifty. They are ten or twelve. They will come to bind us before they take us. That must not be allowed to happen. We will be ready for them and they won't expect us to fight. Thrust for the throat, the stomach or the soft parts.' Her words aroused a murmur of savage approval. 'If we cannot escape at least we can make them kill us.'

Ceris disappeared from the hut and a steady stream of women approached to have their hazel branches sharpened. Some were too long and Tabitha insisted they be snapped in half – a difficult process with such a supple wood – or better still replaced. She was working on one of the final lengths of hazel when she heard a hiss from the doorway.

'Mistress, you should see this.'

She joined Ceris outside in the darkness. At least what should have been darkness. The entire eastern horizon was filled with an eerie blood-red glow that pulsated and flickered as they watched.

'Some druid's sorcery?' Tabitha couldn't keep the anxiety from her voice.

'Or perhaps Agricola is coming? They would not expect a night attack.' Ceris sounded torn between hope and consternation. 'Whatever the reason it will draw the attention of the guards.'

'But not enough of them.' Tabitha pointed to the silhouettes of two men on the wooden platform the Celts had built by the gate. She turned away. 'Whatever it is all we can do is prepare, and wait.'

L

Gwlym felt the blood drain from his face and he put a hand out to steady himself as his acolyte Bedwr described the scene unfolding opposite the Roman cavalry feint. First, a seemingly innocuous pinprick of light had raced south with the speed of a charging horse to become a mile-long inferno as the centre trench, the product of months of work, ignited prematurely. Individually, it meant little – the centre trench lay opposite the dismounted cavalry and its purpose had been to announce to Agricola that his diversion had worked – but the improbability of the event sent a shiver through Gwlym. His suspicions were instantly confirmed when he heard Bedwr gasp.

'What is it?' he demanded.

'The north and south trenches, arch-druid.' Bedwr's voice shook with emotion. In his mind Gwlym pictured the ribbon of fire to his front, and the second far away to his left. The foundations of his defensive strategy knocked away at a single stroke. His orders had been to delay firing the two outer trenches until the first Roman soldier stepped on to the beach. He tried to still his whirling emotions. Had it happened by accident or design?

'Find out who is responsible,' he ordered. 'When they have confessed all they know cast them into the flames. The prisoners from Canovium are in position?'

'Yes, lord, the men only await your word.'

'Then make it so. The flames will burn all the higher for consuming their flesh.' For a moment he considered the implications of what he had just ordered. 'And have the women brought to their places of sacrifice.'

Gaius Quintus Naso had been staring at the black shadow marking the far shore of the strait for what seemed like hours when he saw the extraordinary spear point of light in the far distance, quickly followed by another that seemed so close he should feel the heat of it. It came as less of a surprise than it might, because Valerius had plotted the positions of the fire trenches from the detail he had tortured from the mutilated Celt. He and Naso had agreed the Ninth Hispana should attack half a mile south to sidestep the obstruction, even though the strait widened at that point. They'd also agreed Agricola should be informed that Naso had assumed command of the Ninth in Valerius's absence. Naso had thought long and hard before sending the message – along with the position of the fire trench opposite the Twentieth – because it felt like a betrayal.

The cohorts of the Ninth waited just behind the shoreline where they'd sat in their formations for most of the night. Naso had walked among them while they'd broken fast and drunk from their water skins and they'd called out to him asking when they'd have the chance to get at the enemy. He'd smiled and assured them it would be soon enough and left well pleased with their morale and enthusiasm. A different legion entirely from the whipped ragtag of individuals Fronto had created. And all due to the leadership of Gaius Valerius Verrens, who'd given them an eagle to follow and personally led them into the jaws of the lion. Now Valerius had placed his faith in Quintus Naso and given him command of the most difficult mission the legion had faced since the crossing of the Tamesa in Claudius's day. Oddly, Naso felt neither fear nor the weight of his responsibility. The plan was in place. Ulpius Canalius, the legion's *primus pilus*, would lead the first wave, six centuries of the Second cohort who sat by their boats furthest forward.

He would set up a defensive perimeter while the boats returned for the second wave. Naso would go with the third, along with Claudius Honoratus and the eagle.

Was there anything else he could do? He studied the flickering barrier to his right and the certainty flared inside him. Yes! Yes there was. 'Go forward and tell the *primus pilus* to have his men loaded into the boats and the Batavian crews ready to embark.' His voice quivered with elation. He'd intended to wait until dawn, but the tide was right and the enormous fire provided just enough light to allow the boat crews to make out the beach. 'He may go when he is ready.'

Naso strapped his helmet a little tighter and went to warn the second wave to get ready. He felt perfectly calm. The die was thrown. The fire to the north seemed to gain new strength, sending up great flares all along the line. He wondered what had caused it, then his mind turned to Valerius, presumably somewhere in the darkness beyond. Where was he? Had he been discovered? He remembered Tabitha's smile and the fact that she and young Lucius were in the hands of merciless barbarians. 'Poor bastard,' he whispered.

An awed legionary sentry called Julius Agricola from his tent with a garbled tale about the darkness on the far shore suddenly erupting into an unbroken barrier of flame. The governor was tempted to send an aide, certain the man must be exaggerating. Nothing could be as devastating as he described. Still, he set aside his fury at the dispatch from Naso. Gaius Valerius Verrens would be dealt with later, if he even lived.

The camp lay more than a mile from the strait, in keeping with Agricola's strategy of ensuring the Twentieth legion's preparations lay far beyond prying Celtic eyes. Yet from the moment he left his tent and saw the colour of the western sky the Roman commander was assailed by a superstitious dread. The further he rode west through the waiting ranks of legionary and auxiliary cohorts the brighter the sky and the deeper his concern. What force of nature could have created something like this? It was only when he reached the crest of the little rise overlooking the strait that he understood. Naso's message had contained a warning of some sort of fire pit, but Agricola had been so consumed by anger at Valerius's betrayal he'd taken little notice of it.

He urged his mount down the slope to the shingle beach and studied the long line of fire on the far shore. The light seemed to reach out to them across the glistening surface of the strait. They were close enough to hear the crackle of the burning wood and the roar of the flames that lit up the surrounding beach for a hundred paces. 'Lord,' the commander of his personal bodyguard cautioned. 'We are within *ballista* range of the enemy.'

'Then it's fortunate the Celts don't have any.' That might not be true. There could well have been artillery among the weapons in the armoury at Canovium, but it was difficult enough for an experienced *ballista* crew to hit their chosen target. He doubted the Celts were capable. In any case he would not show fear. His own catapults were positioned among the boats hidden behind the hill. They could be dragged to the crest within moments to cover the crossing. But when would the crossing take place? The positioning of the fire trench proved that his carefully planned strategy of deception had failed. Yet he couldn't simply move the crossing north or south, because the beach opposite was the only suitable landing place for a mile either side. But why had they fired the trench now? Was it some kind of trick to make him hesitate or change his plan? A precursor to some even more devastating ploy?

'What's that?'

Agricola followed the pointing finger. On the far side of the fire pit it was just possible to make out a pair of figures hustling a third man into the firelight. Soon they were joined by a second trio and a third, until finally twenty or more little groups were strung out along a line of about a hundred and fifty paces.

'Jupiter save us,' he heard an aide whisper. 'They're wearing auxiliary tunics.'

'I've had no reports of missing auxiliaries.' His aides stared at him, unaccustomed to hearing panic in the governor's voice. 'Could they be from the Ninth?'

'No, we've had their casualty reports. Dead and injured, but no missing.'

'Then what?'

'We haven't lost any auxiliaries since Canovium.'

A silence descended on the little group as they finally began to understand the implications of what was happening. A cry of stark terror reached them from the far shore and they watched as one of the captive men was dragged struggling towards the flaming pit.

'No,' Agricola heard someone whisper, unaware the word came from his own lips.

The Ordovices hurled their prisoner into the flames.

'There were three hundred unaccounted for at Canovium.'

A moment of disbelieving silence interrupted by an unearthly, inhuman shriek that seemed to go on for ever, rising and falling in volume and pitch as the flames fed voraciously on flesh and bone and sinew and fat, taking new strength from the human fuel. A second figure was dragged forward, struggling for his life.

Agricola forced himself to watch ten men burn to death before he turned away. 'My compliments to Legate Ursus. The crossing will begin as soon as he can get his men in position.'

'But sir, the Ninth . . .'

'I will not stand idly by and watch those animals burn three hundred of my men.' The aides flinched at the savagery in Agricola's voice. He reflected for a moment, struggling to control his emotions. 'When we take Mona there will be no prisoners. I will hunt down every man, woman and child on that island if it takes until next winter. Men will talk of the Druids' Isle as a desert populated by nothing but bleached bones.'

LI

Two guards shared a raised platform by the compound gate. Valerius could just make them out in the dim light of a fire where two others huddled outside a thatched hut. He guessed the rest must be asleep inside. The attentions of the men on the platform were concentrated inside the wooden palisade. Clearly they were more concerned about escape than rescue. The two by the fire were stout greybeards, but the silhouettes on the platform had the spareness of youth.

Valerius crouched among the trees thirty or forty paces from the gate and a little way to the south. Didius Gallus, Aurelius and the Pannonians formed a rough line along the edge of the wood. A well-trodden path ran past the northern wall of the stockade and cut through the wood, providing ready access to the coast about a mile away. Felix and his men were stationed on the far side of the path in a similar formation.

Valerius's hand went to his sword as he became aware of a presence at his side.

'Nervous tonight, lord?' Rufus whispered.

Valerius relaxed. He'd sent the little scout to check for any sign of Ordovice warriors nearby. Their camps were scattered over the island and their presence or otherwise was something he had to take into account. 'Fifty rough shelters a little way north,' Rufus reported.

'But judging by their leavings they haven't been there for days.'

The men on the platform were the problem. They could rush the pair by the hut and kill them and those inside before they could react, but, for all their attention was on the stockade, the two men at the gate remained alert. All it would take was one shout and they'd have a pitched battle on their hands, which was the last thing Valerius wanted. Quick and quiet with no survivors to rush off and raise the country against them.

'We'll use the hut as a shield and come at them from the flank,' he said into Rufus's ear. 'Pass the word to Felix.' Before the little man could move they heard a shout from one of the men on the platform. When Valerius looked he was pointing east and the two men beside the fire were on their feet staring at the sky behind Valerius.

'What's happening?' Rufus whispered.

'I don't know, but tell the others to be ready.'

He glanced over his shoulder and saw that between the skeletal upper branches of the beech trees the sky had turned a flickering orange pink. The men outside the hut had been joined by six others. After a brief conversation they picked up spears from a stand by the doorway and moved in a bunch towards the path.

The glow provided just enough visibility to follow their progress. Valerius held his breath. Not yet. He reached out to touch Sido, on his right, on the shoulder. The Pannonian turned to him and Valerius showed two fingers of his left hand and pointed towards the platform. Sido grinned and repeated the signal to Runoz. Wait. The eight men were opposite him now. He could only pray that Felix hadn't gone to sleep. Wait. He gave them another five or six paces so he was in the blind spot to their rear and on their right flank. His sword was in his hand, though he'd no memory of drawing it, and he moved silently out of the trees with Gallus and Aurelius at his side. The first Ordovice felt a hammer blow on his neck and he was still wondering what had happened as he hit the ground, dead. Valerius flicked the blood from his *spatha* and bore down on his next victim. Aurelius had already killed his man, but the Ordovice's dying shriek alerted his companions. Gallus ran the first

411

through as he tried to turn, but the three still faced five spearmen. If they'd attacked immediately the Celts would have overwhelmed their enemy by sheer weight of numbers. They were veterans of war, old, grey and scarred, but they'd been taken by surprise; three of their number were already dead, and judging by the screams from the direction of the compound more were dying now. So they hesitated, advancing tentatively with spears outstretched, the leaf-shaped iron points seeking out a weakness in the armoured trio who confronted them. At last. With a savage roar, Felix and his men charged from the forest at their back. Valerius took advantage of his opponent's distraction to knock the spear aside and reverse his swing so the edge took the Ordovice across the side of the head, smashing bone and cartilage and leaving brain matter oozing from the wound. Aurelius and Didius Gallus doubled up on another man and he went down with his guts spilling in the dirt. A flurry of violence and two cries of agony as Felix, Aper, Paulus and Maternus combined to finish two others. The last spearman dropped his weapon and ran for the trees. Valerius cursed, but the Ordovice had only taken four steps before he went down like a pole-axed bull with one of the lethal Pannonian throwing darts in his spine.

Sido ran to recover his weapon. Runoz was gleefully cutting the throats of the two gate guards who'd fallen to another pair of darts. In the meantime, Rufus finished off the man whose skull Valerius had smashed.

Valerius was already on his way to the gate. Two men pulled back the oak bar and threw open the double doors and he marched inside. Four huts stood in a half-circle, but even in the dull orange gloom it was clear the rest of the compound was empty. He felt a momentary flare of panic that they were too late. But if the women were gone why would the stockade be guarded?

He opened his mouth, but before he could call Tabitha's name a flood of shadowy figures raced from the huts screaming hatred to surround the little group of men. Valerius found himself at the centre of a ring of crude wooden spears aimed at his throat.

A momentary hesitation before a female voice demanded: 'You're Romans?'

'Father!' A high pitched squeal answered her question as Lucius burst through the crowd of women. 'I knew you'd come.'

Valerius clasped his son to his body with so much force Lucius cried out. 'Father, you're hurting me.'

'I'm sorry, Lucius.' Valerius's vision was blurred and he struggled to speak. 'I was worried about you.'

Lucius grinned. 'Mother would never have allowed them to hurt me.'

Valerius looked up and the women parted to reveal Tabitha, still armed with one of the warped hazel spears, and Ceris at her side.

'This is a fine way to welcome your husband,' he choked.

'Did you think I would let them take me without a fight?'

'Never.'

'So what happens now?'

'Now we get you and your friends off this gods-forsaken island.'

While the women gathered what few possessions they'd been allowed for their comfort, Valerius sent Rufus back to the ring of stones to check if Shabolz and the others had returned. The druids' prisoners were at various stages of pregnancy and it took time to marshal them into a straggling column. When they were ready to set off Tabitha took her place at Valerius's side. 'You make it sound easy.'

'The first rule of leadership.' He smiled gravely as they entered the woods. 'Never show weakness. But in truth we're a long way from out of this yet.'

'They will send for us,' she pointed out. 'Perhaps they already have.'

'That's why we're avoiding the path.'

'And they'll search for us,' she persisted.

'Yes,' he agreed. 'And if they find us we will fight them.'

She turned to face him. 'Promise me you will not let them take us alive, Valerius.' He avoided her eyes, but she persisted. 'Promise me. I will not die for the entertainment of these savages.'

'Very well,' he said gruffly. 'You have my word. But it will not come to that.'

The unearthly light from the fires provided just enough visibility for them to make reasonable progress. Didius Gallus marched at the head of the column with Lucius. He'd given the boy his helmet and the metal helm wobbled on his head as he tried to keep step with the young cavalryman. They were so happy to be reunited neither noticed the shadow move in the bushes.

Cadwal's suspicions had been aroused by the premature lighting of the fire trenches and he'd raced to check that the Roman women had been prepared for sacrifice. He arrived as Valerius was emerging with the freed prisoners and was faced with the choice of staying with them or returning to the coast to raise the alarm. He'd chosen to stay. Now, as the young Roman and the boy became separated from the main body, he saw his chance.

Didius Gallus was grinning at something Lucius had said when the Ordovice champion rose silently from the undergrowth and thrust his spear into the cavalryman's body. Such was the enormous force behind the blow that the point penetrated the metal rings of his chain armour and the leather jerkin beneath to bury itself deep in his vitals. Before Valerius could react to the cavalryman's cry of mortal agony Cadwal dropped the spear and wrapped his massive left arm around Lucius's chest. A dagger appeared in his right hand and he held the razor edge against the boy's throat.

'Drop your swords.' Surprisingly, the order was given in a guttural but comprehensible Latin.

Valerius exchanged a glance with Tabitha and placed his blade on the ground. Her face was grey with fear, but her fists were clenched and he willed her not to rush the hulking warrior.

'If you harm the boy all you will achieve is your own death.' He filled his voice with reason and calm, praying the tone would persuade the Ordovice giant to stay his hand. The man only stared at him. A moment later Valerius saw the focus of his eyes shift and sensed motion at the periphery of his vision. 'No,' he whispered.

Tabitha walked steadily towards the bear-like figure holding her son.

'All you'll do is get both of you killed,' Valerius pleaded. But Tabitha's stride never faltered.

Cadwal smiled.

Valerius barely registered the blur of motion behind the big Celt. How Ceris had managed to come within range without being noticed he would never understand, but now she launched herself from the bushes like a wildcat on to Cadwal's back. Her left arm wrapped around the bull neck at the same time as her right fist pounded at the matted hair on the top of his head. It was an act of incredible courage, but Valerius raged inwardly at the ineffectual, futile assault that meant certain death for his son. It was only when he heard Cadwal's agonized howl and the Celt dropped Lucius to the ground that he understood there was more to the attack than he'd realized. A glint of metal confirmed the small knife in Ceris's fist as every frenetic blow added another bone-shattering puncture to the Ordovice champion's skull. Cadwal clawed desperately at the arm around his throat, but he was already dying, his face a mask of blood and the eyes turning up in his head. With a final despairing cry he toppled on to his face like a falling tree, almost crushing Lucius beneath his body. Tabitha ran to her son and wrapped him in her arms.

Didius Gallus lay on his side, his body shuddering with the agony of the great metal spear point embedded deep in his belly. By the time Valerius reached him his face already wore the familiar parchment-grey pallor of death. He clutched the dying boy's hand in his and Gallus gripped his fingers with a fierce strength. 'Tell my father . . .'

'Didius,' Tabitha whispered.

Valerius shook his head. 'He's gone.'

LII

Some of the women needed assistance over the rough ground between the woods and the ancient stone circle and it took longer than Valerius had bargained for to reach the meeting place. By the time they reached the stones, Rufus had been joined by Shabolz, Nilus and Crescens, but Valerius's heart sank as he saw other faces were missing. Shabolz saw Valerius's enquiring look. 'Bato was taken,' he said quietly. 'They threw him into the fire pit with some auxiliary prisoners. We've seen no sign of Hilario and Candidus.'

'We'll give them until the women are rested,' Valerius said. 'Share out what food and drink we have.'

'Perhaps it would be safer to find somewhere we can defend?' Felix offered. 'On the march we're tied to the speed of the slowest and strung out in the open.' He nodded to where Tabitha comforted Lucius. 'If we're discovered it would be a slaughter.'

Valerius looked from his wife to the huddled groups of women sheltering among the stones. 'We don't have enough swords. It would be a slaughter wherever they found us. Better to be on the move. If we can reach the coast the Ninth will be attacking in less than an hour. I won't stand by and watch my men fight and die from the safety of some hill.'

'The Ninth have already crossed, lord,' Crescens said.

'You're sure? The camp prefect was meant to wait until dawn.'

'We heard the sound of a battle to the south after we slipped away from the fire pit.'

Valerius exchanged a startled glance with Felix. 'If it's true we can reach them in less than an hour.' At last the light from the fire pits was dying, but the jagged peaks of the mountain range on the eastern horizon were silhouetted against the fast approaching dawn.

'Rufus?'

'Yes, lord?' The little man led his horse over.

'Take Shabolz and see if you can scout us a safe route to the Ninth. With Fortuna's favour the Ordovices will be too busy fighting them off to bother with us, but mark any defensible position along the way in case they aren't.'

They walked their horses, with Lucius and the least able of the women perched in the saddles, and using the animals to form a protective barrier on the flanks of the rest. Tabitha walked among them, chivvying and encouraging the exhausted women.

Valerius reckoned the distance to the coast from the standing stones at just over a mile. They must have been close to halfway when Rufus returned at a canter.

'We're clear to the top of the rise,' the scout announced. 'Shabolz will signal if there are any surprises. The Ninth have landed in force a little to the south, lord. You can see them from the ridge. It looks as if the Celts are too weak to hold them and are retreating up the coast.'

Valerius plucked Lucius from the saddle and handed him to Nilus. 'Look after him,' he said, as Tabitha approached. 'It seems your adventures may soon be over, lady.'

'Be careful, Valerius.'

He waved a salute and followed Rufus towards the slope. They reined in and dismounted before the crest. When they slipped over the rise Valerius studied the broad swathe of open ground that fell away gently towards the strait. The land was dotted with the occasional

417

patchwork of woods or a cluster of fields around a small farm. 'Has anything changed?' Rufus called to Shabolz, who stood beside a clump of scrubby trees close by.

'The Ninth has them on the run,' the Pannonian said cheerfully. 'See.' He directed Valerius's attention to an untidy, straggling column of men streaming northwards in apparent disarray. Beyond them Valerius could make out the unmistakable sight of a legion in battle formation, cohorts marching in square with auxiliaries providing a protective screen and cavalry on the flanks. 'There don't seem to be many of them.' Shabolz meant the Celts. 'It looks as if they've kept their main strength in the north.'

'All we have to do is stay out of trouble for an hour.' Valerius felt a surge of relief. 'The camp prefect is bound to send out patrols to check his flanks. I'm surprised we haven't already seen them.'

But Rufus's sharp eyes had noticed something neither of the others had seen. 'On the right, below us,' he said. 'That stream bed.'

Valerius followed his pointing finger. At last he found a shallow gully screened by bushes and the hundred or so men crouching below the banks. Not hiding. Waiting. His eyes went back to the advancing Romans. In a pitched battle the Ninth's eagle would be carried at the centre of one of the cohorts, protected by almost five hundred men, but Naso was apparently so confident of victory he'd kept Honoratus, the *aquilifer*, and his eight-man guard with the command group. They were marching in the midst of the advancing cohorts, but Valerius could see the legion would soon have to divide to pass the gully. The Ninth's eagle would be at the mercy of the Ordovice ambushers.

'Tell the decurion to leave two men to look after the lady Tabitha and the others and bring the rest here as quickly as he can,' he said to Shabolz. The Pannonian mounted and galloped off down the slope. 'Can we get there in time?' The question was as much for himself as it was for Rufus.

'You plan to attack a hundred men with thirteen?' Rufus didn't bother to hide his incredulity.

'Thirteen cavalrymen against a hundred infantry.' Valerius used the time to check the bindings on his saddle. 'And if you can put us in the right place we'll have the element of surprise.'

'You never mentioned that campaigning with you was just one long invitation to commit suicide.'

'Think of it as one long opportunity for glory.' Valerius returned his grin. 'The glory of Rome.'

'The glory of Rome?' Rufus laughed. 'You mean I'll end up in a marble tomb with my name on it?'

'I guarantee it.'

Before Rufus could reply Felix galloped up with the others. The decurion halted by Valerius's mount and handed his reins to Julius Crescens. Valerius waved him forward.

'Thank all the gods for that,' Felix breathed as he saw the advancing legion.

'But we have a problem.' Valerius pointed out the waiting ambush and Felix cursed. 'The question is how we reach them without being seen.'

'The bushes that screen them from the legion will also screen us from them,' Rufus pointed out. 'If we cross the crest a little to the north we should be able to surprise them. The Celts down on the plain might see us, but they'll probably die laughing when they see how few we are.'

'He has a point,' Felix said.

'I won't let them take the eagle.'

'Then how?'

'We'll flank them. We can get into the stream bed there.' He pointed to a brown gash where the steep bank had collapsed a few hundred paces to the north of the waiting men. 'They're packed in like olives in a jar. When a dozen horses come galloping up that gully they won't know what hit them. Think of it as your chance for immortality.'

Rufus gave him a sideways grin and Felix blew out a puff of breath. 'A chance for an Ordovice spear up my arse more like,' he said with more resignation than regret. 'At your orders, legate.'

'Now is as good a time as any.' Valerius led them back to the horses.

They took it slowly, riding in a wide arc that took them in the opposite direction from the stream bed. They saw no one as they mounted the crest and cantered towards the plain, but once on the flat they encountered groups of Ordovice warriors who watched them warily but didn't interfere with their passage. Valerius commented on their lack of belligerence and it was Rufus who came up with an answer.

'If you ask me these are the same warriors we came up against three or four days ago. They know what Roman cavalry and infantry combined are capable of and the last thing they want is to be delayed here and chewed up when the legionary cohorts reach us. They're still brave and they'll stand well enough shoulder to shoulder with ten thousand of their painted brethren, but for now they're content to leave us alone.'

He led them south until they came to a stream. To Valerius it looked much like any other, but Rufus was certain they were in the right place. They dropped the few feet into the gully and turned left. The water was low, with only the occasional deeper pool, but the rocks proved round and slippery, jutting from the water like so many polished skulls. Valerius heard muttering as hooves skidded noisily on the slick granite and horses almost unseated their riders, but he concentrated on the ground ahead. Water from his mount's hooves splashed in great droplets on his face and he dashed it from his eyes. He tried to gauge his position from the view they'd had from above. Four hundred paces? Three? What did it matter? He risked increasing his pace from a trot to a canter and the others stayed with him. The horses must have felt the excitement of their riders because they tossed their heads and would have bolted had the men not curbed them with sharp tugs on the reins. On and on along the gully, three abreast, with the tree branches brushing their heads. They must be close now. Valerius heard the skitter of hooves and a massive splash from behind, but his mind was focused entirely on the next corner. He drew his *spatha*.

His first impression was of a line of astonished, disbelieving faces when the big horses surged into view. They crouched in rows beneath the left bank waiting for the cry that would take them like a dagger into the heart of the Ninth. Every man was a seasoned Ordovice warrior armed with a spear or an axe and if they formed a defensive line Valerius and his little band of troopers were doomed. But the shattering sight of Roman cavalry on their flank froze the Celts in place. It was like a blacksmith's hammer striking a row of children's figures.

Valerius's horse battered two men aside before they could bring their spears to bear and his sword chopped down to kill a third. Most sought sanctuary by scrambling up the bank; others fled in panic along the river bed where their exposed backs were an invitation to Valerius's charging cavalry. The few who tried to make a stand were cut down where they stood, their blood mingling in the sluggish waters of the little stream.

Quintus Naso had been astonished at how easy it had been. Two full cohorts of the Ninth crossed unopposed before the Celts reacted. The enemy defences were concentrated behind the southern fire trench and their right flank was an open invitation of which Canalius, the *primus pilus*, had taken full advantage. They were also fewer in number than Naso expected, a mere blocking force who melted away as soon as they came under pressure. Some even surrendered, but when the first blackened corpses had been brought to him from the fire trench he ordered them executed and no further prisoners taken. The only thing troubling him was whether to continue his advance or consolidate his position. He had crossed earlier than Agricola anticipated and the Twentieth weren't due to embark for another hour, which left the Ninth exposed . . .

The first he knew of the potential ambush was when a stream of warriors erupted like flushed partridges from the stunted trees ahead and raced across his front. A trumpet call rang out as his auxiliary cavalry sighted the fleeing men and gave chase, whooping as they rode. Within minutes not an Ordovice lived and crumpled bodies scattered the plain.

'Enemy cavalry on the left flank, sir,' an aide shouted in warning.

Naso turned to follow his pointing finger to where a dozen horsemen emerged from the same bushes that had hidden the running men. 'The enemy has no cavalry we know of,' the camp prefect said. There was something familiar about the bearing of the leading rider, who seemed to be accompanied by what looked like a small boy. The cavalryman raised his right hand and Naso felt a surge of relief. 'Allow them through,' he ordered with a broad grin. 'I hope I see you well, legate.'

'And you, Quintus.' Naso noticed the blood spattered across his face and left arm. Valerius looked over the massed ranks of legionaries marching past them. 'Things seem to be going well. I hadn't thought to see you for another hour.'

'When they fired the trench it looked like an opportunity.' Naso waved at the bodies carpeting the plain ahead. 'I have a feeling you saved us from a nasty surprise.'

'I think they had designs on our eagle, and perhaps your life.'

Naso's tanned face turned pale and he looked to where the *aquilifer* stood nearby, surrounded by his eight guards. 'Honoratus,' he called. 'You will march with the Third cohort from now on.' Honoratus saluted and trotted off. 'And now I must return your command to you, legate. It has been an honour and a privilege . . .'

Valerius put his hand on the other man's arm and shook his head. 'This is your victory, Quintus. I relinquished command of the Ninth to you and you hold it until the governor returns it . . . or otherwise. I am happy to serve under you, but I would beg the loan of a century or two of auxiliaries to escort my wife and fifty other Roman captives to the mainland. They were destined to be sacrificed to the Celts' gods and are understandably distraught and weary.'

'Of course.' Naso turned to an aide. 'Make sure the legate is given every facility.' They watched him ride off with Rufus at his side giving directions. 'So, Valerius,' the camp prefect continued, 'if I cannot take your orders, may I seek your counsel?'

Valerius immediately recognized the dilemma facing Naso, and gave his opinion readily. 'My advice would be to keep them on the run. Their commanders have concentrated the Ordovice defences on the landing beaches. If they have reserves, they're far away in the west

422

looking out for Agricola's non-existent navy. At best, you'll destroy their power entirely before the Twentieth even lands. At worst you will draw part of their strength against you, which is what Agricola planned in the first place. Use all your cavalry to deny them the high ground, there.' He pointed inland. 'And sweep them from the plain.'

'Of course,' Naso smiled. 'I'm sure I would have thought of it in time. And now you will want to say farewell to your lady wife.'

Valerius saw the small column coming over the rise to meet the auxiliaries who would escort them to the landing beaches. Valerius nodded his thanks and turned his horse towards them.

He hugged Lucius as he explained the situation to Tabitha. 'I will be sorry to leave you, Valerius,' she whispered, 'but not this dreadful place.'

'Wait for me in Londinium.' He took her in his arms, oblivious of Lucius's snort of disgust. 'I will come as soon as I am able.'

'We will not be staying in Britannia?'

'I don't know.' He shook his head. 'It dep—'

'Lord?' Rufus indicated two riders approaching. Valerius saw with relief it was the missing Hilario and Candidus. He was about to call a greeting when he noticed the big cavalryman's evident agitation.

'The Twentieth are in trouble!'

LIII

Julius Agricola knew he'd made a mistake the moment he had his first proper view of the landing beach. By the time the initial waves of legionaries disembarked the sandy foreshore was filled to capacity. The beach was too narrow to hold more than three thousand men, and his soldiers couldn't fight their way off the sands because of the fire trenches. Worse, they were helpless targets. Agricola knew from experience the Celts could always call on the occasional archer or slinger at need, but here they were present in their hundreds, perhaps thousands. The legionaries' big wooden shields, plate armour and iron helmets saved them from the worst of the storm of missiles, but inevitably men would fall with an arrow through the throat or a lead slingshot in the brain. Blood soaked the sand and ran down the beach in little streams until it merged with the gently lapping waves. The governor stood with his senior officers on a floating platform just out of range of the slingers, with a boat to hand to carry them ashore in the event of a breakthrough. Naked, tattooed warriors capered among the trees in the infernal light of the flames, shouting insults. Agricola knew they were attempting to draw a volley of javelins, but he'd decreed the weapons should be hoarded until they were needed most, during the breakout. If they ever achieved a breakout. Every few moments a Celt would run forward to hurl another bundle of pitch-soaked wood into the pit to stoke the fire, causing a great flare of flame that outshone the silvery pre-dawn light. The crackle of burning branches and the screams and jeers and roars of frustration that were the heartbeat of this battle were punctuated every few moments by the hiss of a *ballista* missile or 'shield-splitter' passing overhead, to be absorbed ineffectually by the trees. The boats of the third wave milled in confusion just off the shore, carrying another fifteen hundred men who might have made the difference if only he could get them on land. But the only reinforcements who reached the beach were men called forward by their centurions to replace the fallen, who were dumped unceremoniously in the shallows to make room.

'Have four centuries attempt the flanks again using *testudo*,' he ordered Julius Ursus, commander of the Twentieth. The legionaries could form *testudo* in their sleep, but Agricola registered a glance of disdain, or perhaps something worse, from the legate.

'They've blocked the exits with some kind of abatis designed to break up the *testudo* as soon as it tries to cross it,' he said. 'All we'll do is take more casualties. Even if they cross the obstruction they'll still have to climb a sheer thirty-foot cliff under missile attack.'

'Nevertheless,' Agricola said through gritted teeth, 'I insist we try. We did not come here to sit on the beach collecting seashells.'

Ursus shot him a glance of pure hatred, but he called for an aide and relayed the order.

Agricola ignored him, but inwardly he raged at the knowledge that he'd chosen this landing place for precisely the characteristics that were frustrating his plans. The terrain on the far side was such that the defenders could only oppose the attack with an equal number of warriors as the attackers. Man for man a Roman legionary was worth any three barbarians. If everything had gone as he'd hoped the Ordovices would be sucked into the battle by their own enthusiasm, to die in their thousands on the point of the deadly Roman short swords. The greatest barrier he'd believed he'd face was the piles of their dead.

Yet he couldn't reach them. That inferno of a trench, which stretched

425

the entire length of the beach, might burn for hours, and was too wide for the most agile soldier to leap in full armour. Every time he saw a man fall he was reminded that Roman ingenuity could have overcome this barrier with ease if he hadn't been stung into premature action by the screams of the burning auxiliaries. Back on the mainland his engineers were working frantically to create wood and wicker bridges that would allow the legionaries to pour across once the flames died down, but they wouldn't be ready in sufficient numbers until the sixth hour at the earliest.

A great roar went up from the shore and in the light of the flames he saw a pair of *testudines* jogging from the mass of milling men towards each flank. From here the interlocking shields appeared impregnable, but that failed to take into account the man who'd designed the formidable barriers of felled tree trunks, banks of thorns and sharpened stakes they'd have to cross. The defenders had arranged them in such a fashion that from the moment they tried to mount the barrier the men in the *testudines* were forced apart like the tiles of a marble mosaic in an earthquake. Cohesion was the key to the *testudo* and without that cohesion the men were vulnerable to the missiles that poured into them from the flank and the massive boulders showering them from the clifftop. Agricola saw first one *testudo* disintegrate, then a second, the men crumpling or falling back.

He was so focused on the attack that he didn't see the messenger who arrived by boat from the mainland. Ursus accepted the scroll and studied the text in the dull light through narrowed eyes. 'Perhaps we should consider withdrawal,' he said. Agricola's hand shook as he accepted the parchment. 'A lamp here for the governor,' Ursus growled.

Agricola felt an icy hand grip his stomach as he read: *Gaius Quintus Naso, acting commander Ninth legion Hispana, greets Gnaeus Julius Agricola, proconsul, and begs to report that the Ninth legion crossed the strait in force an hour before dawn, my legion's landing was unopposed and I am consolidating my position while I await orders.*

'If we withdraw now and leave a token force to hold the barbarians

426

in place we can force march to the southern crossing in an hour or two and capitalize on Naso's success,' Ursus persisted.

Agricola crumpled the parchment in his hand. 'Do you really believe Julius Agricola will allow men to say an upstart temporary commander and the Ninth legion took Mona? No, the Ninth's partial success will achieve what I always intended. They will draw defenders away from the Twentieth and you will take this beach. Do you understand, legate?'

Ursus couldn't bring himself to speak. He answered with a curt nod.

'Have the engineers send forward what temporary bridges they've constructed. And buckets. If the men can't fight they can form chains to damp the flames. Do I have to think of everything?' Agricola snarled at his aides.

'There's no point in using the bridges in ones and twos.' Ursus risked more criticism. 'We need to attack them in a hundred places. Two hundred.' He decided it wasn't worth pointing out that a few buckets of water wouldn't have the slightest impact on the inferno in the trench.

An hour later he watched in silence as he was proved right. The engineers had managed to supply ten or fifteen wood and wattle platforms of sufficient scale to bridge the fire pit. Teams of twenty legionaries rushed forward, raised them upright and used ropes to lower them into position. The Ordovices defended the bridgeheads by the simple expedient of sending groups of warriors forward to hurl pitch-soaked bundles where the bridge would fall. One by one they were consumed in columns of flame. A few legionaries, as always the bravest and the best, managed to cross, only to be slaughtered on the far side, and a few more burned to death when the bridges inevitably collapsed. The Ordovices died in their scores, because Agricola had ordered the attacks to be covered by javelin throwers, but Ursus had the feeling they were content with their sacrifice.

'We will try again.' Ursus decided that Agricola sounded like a child whose puppy had pissed on his best sandals.

Gwlym listened to Bedwr's exaggerated description of the Twentieth legion's agony and felt a flare of exultation. Despite the early ignition of the fire trenches everything was going to plan. The Romans had managed to land less than half their force and they were dying by the dozen with every passing moment. Soon he would send his warriors to push them back into the sea, there to be consumed by the next riptide. But first they must be driven to the very brink of madness and despair. It was time to appease the Mother Goddess.

'Where are the Roman harlots?'

'They have been sent for, arch-druid.'

'Then send for them again. I want to hear them screaming.'

He focused on the noise of the battle below, taking satisfaction from the shrieks of the dying and the increasingly audible frustration of the Roman soldiers. It was the sound of impending victory. The first rallying cry in the great rebellion that would drive the red filth from the shores of Elfydd. He found the thought mesmerizing and it took time to realize that a frantic whispered conversation was taking place nearby.

'What is it?' he demanded.

'Bedwr is receiving news, arch-druid,' Aymer told him. Gwlym sensed he was forcing himself to keep his voice steady, but to the druid's sensitive ears it held a shrill edge of concern close to panic.

'Bedwr,' he snapped.

'Yes, arch-druid?'

Gwlym felt his heart thunder in his chest and it was a moment before he understood why. 'The women. Where are the women?'

'They . . .' Bedwr sounded as if he was choking on the words. 'They . . . are missing.'

'Missing,' Gwlym shrieked. 'How can they be missing? They were guarded. I ordered that no man come near them. Cadwal . . .'

'Cadwal is dead.'

Gwlym flew at the source of the disastrous news, his long nails searching for Bedwr's eyes as the druid mewled in terror. Strong arms pulled Gwlym away. 'You will pay for this with your soul, Bedwr Ap Ban,' Gwlym shrieked.

'There is more, arch-druid,' Aymer whispered. 'The Romans

428

bypassed the southern fire trench and Madog's men were taken by surprise. He says he is withdrawing until he finds a place to defend. He is confident he can hold the enemy if you send him Tudfic's warriors to fight at his side.'

'The Romans came for their women? How? How could they have known?'

'No one knows, arch-druid. It was as if they were ghosts.'

'How many?'

'Perhaps thirty.'

'Not those who took the women,' the arch-druid screamed. 'The others.'

'Madog says five thousand infantry and a few cavalry.'

'I gave Madog eight thousand men.'

'Madog was with Owain Lawhir on the ridge,' Aymer said carefully. 'He has seen the Romans fight.'

'So have I,' Gwlym spat. But he knew the only way to put some spirit back into Madog was to give him more men. 'We have two thousand men in reserve at Pencerrig. Tudfic will lead them.'

'But they are needed here. Our men are already tiring.'

Gwlym ignored the desperation in Aymer's voice. 'Madog must do more than hold the Romans – he must defeat them. When he has done that they will return here and help Dafyd drive the Romans into the sea. Have Tudfic come to me for instructions.'

The tall young warrior appeared a few minutes later. Tudfic snorted when he heard about Madog's incompetence and his nervous retreat. He had been on Mona since the raid on Canovium and his head was still filled with the victory. Yet stories of the battle on the ridge had reached him and they made him uneasy. 'When you have defeated the Romans you will find the women and bring them to me,' Gwlym said.

'You may count on me, arch-druid,' Tudfic assured him. He took his bodyguard to where the Ordovice sub-tribe waited. 'We are to join Madog and together we will destroy the Romans,' he assured them.

But as they marched south, he found his confidence wavering. He knew of the importance Gwlym placed on the deaths of the women and the means of it, and it made him uneasy. This was the kind of treatment the Romans would never forget or forgive. They would hunt down and slaughter every man they believed was involved. He called for the head of his personal bodyguard and issued a short instruction. A little later a messenger arrived urging him to return for fresh orders.

Tudfic delegated responsibility to a tribal elder and told him to carry on until he met Madog's warriors. 'I will join you soon,' he assured him. Then he took his bodyguard and marched west to the settlement where Gwlym had insisted the women of his tribe stay during the defence of Mona. From there it was just a short journey to the sheltered bay where his ships waited.

LIV

The further north the Ninth marched the more the opposition to their advance stiffened. Clearly someone had learned of the threat to the south and was calling up what reinforcements he could. Little bands of Ordovice warriors appeared from ditches and wooded valleys and launched themselves at Naso's formations like vengeful wasps. Valerius watched with approval how the camp prefect allowed them to spend themselves against the shields of the legionary cohorts and used his auxiliaries to slaughter them as they retreated exhausted. He felt no need to interfere and would not have done so in any case. This was Naso's battle and it would be his glory – or defeat. He kept his cohorts in square in broken country that would have destroyed the cohesion of a battle line, and, as Valerius suggested, he used the bulk of his cavalry to dominate the hills on his west flank. The strait would guard the east.

Madog was no fool and no coward. He knew he was fighting for his survival and that of his tribe. He'd been lulled by Gwlym's insistence that his eight thousand warriors only had to hold their line behind the fire pit, and it had unnerved him when that strategy proved so disastrous. After the battle on the ridge, the knowledge that the Romans were on their flank panicked his men. It was all he could do to hold them, but hold them he did and now they had recovered some of their confidence. When he heard he was to have another two thousand under Tudfic he decided he could do more than just hold the Romans. After all, he outnumbered them at least two to one. He knew where he would make his stand. It was closer to Gwlym's position than the arch-druid would like, but the only place he was confident he wouldn't be outflanked. A low ridge with a river to cover his right wing and a steep, tree-covered slope that fell to the sea on his left. If he calculated correctly his battle line would either outstretch the Romans' or be two or three ranks heavier. Either case gave him the advantage. When the head of the first of the clans he had been promised appeared he had already begun placing his men. He told the chief his plan and ordered him to take his people and defend the place of honour on the right wing, with his flank against the riverbank. It surprised but didn't concern him that there was no sign of Tudfic; he would appear soon enough.

Word came back to Naso and Valerius that the enemy had stopped running and they rode forward to survey the position. 'Sensible from his point of view,' Naso said conversationally as they looked up at the endless ranks of warriors lined up at the top of a long, sloping piece of pasture-land. He checked the flanks and nodded. 'Quite clever for a barbarian.'

'Perfect,' Valerius agreed.

Naso grinned. 'We'll keep it simple, I think.' He raised his voice so his aides could hear his confidence. 'Seventh cohort will act as reserve along with the First Tungri. First Pannonia will replace the Seventh in the line. Sound form three ranks and send word to the cavalry to maintain their station until they hear my signal.'

Valerius called Felix across. 'No point in having the horses just stand-ing about when there's work to be done. It's time you and your lads had a bit of freedom, Cornelius. It can't have been much fun being tied to me for the last three months. Take them across there,' he pointed to where the auxiliary cavalry were lined up on the left flank, 'and attach yourself to a squadron.' He saw Felix was about to protest. 'I'll be safe enough at the centre of the legion. I promise to stay out of trouble.'

Felix saluted with a grin and rode off shouting orders. Valerius received a couple of curious glances from his troopers. Gaius Rufus hesitated as the others rode off, but Valerius waved the scout away and he turned to join them.

The *cornicen* waited long enough for the reserve cohort and its replacement to be given their orders before putting his curved trumpet to his lips and sounding the triple blast that signalled the camp prefect's chosen formation. With swift choreographed movements, made routine by years of mind-numbing daily practice, the cohort squares flowed into their positions. Soon three unbroken lines filled the broad pastureland from river to sea with a solid wall of painted shields. A roar of defiance rose from the waiting Ordovices at the sight and Valerius heard the harsh, intimidating bray of the carnyx, the distinctive bronze Celtic war trumpet. Individual warriors dashed out from the straggling lines shouting ritual challenges that went unanswered.

The long lines of waiting legionaries stood silent and motionless, displaying an air of almost unearthly calm. Valerius, in the centre of Naso's command group, recognized the serenity for the illusion it was. There wasn't a man in those three ranks whose heart didn't thunder as if to escape his chest. Centurions would be snarling at men whose only ambition was to get at the enemy and avenge the auxiliaries whose charred bodies they'd watched being dragged from the fire pit. Men would be vomiting on the rough grass. Some would piss themselves, or worse. The moments before battle brought a variety of reactions that had nothing to do with bravery or cowardice. A coward didn't last long in the legions. What mattered was that the man next to you knew he could depend on you to hold your shield high and locked tight with his. That you would stick your *gladius* into your enemy's guts until he put a spear through your throat or cut your aching arm off at the elbow. That you would fight until your last breath and your final heartbeat. Valerius had given many a stirring speech urging men to fight for Rome and their emperor, but the truth was that they fought for each other, a more powerful bond by far. He had been in the enemy's position and he could almost feel their unease at the stillness of the long, achingly slim Roman lines.

A single blast rang out and the six cohorts brought their shields up to chest height, braced by the left arm. The pair of heavy *pila* they clutched in their right hands came to rest on the right shoulder where they couldn't get tangled with any other piece of equipment. A second blast and they stepped out at a steady unhurried pace over the tussock grass. Centurions craned their necks and growled at their men to keep a straight, unbroken line, using their vine sticks where necessary to reinforce the orders. The lines wove and rippled for a few steps until men found their rhythm and their training overcame any other concerns.

The two reserve cohorts marched in squares twenty wide and twenty deep, two hundred paces apart and fifty paces behind the fighting line. The spacing was designed to keep them close enough to react to any sudden crisis or supply replacements for casualties at need. Naso's command group, along with Valerius, rode between them, their elevated position in the saddle providing an uninterrupted view of the field.

Valerius studied the untidy mass on top of the low hill for signs of movement. The enemy's best chance of breaking the Roman line was to launch an all-out charge when the first line reached the bottom of the slope. Momentum and the sheer weight of the attack would give them the advantage, but it would be lost if they allowed the legionaries to advance much further. Instead, they stayed in their positions screaming insults and taunts and hurling the occasional missile that usually dropped short of the marching legionaries. By now the centurions would be dispensing their familiar, homely advice. The old mantras rang unbidden in Valerius's head. 'Keep your discipline. Don't rush. Your shield will protect you when you're in line, but get isolated and you'll have a spear up your arse before you can blink. Don't waste your breath shouting insults. A legionary does his talking with a *gladius*. Three inches of iron in the right place is worth a foot somewhere else.'

They were halfway up the long slope and the pace never faltered, legs accustomed to marching fifteen miles a day barely noticing the incline. The Britons became more agitated, the screaming reached a new pitch and more and more men darted threateningly from the line, shaking their spears at the advancing legions.

'Soon,' Valerius heard Naso whisper. 'It must be soon.'

Valerius wanted to assure the camp prefect that everything was going to be all right – Julius Ulpius Canalius and his centurions knew their business and they had their orders – but he kept silent. No point repeating what Naso already knew.

A new, more powerful rasping challenge from a carnyx, taken up by others all along the Ordovice line. The barbarian warriors charged. One moment they were a shadow stretching across the top of the slope, the next they were a wave pouring down it. Just fifty paces separated them from the advancing Romans. 'Throw,' Naso hissed through gritted teeth.

At thirty paces the sky above the Roman lines darkened as the legionaries launched two thousand weighted javelins into the charging ranks. Valerius was close enough to hear the dull slap as the heavy spears landed and the screams of their victims. From behind it was as if the entire mass tripped. All along the mile-long line men fell with *pila* piercing chest and throat and skull, rib and thigh, and bringing down others in the ranks behind. Yet the trip was an illusion, because the charge absorbed the missiles without pause and enough Ordovices raced on to collide with the legionary line and throw the front rank back on its heels. A thunderous clash split the air as warriors hammered into the wall of shields. The entire line rippled and bowed, but the ranks behind pushed into those in front and helped soak up the impact. Gradually the line restored its integrity. Then the slaughter began.

As long as a man's arm from elbow to the tip of his middle finger and with a needle-sharp triangular point, the *gladius* had evolved to become the perfect close quarter killing weapon. Celtic swords were similar to the cavalry *spatha*, long, heavy and unwieldy. The Ordovices who could afford them used them like bludgeons, smashing at Roman shields and helmets. Their spearmen, driven on to the shield wall by those behind, were forced to seek out any unprotected flesh and the iron points jabbed at throats and eyes. As long as a legionary held his discipline and kept faith in the men to left and right and at his back he could hunch down behind his big, curved *scutum* and know he had a fair chance of surviving. But that was only the start. Valerius heard a centurion shout an order. With a mighty heave the Roman shields smashed forward as one, momentarily disconcerting the enemy and angling to leave a gap on the right. The legionary darted his *gladius* through the gap into the unprotected flesh of the warrior to his front right. Three inches of bright iron in the right place, a fearsome twist of the wrist to withdraw and the warrior slumped to the grass vainly trying to return his guts to their cavity. Steam from thousands of bodies misted the air. Minutes into the fight men could barely see for the sweat in their eyes and their hands struggled to grip their sword hilts. The air was filled with the sewer stink of torn bowels and the acrid scent of freshly spilled blood. They struggled to stay upright as their feet slipped on blood-slick grass, lengths of intestine or the squirming body of one of their earlier victims. It was happening all along the line and Valerius could hear the disbelieving shrieks of the eviscerated Ordovice warriors and the grunts as the legionaries heaved their shields and plunged their points into their next victims. With every heave the Roman lines advanced another few inches. In the second line men kept their swords sheathed and used the length of the *pilum* to keep enemy spearmen from killing their comrades in the front rank. If a Roman fell or spun away injured the man behind automatically stepped into his position. Soon a broad line of scarlet and the fallen bodies of bare-chested warriors marked their passage up the green sward of the pasture.

Madog watched the battle from the crest like a hungry wolf seeking out the weakest goat in the flock. A worm of unease wriggled inside him that had its origin in Prince Tudfic's continued absence, but he drove it from his mind and waited for his opportunity. It came when he saw four of his men drag a big Roman from the front rank and plunge their spears into the fallen body. The legionary lost his helmet as he fell and Madog saw the flash of scarlet of an officer's horsehair crest. A roar of triumph went up from the Ordovices and he felt a bolt of exhilaration. Instinct more than conscious thought set him in motion as he heard the howl of dismay from the Roman line. He'd kept twenty of his personal guard in reserve and now he waved his axe and led them forward, bounding down the slope to where the Roman had fallen.

'The *primus pilus* is down.'

Valerius heard the panicked shouts at the same time as he noticed the compact group of warriors racing from the crest like a Roman 'Boar's Snout' wedge. He knew how effective the wedge could be against a weakened line and that the loss of their centurion would have shocked even the most experienced legionaries. He looked desperately towards the reserves of the Seventh, but by the time he fetched them the Ordovices would have struck. He dropped from the saddle and dashed for the slope, picking up a *scutum* dropped by a wounded man on the way and locking it on to the wooden fist that had been designed to fit the grip. A *pilum* was stuck point first in the trampled grass behind the Roman line and he plucked it free as he ran. He fought his way through the rear rank, meaning to do what he could to bolster the second file before the Ordovice wedge struck. Too late. The line bulged back towards him under the fierceness of the assault by Madog's champions and he heard the screams and curses of Roman soldiers dying. A flurry of movement to his front and jagged splinters of wood stung his face, disbelief as the front file's shield disintegrated before his eyes and the man reeled away with his face a mask of blood. Valerius pushed him aside just in time to take Madog's next attack on his shield boss and fill the gap in the line. The force of the blow would have broken a normal man's wrist, but the thrice-tanned cowhide stock of his wooden fist absorbed some of its power. Madog howled and launched another frenzy of axe blows, maddened and filled with a visceral joy by the taste of Roman blood on his lips. Valerius instinctively met violence with violence, stepping forward into the axe and giving Madog less room to swing. Mars' sacred arse, he hadn't even had time to draw his sword. What was he thinking of? He was too old for this. When he heaved forward there was a loud clang and his head seemed to explode. He understood the axe had smashed into his helmet, but he knew that to ease the pressure was to die, so he closed his eyes and pushed. Another enormous blow split the shield in two, leaving Valerius with the boss and an eighteen inch strip of oak. He saw his death in Madog's crazed eyes and heard someone telling him to get back. Instead, as the Ordovice war chief raised his axe for the killing blow, Valerius launched himself forward and smashed the strip of shield into Madog's throat, knocking him backwards. Suddenly they were down among the blood and the shit clawing at each other amid a forest of feet. Valerius knew that the Celtic spears would be seeking him out, but all he felt was the fierce visceral joy of battle. It came to him that this was what Serpentius had always felt and he laughed. He saw puzzlement and something more in Madog's eyes. This was the way to die. In single combat with a man worth killing. He was surprised when the sky went black. For a moment he wondered if he were already dead, but his dazed mind told him the line had moved forward with him and these were Roman shields. He was holding Madog by the throat with his left hand. The Celt lashed at his eyes and hammered at the fingers that were choking him, but Valerius seemed to have the strength of ten men. As the Ordovice squirmed beneath him the Roman pummelled his face with his wooden fist until the features were no longer recognizable and the only sign of life was the bloody bubbles bursting close to what had been his enemy's nose. He struggled to his feet and somebody thrust a shield at him. He locked it in place and drew his sword before he noticed that men were looking at him with a kind of religious awe. 'Kill them.' His voice sounded odd. 'Kill every last one of them.'

The Ordovices who held the right flank had been fighting for fifteen minutes and were close to exhaustion, always conscious of the cavalry formations waiting patiently like so many hawks on the ridge to the west. Like Madog, they were uneasy at Tudfic's absence. A few of them had already persuaded themselves that this was reason enough for them to withdraw from the fight and more were joining them with every passing second. When they heard the enormous shout from the east and saw warriors streaming up the slope the trickle became a flood and retreat became a rout. In the centre the Ordovices had been more

438

than holding their own, but when their right and left flanks collapsed there was nothing to do but join the retreat. The Roman line advanced behind the defeated barbarians, determined not to allow them a breathing space.

A trumpet sounded.

This was what cavalry lived for. A broken battle line and an endless supply of victims. The auxiliaries swooped from their hill and drove the fleeing Ordovices like cattle, selecting their victims by status and competing to see who could do the most slaughter. Valerius's escort were as active as any and they would kill until their arms could swing no more. Days like this made Gaius Rufus feel like a giant, but as always he felt a pang of guilt when he remembered his father, a fundamentally gentle man. He quickly tired of the butchery. His place was with Valerius Verrens. He found Valerius at the centre of the command group, but sensed that though he was with them he was not of them. Why became clear when he saw the gore-caked mail and the blood that coated his commander's face and head. 'You have a strange way of staying out of trouble, lord,' the little scout said.

Valerius tried to smile, genuinely pleased to see him, but something in the Roman's eyes told Rufus this was not the man he'd left less than an hour earlier. 'I am glad to see you well, Gaius Rufus, and your timing could not be better. We have our victory, I think.' Valerius looked to the eagle which Claudius Honoratus still held high at the centre of the reserve cohort and something welled up inside him. He'd felt melancholy after battles in the past once the euphoria of victory faded. Every soldier experienced it. But this was different. A combination of something beyond physical exhaustion and an emptiness that made him shudder. He remembered the Ordovice chieftain's face disintegrating under his wooden fist and shook his head to clear it of whatever *it* had been.

'Lord?'

'Somewhere on this island is a priest called Gwlym. Lead on. Let us find this druid who has taken such an interest in my family.'

*

The first Gwlym knew of his utter defeat was when Aymer reported first dozens, then hundreds of Ordovices retreating from the south in disarray, crying the gods had abandoned them.

'Can no one rally them?' the arch-druid whispered. 'Where is Madog? Where is Tudfic?'

'They say Madog is dead. Tudfic . . .' He left Tudfic's fate unsaid, but Gwlym could read his meaning clearly enough.

'Prince Dafyd?'

'Prince Dafyd does not know how long he can hold them without Tudfic's men. The fires are burning low. He urges you to leave.'

'Leave?'

'Mona is lost,' Aymer said brutally. 'But it is not lost for ever as long as you live. You are the font of our knowledge, our wisdom and our rites. Without you there is no future.' He laid a hand on the old man's shoulder. 'We have a ship.' Gwlym's mind seemed to have gone blank and he didn't resist the hands that led him away.

Rufus led Valerius to a height overlooking the beach where the legionaries of the Twentieth still streamed ashore and formed up to advance into the centre of the island. Someone had told the men of the Ninth to hold their positions and no one seemed to have the energy to argue. Valerius could see bodies rocking gently in the shallows below. A surprisingly large number of bodies. The smell of cooking meat filled the air, but no one had lit a fire.

A corpse in a dirty white robe lay close by and Rufus dismounted and turned it over. 'You were looking for a druid, lord?'

'Not this one.' They had torn Bedwr's eyes from his head before they cut his throat. 'It's true Gwlym is blind, but this druid is too young.' He looked down and saw Agricola sitting on the stump of a tree among a group of his officers. His freshly polished armour shone like gold in the sun. Valerius had experienced a moment of trepidation when he considered the inevitable meeting, but suddenly none of it mattered any more. The conference seemed to be breaking up. 'If you are ever in need, Gaius Rufus, seek out Gaius Valerius Verrens.'

'You won't get rid of me that easily, lord,' the little man grinned. 'The last survivors of the Temple of Claudius should stick together.'

Agricola was still seated on the stump looking thoughtfully over the beach and the bodies towards the mainland.

'I doubt you would enjoy Rome, scout. Too many people.' Valerius set his horse down the slope. 'See if you can round up my escort. I may be needing them.'

Four hard-eyed bodyguards stepped in front of Valerius as he rode into the hollow where Agricola sat. 'Leave us,' the governor ordered, waving the men away. He looked up and noticed for the first time the bloodstained features and gore-clogged mail. 'But don't go far.' He waited until Valerius dismounted before he got to his feet. 'I suppose you expect me to thank you?'

'Actually, I was expecting you to arrest me.'

'Arrest?' Agricola produced a snort of bitter laughter. 'I'd be within my rights to have you executed on the spot.'

'But you won't?'

'Tabitha and Lucius?'

'Safe.' The words *no thanks to you* were left unsaid, but Agricola knew they were there.

He nodded. It was all the acknowledgement or apology Valerius would ever get.

'Not won't.' He started off towards the beach, saw something that changed his mind and spun to walk up the slope. 'Can't. It would make me look a fool.'

Valerius followed him and Agricola handed him the scroll he'd been reading. Valerius unrolled it and read. *Titus Flavius Caesar Vespasianus Augustus confirms the appointment of his beloved subject Gaius Valerius Verrens as legatus of the Ninth legion Hispana and directs him to give all support to his proconsul of Britannia, Gnaeus Julius Agricola, in his campaigns in the next marching season and beyond.* There was more, about honour and duty and the peril of failing the Emperor, but the words all seemed to blur together.

'The Ninth is yours, Valerius, for good or ill. I'm not sure I altogether trust you and I know you don't trust me, but none of that matters. It will cost blood and sweat, but together we will give Rome what it craves, a Britannia subdued and at peace for generations to come. Go to Lindum and prepare your legion. In the spring we march north.'

Your legion.

For all the doubts he harboured about Agricola and his inner circle the words still lit a fire in Valerius's heart. What more could a soldier want?

Gaius Valerius Verrens. Legate of Rome.

Gwlym felt old and faded, but it had nothing to do with the motion of the boat. Part of him wished he'd stayed to die on Mona with the Ordovices. 'The boatman wishes to know where you would like to land on Hibernia, arch-druid?' Aymer said respectfully.

Hibernia? Gwlym hadn't thought about their destination. In Hibernia the cult of the druids was still strong . . .

'Not Hibernia,' he said. 'North. Eventually the Romans must go north. I have unfinished business with Rome.'

Historical note

Every writer who chooses to focus on the Roman presence in Britain at the end of the first century must acknowledge a debt to the historian Publius Cornelius Tacitus, son-in-law of Julius Agricola, governor of the province from AD 78 to AD 85. Tacitus's *Life of Julius Agricola*, published in AD 98 after Agricola's death, provides a unique and privileged window into the world of a Roman official of proconsular rank and the impact he had on the lives of those he ruled. Modern historians have questioned the true value of *Agricola*, on the grounds that it is a eulogy and Tacitus was unlikely to paint a less than flattering picture of his late father-in-law. His view may also have been influenced by the political climate in the wake of the death of the Emperor Domitian, whom he blames for throwing away Agricola's legacy. What can't be denied is that, as a chronicler of events, Tacitus can be frustratingly obscure when it comes to chronology and geography. Therefore we know that Agricola's campaigns took place over several campaigning seasons, but not precisely which advances are linked to which year. We know that he contemplated an invasion of Ireland, but not his precise location when he envisaged it. We know he had to fight battles, but, apart from the original campaign against the tribes of north Wales which is a central feature of *Glory of Rome*, not where or when. However, what he does tell us gives a fascinating insight into the Roman world and the mindset of the bureaucrats who were the cement that bound it, even if it requires careful reading. Some time in the late summer of AD 78 word reached Londinium that a Roman cavalry fort in Ordovice country had been attacked and the garrison all but wiped out. Despite the lateness of the season and the difficulty of the terrain, Agricola put together a force capable of destroying the power of the Ordovices and the druidic cult on Mona he believed was the guiding hand behind the attack. The fort has never been identified, but I thought Canovium (Caerhun), in the Conwy valley, was as likely a candidate as any. Its later stone incarnations were manned by auxiliary infantry, but it's perfectly possible Canovium originated as a cavalry post. My research also revealed that archaeologists have recently discovered evidence of extensive burning associated with the early fort. According to Tacitus, Agricola's reaction was swift and merciless, but his suggestion that the Ordovices, probably a numerous, widespread tribal federation, allowed themselves to be penned together in a single hill fort and slaughtered seems unlikely. Agricola himself is portrayed as a rather two-dimensional character who treated his soldiers well, but punished infractions severely, and was promoted by Vespasian for his superior qualities and dismissed by Domitian, Tacitus would have us believe, because of jealousy. Three legions took part in Agricola's campaigns, but we learn little of their individual feats and the names of their commanders are never mentioned. It seems no other major figure could be allowed to diminish Agricola's lustre. The Ninth legion Hispana was one of the units, but the exploits and trials featured in this book are purely fictional. Whether it had a reputation for bad luck is conjecture on my part. What can't be denied is that it was targeted by Julius Caesar for decimation – a brutal punishment where one man in ten was chosen by lot to be killed by his comrades – though the order was rescinded; it was one of the legions that mutinied before Claudius's invasion of AD 43, and it lost a substantial part of its strength in an ambush by Boudicca's warriors.

Emperor Claudius's last command to his governor, Aulus Plautius, in AD 43 was to 'conquer the rest'; now, almost forty years later, that responsibility falls to Julius Agricola . . . and his faithful legate of the Ninth legion Hispana, Gaius Valerius Verrens.

Soon, Valerius will march north to take on the might of the fearsome Caledonians, always mindful that the deadly enemies at his back are growing in strength and power.

Glossary

Ala milliaria – A reinforced auxiliary cavalry wing, normally between 700 and 1,000 strong. In Britain and the west the units would be a mix of cavalry and infantry, in the east a mix of spearmen and archers.

Ala quingenaria – Auxiliary cavalry wing normally composed of 500 auxiliary horsemen.

Aquilifer – The standard-bearer who carried the eagle of the legion.

As – A small copper coin worth approx. a fifth of a **sestertius**.

Aureus (pl. Aurei) – Valuable gold coin worth twenty-five **denarii**.

Auxiliary – Non-citizen soldiers recruited from the provinces as light infantry or for specialist tasks, e.g. cavalry, slingers, archers.

Beneficiarius – A legion's record keeper or scribe.

Caligae – Sturdily constructed, reinforced leather sandals worn by Roman soldiers. Normally with iron-studded sole.

Century – Smallest tactical unit of the legion, numbering eighty men.

Cohort – Tactical fighting unit of the legion, normally contained six centuries, apart from the elite First cohort, which had five double-strength centuries (800 men).

Colonia – A colony of retired legionaries set up and given special rights and dispensations on the orders of the Emperor.

Consul – One of two annually elected chief magistrates of Rome, normally appointed by the people and ratified by the Senate.

Contubernium – Unit of eight soldiers who shared a tent or barracks.

Cornicen – Legionary signal trumpeter who used an instrument called a *cornu*.

Decurio – A junior officer in a century, or a troop commander in a cavalry unit.

Denarius (pl. Denarii) – A silver coin worth four **sestertii**.

Domus – The house of a wealthy Roman, e.g. Nero's Domus Aurea (Golden House).

Duplicarius – Literally 'double pay man'. A senior legionary with a trade or an NCO.

Equestrian – Roman knightly class.

Fortuna – The goddess of luck and good fortune.

Gladius (pl. Gladii) – The short sword of the legionary. A lethal killing weapon at close quarters.

Governor – Citizen of senatorial rank given charge of a province. Would normally have a military background (see **Proconsul**).

Jupiter – Most powerful of the Roman gods, often referred to as **Optimus Maximus** (greatest and best).

Legate – The general in charge of a legion. A man of senatorial rank.

Legatus iuridicus – Legal official of senatorial rank appointed to aid the governor of a province.

Legion – Unit of approximately 5,000 men all of whom would be Roman citizens.

Lictor – Bodyguard of a Roman magistrate. There were strict limits on the numbers of lictors associated with different ranks.

Lituus – Curved trumpet used to transmit cavalry commands.

Manumission – The act of freeing a slave.

Mars – The Roman god of war.

Mithras – An Eastern god popular among Roman soldiers.

Ordo – The council of a hundred leading citizens responsible for running a Roman town.

Ordovices – Celtic tribe which inhabited the mountainous area of north Wales.

Pannonians – Members of a powerful Balkan tribe which lived in what is now Hungary. Provided auxiliary units for the Roman Empire in return for relief from tribute and taxes.

Phalera (pl. Phalerae) – Awards won in battle worn on a legionary's chest harness.

Pilum (pl. Pila) – Heavy spear carried by a Roman legionary.

Praefectus Castrorum – Literally camp prefect, the second in command of a Roman legion, often a soldier who had risen through the ranks.

Praetorian Guard – Powerful military force stationed in Rome. Accompanied the Emperor on campaign, but could be of dubious loyalty and were responsible for the overthrow of several Roman rulers.

Prefect – Auxiliary cavalry commander.

Primus Pilus – 'First File'. The senior centurion of a legion.

Principia – Legionary headquarters building.

Proconsul – Governor of a Roman province, such as Britannia or Syria, and of consular rank.

Procurator – Civilian administrator subordinate to a governor.

Quaestor – Civilian administrator in charge of finance.

Scutum (pl. Scuta) – The big, richly decorated curved shield carried by a legionary.

Senator – Patrician member of the Senate, the key political institution which administered the Roman Empire. Had to meet strict financial and property rules and be at least thirty years of age.

Sestertius (pl. Sestertii) – Roman brass coin worth a quarter of a **denarius**.

Signifer – Standard bearer who carried the emblem of a cohort or century.

Spatha – Sword wielded by Roman cavalry. Longer and heavier than the **gladius**.

Testudo – Literally 'tortoise'. A unit of soldiers with shields interlocked for protection.

Tribune – One of six senior officers acting as aides to a Legate. Often, but not always, on short commissions of six months upwards.

Tribunus laticlavius – Literally 'broad stripe tribune'. The most senior of a legion's military tribunes.

Vexillatio – A detachment of a legion used as a temporary task force on independent duty.

Victimarius – Servant who delivers and attends to the victim of a sacrifice.

Victory – Roman goddess equivalent to the Greek Nike.

Acknowledgements

Once again I'm indebted to my editor, Simon Taylor, Vivien Thompson and the team at Transworld, and my wonderful copy-editor, Nancy Webber, for helping make this book what it is, and my agent, Stan, of Jenny Brown Associates, for his constant support and encouragement. I wouldn't be a writer without the support of my wife Alison and that of my children, Kara, Nikki and Gregor. John Wacher's *The Towns of Roman Britain* and Philip Crummy's *City of Victory* helped me navigate the changing landscape of post-Boudiccan Britannia. *Roman Military Equipment* by M. C. Bishop and J. C. N. Coulston was invaluable for recreating an authentic Roman military, and *Exploring the World of the Celts* by Simon James and Miranda J. Green's *The Druids* performed a similar function for my depiction of the rites and religious traditions of the native inhabitants of Roman Britain and Wales.

ABOUT THE AUTHOR

A journalist by profession, **Douglas Jackson** transformed a lifelong fascination for Rome and the Romans into his first two highly praised and bestselling novels, *Caligula* and *Claudius*. His third novel, *Hero of Rome*, introduced readers to his new series hero, Gaius Valerius Verrens. Seven more novels recounting the adventures of this determined and dedicated servant of Rome have followed, earning critical acclaim and confirming Douglas as one of the UK's foremost historical novelists. An active member of the Historical Writers' Association and the Historical Novel Society, Douglas Jackson lives near Stirling in Scotland.